THE NIGHT SWIM

THE NIGHT SWIM

MEGAN GOLDIN

WHEELER PUBLISHING
A part of Gale, a Cengage Company

GALE
A Cengage Company

Wheeler Publishing® Large Print Hardcover.
The text of this Large Print edition is unabridged.
Other aspects of the book may vary from the original edition.
Set in 16 pt. Plantin.

LIBRARY OF CONGRESS CIP DATA ON FILE.
CATALOGUING IN PUBLICATION FOR THIS BOOK
IS AVAILABLE FROM THE LIBRARY OF CONGRESS.

ISBN-13: 978-1-4328-8410-9 (hardcover alk. paper)

Published in 2020 by arrangement with St. Martin's Publishing

Printed in Mexico
Print Number: 01   Print Year: 2020

To Bernard and Suzanne

'Twas a thousand pities that it should have happened to she, of all others.

— Thomas Hardy,
Tess of the D'Urbervilles

1
HANNAH

It was Jenny's death that killed my mother. Killed her as good as if she'd been shot in the chest with a twelve-gauge shotgun. The doctor said it was the cancer. But I saw the will to live drain out of her the moment the policeman knocked on our screen door.

"It's Jenny, isn't it?" Mom rasped, clutching the lapel of her faded dressing gown.

"Ma'am, I don't know how to tell you other than to say it straight." The policeman spoke in the low-pitched melancholic tone he'd used moments earlier when he'd pulled up and told me to wait in the patrol car as its siren lights painted our house streaks of red and blue.

Despite his request, I'd slipped out of the back seat and rushed to Mom's side as she turned on the front porch light and stepped onto the stoop, dazed from being woken late at night. I hugged her withered waist as he told her what he had to say. Her body shuddered at each word.

His jaw was tight under strawberry blond stubble and his light eyes were watery by the time he was done. He was a young cop. Visibly inexperienced in dealing with tragedy. He ran his knuckles across the corners of his glistening eyes and swallowed hard.

"I'm s-s-sorry for your loss, ma'am," he stammered when there was nothing left to say. The finality of those words would reverberate through the years that followed.

But at that moment, as the platitudes still hung in the air, we stood on the stoop, staring at each other, uncertain what to do as we contemplated the etiquette of death.

I tightened my small, girlish arms around Mom's waist as she lurched blindly into the house. Overcome by grief. I moved along with her. My arms locked around her. My face pressed against her hollow stomach. I wouldn't let go. I was certain that I was all that was holding her up.

She collapsed into the lumpy cushion of the armchair. Her face hidden in her clawed-up hands and her shoulders shaking from soundless sobs.

I limped to the kitchen and poured her a glass of lemonade. It was all I could think to do. In our family, lemonade was the Band-Aid to fix life's troubles. Mom's teeth chattered against the glass as she tilted it to her mouth. She took a sip and left the glass teetering on the worn upholstery of her armchair as she wrapped her arms around herself.

I grabbed the glass before it fell and stumbled toward the kitchen. Halfway there, I realized the policeman was still standing at the doorway. He was staring at the floor. I followed his gaze. A track of bloody footprints in the shape of my small feet was smeared across the linoleum floor.

He looked at me expectantly. It was time for me to go to the hospital like I'd agreed when I'd begged him to take me home first so that I could be with Mom when she found out about Jenny. I glared at him defiantly. I would not leave my mother alone that night. Not even to get medical treatment for the cuts on my feet. He was about to argue the point when a garbled message came through on his patrol car radio. He squatted down so that he was at the level of my eyes and told me that he'd arrange for a nurse to come to the house as soon as possible to attend to my injured feet. I watched through the mesh of the screen door as he sped away. The blare of his police siren echoed long after his car disappeared in the dark.

The nurse arrived the following morning. She wore hospital scrubs and carried an oversized medical bag. She apologized for the delay, telling me that the ER had been overwhelmed by an emergency the previous night and nobody could get away to attend to me. She sewed me up with black sutures and wrapped thick bandages around my feet. Before she left, she warned me not to walk, because the sutures would pop. She was right. They did.

Jenny was barely sixteen when she died. I was five weeks short of my tenth birthday. Old enough to know that my life would never be the same. Too young to understand why.

I never told my mother that I'd held Jenny's cold body in my arms until police officers swarmed over her like buzzards and pulled me away. I never told her a single thing about that night. Even if I had, I doubt she would have heard. Her mind was in another place.

We buried my sister in a private funeral. The two of us and a local minister, and a couple of Mom's old colleagues who came during their lunch break, wearing their supermarket cashier uniforms. At least they're the ones that I remember. Maybe there were others. I can't recall. I was so young.

The only part of the funeral that I remember clearly was Jenny's simple coffin resting on a patch of grass alongside a freshly dug grave. I took off my hand-knitted sweater and laid it out on top of the polished casket. "Jenny will need it," I told Mom. "It'll be cold for her in the ground."

We both knew how much Jenny hated the cold. On winter days when bitter drafts tore through gaps in the patched-up walls of our house, Jenny would beg Mom to move us to a place where summer never ended.

A few days after Jenny's funeral, a stone-faced man from the police department arrived in a creased gabardine suit. He pulled a flip-top notebook from his jacket and asked me if I knew what had happened the night that Jenny died.

My eyes were downcast while I studied each errant thread in the soiled bandages wrapped around my feet. I sensed his relief when after going through the motions of asking more questions and getting no response he tucked his empty notebook into his jacket pocket and headed back to his car.

I hated myself for my stubborn silence as he drove away. Sometimes when the guilt overwhelms me, I remind myself that it was not my fault. He didn't ask the right questions and I didn't know how to explain things that I was too young to understand.

This year we mark a milestone. Twenty-five years since Jenny died. A quarter of a century and nothing has changed. Her death is as raw as it was the day we buried her. The only difference is that I won't be silent anymore.

2
RACHEL

A single streak of white cloud marred an otherwise perfect blue sky as Rachel Krall drove her silver SUV on a flat stretch of highway toward the Atlantic Ocean. Dead ahead on the horizon was a thin blue line. It widened as she drove closer until Rachel knew for certain that it was the sea.

Rachel glanced uneasily at the fluttering pages of the letter resting on the front passenger seat next to her as she zoomed along the right lane of the highway. She was deeply troubled by the letter. Not so much by the contents, but instead by the strange, almost sinister way the letter had been delivered earlier that morning.

After hours on the road, she'd pulled into a twenty-four-hour diner where she ordered a mug of coffee and pancakes that came covered with half-thawed blueberries and two scoops of vanilla ice cream, which she pushed to the side of her plate. The coffee

15

was bitter, but she drank it anyway. She needed it for the caffeine, not the taste. When she finished her meal, she ordered an extra-strong iced coffee and a muffin to go in case her energy flagged on the final leg of the drive.

While waiting for her takeout order, Rachel applied eye drops to revive her tired green eyes and twisted up her shoulder-length auburn hair to get it out of her face. Rachel was tying her hair into a topknot when the waitress brought her order in a white paper bag before rushing off to serve a truck driver who was gesticulating angrily for his bill.

Rachel left a larger than necessary tip for the waitress, mostly because she felt bad at the way customers hounded the poor woman over the slow service. Not her fault, thought Rachel. She'd waitressed through college and knew how tough it was to be the only person serving tables during an unexpected rush.

By the time she pushed open the swinging doors of the restaurant, Rachel was feeling full and slightly queasy. It was bright outside and she had to shield her eyes from the sun as she headed to her car. Even before she reached it, she saw something shoved under her windshield wiper. Assuming it was an

16

advertising flyer, Rachel abruptly pulled it off her windshield. She was about to crumple it up unread when she noticed her name had been neatly written in bold lettering: *Rachel Krall (from the* Guilty or Not Guilty *podcast).*

Rachel received thousands of emails and social media messages every week. Most were charming and friendly. Letters from fans. A few scared the hell out of her. Rachel had no idea which category the letter would fall into, but the mere fact that a stranger had recognized her and left a note addressed to her on her car made her decidedly uncomfortable.

Rachel looked around in case the person who'd left the letter was still there. Waiting. Watching her reaction. Truck drivers stood around smoking and shooting the breeze. Others checked the rigging of the loads on their trucks. Car doors slammed as motorists arrived. Engines rumbled to life as others left. Nobody paid Rachel any attention, although that did little to ease the eerie feeling she was being watched.

It was rare for Rachel to feel vulnerable. She'd been in plenty of hairy situations over the years. A month earlier, she'd spent the best part of an afternoon locked in a high-security prison cell talking to an uncuffed serial killer while police marksmen pointed automatic rifles through a hole in the ceiling in case the prisoner lunged at her during the interview. Rachel hadn't so much as broken into a sweat the entire time. Rachel felt ridiculous that a letter left on her car had unnerved her more than a face-to-face meeting with a killer.

Deep down, Rachel knew the reason for her discomfort. She had been recognized. In public. By a stranger. That had never happened before. Rachel had worked hard to maintain her anonymity after being catapulted to fame when the first season of her podcast became a cultural sensation, spurring a wave of imitation podcasts and a national obsession with true crime.

In that first season, Rachel had uncovered fresh evidence that proved that a high school teacher had been wrongly convicted for the murder of his wife on their second honeymoon. Season 2 was even more successful when Rachel had solved a previously unsolvable cold case of a single mother of two who was bashed to death in her hair salon. By the time the season had ended, Rachel Krall had become a household name.

Despite her sudden fame, or rather because of it, she deliberately kept a low

18

profile. Rachel's name and broadcast voice were instantly recognizable, but people had no idea what she looked like or who she was when she went to the gym, or drank coffee at her favorite cafe, or pushed a shopping cart through her local supermarket.

The only public photos of Rachel were a series of black-and-white shots taken by her ex-husband during their short-lived marriage when she was at grad school. The photos barely resembled her anymore, maybe because of the camera angle, or the monochrome hues, or perhaps because her face had become more defined as she entered her thirties.

In the early days, before the podcast had taken off, they'd received their first media request for a photograph of Rachel to run alongside an article on the podcast's then-cult following. It was her producer Pete's idea to use those dated photographs. He had pointed out that reporting on true crime often attracted cranks and kooks, and even the occasional psychopath. Anonymity, they'd agreed, was Rachel's protection. Ever since then she'd cultivated it obsessively, purposely avoiding public-speaking events and TV show appearances so that she wouldn't be recognized in her private life.

That was why it was unfathomable to Rachel that a random stranger had recognized her well enough to leave her a personalized note at a remote highway rest area where she'd stopped on a whim. Glancing once more over her shoulder, she ripped open the envelope to read the letter inside:

Dear Rachel,
I hope you don't mind me calling you by your first name. I feel that I know you so well.

She recoiled at the presumed intimacy of the letter. The last time she'd received fan mail in that sort of familiar tone, it was from a sexual sadist inviting her to pay a conjugal visit at his maximum-security prison.

Rachel climbed into the driver's seat of her car and continued reading the note, which was written on paper torn from a spiral notebook.

I'm a huge fan, Rachel. I listened to every episode of your podcast. I truly believe that you are the only person who can help me. My sister Jenny was killed a long time ago. She was only sixteen. I've written to you twice to ask you to help me. I don't know what I'll do if you say no again.

20

Rachel turned to the last page. The letter was signed: *Hannah.* She had no recollection of getting Hannah's letters, but that didn't mean much. If letters had been sent, they would have gone to Pete or their intern, both of who vetted the flood of correspondence sent to the podcast email address. Occasionally Pete would forward a letter to Rachel to review personally.

In the early days of the podcast, Rachel had personally read all the requests for help that came from either family or friends frustrated at the lack of progress in their loved ones' homicide investigations, or prisoners claiming innocence and begging Rachel to clear their names. She'd made a point of personally responding to each letter, usually after doing preliminary research, and often by including referrals to not-for-profit organizations that might help.

But as the requests grew exponentially, the emotional toll of desperate people begging Rachel for help overwhelmed her. She'd become the last hope of anyone who'd ever been let down by the justice system. Rachel discovered firsthand that there were a lot of them and they all wanted the same thing. They wanted Rachel to make their case the subject of the next season of her podcast, or at the very least, to use her considerable investigative skills to right their wrong.

Rachel hated that most of the time she could do nothing other than send empty words of consolation to desperate, broken people. The burden of their expectations became so crushing that Rachel almost abandoned the podcast. In the end, Pete took over reviewing all correspondence to protect Rachel and to give her time to research and report on her podcast stories.

The letter left on her windshield was the first to make it through Pete's human firewall. This piqued Rachel's interest, despite the nagging worry that made her double-lock her car door as she continued reading from behind the steering wheel.

It was Jenny's death that killed my mother [*the letter went on*]. Killed her as good as if she'd been shot in the chest with a twelve-gauge shotgun.

Though it was late morning on a hot summer's day and her car was heating up like an oven, Rachel felt a chill run through her.

I've spent my life running away from the memories. Hurting myself. And others. It took the trial in Neapolis to make me face up to my past./That is why I am writing to you, Rachel. Jenny's killer will be there. In that town. Maybe in that courtroom. It's time for justice to be done. You're the only one who can help me deliver it./

The metallic crash of a minibus door being pushed open startled Rachel. She tossed the pages on the front passenger seat and hastily reversed out of the parking spot./

She was so engrossed in thinking about the letter and the mysterious way that it was delivered that she didn't notice she had merged onto the highway and was speeding until she came out of her trancelike state and saw metal barricades whizzing past in a blur. She'd driven more than ten miles and couldn't remember any of it. Rachel slowed down, and dialed Pete.

No answer. She put him on auto redial but gave up after the fourth attempt when he still hadn't picked up. Ahead of her, the widening band of blue ocean on the horizon beckoned at the end of the long, flat stretch of highway. She was getting close to her destination.

Rachel looked into her rearview mirror and noticed a silver sedan on the road behind her. The license plate number looked familiar. Rachel could have sworn that she'd seen the same car before over the course of her long drive. She changed lanes. The sedan changed lanes and moved directly behind her. Rachel sped up. The car sped up. When she braked, the car did, too. Rachel dialed Pete again. Still no answer.

"Damn it, Pete." She slammed her hands on the steering wheel.

The sedan pulled out and drove alongside her. Rachel turned her head to see the driver. The window was tinted and reflected the glare of the sun as the car sped ahead, weaving between lanes until it was lost in a sea of vehicles. Rachel slowed down as she entered traffic near a giant billboard on a grassy embankment that read: WELCOME TO NEAPOLIS. YOUR GATEWAY TO THE CRYSTAL COAST.

Neapolis was a three-hour drive north of Wilmington and well off the main interstate highway route. Rachel had never heard of the place until she'd chosen the upcoming trial there as the subject of the hotly anticipated third season of *Guilty or Not Guilty.*

She pulled to a stop at a red traffic light and turned on the car radio. It automatically tuned into a local station running a talkback slot in between playing old tracks of country music on a lazy Saturday morn-

24

ing. She surveyed the town through the glass of her dusty windshield. It had a charmless grit that she'd seen in a hundred other small towns she'd passed through over her thirty-two years. The same ubiquitous gas station signs. Fast-food stores with grimy windows. Tired shopping strips of run-down stores that had long ago lost the war with the malls.

"We have a caller on the line," the radio host said, after the final notes of acoustic guitar had faded away. "What's your name?"

"Dean."

"What do you want to talk about today, Dean?"

"Everyone is so politically correct these days that nobody calls it as they see it. So I'm going to say it straight out. That trial next week is a disgrace."

"Why do you say that?" asked the radio announcer.

"Because what the heck was that girl thinking!"

"You're blaming the girl?"

"Hell yeah. It's not right. A kid's life is being ruined because a girl got drunk and did something dumb that she regretted afterward. We all regret stuff. Except we don't try to get someone put in prison for our screw-ups."

"The police and district attorney obviously think a crime has been committed if they're bringing it to trial," interrupted the host testily.

"Don't get me wrong. I feel bad for her and all. Hell, I feel bad for everyone in this messed-up situation. But I especially feel bad for that Blair boy. Everything he worked for has gone up in smoke. And he ain't even been found guilty yet. Fact is, this trial is a waste. It's a waste of time. And it's a waste of our taxes."

"Jury selection might be over, but the trial hasn't begun, Dean," snapped the radio announcer. "There's a jury of twelve fine citizens who will decide his guilt or innocence. It's not up to us, or you, to decide."

"Well, I sure hope that jury has their heads screwed on right, because there's no way that anyone with a shred of good old-fashioned common sense will reach a guilty verdict. No way."

The caller's voice dropped out as the first notes of a hit country-western song hit the airwaves. The announcer's voice rose over the music. "It's just after eleven A.M. on what's turning out to be a very humid Saturday morning in Neapolis. Everyone in town is talking about the Blair trial that

starts next week. We'll take more callers
after this little tune."

3
RACHEL

The moment the traffic light turned green, Rachel put her foot on the gas and shot out across the intersection toward her hotel. It was a modern four-star hotel on a beach road, opposite the town's new marina, where day cruisers were docked in a gleaming white row. Hanging off the biggest boat was a giant red banner offering the cheapest prices in town for day trips and game-fishing cruises.

Rachel gave her car to the hotel parking valet and wheeled her suitcase to the reception desk. Check-in wasn't for an hour, but the hotel had promised to make her room available early.

Rachel had deliberately arrived in Neapolis days ahead of the trial to cultivate sources and get to know the people and the rhythm of the town. She was under enormous pressure to make Season 3 better than the last two seasons. A flood of imitation

28

podcasters were copying her original format, with varying results. She had to keep *Guilty or Not Guilty* fresh and groundbreaking, or risk the podcast falling into obscurity as ambitious rivals overtook it. In short, she had to deliver a podcast that ran rings around the first two seasons. There was no room for failure and Rachel knew it. That was why she'd selected a case for Season 3 that was topical, controversial, and had the potential to spark conversations at water coolers and dinner tables alike.

For the first time *Guilty or Not Guilty* would cover an active trial while it played out in court. The previous seasons had rehashed old cases from years earlier, where everything was viewed through the twenty-twenty lens of hindsight, and with masses of information available online.

Covering a trial while it was under way would put the audience in a virtual jury box. Rachel would give her listeners the testimony and the evidence in real time as it came out in court, as if they were real jurors. Every listener would reach his or her own verdict based on the evidence as the jury deliberated.

Season 3 would test Rachel's endurance more than ever. She planned to attend court during the day and record podcast episodes at night, as well as post on the podcast website daily summaries of each day's hearings and transcripts of testimony, whenever possible. She'd have to do it all without Pete at her side. He'd been in a motorcycle crash and couldn't join her for the trip. Although he'd insisted that he'd help all he could from his hospital bed.

Rachel's first interview was scheduled for later that afternoon, and she wanted to freshen up and change into clothes better suited to the sticky heat. Mostly she wanted to unpack so she could explore the town before her hectic work schedule began. Her heart sank a little when the hotel reception clerk said that her room was still being cleaned.

Rachel headed to the lobby cafe, sitting at a small, round table while she waited for her room. Behind her was a gilded birdcage. She assumed it was ornamental until she heard a rustling noise and turned around to see a brown bird with a reddish tail scratching listlessly at birdseed. A waiter passed by. She called him over and ordered a glass of freshly squeezed orange juice.

"What kind of bird is that?" Rachel asked the waiter when he returned with her drink.

"It's a nightingale," he said. "The manager thought it was a cute idea to have a songbird

30

in the lobby. The problem is that bird doesn't know how to sing. I've never heard it so much as <u>tweet</u>. It's not much to look at, either. Between you and me, I think it's a <u>fake</u>. I don't think it's a nightingale at all."

"Well, I'm hardly a bird expert, but even I can tell that's one unhappy bird," Rachel said.

"Maybe," the waiter said, shrugging helplessly as if to tell her that he had no influence when it came to the bird's welfare. "You're here for the trial, aren't you?" he asked, changing the subject.

"What makes you think that?" Rachel responded, suddenly on guard.

"You don't have a vacation vibe. The manager said we'd be getting some guests staying here for the trial. Media types. Lawyers too."

Rachel could tell he was fishing to find out which category she fell into, but she had no intention of satisfying his curiosity. She'd booked into the hotel using Pete's family name for a reason. She didn't want anyone at the hotel to know her true identity.

"I gather the trial is an emotional topic around here," she said.

"It can get heated," he agreed. "Everyone knows the boy involved. Some personally and some by reputation. He's pretty famous around here. And this town is small enough that people can pretty much guess who the girl is, even though her name has been kept out of the newspapers."

"If everyone knows everyone, I'm surprised the trial wasn't moved to a different jurisdiction."

"I heard the judge refused to allow it to be moved. Said he had faith in the jurors. I think he's right. They'll be fair. I don't think it's true that everyone knows everyone here. Maybe once. Neapolis isn't a small town anymore."

"Have you lived here long?" Rachel asked.

"My parents moved here when I left for college. I visit them in the summer and work at the hotel during the tourist season." He wiped the table next to Rachel's as he spoke.

"You must like the place if you come every summer?"

"It's great for kids and old people. Not much to do here if you're my age. Nothing in the way of jobs, that's for sure," he said. "My dad says this town never got a break. The factories are struggling. Fishing and tourism are the big money earners. Neither are reliable. The fishing used to be good. Not so much anymore. The tourism, well, that depends on the hurricane season."

Rachel's phone rang. The call was from

Pete. The waiter inched away, straightening chairs that didn't need to be straightened. Rachel could tell that he was listening in to her conversation. He had a perplexed expression that suggested he was trying to figure out why her voice sounded so familiar.

It was a common reaction. Rachel's soft, breathless broadcast voice was instantly recognizable. It was her signature. That and her tendency to break the fourth wall with reflections on the miscarriages of justice that she investigated for the podcast. The combination made the podcast addictive.

"Rachel Krall has sexualized true crime in the same way that Nigella Lawson has given sex appeal to frying eggs," one newspaper columnist wrote. "Krall's seductive voice and out-loud musings give her true-crime podcasts the intimacy of pillow talk. It's no wonder that it's the most successful podcast in the country. I suspect Ms. Krall could record a podcast on paint drying and people would be hooked on her every intonation and the silky cadence of her bedroom voice."

"I couldn't hear your voice mails properly, Rach. The connection was horrible. I did hear you mention finding something on your car? What was it?" Pete asked.

33

"Someone left a letter on my car while I went for breakfast at a truck stop. It was addressed to me. By name," Rachel said, cupping the receiver of her phone so the waiter wouldn't overhear.

"Were there any threats?" Pete asked.

"It wasn't the content of the letter so much as the way it was left for me under my windshield wiper," she said. "Someone recognized me, Pete."

"It was bound to happen," sighed Pete. "You are a household name."

"I'm not a household face. People don't recognize me so easily, and this place was truly in the middle of nowhere. I don't think anyone here has ever heard of the podcast. It's so remote."

"What was in the letter?" Pete asked.

"Something about a girl called Jenny who was murdered here in Neapolis decades ago," Rachel told him. "The writer claims to have emailed us in the past asking me to investigate. We must have sent back one of those rote letters I hate so much. We should stop sending them, Pete. They're soul destroying. Better to not respond than brush people off."

"Let me get this right," said Pete. "After writing to you several times and getting a rejection letter, this person just by chance happens to see you at a truck stop in the middle of nowhere, recognizes you, and leaves you a letter on your car while you're eating breakfast." A note of worry inflected Pete's voice. "That seems awfully coincidental."

"Yes. That's exactly my point," Rachel said. "I didn't even know myself that I was going to stop until I saw the restaurant sign on the highway. What's the probability that someone who sent me fan mail months ago and received your very polite 'thanks but no thanks' letter happened to be at an isolated rest stop area at the exact time that I made an unplanned stop?"

"Whoever left the letter must have followed you," answered Pete. "Did you notice being tailed on the drive down?"

"I'm pretty sure I saw the same car off and on for a good part of the drive. I lost it when I hit heavy traffic as I drove into Neapolis," Rachel said.

"Did you get a description? License plate?"

"You know me, Pete. I can't tell a Mazda from a Toyota, and don't even get me started on European cars. The way I figure it, there's only one word for someone who followed me across three states to leave a note on my car."

"A stalker," said Pete.

"That's why I'm just slightly freaked out. Not from the letter. The letter intrigues me, to tell you the truth. It's the way it was left for me. The familiarity of its tone. And the fact that whoever left it must have followed me," said Rachel.

"I could ask the cops to look into it. See what they can find out," Pete offered. "My contact at the FBI said we shouldn't hesitate to file a complaint after the death threats you got last year. I still have his card with his direct number," he added. "Send me a copy of the letter. I'll see what I can do."

"Let's keep the letter between us for now. I don't want cops involved. Not yet, anyway. I don't want to be the girl who cried wolf," said Rachel.

"If you insist," said Pete reluctantly.

"I'm sorry, Pete. I shouldn't bother you with this stuff. You're in the hospital and you're probably in agony."

"Nah, they've given me stuff for the pain. Trust me, anything I can do to take my mind off my current predicament is fine by me. Send it over, Rachel; I am actually begging you. I can safely say that if I die here, it will be only of boredom."

"I feel like an idiot, Pete. I'm sure it's nothing."

"Better to be paranoid than to lower your guard, Rach. There are a few nutjobs out there and I am betting that you are right at the top of their crazy list. You need to watch your back."

After hanging up, Rachel took a photo of the letter with her phone and emailed it to Pete. It was only when she was stuffing the pages back into the envelope that she noticed writing scribbled on the corner of the envelope, almost as an afterthought.

Maybe we should talk in person. I'll wait for you at the Morrison's Point jetty at 2 p.m. sharp.

Rachel tore the envelope into strips. She had no intention of rendezvousing with an anonymous fan and possible stalker at an old jetty. Pete was right. She needed to be careful. The first episode of Season 3 had been released. Her fans knew she was in Neapolis to cover the trial. So did everyone else.

4
GUILTY OR NOT GUILTY

SEASON 3, EPISODE 1: VICTIM
BLAMING

Ever since I announced that I'm covering a rape trial for Season 3, I've been inundated by people asking me why. My mother. My brother. My producer. Even my ex called to express his reservations.

The phrase "Rachel, are you crazy?" came up a lot. They're worried that no matter how I report on the trial, I'm going to rile people up. I'm going to offend people. I'm going to get hate mail and abuse. And, perhaps most frighteningly, I'm going to get crucified on Twitter.

Because rape, for a reason that I can't understand, is divisive.

Murder is a piece of cake by comparison. Everyone agrees that murder is heinous. There's no argument about that. There's no difference of opinion. The Bible says it straight out: "Thou shalt not kill."

When it comes to rape, the Bible is more ambivalent. Much like rape laws have been for millennia.

Raping women was considered a legitimate spoil of war throughout much of human history. It wasn't that long ago when a husband could rape his wife without breaking the law in some states. In some countries, a husband can still rape his wife, or even a random woman or girl. As long as he marries her afterward.

That's why I chose this case rather than cover another murder trial for Season 3. I want to make you think about how rape and the threat of rape affect the lives of women in a hundred different ways.

I suppose there's another reason why I chose to cover this case. Long before I heard about the rape trial in Neapolis, there was another case I worked on that, well, I'd be lying if I didn't tell you that it got to me. Even today, I get kind of teary. And emotional. As you can probably hear . . . Damn, I promised I wouldn't cry when I told you the story.

The victim was my age. She lived on my block. We shopped at the same supermarket. We took shortcuts through the same park at night. We took the same train from the same platform. So, yeah, her death felt personal.

It was my park. My neighborhood. And she

died there, on a damp stretch of grass where my friends and I would play Frisbee in the summer.

But . . . if I'm honest, I think there was more to it than that awful, selfish thought that "but for the grace of God go I." Her story, out of all of the stories that I covered as a crime reporter, tore me up because of the way she was treated after her death.

I won't say her real name, but let's call her Cat Girl. She loved cats. She had a miniature sphinxlike cat tattooed on her shoulder. That was how she was identified — through that tattoo. She worked at an animal shelter on Sundays and at a soup kitchen on Wednesdays. She was kind and funny. By all accounts, she was a talented jazz musician with a husky, evocative voice that put chills down my spine the first time I heard a recording of her singing. If that wasn't enough, she played some seriously good sax.

Cat Girl worked at a little jazz club in Carytown, in downtown Richmond. Music lovers went there for the jazz. College students went there for the Happy Hour specials. The bar was a hole-in-the-wall sort of place. Narrow wooden stairs at a side-street entrance leading down to a basement bar. It had midnight blue walls and grungy water-stained tables with mismatched chairs. Nobody noticed because the place was too dark to see anything except the stage.

It was a Thursday night. Cat Girl performed a few songs in between serving tables. At some point, a big-shot record producer who was out scouting talent gave her his business card and invited her to audition for a band he was putting together. It was the biggest break she'd ever had. His business card was listed in her personal effects in the autopsy report. It was a sobering reminder that her life went from elation to tragedy in the space of hours.

When the bar closed, she walked home instead of taking a cab. Maybe she wanted to unwind. It was early summer. A perfect night for walking. So she walked. Why not. Right?

It took fifteen minutes for her to walk home. The last part was a little dicey. Remember, it was my neighborhood. I knew it like the back of my hand. Before she cut through the park, she texted her friend to say she was almost home. I guess you can figure out the rest.

Her body was found by a jogger. She was lying on the grass in the middle of the park. Her clothes and hair were wet. It had rained overnight. Her underwear lay in a ball in a puddle and her skirt was hiked up. There were bruises around her throat. She'd been raped and strangled.

It was the way that she'd been left exposed

41

by her killer that sickened me most. He'd taken everything from her. He'd taken her life. Yet even in death, he had to degrade her in one final act of humiliation.

The area where she was murdered was a popular neighborhood for college students living in off-campus apartments. Rumors spread like wildfire that she was killed by a serial killer. Well, you can imagine the hysteria.

It didn't help any when the cops told women living in the area to take precautions. You know, the usual stuff. Hold your keys between your fingers to use as a weapon. Keep your phone in your hand and dial nine-one-one if you're being followed or feel afraid. If every woman who felt afraid called nine-one-one, the switchboard would melt. That is what women live with every day of our lives.

A lot of women felt the cops were blaming Cat Girl instead of her rapist and killer. These women argued that women should be able to walk wherever they want, whenever they want. If they walk home late at night through a park, they shouldn't be criticized for it. And they sure as hell shouldn't be raped and murdered for it.

When school kids are shot by a random shooter, nobody asks whether the victims should have taken more precautions. Nobody suggests that maybe the victims should have skipped school that day. Nobody ever blames the victims.

So why is it that when women are attacked, the onus is on them? "If only she hadn't walked home alone." "If only she hadn't cut through the park." "If only she'd taken a cab."

When it comes to rape, it seems to me "if only" is used all the time. Never about the man. Nobody ever says "if only" he hadn't raped her. It's always about the woman. If only . . .

As I was researching possible cases for Season 3, I thought a lot about Cat Girl and what happened to her. Mostly I thought about the way she was blamed for her own rape and murder.

Then I heard about the upcoming trial in Neapolis. Something about it moved me so deeply that I couldn't get it out of my mind. It reminded me of the Cat Girl case even though the Neapolis case is different in so many ways. In almost every way.

There is one thing that is exactly the same. That's the blame-the-victim game. That hasn't changed at all. Just like with Cat Girl, I kept hearing people blaming the girl at the center of this case in Neapolis.

This trial isn't about the victim. It's about the man accused of raping her. Yet somehow you could be mistaken for thinking that the victim

43

is on trial, too, because, like most rape trials, the case largely rests on his word against her word. The alleged rapist and the alleged victim. Which one of them is speaking the truth?

The trial starts next week. We're in this together. Let's see where the evidence takes us.

I'm Rachel Krall and this is *Guilty or Not Guilty,* the podcast that puts you in the jury box.

5
RACHEL

Rachel had to stand on her tiptoes to get a glimpse of the sea from her hotel room window. The reception clerk had told her that she'd been upgraded to an ocean view room when he handed her the key card downstairs. He hadn't mentioned the view would be obstructed by the smokey gray glass of the marina restaurant complex across the road.

Rachel let go of the white netting of the drapes, disappointed by the uninspiring view. She returned to unpacking her suitcase and settling into what would be her home and office for the duration of the trial.

There was a desk, a coffee-making nook, and a brocade armchair alongside a bronze lamp on the blue-gray carpet. In the bathroom was a glass-enclosed shower with a pile of fluffy white towels and an assortment of miniature bottles of translucent body wash and shampoo. The room smelled of

45

carpet deodorizer, vacuum cleaner fumes, and cleaning spray.

Rachel stifled a yawn as she slipped off her shoes and collapsed on the starched white sheets of the king-size bed, staring up at the ceiling until her eyes blurred. She'd been driving since the middle of the night. She longed for sleep and was tempted to take a nap, but she reminded herself that she had work lined up later that afternoon and couldn't risk oversleeping.

She reluctantly climbed off the bed and finished hanging her clothes in the wardrobe before arranging her files on the desk along with her laptop and power chargers. When she was done, she changed into shorts and a T-shirt and went downstairs for a brief walk to loosen up her body, stiff from hours sitting behind the steering wheel.

It was a relief when she was finally outside the hotel, strolling in the sunshine along the boardwalk. After a while, Rachel sat on a bench and soaked up the almost blinding explosion of color from neon-clad swimmers in the blue water and rows of striped beach umbrellas across the strip of golden sand. She felt so relaxed that she briefly wondered how she'd get any work done She had to remind herself that Neapolis might be a vacation town, but she was there for business.

A white-haired couple walking arm in arm smiled at Rachel as they went past. She smiled back and then surprised herself by calling out to ask them where she could find the Morrison's Point jetty. She regretted each word as she said it.

"Morrison's Point," repeated the man. "Haven't heard it called that for a long time. It's past the headland over there." He pointed to the south. "Nobody goes there much. Not since they built the marina and fixed up the beaches around here."

"Except for fishermen," his wife corrected. "Always plenty of fishermen. Just like the old days."

"Yup," her husband said. "Fishing's still good down there."

"Is it far? Can I walk?"

"Sure can. Keep walking till you can't walk anymore. You'll see it across the beach. Can't miss it."

As Rachel walked, she told herself that she was breaking a cardinal rule for true-crime podcasters: Never rendezvous with fans who leave notes on your car windshield. Never.

Rachel had a tendency to break cardinal rules, so she kept walking. Her feet hit the concrete of the boardwalk faster and faster

47

in her determination to get there on time. The boardwalk ended and Rachel jumped down onto the sand. She took off her shoes and jogged by the shoreline, jumping over seaweed while trying to keep out of reach of the lapping waves.

She had a clear view of the Morrison's Point jetty from the next headland. It looked old and decrepit from a distance, but when Rachel came closer she saw that it was solidly built from aged timber.

A handful of fishermen were scattered across the jetty, their eyes fixed on the tension of their nylon lines. One fisherman sitting on a red cooler box gripping a fishing rod looked half-asleep, with a canvas hat slouched over his head.

Rachel walked to the end of the jetty and leaned against the rails as she watched a sailboat maneuver in the distance as sunlight hit the water.

"Have you caught anything today?" Rachel asked a nearby fisherman whose face was creased in concentration as he hunched over his rod. In answer, he kicked open the lid of a white bucket next to his stool. Rachel peered inside. Two silver fish sloshed around in circles.

"Pulled in a flounder earlier. Threw it back. Too small," he said, indicating the size of the fish with his hands.

"Seems big to me," said Rachel.

"Nah, that's nothing," he said. "When I was a kid, we'd get fish three times the size without even trying. Best place to fish for miles. No rocks here. It's all sand. On a windless day when the water is clear, you can actually see the fish through the water. They've got nowhere to hide."

"Sounds like you've been fishing here for a long time?"

"Used to come with my great-granddaddy. This jetty has been here for over a hundred and twenty years. It's survived more hurricanes than you can poke a stick at. We thought it would get blown away when Sandy hit. But it held up good."

Rachel turned around to look for Hannah. She'd made it to the jetty by the deadline. But there was nobody around other than the fishermen and a man with a shaved head jogging along the beach. His dog trailed behind, yapping at the waves.

Rachel examined a brass plaque inset into a timber rail on the jetty. It was engraved with a brief dedication to the crew of a trawler who'd died in a storm in 1927. There were other plaques, too, in memory of sailors whose boats had gone down in storms over the years. The most prominent

49

was a plaque dedicated to a merchant ship torpedoed in nearby Atlantic waters by a German U-boat during World War Two.

"The coast around here is a graveyard. My daddy used to say it was haunted. At night the ghosts of —" The fisherman's rod jerked and he abruptly stopped talking as he quickly reeled in the line until an empty hook emerged from the water. "Got away," he muttered, rehooking his line with fresh bait and shuffling to his feet to recast it into the water.

"Did you see anyone waiting?" Rachel asked once his line was set. "I'm supposed to meet someone here. A friend," she added, looking around again. "I don't see her anywhere."

"Can't say that I've seen anyone standing around. Except you. But that's not to say that nobody's been here. I keep my eyes on my line," he said. "Got to be quick or you lose 'em."

Rachel could feel her skin starting to burn as she waited. The sun was strong. She regretted not putting on sun lotion. She hadn't expected to be out that long and certainly never planned to wait at the jetty for Hannah to turn up. Rachel didn't even know why she'd come. She was in Neapolis to cover the trial for the podcast. She

50

couldn't help Hannah. She didn't have the time. The trial would take up all her focus and energy.

Still, she didn't leave. She looked across the beach. There was nobody heading toward the jetty. The beach was deserted now that the man and his dog had disappeared. The old couple who'd given her directions earlier were right. Nobody came there except for fishermen.

A gull squawked. Rachel swiveled around to watch it swoop down toward a school of silver perch. The fish darted under the jetty to take cover. Other gulls swept in and hovered over the water, but the perch remained stubbornly under the jetty.

This is ridiculous, Rachel thought. She'd wasted a good part of the afternoon and she wasn't going to waste another second. She was done waiting.

As she walked back down the jetty, she noticed a gleam of metal. It was a pocket-knife, stuck into the post of a timber rail. Rachel squatted down to take a closer look. The pocketknife was skewering an envelope into the timber. The knife's blade was pushed into the wood so deeply that Rachel had to use all her strength to tug it free, grabbing the paper before it fell between the slats of jetty. It was an envelope. Her name was written on it in what was becoming familiar handwriting.

Rachel closed the knife and put it in her pocket. She took a closer look at the timber post. Someone had carved a heart into the timber exactly where the envelope had been pinned. An inscription had been painstakingly pried into the wood with the sharp tip of a knife: *In loving memory of Jenny Stills, who was viciously murdered here when she was just 16. Justice will be done.*

Rachel remembered seeing a fisherman slouched on a red cooler box in the same spot earlier. The fisherman was gone.

She sat down on the timber decking. Her legs hung over the side of the jetty as she opened the envelope. It had a big hole through it from being pierced by the knife.

Rachel heard the faint ring of her phone. She retrieved it from her bag. It was Pete, but he had already hung up by the time she answered it. He'd left her a voice mail message. She pressed her phone hard against her ear to listen to his message above the wind.

"Rach, I called Tina, the student who interned for us in the spring. She remembers getting emails asking you to investigate the death of a girl called Jenny. She sent back the usual form letter. The writer wasn't happy. She wrote back. Begged us to help her. Tina sent another 'rejection' note. Then the writer stopped emailing us —"

The last part of Pete's message was drowned out by a sudden peal of laughter. Teenagers were running onto the jetty, making it sway as they climbed over the handrail and jumped into the waves with loud whoops. One splash followed another until they were all in the water except for a girl with long blond hair, who stood uncertainly on the narrow ledge, her back to the rails. The others treaded water, waiting for her to jump.

"Come on," someone shouted.

The girl hesitated.

"Jump already!"

The girl took a deep breath and jumped into the water, splashing Rachel and the note. The paper was damp and the ink was bleeding as Rachel began to read.

6
HANNAH

Rachel, I wrote to you about my sister Jenny five months ago. I received a response from your office. It was signed by you, but I got the impression that you didn't write it. In the letter, you said that you were deeply sorry to hear about my tragedy but that you weren't able to help. You wished me the best of luck and said that you hoped that I'd get justice for my sister.

I appreciate the sentiment. I really do. At the same time, and I hope you don't mind me saying so, I don't see how that could possibly happen. Not without your help. The cops gave up a long time ago. You're the only person who can help me now. If I didn't believe that then I wouldn't have left you that letter at the rest stop. You looked flustered when you found it. I wasn't sure whether you'd read it. But you did. Otherwise you wouldn't have come to the jetty and you wouldn't be reading this note.

I know that Jenny is just a name to you, so I want you to understand what she meant to me. Perhaps then you'll reconsider.

Jenny had long blond hair the color of corn and the same pale blue eyes as our mother. Light freckles flecked her nose and cheekbones. She had a wide smile with a slight gap between her front teeth that she hated. I always thought it was her most beautiful feature.

Jenny was more than my big sister. She took care of me when our mother was at work, which was often, since Mom worked two jobs until her health waned. Jenny picked me up from school and took me to the supermarket, where we'd do homework in the staff room until Mom's shift was over. Sometimes if Mom worked late, we'd take the bus home and Jenny would fix dinner. My sister's loss left a gaping hole in my heart that has never healed.

After Jenny's funeral, Mom's decline was quick. Her complexion faded into the lifeless gray of a dying tree. Her eyes were flat. She moved slowly with the listlessness of an old woman. Most troubling of all, for the first time since she'd been diagnosed she made no effort to hide her suffering.

Before Jenny died, Mom would pick lemons from our tree and juice them by hand to make a pitcher of lemonade. All the while, she'd talk enthusiastically about plans for the summer and a promised road trip the following year. Though maybe even then she knew that it would never happen.

After Jenny died, there was nothing. No hope. No plans. No thoughts about the future. Mom stopped fighting. She capitulated. Without a will to live, those relentless invaders surged through her body, leaving devastation in their cancerous wake.

Day and night, she lay in bed facing the wall, staring at photos of Jenny. It was almost as if she turned her back on life. And me. Within weeks of Jenny's death, my mother's casket was lowered into the ground alongside Jenny's grave. I wasn't there for the funeral. I was in the hospital.

When I was feeling better, the psychologist, a pretty woman with a heart-shaped face and short dark hair whose name I have long forgotten, offered to take me to the cemetery so I could lay flowers at their graves. She said it was important to say goodbye. I ignored her offer as I sat in my usual spot on the floor by the hospital windows, hugging my knees to my body as I looked through the glass panes at hedges clipped to rectangular perfection.

I haven't told this to a living soul, but if

I'd gone to the cemetery and stood by my mother's and sister's graves then I would have found a way to join them/ For they were the only family that I had ever known and the pain at their loss sears my soul to this day./

I never returned home, though I remember every nook and cranny of our simple house. We lived south of town, inland from the beach. Mom called it no-man's-land, because there was nothing much there except for us./

It was an old two-bedroom house with a rusty flat roof that leaked when it rained hard. We had an overgrown garden of fruit trees in the back. Hanging from an apple tree was a rope tied to an old tire that I'd swing on while Mom hung clothes on the washing line. That house and her beaten-up station wagon were about all we had in the world./

I don't remember much about my time at the hospital. I sat by the bay window most days, thinking about home/ It was from my usual perch that I saw a man and woman arrive one afternoon. He walked with a pronounced limp. She was soft and ached with a maternal need that I could sense as I watched them through the glass window./

They shuffled across the sloping lawn to

the hospital entrance. Their pace was excruciatingly slow. I silently urged them on. She held his arm to support him as they climbed the stairs to the main doors, and then disappeared out of my line of sight.

I knew without having to be told that they were the couple who had offered to foster me. I'd already informed the psychologist in no uncertain terms that I would not live with strangers. She said that I needed a family that would love me as their own. I told her that no family would love me the way my real family had done.

It took time, but eventually I realized I couldn't stay at the hospital forever. A foster family was my only option. I had no relatives that I knew of. I asked the psychologist if the couple she'd told me about had other children. She said they hadn't been blessed in that way. I asked why and she told me that she guessed it was because he'd been hurt in a war and that it had taken a long time for him to heal.

I learned much later that Henry was injured five weeks into his first tour of Vietnam, when a grenade exploded in a ditch not far from where he lay. He spent more time in rehabilitation than he had on the battlefield.

A surgeon at a U.S. military hospital saved

him by stopping the bleeding and removing whatever shrapnel he had time to pull out in the meatball surgery they did in those battlefield hospitals. The shards he left behind caused Henry terrible pain for the rest of his life. Henry was a kind man who spoke little and left it to his wife to run the household. Her name was Kate. Henry always called her Kitty.

On the day I first met them, they walked into the hospital recreation room, their eyes only on me as I stood uncertainly while introductions were made. Before I could say a word Kitty embraced me with plump arms and the scent of jasmine. It was probably only a second or two, but I could have stood like that for hours. In her arms. For the first time since Jenny died, I felt safe. When Jenny died, my mother surrendered to death. Now I embraced life. I cherished it and protected it as if it were the sputtering flame of a candle. I couldn't look back. Only forward. Or my life would be unendurable.

In the months that followed I moved to Kitty and Henry's graceful home across the state, near the Appalachian foothills. I wore pretty cotton clothes in shades of pastel and white. I slept in a cream four-poster bed in an upstairs bedroom. Henry painted the walls a dusty pink. Kitty plaited my hair and drove me to school and dance class and soccer practice. Nothing was too much for them.

When my art teacher told Kitty that I had talent, Kitty arranged extra classes with a private teacher. She covered her living room walls with my creations, even those that only a parent could love. Time passed and we blended into a family. I can't remember exactly when the adoption went through. I must have been around thirteen.

During those first weeks, Kitty slept on an armchair in my room when I woke screaming during the night. Eventually they bought me a night-light. I used that night-light throughout my childhood out of politeness. It never stopped the nightmares. Not once.

My night terrors became so bad that when I went to college my roommate asked to be reassigned. She said that she couldn't live with someone who screamed as if she were being murdered. I learned to stifle my screams by burying my head in my pillow.

I made an appointment at the college campus medical clinic and asked the doctor for a prescription for sleeping tablets. He suggested I consider therapy. I told him that I was just fine with the medication. I fooled him. I didn't fool myself.

7
GUILTY OR NOT GUILTY

SEASON 3, EPISODE 2: THE SHORTCUT

I'm starting to get a feel for Neapolis. The population here is just over ninety-six thousand. Around a quarter of that are the original townsfolk. The rest are imports, mostly military families — there are two military bases near town — and retirees. There's a cottage industry of retirement homes for older folk drawn to this isolated but beautiful coastal strip by affordable beachfront property and the relaxed lifestyle of a sleepy seaside town.

Before the relatively recent population spike, Neapolis was your classic small town. Everyone knew everyone. In fact, it still has that small-town vibe. The town is on a weather-beaten stretch of North Carolina coast. It gets pummeled by storms, and occasionally by hurricanes. Cartographers can never properly chart the coastline. It changes every year.

The locals love their water sports; fishing,

sailing, windsurfing, and sea kayaking. There are shipwrecks along the coast for scuba divers, and a golf course for those who prefer to keep their feet on dry land.

Despite its beautiful beaches and laid-back atmosphere, Neapolis hasn't taken off in a big way with vacationers. I'm not sure why. Maybe it's because it's never been able to shake off its blue-collar roots. Or maybe it's because it's hard to get here. There's no commercial airport nearby. No train. It's at the end of a dead-end offshoot that is itself an offshoot of Interstate Ninety-five.

There's a decent-size hospital. A courthouse and a local paper, the *Neapolis Gazette.* Flip through its pages and it quickly becomes apparent that the political bent here is more red than blue.

Local cuisine? I'll have to get back to you on that one, but I've been told the crabs around here are something special.

They have a languid way of talking in these parts. As if they have all the time in the world. Which they sort of do, because the rat race feels very far away. Neapolis is surrounded by national parks, a marine reserve, and some expansive beaches. The locals say they're the prettiest beaches anywhere. From what I've seen so far, they could well be right.

Speaking of sweeping landscapes, you've

probably heard background noise behind me as I talk. I'm not in the studio right now. Maybe you can figure out where I am?

I'll hold out the microphone so you can hear the ambient noise. Listen real hard.

Can you hear it?

It's loud. Right?

There's a definite whoosh. Like a waterfall.

Except there's no water here.

I'm actually in the middle of a barren field of long wild grass. That whoosh you hear is grass swaying in the wind. We forget how loud nature can be when there are no car engines to mask the magical sound of a windblown field.

I want you to hear the rustling of wild grass because I want you to hear what K heard when she walked through this very field on that fateful night.

K is the name of the victim — sorry, *alleged victim* — in the case we will be following this season. This podcast follows accepted practice by media outlets to withhold the names of victims of sexual assault. So I won't be using her real name in the podcasts. We're going to refer to her as K.

It was a Saturday afternoon. Nearly dusk. The sun was low and the light was ebbing. It was fall. The field I am walking through right now was burnished in rusts and dark autumn

63

gold. Running along the side of the field is a row of dark green fir trees that give it a forbidding air reminiscent of a Brothers Grimm fairy tale.

You're probably wondering what brought a sixteen-year-old girl to a desolate field close to nightfall. It was something very simple that I bet happened to you all at least once in your lives: she missed her bus.

K was heading to her best friend Lexi's house for a sleepover. By the time she reached the bus stop, the bus had gone. Happens to the best of us, right? So K walked.

She had two choices. She could walk along the main road. It would take three-quarters of an hour. Or she could cut through this field. It would take fifteen, twenty minutes tops. She chose the narrow track where I'm walking right now. You can probably hear my feet crunch on the dirt as I walk down the path.

Let me describe where I am right now. On each side of the path is tall wild grass that reaches my waist. Maybe even higher. I'm just short of five foot eight, so that grass is pretty darn tall.

If I spin around and look in every direction, all I see is long burnished grass and the forest beyond. There's no sign of civilization. No houses. No roads. It feels stark and desolate in a way that kind of makes me nervous. I suspect K felt the same way.

I have no reason to be scared. I'm here in the afternoon. The sun is shining, and my producer, Pete, who's in the hospital recovering from a car accident, is on speed dial.

That's not how it was for K. She was here at dusk. Alone. Nobody knew she'd come this way.

Slung over K's shoulder was a backpack, heavy from the weight of beer bottles she'd brought from home. Her parents were out, so she scrawled a note explaining that she was sleeping at Lexi's house. She left it under a magnet on the kitchen fridge.

What K didn't mention in the note was that Lexi's parents were away until the following evening. They'd left Lexi's twenty-year-old brother, Miles, in charge. He told Lexi he was out for the night and that she'd better invite a friend to keep her company. That's why Lexi invited K.

Through a series of texts between the two girls over the course of the afternoon, they decided they would throw a party. Nothing crazy. A dozen friends. Music. Beer. Maybe they'd all chip in money and order pizza. K was rushing to Lexi's house to get ready for the party when she took this shortcut.

I wonder if she found it menacing?

I do. I saw a discarded crack pipe earlier.

65

Right near me is an empty liquor bottle tossed on the path. It says a lot about the kinds of people who hang out here. At some point, K would have felt vulnerable. Perhaps she sped up. Moved from a fast walk to a jog. Maybe even a sprint. The beer bottles in her backpack would have rattled loudly as she ran down the lone field, pursued by the wind.

By the way, I walked both routes from K's house to Lexi's. I can tell you that from a personal safety perspective, both options have potential dangers. Sure, the shortcut through the field is isolated. But the main road isn't exactly safe. It's a quiet rural road. Several cars honked their horns when I walked that way earlier. One car slowed down and the driver leered at me as he drove by. At least it felt that way.

Two men stopped and offered me a ride in their open-back truck. They seemed nice enough. They shrugged when I declined, and drove on. Fact is, though, that there wasn't anything I could have done if they'd wanted to force me into their truck on that lonely stretch of road. I was at their mercy.

It's a coin toss which route is safer. The shortcut versus the main road. Heads you get there alive and well. Tails you don't.

I'm Rachel Krall. This is *Guilty or Not Guilty,* the podcast that puts you in the jury box.

8
RACHEL

The night clerk issued a strained "good evening" as Rachel entered the hotel lobby through the revolving glass doors and passed the reception desk. "Good morning" might have been more apt, given it was well after midnight, thought Rachel, flashing a tired smile in return. She had spent most of the evening in a studio she'd rented at the local radio station, recording her latest episode.

As Rachel moved farther into the lobby, she understood the reason for the night clerk's unease. An unruly group of real-estate conference attendees were drinking beer and shots bought before the hotel bar closed for the night. There was no staff around to break it up, except the night clerk and a porter, a gangly young man who was half-asleep.

Someone in the drunken group finished telling a foulmouthed story as Rachel walked by. The raucous laughter that exploded after the punch line bounced off the faux marble walls. The porter glanced up unhappily, too intimidated to ask them to keep it down.

One of the men stumbled drunkenly to the birdcage. He pressed his flushed face against the gilded bars.

"Sing," he bellowed. "Sing, goddamn it. What kind of stupid nightingale are you?"

When that didn't work, he sang a line from a song as his friends laughed. The bird was silent. The man whistled and then tapped the cage with his knuckles. The bird fluttered, visibly distressed.

"If I heard your singing voice up close, Marty, I'd be terrified, too," someone called out from their table. More laughter. It faded as Rachel entered the elevator and the doors closed.

Rachel's floor was dimly lit when she stepped out of the elevator and walked down the long carpeted corridor to her room, passing room service trays left for collection on the carpet outside hotel room doors. Rachel entered her room and locked the door behind her, leaning against it as she sighed heavily. It had been an incredibly long day.

A sharp stab in Rachel's stomach reminded her that she hadn't had time to eat while she wrote and recorded the podcast all evening. She considered ordering room service but decided she'd make do with the food in the minibar. She ate a packet of cashews and drank a beer straight from the bottle as she listened back to the recording she'd just finished. Satisfied with what she heard, Rachel emailed the audio files to Pete to edit when he woke in the morning.

Pete had insisted that he'd edit the podcast episodes on his laptop while in the hospital. He told her there was nothing in his job description that he couldn't do from a bed. Anyway, he'd joked, it was the least he could do after picking the worst possible time to get himself almost killed. A few days before Pete had been due to travel to Neapolis, he was sideswiped by a delivery van while riding his motorcycle to work. His bike spun out of control and he was thrown into the street. He rolled into the gutter and promptly lost consciousness as the traffic light changed to green.

A few seconds earlier, or later, and Pete would have been crushed to death before he could get clear of the incoming traffic. He was lucky, but not lucky enough to walk away unscathed. He'd sustained a fractured shoulder and multiple breaks in his left leg.

Pete was in traction in the orthopedic ward, where he was expected to remain for a few more days before being sent home to continue his recovery.

Pete had been with Rachel from the start of her journey into podcasting. She'd had a background as a newspaper reporter and zero experience making podcasts when she started Season 1. Pete taught her everything he knew about producing a podcast. In return, she gave him a crash course in investigative journalism.

They made a good team. Rachel was intense and focused. She could occasionally be wracked with self-doubt, but she was incredibly tenacious. Pete knew audio production like he had been born mixing sound. If that wasn't enough, he had a real knack with social media. Most important, he took care of all the distractions so that Rachel had the time to dive deep into an investigation.

Rachel was quietly relieved at Pete's determination to keep working despite his injuries. He'd done a huge amount of work setting up the new season, and she felt it was wrong to replace him with another producer.

Rachel checked her computer. The audio files had gone through. She loosened her hair and arranged her pajamas for bed.

A housekeeping attendant had come into her room to do turndown service while Rachel was recording at the radio station. The drapes Rachel had left open were drawn and the crisp sheets of her bed were neatly folded down. A miniature box of chocolates sat on her pillow.

Alongside the box was a letter from the hotel, informing her that the tourist brochure she'd requested was attached. Someone on the hotel staff must have mixed her up with another guest she thought as she opened a glossy leaflet attached to the cover letter.

It was a brochure of the local cemetery, which the front cover described as one of the town's heritage highlights. According to the brochure, the cemetery dated back to the Revolutionary War and there were a number of graves of historic interest.

The brochure included a double-page spread with a map of the cemetery on one side and a list of notable graves on the other. Rachel's heart skipped a beat when she saw that a name had been added at the bottom of the list. Someone had written *Jenny Stills* in blue pen. A corresponding grave was circled with the same blue ink on the map.

This time Hannah had crossed a line. There was something insidious about the way this message had been sent to Rachel, left on her bed. It was as if Hannah wanted Rachel to know that she could get to her anywhere, even in the privacy of her hotel room.

If this was supposed to intimidate Rachel then it failed badly. It infuriated her. She marched to the lobby. The drunken guests from earlier were gone, their used shot glasses strewn across their tables. Discarded beer bottles lay on their sides, amber liquid trickling out. The night clerk at Reception looked up in surprise as Rachel approached.

"I'm in room four-oh-one-four," Rachel said. "Do you know why this brochure was left in my room?"

The night clerk took a moment to retrieve the computer records associated with Rachel's room. "There's a note in the system that says you called the reception desk at six P.M. and asked for the brochure to be brought to your room," the clerk said with a neutral expression that didn't quite hide the fact that she thought Rachel was a raving lunatic for making a fuss over a brochure.

"It wasn't me," said Rachel. "I didn't contact the hotel today at all."

"Then it must be for another guest and

72

our staff mixed up the room numbers," said the clerk, confused at how such a mistake might have happened. "Either way, I'm terribly sorry for any inconvenience."

Rachel knew it wasn't a mix-up and she didn't like the situation one bit. First the note on her windshield. Then the letter skewered to the jetty with the blade of a pocketknife. Now a tourist map left on her hotel room pillow with Jenny Stills's grave clearly marked on its pages.

"Do you record all your calls for training and quality purposes?" Rachel asked the clerk.

"Yes, we do, ma'am."

"I'd like to listen to the call from earlier in which I supposedly called to request the brochure," Rachel said.

The clerk retrieved the recording of the call from the computer and played it back for Rachel, who had to lean over the counter to hear the audio properly. A woman had called the hotel and in a poor attempt at mimicking Rachel's voice had asked for a brochure that had been left for her at the concierge's desk to be brought up to her room.

"Does that person sound like me?" Rachel asked when the recording was over.

"No, ma'am. It doesn't," said the reception clerk, swallowing nervously. "It's very strange. I'll ask the manager to look into it first thing in the morning."

Rachel asked the clerk to note in her file that moving forward, nobody had her permission to enter her room other than the morning cleaner. No turndown service. No room access. No mail or messages left for her in her room. She'd collect it all in person from Reception. "And, please," she added, "make sure that my room number is not divulged to anyone."

With that she went back to the elevator, her eyes blurred from exhaustion. When Rachel reached her floor, she walked down the corridor, passing the peepholes of one closed door after the next. The room service trays had been collected. Only one tray was left lying on the carpet. It was on the floor right outside Rachel's door.

Rachel picked up the tray and removed the stainless-steel cloche to reveal a hamburger and fries. It was exactly what she would have chosen if she'd ordered room service. Under the cutlery was an envelope. With her name on it.

Rachel turned around. The corridor moved out of focus as she looked down the long, silent passageway of flickering lights and rows of peepholes that seemed to be watching her. The elevator chimed, but the doors didn't open.

9
HANNAH

I hope you're enjoying Neapolis, Rachel. It's a majestic coastline. Postcard pretty. Don't let that lull you into a false sense of security. Always remember that it's beautiful on the surface. Underneath, it's treacherous. It should never be underestimated.

I owe you an apology, Rachel. It was terrible manners on my part, inviting you to the jetty and then standing you up. The invitation was sincere. I truly hoped we could meet in person. In the end, I found it too overwhelming, returning to Morrison's Point. I had a sudden flash of memory. It left me shaking and sucked the breath out of me. I couldn't stand to be there a moment longer. I had to leave. You can't imagine what she went through that night, Rachel.

For me, the past is like an overexposed photograph: so blindingly bright that it can't be looked at with the naked eye. Filled with

76

moments too painful to recall, beyond the faint taste of a bittersweet memory lost in time.

Being here in Neapolis for the first time since I was a child, I've come to the conclusion that to overcome my past, I must remember it. Every detail. From the poignant, to the trivial, to, yes, even the horrifying.

When I return to a familiar place, or stumble across a scent that takes me back to my early childhood, or even taste a food I haven't eaten since I was young, I glimpse a snapshot of forgotten memories. It helps me remember. Funnily enough, writing you these letters helps as well.

It's excruciating, this lancing of my emotional wounds. If I'm asking too much of you to share the burden then feel free to rip up my letters. I won't judge you. But I'll keep writing, nevertheless. I find these letters cathartic. It may take me a while to get my story out. Some of it is buried so deep that I need time to digest it before formulating it into words.

So where were we, Rachel? I remember now. I was telling you about my mom. At first she waved off her diagnosis as a blip. Another obstacle to overcome in a lifetime of hurdles. Eight months after her diagnosis, she was sicker than ever and trying to pretend there was nothing wrong.

On the first day of the school vacation, Mom insisted on dropping us at the beach. She stopped her beat-up sedan in the dirt parking lot, leaving the spluttering engine running while she popped the trunk. Jenny went out to retrieve our beach bag and towels.

With Jenny temporarily distracted, Mom slipped me cash.

"Ice-cream money," she whispered. "Don't tell Jenny where it came from. She'll make you give it back." I bunched it up in my fist.

"Have fun," Mom said, blowing us kisses as she jerked the car into motion. She was heading to the hospital for an appointment. "I'll expect you both at dinnertime. Not a second before."

"Sure, Mom," said Jenny. Her voice was drowned out by the rattle of the car. It badly needed a repair that it wouldn't get unless it broke down entirely. Mom hadn't held down a regular job since she was diagnosed. She worked when she was able, which was becoming less and less frequent. When she did get a shift, she came home ashen. It would take her days to recover.

Jenny must have seen me slip the money

78

secretly into the pocket of my shorts as we walked down the path toward the beach. She knew my mother better than me.

"Give it up." Jenny held out her hand.

"Give what up?" I asked, feigning innocence.

"You know what."

"Mom gave it to me. It's for ice cream."

"We don't need ice cream." Jenny held out her palm for the money.

I handed over the crumpled note. Mom's little gambit hadn't worked. Sometimes it felt as if Jenny were the only grown-up in our family.

Jenny and I found a spot on the sand not far from the Morrison's Point jetty. Her school friends arrived throughout the morning. They congregated near us in small satellite groups of teenagers, lying on towels and listening to music on boom boxes.

The boys wrestled with each other or kicked around balls on the sand. The girls rubbed each other's backs with coconut oil and compared tan lines while watching the boys surreptitiously through the tint of their sunglasses.

Oblivious to the antics of teenagers, I built an elaborate sand castle with turrets, which I decorated with shells. When the heat intensified, Jenny's friends abandoned their towels to cool down in the water.

The jetty was high and the water was deep, so that only the bravest dived in. The boys egged on each other to jump, hooting in derision if someone chickened out. The girls mostly waded in their bikinis into the waves, where they swam and splashed each other.

Jenny lay on her towel, reading a book and listening to music on our transistor radio. Occasionally she lifted up her head to glance wistfully at the sea.

Eventually, she asked if I was all right playing alone on the sand while she swam. I shrugged. It didn't matter to me either way, so long as Jenny didn't make me join her. I hated swimming. Still do. Mom and Jenny tried to teach me, but I always flapped about and swallowed seawater until I ran out of the waves in tears, vowing never to swim again.

Jenny tossed her sunglasses onto her towel and told me not to go anywhere. I nodded without looking up as I contoured a sand castle with the edge of a shovel.

Some boys who'd been jumping from the jetty wolf-whistled as Jenny walked down the sand in her coral bikini. I sensed her self-consciousness, though she tried to hide it by standing taller and pushing her long golden hair behind her shoulders.

Jenny didn't wade into the water like the other girls. She went to the jetty and climbed to the top of the wooden rails. She balanced like a flamingo before diving into the water in a low racing dive that skimmed under the surface with barely a splash. I had the impression that it was her way of telling those boys to leave her alone. She emerged a distance away among her school friends, who were chatting as they bobbed in the waves.

I returned to working on the outer walls of my sand castle. A shadow fell across the sand. Looming over me was one of the boys who'd wolf-whistled at Jenny. He had dirty brown hair and pale gray eyes. He held a lit cigarette casually between his fingers. His friends up on the slope of the beach seemed to be watching him with rapt attention. I had a feeling that he'd been sent to talk to me on a dare.

"Nice castle," he said.

"Thanks." I pressed my last shells into the sand to decorate the turrets.

"My friend wants to know your phone number," he said.

"Why? What does he want to talk to me about?"

"He doesn't want to call you," he said,

kicking at the sand. "It's your sister. What's your number?"

"I don't know. And even if I did, it wouldn't matter because our phone's not working," I said.

He shrugged and walked back to his friends up on the dune, leaving a trail of cigarette ash behind. When he reached his friends, he angrily slapped the money into their hands as if he'd lost a bet.

Jenny came out of the water not long after.

"What did he want?" she asked, wiping the salt water off her face with her beach towel.

"Nothing," I said, deep in concentration as I used my hands to compress sand into a moat.

10
GUILTY OR NOT GUILTY

SEASON 3, EPISODE 3: THE PARTY
Lexi lives in a subdivision a few miles out of Neapolis. It's called Crystal Cove./Sounds to me like the name of a beachfront community./ Except when I visited Crystal Cove, the first thing I noticed was that the ocean was nowhere to be seen. The subdivision, with its cute nautical name, is cut off from the coast by a forest. There's no crystal in the neighborhood, and definitely no cove.

Crystal Cove was built on scrubland by a developer with little imagination./ The houses look freakishly like clones. They're all light blue-gray clapboard with white trim. /They have double garages and attic windows./ Even the gardens are identical. The place feels like a social-engineering experiment gone wrong./

When I visited, there were no kids riding bikes. Nobody tending garden beds or mowing lawns. No dogs barking./

I rang Lexi's doorbell. She opened it wearing jeans and a black crop top with a pink sparkly motif. She's cheerleader pretty. Shoulder-length blond-streaked hair, bright blue eyes. She was friendly enough. We talked for a bit, but she asked me not to record her.

Lexi has good reason for wanting to keep a low profile. You'll learn why later. For now, let's just stick with the idea that Lexi is the girl next door. A pretty one with lots of cool friends and a fair bit of attitude.

When K arrived at Lexi's house late that afternoon, they pulled the sofas out of the way and rolled up rugs to prepare for the party. They made a huge bowl of popcorn, chose a playlist, and tested out the sound system. The first ring at the door came just after eight P.M.

By nine P.M., the party was officially out of control. They'd invited fifteen people. Four times that number turned up. Half the guests they didn't know. Many were college aged. Some were even older.

Almost everyone brought alcohol. The kitchen counter was laden with bottles of liquor and beer. Pieces of popcorn littered the floor like white confetti.

At some point in the night, someone, nobody ever knew who, poured cheap vodka into all the half-drunk bottles of soda in the kitchen. Not any vodka, either. It was a backyard

84

moonshine that could strip paint off a wall. K drank several cups of soda. She had no idea that it was spiked. By the time she realized it, she was already drunk.

A lot of what I know about the party is taken from videos some of the kids posted on their social media feeds that night. In the videos that I've seen, K is unsteady on her feet. She pushes through the crowd in the living room, pausing to laugh and talk with friends. She looks visibly drunk. In the corner of the frame of one video, she can be seen losing her balance and stumbling into someone.

The person she bumped into was Lou Lowe. He's a baseball pitcher on the high school varsity team. He's tall, with freckles and strawberry blond hair. Lexi had dated him a few times. She considered him an ex-boyfriend. She would sometimes tell her friends that she wanted to get back with him. That he was the love of her life. Her friends say that she talked that way about all her exes. It was Lexi's way of putting up a "no trespassers" sign.

Lou remembers that night well because of what happened afterward. Here's what Lou Lowe said when I spoke with him earlier today.

"I had a training session real early the next morning, so I couldn't drink. Not even a beer. I guess I was maybe one of the only people at the party who wasn't drunk. I remember that she knocked into me and said something like 'my bad.' I made some joke about how she could bump into me any time. She thought that was funny and we started talking."

After a while, Lou pulled the classic line. He told K that it was too noisy to talk over the music. He took her by the hand, supposedly to find somewhere quiet to talk.

K allowed him to pull her out of the throng of partygoers down the corridor. They went to the laundry room, where a glass sliding door led to an outdoor courtyard. Several people saw them disappear together. Word spread like wildfire. The rumors reached Lexi. She stormed through the house looking for them, furious that her best friend had disappeared with the boy who she had suddenly decided was the love of her life.

Lexi claims that she found them making out under the laundry line, between hanging bedsheets. She tore into K with a slew of accusations. Most of them were incomprehensible. Lexi was drunk and barely coherent.

Lou walked off in the middle of Lexi's rant. He left K to take the brunt of her friend's drunken fury. He feels bad about that now. He wonders if things would have turned out differently if he'd stayed. By the way, he says it's not true that they were making out. He insists that Lexi made the whole thing up to try to justify her actions afterward and to paint K in a bad light.

When Lexi ran out of insults, she went inside, locked the glass sliding door, gave K the finger, and for added measure pulled down the blinds. K was alone in the dark in Lexi's backyard. It was cold out. Her jacket was inside, along with her backpack and her cell phone.

K walked around the house to the driveway, where she waited to catch a ride home with someone leaving the party. Nobody left. She stood in the cold as people gawped and laughed at her through the living room windows. Lexi moved among the onlookers, whispering her version of what had happened.

K was too proud to beg Lexi to let her in, or to ask someone to call her parents and deal with their questions when they picked her up. She'd get home by herself. She walked down the street toward the path she'd taken that afternoon. This time, it wasn't dusk. It was nearly midnight. More dangerous than ever.

It's a calculation women make all the time. Cat Girl, whom I mentioned in Episode 1, had to make the calculation, too. Should she walk home from the bar, or take a taxi? Should she cut through the park, or take the long way around? Should she speed-dial nine-one-one when she thought someone was following her? Should she . . .

Well, you could go on endlessly. Women, girls, we make these decisions all the time. Convenience versus safety.

Most of the time things work out fine.

Occasionally something terrible happens.

I'm Rachel Krall. This is *Guilty or Not Guilty*, the podcast that puts you in the jury box.

11
RACHEL

Neapolis's old cemetery looked more like a secret garden than a burial ground. It was surrounded by black cast-iron fences choked by overgrown ivy. As Rachel pulled her car into the empty parking lot, she knew it wasn't the smartest thing she'd ever done, taking the bait and turning up at the cemetery first thing in the morning. Curiosity was Rachel's kryptonite. Always had been. Always would be.

Her mother used to warn her that her curious streak would get her into trouble one day. She was wrong about only one thing: it had done so not once but many times over the years. It was also the secret of Rachel's success.

It was Rachel's inquisitive nature that drew her to journalism, and it was her indefatigable curiosity that pushed her to investigate the case of a teacher jailed for murdering his wife on their second honeymoon. Rachel found new witnesses who were never contacted by police, and other evidence that strongly indicated the husband, a well-loved high school coach, had been wrongly convicted.

She turned it into the first season of her podcast. It brought her to national prominence and revived her flagging career just as she was contemplating quitting journalism and finding what she jokingly called a real job. It also caused a torrent of hate mail from people convinced she had helped a murderer go free when his conviction was vacated and he was allowed home pending a retrial.

That was why Pete was so concerned for her safety. He would have had a fit if he'd known she was at the graveyard alone. Going there was potentially reckless, Rachel granted as she turned the handle of the gate to enter the cemetery. But she couldn't bring herself to stay away.

The gate creaked as Rachel pushed it open. She paused, still holding on to the handle as she surveyed shadowy tombstones covered with creepers. They gave the impression the cemetery was more alive than dead.

A sudden rustle of leaves startled her. The gate slipped out of her grasp, slamming shut behind her with a clang that sent birds flying into the overcast sky. Their panicked wings mimicked Rachel's quickening heartbeat as she moved deeper into the cemetery. Tree branches interlocked into thick canopies, giving the place a dark soulfulness that might have been quaint under different circumstances.

The map flapped in her hands from the wind as Rachel walked along the cracked, cobbled path, trying to get her bearings. The crumbling ivy-covered gravestones were arranged in no particular order. The plots had been dug randomly in past centuries, before the practice of arranging the dead in neat, parallel rows. In the old days, the dead were buried in whatever patches of soil were softest and easiest to dig out. As a result, the cobbled path meandered unpredictably into a series of dead ends. Rachel had to retrace her footsteps more than once.

The map listed a trail of notable graves, all marked with numbers that corresponded to a short historical description. Among them was the grave of an eighteenth-century cabin boy who served on the pirate Blackbeard's ship and was captured and executed for piracy. He was buried in a rum barrel in lieu of a coffin.

Farther along were graves of local figures,

a senator, a nineteenth-century industrialist, and a cousin of the Wright brothers who'd invested in the aviators' early aeronautical adventures. There was also a section from the Civil War that included the graves of eleven members of an all-black battalion of Union soldiers.

Rachel found a path that took her through a row of sycamore trees into the new section of the cemetery. It was a bleak stretch of identical rows of headstones, vastly different from the historic graveyard. The lawn was neatly mowed. The headstones were machine carved. There were no creepers, or overhanging oaks. It was orderly and sterile.

Wilting wreaths and flower arrangements lying on graves reminded Rachel that these deaths were still mourned by loved ones. A weathered teddy bear was propped on the grave of a stillborn child. A rusty train engine was perched on the tombstone of a young boy, its red paint peeling. The sky rumbled. Rachel looked up. Dark clouds were rolling in like waves about to crash.

Rachel hadn't brought an umbrella. She hoped the rain would hold off until she left. She hastily followed the map until she found the row where Jenny Stills's grave had been marked at the far end. She walked down the row until she reached two connected tombstones carved from a simple gray granite.

The dedications inscribed in the headstones confirmed at least some basic facts. *Jenny, beloved daughter of Hope and sister of Hannah. Hope, beloved mother of Jenny and Hannah.* One grave alongside the other. A mother and a daughter who died within three weeks of each other.

Fresh wild yellow daisies were scattered across both graves. Someone had been there recently. It must have been Hannah, thought Rachel. She squatted down to take a closer look and immediately noticed fading graffiti on the bottom of the headstone. She wiped off a thin coating of dirt until she was able to make out the faint outline of a word on Jenny's tombstone: *WHORE.*

A cold chill ran through Rachel. Twenty-five years had passed and someone still went to the trouble of stopping by Jenny Stills's grave, not to lay flowers but to insult her. To dehumanize her. Rachel had heard the same word used to describe Kelly Moore, the complainant in the Scott Blair trial. Would Kelly have to spend the rest of her life being smeared as well?

Rachel saw no other graffiti, although she did find a faded two-toned blue ribbon among old leaves piled up at the corner of

Jenny's grave. It was tied around a bouquet of flowers so desiccated that the dry petals turned into dust in Rachel's hands when she picked it up. Attached to the ribbon was a water-stained card; the ink had run and the message was unreadable.

It began to rain. Lightly at first, and then with a ferocity that forced Rachel to run for cover. It felt as if the elements were pursuing her as she ran, deafened by the crackle of rain hitting hard, unyielding gravestones.

Rachel sprinted through the cemetery gate to her car. She clambered into the driver's seat, dripping wet, still holding the ribbon and faded card from the old bouquet she'd found at the grave. She shoved them into her glove box.

The downpour was heavy as Rachel backed out. Yet through the thick relentless pelting of raindrops again her car, something caught her eye in the rearview mirror. It was a woman standing by the cemetery gate, watching her. When Rachel turned around for a better look, there was nobody there.

12
GUILTY OR NOT GUILTY

SEASON 3, EPISODE 4: INTO THE NIGHT

I'm a visitor in this town. I don't know anyone at all. So when I'm not working, I'm listening to local talk radio. It keeps me company. That and my calls to my producer, Pete, who, incidentally, for those who have written to ask, is on the mend. He should be out of the hospital very soon.

I miss Pete. It's lonely being on the road without him. Local radio has become my companion. Pathetic, right? Aside from keeping me company, it helps me take the temperature of this town. I can tell you that it's fever pitch ahead of the trial.

One theme that keeps coming up is opinions from some people — by no means all — suggesting that K kind of brought this on herself. Drinking. Hanging out with boys. You know, the usual BS we hear about rape victims. This is a small town and there has been lots of

95

gossip about what happened that night. Lots of speculation.

Today I was at the supermarket to buy candy to feed that sweet tooth of mine. An argument broke out in the checkout line next to me over whether Scott Blair was guilty. And even if he was guilty — to quote the lady in front of me in the line — "whether his life should be ruined over one dumb night with a girl who knew what she was getting herself in for the second she got into his car?"

I managed to record part of the argument that broke out on my phone. I want to play it to you so you can get a sense of how the locals feel about this case.

"She was drunk. Means she couldn't consent."

That was from a mom with a toddler sitting in the back of a shopping cart.

"He was drunk, too. How could he know she didn't consent if he was drunk? It goes both ways. Anyway, his life is ruined. What happens if some slutty girl tries to ruin my kid's life by making stuff up?"

"Watch your mouth, mister."

"Hey! You watch it."

"If she says it happened, then I believe her."

This was from the lady working the checkout.

It went on like that for a while until voices

96

were raised so loud that the store manager threatened to call the cops. This town is so wound up about the trial that it will almost be a relief when it finally starts. Everyone has an opinion, but nobody seems to know any facts. So let's talk about what did happen that night.

It was close to midnight when K entered that barren field of wild grass after being kicked out of Lexi's party. The path was slick and muddy. It had rained earlier. K would have had to walk slowly so as not to slip.

The cold air might have sobered her. Perhaps enough to realize that it was a really bad idea, walking there alone. She probably considered turning back. In the same situation, I might have turned back. At least, the sober me would have turned back.

The drunk me, scared and humiliated, emboldened by alcohol, probably would have done exactly what K did. Yeah, if I think about myself in that situation, then I would have kept going. Turning back would have amounted to defeat. K wouldn't have wanted to give Lexi the satisfaction.

At around the halfway point, K heard footsteps. Someone was running toward her. A tall, broad-shouldered man emerged from the dark.

Have you ever heard of the "fight-or-flight" response? It's an instinct hardwired into humans to either fight or flee from danger. Except turns out that "flight or flight" isn't the whole story.

Experts now know that when faced with extreme danger from which we can see no way out, humans freeze. Just like lizards freeze in the hope their camouflage will protect them from a predator. That's why it's now called the fight, flight, or freeze response.

So from what I've learned, K didn't run. She didn't hide. K froze. Right there on the path as the man came closer. When she saw his face, a rush of relief would have run through her. He was a familiar face, a senior from school with a nice-guy reputation.

Harris Wilson has darkish hair that flops over his forehead. That night, he wore a denim jacket over a gray T-shirt and black skinny jeans. According to a phone interview I did with him several weeks ago, he told K that she shouldn't be walking there alone.

"And you should?" she responded.

"Probably not. I thought I'd keep an eye on you. Make sure you get home safe."

"I don't need company," she replied. "It's no big deal. You can go back if you're scared."

She walked off, leaving him behind for a second until he caught up. Silence followed until K asked how he ended up at Lexi's party. He said he and a friend heard about the party

98

on Instagram and decided to check it out. The friend wanted to stay. He thought the party was boring and left.

Eventually, the path came out alongside a neighborhood playground surrounded by hedges. Harris lived diagonally opposite the playground. K lived three blocks away.

They hung out in the playground, rocking gently on adjacent swings as they talked about Lexi, and the party, and school.

Harris had a flask of bourbon in his jacket pocket. They shared it. It burned her throat, but it made her drunk again and restored the euphoria she'd felt at the party.

They listened to music on Harris's phone. He showed her funny memes. They drank more whiskey. Between the two of them, they finished the flask.

Emboldened by the alcohol, Harris kissed her. He said she kissed him back. They messed around for a bit. Nothing serious. When he tried to take things further, she pulled away and pushed off on the swing until she was airborne. He said he was going home to get a joint from his bedroom. Remember, his house was right across the road.

"I'll wait for you here," K promised. She put her head back and stared at the stars as she swung through the air, while Harris ran home, leaving her alone in the playground in the middle of the night. The wind whooshing into her ears would have been so loud that she probably didn't hear footsteps approach until the intruder was standing right there.

What happened next is at the center of the trial that starts next week. We'll talk about it in the next episode of *Guilty or Not Guilty,* the podcast that puts you in the jury box. I'm Rachel Krall.

13
RACHEL

Rachel pulled the fleece hood of her sweatshirt over her head before climbing out of her car in a nondescript street in Neapolis. It was after 11:00 P.M. Most people in the neighborhood had turned in for the night.

Bedroom lights shone dimly behind pulled-down blinds on the upper floors of houses. The lights of a TV set flickered from a window as Rachel turned a corner onto the next street. She counted three houses, all shrouded in darkness. The fourth house had a light turned on above the garage. She walked toward the light and then down a path alongside the garage into the back of the house, where a glass sliding door had been left unlocked.

Kelly Moore's father, Dan, was sitting on the leather armchair in the corner of his office. His eyes were closed and his hands were pressed together against the profile of his face as if he was deep in thought. He had light hair, dark blond with a sprinkling of gray, and a tanned face. Laugh lines permanently crinkled the corners of his eyes.

When he opened them to greet Rachel, his pale blue irises were filled with bewilderment and exhaustion. He'd taken his daughter Kelly's rape very hard. Rachel knew this because she'd spoken to him on the phone half a dozen times as she tried to convince him to meet with her.

Rachel pulled off her sweatshirt hood to reveal her slightly rumpled shoulder-length auburn hair. Her cheeks were glowing from the nighttime walk.

"Sorry about making you park a block away." He stood up abruptly and quietly shut the door that connected his home office to the rest of the house. "I didn't want anyone to see your car near our house. People talk. Especially now."

Dan Moore's office mirrored his personality. Everything was arranged with razor precision. There was a sitting area with a wide-screen television on the wall, a leather sofa, and two armchairs. On the other side was an L-shaped desk and metal filing cabinets. The walls were decorated with photos of his wife and two children and his naval service, all arranged with geometric precision. He was neat, disciplined, and clearly took great pride in all he'd accomplished. Especially his family.

It had taken Rachel weeks to convince Dan to talk to her. It was easy enough getting the defendant's side. Scott Blair and his family had done several media interviews. Even though their new trial lawyer had banned further interviews, the Blair family still worked the media by drip feeding leaks from their inner circle. Leaks that were designed to whip up sympathy for Scott and portray him as an innocent young man who was the victim of a vindictive girl.

It was an open secret in Neapolis that Kelly Moore was the complainant in the Blair rape trial, even though the media was withholding her name from publication. Theoretically, the anonymity gave her a measure of privacy, but Dan told Rachel when they'd last spoken on the phone that it was a double-edged sword. It silenced Kelly and her family at a time when the Blairs were using every means possible to win public relations points ahead of the trial.

It didn't help that the prosecutor's office had insisted that the Moore family refuse all media requests until after the trial, even requests from TV news networks promising to film Kelly and her parents as dark silhouettes and disguise their voices to maintain Kelly's anonymity. "The prosecutor's office is worried it could backfire. Hurt the case. We can't let that happen," he'd told Rachel in a past conversation when she'd pressed for an interview.

Dan Moore's view had changed that morning when he read an article in the *Neapolis Gazette* that quoted "friends of the Blair family" as saying that Scott was severely depressed. "He's lost everything. His career. His friends. His good name. There are days when he wonders if there is anything left to live for. He is struggling to cope. It's heartbreaking seeing him like this," an unnamed family friend told reporters.

When Dan saw the article, he felt as if he'd been sucker-punched. His daughter, with whom he'd always had a close relationship, now shrank if he came near her. He couldn't so much as bend toward her to press a goodnight kiss against her temple without her flinching. She'd sit for hours scratching her arms until the skin was raw. She barely ate. She was morose. Uninterested in everything. She'd changed almost beyond recognition since she was raped.

Dan was so furious that Scott Blair was being presented as the victim to the public that he telephoned Rachel that afternoon, his voice still trembling with anger when she answered his call. He told her that he was ready to talk. She wasn't allowed to quote him, but at least she'd know Kelly's side of the story. The only proviso was that Rachel had to come to his house and she had to do it late at night after his wife and daughter were asleep.

Rachel helped Dan get comfortable with her by asking a string of questions about Kelly's childhood. He reeled off his daughter's many accomplishments. She was a good student, athletic, and a great dancer. She'd won a lead role in the school musical in junior high. He told Rachel that one of his proudest moments as a father was when Kelly asked her friends for donations for hurricane victims in Haiti in lieu of presents for her fourteenth birthday. "Kelly was always full of energy. She wanted to change the world," he said. "These days she can barely get out of bed."

Rachel examined a framed photo of Kelly with her parents, taken after the junior high musical. Kelly had the same lustrous dark hair and dimples as her mother. Her hazel eyes sparkled in the photo as she smiled for the camera.

"You wouldn't recognize Kelly now. She's

a different girl. In appearance and in person-ality. All that confidence; gone. She's gaunt and so on edge we worry she's going to shatter," Dan said.

"It sounds as if the past few months have been incredibly difficult. Not just for Kelly but for the rest of the family as well," said Rachel sympathetically.

"You can't begin to imagine," said Dan, unconsciously rubbing his temple. "The family of that animal have hired a public relations company to help them portray Scott as a victim of an unhinged teenage girl who turned on him when he dumped her. They'll lie their way to an acquittal. People will believe them. They already do."

"What happened that night? I've heard scraps of information, but I haven't heard Kelly's story."

"I told you on the phone, the prosecutor specifically said we shouldn't discuss Kelly's testimony. I can't say anything that could jeopardize our case."

"I won't tell the DA's office, if you don't," Rachel pushed.

"My dad was a cop. I was taught to respect officers of the law," he responded.

Rachel had been in town long enough to learn that Dan Moore's dad was the town's legendary police chief, Russ Moore, who'd served for nearly two decades. A street had been named after Russ Moore when he retired from the force. Some of the locals in the Blair family camp said the case against Scott Blair was so weak that he would never have been charged if Kelly hadn't been Russ Moore's granddaughter. Rachel was curious to see what Russ Moore looked like, and she was a little disappointed that Dan didn't have a single photograph of his renowned father in his collection of framed family photos on display.

"You didn't want to follow in your dad's footsteps and go into law enforcement?" Rachel asked.

"It wasn't easy being the son of the police chief. I needed to find my own way," Dan explained. "The navy gave me that opportunity."

Dan had returned to Neapolis after leaving the navy and started a moderately successful tour boat business. He employed five people full-time and another ten during the tourist season. He had four cruisers and a couple of speedboats. They were owned mostly by the bank.

"I've been throwing myself into work the last few months. It's peak season. Even though the trial is coming up, there's not much I can do except be there for Kelly.

I'm grateful we have the best prosecutor around on the case. If anyone can get that son of a bitch locked up, then it's Mitch Alkins. He's always been a fighter. Even when he was in preschool."

"So you knew Alkins growing up?" Rachel asked.

"Oh, sure. We were in the same grade at school. Then he went off to Georgetown and became a hotshot defense attorney. Made a lot of money and a big name for himself. Now he's back here as DA. Said he missed the old place. Gave it all up to come home."

Rachel knew Mitch Alkins by reputation only. He had been a gun-for-hire defense attorney whose client list read like a "Who's Who" of scumbags. All rich. They had to be, to pay his fees. Nobody else could afford him. Then about three years ago, he threw it all in, returned to his hometown, and left criminal defense law to become a prosecutor.

"You don't find it strange that Mitchell Alkins is prosecuting a rape case after spending most of his career defending some of the most savage rapists and murderers imaginable?" Rachel asked.

"I don't rightly know why Mitch became a prosecutor. I don't care, either. He is back on the side of good. If anyone is going to get a conviction in this case, it's Mitch. He's the best of the best. I've known him since we were this high." He held his hand up to knee level.

"Does everyone know each other here?"

"Not everyone. Newcomers have been pouring in over the past few years. But sure, those of us who grew up here and whose parents grew up here know each other. More than we would like sometimes."

"The defendant's father grew up here, too. Greg Blair. Did you know him as a kid?" Rachel asked. The question prompted an awkward silence from Dan Moore.

"Greg and I were friends when we were young," he answered stiffly. "We grew up to be very different people. We haven't been friends for a long time. He tried to contact me after it happened. I think he wanted me to ask the police to back off so we could sort it out between us. I don't know what he was expecting, that Scott could apologize to Kelly for what he did? That all would be forgotten? I told him where he could shove it."

"You both went to Neapolis High?"

"In those days there was only one high school. Even Judge Shaw went there. He was four years ahead. I never knew him except to say 'hi.' You look shocked." He laughed, taking in Rachel's surprised expression. "Go ahead and say it: this town is inbred. No doubt about it."

"What was Alkins's reputation like at school?" Rachel asked.

"Even at school, Mitch was intimidating. He was smart as a whip with a gilded tongue to boot. That is a lethal combination. He will get a guilty verdict," he assured Rachel. "Strange how life brings old friends back together. Before this trial, we hadn't been in touch since school. That's a good twenty-five years ago. I graduated in '92."

Rachel thought back to Jenny Stills's gravestone in the cemetery. The summer of '92 was the summer that Jenny Stills had died. It was a small enough town in those days that her death was surely ingrained in the memories of her schoolmates. Or maybe not? Rachel figured it couldn't hurt to ask.

"When you were at school, did you know a girl called Jenny Stills? She was probably a sophomore when you graduated."

"Jenny Stills?" He paused, deep in thought. "I'm sorry." He shook his head. "School was a long time ago. I don't remember a lot of people. Why are you asking?"

"She died the summer you would have

graduated. I thought maybe you know what happened."

"I wasn't around that summer. Left for vacation not long after graduation. By August, I was in the navy. Boot camp. They ran us so hard I don't remember anything other than the pain."

By the time they were finished talking, it was well after midnight. Dan offered to walk Rachel to the car, but she refused. Rachel wouldn't be cowed. It was a promise that she'd made to herself years earlier when the cops told all the girls in the neighborhood not to walk around at night after Cat Girl had been viciously raped and strangled near her apartment.

Rachel had decided then that she would not be intimidated. Not by anything. Or anyone. Certainly not by the dark.

Dan let her out through the front door, turning on the porch light as he watched her navigate down the garden pathway. As she reached the street, she heard the door close and the metallic click of a bolt. Leaves scraped against the asphalt in the light breeze as Rachel walked into a cloak of darkness, down the deserted street toward her car.

After she turned the corner, she heard footsteps behind her. It sounded as if she was being followed. When she turned around, she saw nothing but shadows. She walked faster. More footsteps. She wondered if they were her own and she was scaring herself.

She crossed the road on a diagonal and clicked her keys to unlock her car. It beeped and the lights turned on. Rachel jumped inside and drove back to the hotel.

14
RACHEL

Rachel didn't so much as twitch when her cell phone first rang. Eventually, the familiar ring tone registered somewhere in her exhausted brain. She reached out her hand from under the covers and turned off the phone without waking. She buried her head under a white pillow and sank back into a heavy sleep.

The old-fashioned peal of her hotel room phone rudely woke her a few minutes later. Rachel jerked the phone console toward her. It toppled onto the bed as she randomly pressed buttons with her eyes closed. All she wanted to do was shut the thing up and go back to sleep. When nothing worked and the insistent ringing continued, she pulled the phone under the covers.

"Who's this?" she croaked.

"It's Pete."

"Pete? Why're you calling me in the middle of the night?" she asked, her eyes still closed.

"It's morning, Rach," said Pete. "You asked me to wake you early so you could go for a run. Remember?"

Rachel opened her eyes and peeped out of the covers. Bands of bright sunlight at the edges of the drapes indicated it was well into morning.

"So it is," she said. "I'm so exhausted. I fell asleep at three A.M."

Rachel sat up and rested her head on a pile of pillows. The green fluorescent numbers of the clock radio told her it was three minutes before seven in the morning. She'd slept for four hours.

"How did it go with Dan Moore?" Pete asked.

"Not sure." She yawned. "He was reluctant to talk about anything that might come up in court. He mostly told me what happened when he and his wife found out that Kelly was missing."

"Why make you meet with him in the middle of the night if he wasn't going to dish dirt?"

"Don't know. What I do know is that he made me park a block away and sneak into his house after his wife had gone to sleep. He said he didn't want her or the prosecu-

114

tors to find out that he was talking to me. I don't know why anyone would care. It's not like he told me that much. In fact, he was very —" She heard a murmur of voices over the phone line.

"Rach, my surgeon just arrived for ward rounds. I'll call you back as soon as he leaves."

Rachel stifled a yawn and the overwhelming desire to return to sleep. Instead, she rolled out of bed and had a hot shower to wake up while she waited for Pete to call back. She dressed and was pulling open the drapes when her cell phone rang.

"What did the surgeon say?" Rachel asked.

"I need to stay until the end of the week. Between you and me, I'm thinking of staging a prison break. I am so over it," he said, his lighthearted tone not quite hiding his despondence. "Tell me what Dan Moore said."

"I'll do one better. I'll read you his quotes. Verbatim," said Rachel, taking out her notebook and sitting cross-legged on her unmade bed as she turned to the first page.

" 'We were driving up to Norfolk to see John, my son. He's an ensign in the navy. His base was open for family visits that Sunday. We stopped at Lexi's house to get

Kelly. Since Kelly wasn't answering her phone, I went inside to get her.

" 'It was obvious there had been a party. There were yellow trash bags overflowing with beer cans piled up by the garage doors. Someone had thrown up in a garden bed. I was surprised Lexi's parents allowed a party, because they'd only moved into that house a few months earlier. No adult in their right mind would knowingly let their kid throw a party in a brand-new house. It made me immediately suspicious.' "

Rachel climbed off the bed and turned on the kettle. She tore a coffee packet with her teeth and poured the freeze-dried granules into her mug while she read.

" 'The front door was off the latch. I pushed it open. Two teenagers were sleeping in the living room. One was lying on a sofa, fully clothed in jeans and boots. Another was curled under a coffee table with a jacket thrown over his, or her, head. Popcorn and chip crumbs were ground into the carpet.

" 'I followed the sound of vacuuming to the dining room, where I found Lexi. Her makeup was smeared and she was wearing lounge pants and an oversized gray T-shirt. Her feet were bare. There was a wine stain on the carpet near the dinner table. I glanced at it. She blushed like she'd been caught red-handed.

" 'She said it wasn't her fault. That they'd come uninvited and she couldn't get rid of them. It sounded to me as if she'd been practicing her excuse for most of the night. I asked her to tell Kelly to come downstairs. She looked at me as if I was crazy. She said something like, "Kelly?" And I said, sort of sarcastically, "Yeah, Kelly, my daughter. Don't tell me she's still asleep?" Lexi looked confused. She told me that Kelly wasn't there. That she'd gone home the night before.' "

Rachel paused to pour boiling water into her mug. She added creamer and sugar and stirred as she remembered the pain in Dan Moore's voice as he struggled to find words to explain what had happened on the morning his family's charmed life changed for good.

" 'I panicked,' " Rachel continued reading to Pete. " 'We hadn't seen any sign of Kelly coming home. Usually she leaves lights on, or dishes in the kitchen. She always leaves her keys on the hall table. Her keys weren't there. The house had been exactly as we'd left it when we went to sleep the night before. I asked Lexi how Kelly got home. That's when she got real weird. Swallowed.

117

Went pale. I could tell that she felt guilty about something.

" 'Lexi rambled about how she'd heard from other people that Kelly and some kid from school, Harris, left the party on foot. I asked Lexi which direction they'd walked. At first she shrugged and then she said she guessed they took the shortcut through the field. She said that's the way Kelly had arrived. Lexi opened the hall closet and gave me Kelly's bag.

" 'When I saw that Kelly had left behind her backpack with her things and her phone, I knew that Lexi had thrown her out. Kelly would have called me to pick her up if she'd had her phone. I never liked Lexi much. That girl has a vicious streak a mile wide.' "

Rachel turned to the next page and took a sip of coffee. She remembered how Dan had stood up abruptly and paced across his study when he'd told her the next part.

" 'We had to retrace Kelly's footsteps as quickly as possible. Time was working against us. I drove the car down to the field. I saw muddy footprints at the start of the path. There were more than one set of footprints in the mud. If Kelly had been there, then other people had been there, too. I panicked. That isn't at all like me. I've seen combat. I don't panic. But when it's your little girl gone missing, well, that's a whole other story.

" 'I threw the car keys to Christine and told her to drive home to look for Kelly while I retraced her footsteps through the field. A person could disappear in that long grass. I didn't see any sign of Kelly. But I saw things that scared me: a row of beer cans nailed into a log, with holes in them from air rifle pellets. That told me more than I wanted to know about the sort of people that hung out there. The thought that my little girl had walked through there at night made me physically sick. By the time I got home, Christine was sitting on the porch steps crying. Kelly's bed hadn't been slept in. We searched the house from the basement to the attic. The backyard, the garage, the shed. Christine even checked the alarm system computer logs. Nobody had come into the house during the night. That told us for sure that Kelly never arrived home.

" 'I sat down next to Christine. We held hands and put our heads down in prayer. Our daughter was gone and we had no idea what had happened to her.' "

Rachel tossed her notebook on the bed. "That's more or less everything Dan told me," she told Pete, eyeing the alarm clock

119

next to her bed. "I better get going. I have so much to do today. If there's time, I want to find out more about Hannah's sister's death. Somebody must remember something."

"You know that I don't like this one bit," said Pete. "The way she's been leaving those letters for you crosses a line. You don't know anything about her."

"That's exactly why I want to talk to Hannah."

"Look, Rachel," said Pete carefully. "The trial starts in, what, four days? Put this Hannah thing aside and focus on the podcast. We can always look into it later."

"Don't worry," said Rachel. "The podcast is my first priority. I wrote the script when I returned from meeting Dan Moore last night and I've booked the studio to record this afternoon. It would really help if you would keep digging for information on Jenny Stills. Anything you can find."

"I'm digging, believe me," said Pete. "In fact, that reminds me of something interesting. Hannah Stills has no digital footprint. No birth certificate. No social media accounts. It's almost as if she doesn't exist."

"She probably uses her adoptive parents' name. I'm betting those records are sealed," said Rachel. "What about the local newspapers? I ran a few searches but didn't find anything. Were you able to check the regional newspaper databases? Did the local papers print any articles on Jenny's death?"

"I couldn't find a single thing online."

"I'll stop at the Neapolis library this morning. See if I can find old newspaper editions in the reference section."

"Rach, I still don't get why you're so obsessed about this thing. Because Hannah stood you up at the jetty?"

"No," said Rachel. "Because I let her down. She wrote to me, desperate for help, and I ignored her. Just like people ignored Kelly Moore when she stood outside that party waiting for help. I won't be indifferent, Pete. I can tell Hannah is desperate. Otherwise she wouldn't be trying so hard to get my attention."

"You can't save the world, Rachel," said Pete quietly.

"Maybe not. But I can save one person at a time."

15
RACHEL

Neapolis's central library was a light brick building with enormous windows overlooking a brick-paved plaza of cafes and specialty stores.

Rachel took her place fourth in line at the information counter. The librarian on duty was showing an elderly lady how to use the automatic book-borrowing machine. Eventually, the librarian gave up and scanned the books for the lady before returning to the counter to assist with the next query.

"Where can I find your newspaper archives?" Rachel asked.

"We're now a lending library only. Not a research library," the librarian explained. "All our archives and research materials have been moved to the City Hall archive. It's open two mornings a week. Today until noon and Friday morning." She looked at her watch. "If you want to go there now then you'd better hurry. It closes in an hour.

Otherwise you'll need to wait until Friday."

Friday morning was out of the question for Rachel. The trial would have begun by then. Rachel hurried out of the library, determined to get to the archive before it closed for the day. The fastest way to get there was to run through the city park. It separated the new section of town from the graceful heritage area, where the nineteenth-century City Hall building, courthouse, and other administrative buildings were situated along a tree-lined boulevard. Rachel crossed the road and ran across the green lawns, past an ornamental pond filled with ducks and lily pads in the heart of the city park, and up a cycling track that came out at the top of the boulevard.

Rachel was sweating by the time she jogged up the stairs into the air-conditioned coolness of the white, classical City Hall building. It was the first real exercise she'd had since arriving in Neapolis. She saw an information map on the wall by the entrance and followed the directions down to the basement, where the archive office was located at the end of a long windowless corridor.

A slender man with gray hair looked up from his computer screen as Rachel entered the austere office. Beyond him were tables with old-fashioned equipment for viewing microfilm.

"I'm looking for old newspaper clippings from the *Neapolis Gazette*," Rachel told him, still standing even though he motioned to her to sit down. She was in a rush and standing would give some urgency to her request.

"We have newspaper records going back over a century," he said. "You need to make an application to access the original copies in the archive. It takes a week to get permission. Or if you like, you can look at microfilm copies without an appointment. What period are you looking for?"

"Summer of '92," she said.

"In that case, you'll have to go through the microfilm. Those records haven't been scanned yet into our digital system."

"How do I access the microfilm?" Rachel asked.

"We're closing soon. It would be better if you come on Friday when we're next open. That way you'll have time to go through them properly," he said, making no effort to hide his irritation at her last-minute arrival.

"Today's the only day I have," said Rachel, glancing at the wall clock. There were forty minutes left until the archive closed. "There's still time for me to find what I'm

124

looking for," Rachel insisted.

"All right," he said reluctantly. "What dates do you want?"

"June to December of '92."

The archivist turned on an old-fashioned microfilm machine and went through a catalog of slides with a slowness that Rachel found excruciating as she kept an eye on the wall clock. Eventually, he found the slides in question and loaded them into the machine.

Rachel used the toggles of the machine to skim read the daily editions of the *Neapolis Gazette.* She found a number of articles about two local boys who'd been killed in a car accident that summer. There were no articles about Jenny Stills's death until Rachel stumbled across a brief paragraph on an inside page in a local news summary section. It was so small she almost missed it:

NEAPOLIS TEENAGER
DROWNS NEAR JETTY

A 16-year-old girl drowned at the Morrison's Point beach yesterday. She was taken to Neapolis General Hospital, where doctors pronounced her dead on arrival. The victim's name has not yet been released. The beach was closed following the incident. It has since reopened. Police are urging swimmers to show caution in the water.

Rachel's suspicion that the drowned girl was Jenny Stills was confirmed in a newspaper article published a few days later. It too was buried in an inside page in the newspaper:

A local teenage girl who drowned at the Morrison's Point beach has been identified as Jenny Eliza Stills. Police say the girl hit her head on rocks when she jumped off the jetty while swimming at night. Funeral details have not been released by the family. Police and city officials are urging teenagers not to swim near the jetty at Morrison's Point.

Rachel could find nothing else on Jenny's death. There were several more updates on the two boys involved in the fatal car crash. Both boys were from obviously prominent families and the coverage, eulogies, and obituary notices on their deaths were extensive. There were also several updates on the condition of an unnamed third boy, believed to be the driver, who was fighting for his life in intensive care. There was nothing more on the drowned girl.

Rachel's attention was briefly caught by a

photograph from a candlelit memorial service, held a week after the fatal car accident. It was on the front page of the newspaper under a headline that said: NEAPOLIS MOURNS. Rachel squinted at a hazy black-and-white photo of the police chief, Russ Moore, standing on a podium beside the mayor. The police chief held his arms ramrod straight and stuck out his chest during what the photo caption described as a moment of silence for the two dead boys. One of the boys was the mayor's nephew. The other was the only son of a prominent businessman in the town.

Police Chief Moore seemed larger than life, a powerful presence that overshadowed the gray-haired mayor standing alongside him in the photo. In another photo, Rachel recognized a young Dan Moore, his arm in a sling, with his dad.

Rachel toggled through the news clippings faster and faster, aware that she was running out of time. She was disappointed there was no more information on Jenny Stills beyond those two small articles.

The archivist was making a big performance of shutting down the office, noisily turning off the other machines and packing his briefcase. Rachel was not so obtuse that she didn't realize it was his way of telling her to hurry up. She ignored him and kept toggling through articles, determined to eke out every second that she had left until the archive closed. She was glad that she did when she found an article in a newspaper later that year.

CASE CLOSED ON NEAPOLIS DROWNING

A teenage girl who was found dead in the water at Morrison's Point last summer died from accidental drowning after jumping off the jetty and hitting rocks, said the medical examiner's office, which officially closed the case yesterday.

The girl's mother, who is since deceased, had demanded police launch a homicide investigation into the circumstances of her daughter's death. But the medical examiner's office said no further investigation was warranted as the girl tragically drowned while swimming in rough waters at night.

City officials say they have long warned teenagers against jumping from the jetty and promised that warning signs would be erected to prevent future tragedies.

"You'll have to finish now."

Rachel looked up. The archivist was standing by the door with his hand on the light switch. She was out of time.

As Rachel left the building and jogged back to the library, where she'd left her car, she was more curious than ever and frustrated that she wouldn't have much time to look for answers. Not with the trial about to start.

The paltry information and sparse newspaper coverage about Jenny Stills's death had raised more questions for Rachel than it answered. There was a marked difference between the way the newspaper had covered Jenny's death compared to those of the two boys. Maybe it was because of how Jenny had died in an accidental drowning, rather than a fiery multi-casualty car crash. Or because Jenny and her family, Rachel had surmised from Hannah's letters, ranked low in the town's social hierarchy and the boys killed in the car accident were from influential families.

It wasn't only the lack of public interest in Jenny's death that bothered Rachel. She couldn't stop wondering what had troubled Jenny's mother enough to muster whatever remained of her strength in her dying days to demand her daughter's death be investigated as a possible homicide. What made Hope Stills think that Jenny might have been murdered when the authorities were certain that she had died in a tragic drowning?

Rachel had enough time for a quick stop at the nearby police station to see if she could find some answers. It was a flat-roofed seventies-style building two blocks from the library. Rachel handed her reporter's accreditation card to the duty officer and explained that she wanted to speak to a veteran policeman who might have investigated a drowning case from several decades before. Failing that, she wanted to access copies of the police and autopsy reports.

"Do you have a case number? Or a name of the victim?" the police officer asked.

"Jenny Stills," she answered.

He typed the name into the system.

"I'm sorry," he said. "That name doesn't appear in our files."

16
RACHEL

Detective Nick Cooper was on his hands and knees prepping the deck of his two-master schooner with an electric sanding machine when Rachel climbed onto his boat. Realizing there was no chance he'd ever notice she was standing there over the deafening roar of the machine, Rachel pulled the sander plug out of the socket and cut the power.

The high-pitched screech ended abruptly, leaving the tranquil sound of water lapping against the boat in its wake. Detective Cooper removed his noise blockers and protective eye mask as he stood up to find out why his sander had abruptly stopped working.

He saw Rachel and wiped his sweaty palms on his khaki work pants before reaching out to shake her hand. His light hair and stubble contrasted with his deep tan and black T-shirt.

"Was it hard to find my boat?" he asked, putting the sander aside.

"I followed the cloud of dust just like you told me," Rachel said. "Looks like you have a big paint job ahead of you."

"It's the price I pay for having a timber sailing boat. More maintenance, but there's nothing like sailing this baby when the wind is up," he said, taking two sodas covered in condensation out of a cooler box. He tossed one to Rachel before opening his own with a hiss.

"What is it you want to talk about?" he asked, moving aside a two-gallon can of paint so there was space for Rachel to sit on a bench.

"Everything you know about the Scott Blair case," Rachel replied.

Detective Cooper sat on the edge of the boat and took a long sip of his drink. "Nice try," he said once he'd swallowed. "You know I can't talk about the case before it gets to trial. Anyway, the case wasn't handled by me. It was handled by our sex crimes unit. All I did was make initial inquiries in the hours after Kelly Moore went missing. Like I told your producer, I'm willing to talk about that if it helps. As long as I'm not quoted."

"Go ahead," said Rachel. "Tell me whatever you're able to tell me."

"I'd planned to sail out to Ocracoke that Sunday morning when I got a call from the duty officer down at the station. A teenage girl had been reported missing. Her dad called it in. They asked me to make some inquiries."

"Her dad being Dan Moore," said Rachel. "The son of the former police chief, Russ Moore?"

"I see you've brushed up on your local history."

"As best as I could," said Rachel, thinking that there was a fair chunk of local history she hadn't been able to piece together yet. Such as how Jenny Stills had died. "I am betting the investigation was fast-tracked out of respect for Russ Moore."

"No comment," Detective Cooper said, taking another sip of his soda.

"What steps did you take once they asked you to find out what happened to Kelly?"

"In these cases, you really want to speak to the last person to have seen the missing person. In this instance, it was a kid called Harris Wilson. My first stop was his house."

Harris's dad, Bill Wilson, was in the driveway polishing his car when Detective Cooper arrived. The detective was dressed in

133

canvas shorts and a T-shirt. He'd been on his way to his boat when he'd received the call about Kelly Moore and didn't have time to go home and get changed.

"Harris around?" he called out to Bill as he walked down the driveway.

"Who's asking?" asked Bill.

Detective Cooper flashed his police badge. "I'm looking for a girl who went missing last night. Harris's friends say he might have seen her before she disappeared."

"Harris is asleep," Bill said, furiously polishing the hood of his car.

"Can you wake him up?" Detective Cooper asked. "It's kind of important."

"With pleasure. 'Bout time he woke up." Bill tossed the rag onto the car hood as he led the way into the house.

He left Detective Cooper sitting at the pine kitchen table, flipping through the sports section of the newspaper while he went upstairs to wake his son. A few minutes later, Harris shuffled into the kitchen in bare feet. His hair was a mess. His clothes were creased, like he'd literally thrown them on. He couldn't meet Detective Cooper's eyes at all as he pulled out a chair and sat alongside his dad at the kitchen table. Detective Cooper took one look at him and tossed the newspaper aside.

He had dealt with scores of missing-persons cases during his years on the force. The scenario was almost always the same: A teenager runs away and the parents immediately expect a missing-persons file to be opened and no stone to be left unturned in the search for their kid. The kid inevitably turns up hours or days later. It's discovered he, or she, was staying with friends after a fight at home. Sometimes the pattern repeated itself when the kid ran off again after another argument.

He'd assumed this would be one of those cases. That is, until he set eyes on Harris. His eyes were bloodshot and he was showing an inordinate amount of interest in the floor. More troubling, Harris reeked of alcohol and weed. Detective Cooper smelled it even before Harris reached the kitchen table.

Rightly or wrongly, in the unofficial barometer of guilt by which detectives measured potential suspects Harris was in the red zone.

Harris took a green apple from the fruit bowl on the table. He looked for a moment as if he was about to take a bite, then changed his mind and threw it from one hand to the other like he was preparing to pitch a ball. It didn't look good. A girl was missing and he was messing around, fidgeting and looking like he wished he were anywhere else.

Harris's father gently kicked Harris in the calf to get him to cut it out. Harris looked at his dad and shrugged. He must have known that he stank of marijuana and cheap liquor. Not exactly the way to impress a cop who'd heard that he was the last person to see a missing girl before she disappeared.

Harris tossed the apple around again and then took a bite with a pronounced crunch. Detective Cooper watched him closely, pushing back his chair so he could get a better view of the teenage boy sitting across the table from him.

One thing was certain in his mind: Harris Wilson had gone from a possible witness to a key suspect before he had answered a single question.

"Thanks for talking to me, Harris," Detective Cooper said, deliberately sounding casual. "I only have a few questions. It won't take long." The teen shrugged as if it made no difference to him.

"Are you aware that Kelly Moore is missing?"

"My dad told me. When he woke me up. That's the first I heard of it," he said, his eyes downcast. He shifted the apple from one hand to the other. "What do you mean by 'missing'?" He looked up. Detective Cooper noticed an uncertain catch in his voice. Harris was afraid of something.

"Missing as in nobody knows where she is," said Detective Cooper, watching him closely. "Some people say they saw you leaving a party with her. Did you leave a party with Kelly last night?"

"Kind of." Harris squirmed at the question.

"What do you mean by 'kind of'?"

"Kelly left the party after Lexi locked her out of the house. I saw her walking off down the street in the dark. A lot of us did. I followed her from the house."

"You followed her?"

Bill Wilson sat up so abruptly that his chair squeaked. He seemed to register for the first time that Detective Cooper's sudden interest in his son was not as innocent as he had presumed.

"I didn't think it was right that she was walking alone at night. Lexi was being an outright bitch to her. So I went after Kelly and walked back to town with her. I was leaving anyway. The party was lame."

Harris told Detective Cooper how they went to the playground and sat on the swings for a while until he left Kelly there to go to his house to get something. He was gone for only a few minutes.

"What exactly did you get from your room that was so important that you had to leave a teenage girl alone at a park in the middle of the night?"

Harris examined his nails with the utmost fascination before raising his head. "I got something to smoke," he said eventually.

"A cigarette? Or something stronger? Like marijuana? Don't worry. I'm not here on a drug bust. I'm only here to find Kelly."

"The other thing," muttered Harris.

"I have a feeling there's more," said Detective Cooper, who had no such feeling but knew how to keep a suspect talking. "What else did you take?"

"I refilled my flask," Harris said, looking at his dad guiltily.

"And?" Detective Cooper asked, fishing for more.

"I got a condom." Harris exhaled loudly as he stared at his bare feet.

"So you thought you'd get lucky with Kelly?"

"I figured it was worth having. In case."

"And did you get lucky?"

"No," said Harris. "She wasn't there when I got back. Like I told you before."

Detective Cooper sighed. He would have

138

loved to pursue that line of questioning further, but he had to restrain himself. Harris was still technically a witness, not a suspect, and Detective Cooper hadn't read him his rights.

"What happened when you saw that Kelly wasn't at the park?"

"I sat on the swing and smoked my joint."

"You got high? You didn't look for her?"

"Sure, I looked for her. I called her name. No answer. I figured that she'd gone home. That she'd stood me up. I stayed for a bit, smoked, and went home."

"That's right," his father interrupted. "Harris knocked over a pile of recycling when he came in at around two thirty A.M. I went to check on him not long after. He was in bed. Asleep."

"It would be helpful if you'd come down to the police station, Harris," said Detective Cooper, treading carefully. "So we can talk some more. There might be other things you saw that could lead us to Kelly."

"Is that really necessary?" Bill Wilson said. "You said you only had a few questions."

"I did. But a girl is missing. Based on what Harris has told me, there are more questions that need to be asked. That's best done at a police station rather than here."

Harris's dad picked up a pack of cigarettes

and lit one. "Do we need a lawyer?" he asked once he exhaled.

"It's up to you."

"Are you saying that my son is a suspect?"

"Until we find Kelly Moore, everyone is a suspect. Especially the last person to have seen her alive. Right now that appears to be your son."

Detective Cooper squashed his empty soda can and tossed it into the trash. Rachel's time was up. He needed to get back to his work.

"Do you think that Harris was involved? That he and Scott did this together?" Rachel asked, reluctant to budge until she'd squeezed as much information as she could get out of him.

"Harris was charged with aiding and abetting. That's a serious offense. I guess you heard on the local news that he cut himself a deal. Now he won't stand trial."

"Harris must have been involved. Otherwise, why would he take a plea deal?" Rachel pressed.

"There are lots of reasons why a suspect takes a plea deal. Maybe he's guilty. Or he's innocent but doesn't think he can prove it to a jury. Or, third option, his family can't afford to pay the going rate of a good trial

140

lawyer," he said, inserting a fresh piece of sandpaper into the sander as he prepared to resume his work.

"Even then, it's hard to believe that a person would admit to doing something if he didn't do it," said Rachel.

"Justice is expensive. You've got to have serious money if you want to put up a halfway decent defense. Maybe his family and lawyers did the math and figured they didn't want to risk a long prison sentence for Harris," he said. "That sort of horse trading happens all the time. Otherwise the court system would be clogged to paralysis. I've seen more plea deals than trials in the twenty years I was a detective in Rhode Island, and then the past two years here in Neapolis."

"You're a recent arrival!" said Rachel in surprise. She'd intended to ask him about Jenny Stills in case he knew what had happened to her, but didn't bother in light of his revelation that he was a relative newcomer to the town. "What made you move here?"

He hesitated. "My marriage broke up. I figured I'd leave the force, set up a business taking tourists on diving trips. I'm a master diver. Ended up getting offered a detective job. Now I'm a working cop again. Believe me, there's nobody more surprised than me," he said, plugging in the sanding machine.

Detective Cooper put on his earplugs as Rachel climbed off the boat onto the jetty to the sound of the high-pitched whine of the sander scraping the deck.

She walked down the jetty, passing a line of moored cruisers until she reached the marina complex, where there were several seafood restaurants with tables that spilled out onto a waterside deck. Rachel hadn't tried any of them even though they were across the road from her hotel. They were always crowded and she didn't have the luxury of time to wait for a table.

As Rachel passed the Blue Sea Cafe, she spotted a small table overlooking the water. She decided that for once she'd have a proper lunch instead of eating takeout on the go. Rachel chose the seat facing the sea and put on her sunglasses to block the glare of the sun.

When the waitress came around, Rachel ordered the crab burger from the specials chalkboard. It came with chips, a side of salad, and an artfully presented sliced avocado with a squeeze of lime. Rachel ate it all. She opted not to order dessert or coffee. She'd dawdled enough. When the waitress came around with an American Express folder containing the check, Rachel slipped her credit card inside without looking at the bill.

"Oh, I don't need your card," said the waitress. "Your bill has been paid in full."

"By who?" Rachel opened the folder to find out. Inside was a cash register receipt stapled to an envelope with her name scrawled on it.

"Don't know," the waitress answered as she stacked Rachel's dishes into a neat pile. "It was paid for at the counter."

17
HANNAH

Rachel, have you ever done something you regretted so badly that you'd sell your soul to go back in time and reverse it?

Maybe for you it was getting married to your college boyfriend and then divorcing him six months later when you realized that you'd married your best friend, but not the love of your life. You mentioned that in an interview you gave to some magazine. I forget which one.

For me, it was three weeks into our summer vacation. I'd fallen asleep on the beach to the sound of summer hits playing loudly on the radio, and a constant trill of laughter woven between the crash of breaking waves.

When I awoke, everything felt different. It was still, and very quiet. The ocean was oddly subdued, on its best behavior. The light was soft. The clear blue sky had been replaced by billowing gray clouds. The temperature was cooler. I sat up and saw that we were the only people lying on the beach. Everyone else had gone home, taking their towels and umbrellas with them. Down the headland, surfers with longboards and half-zipped wet suits emerged from the water and crossed the beach in a raggedy procession as they wrapped up their day.

Jenny was putting on a tie-dyed turquoise beach dress over her bikini. Her damp hair hung loose. I packed my things into the beach bag and we began the long walk home. Our hair knotted with salt and our flushed skin sprinkled with sand.

When we passed the gas station at the Old Mill Road, I asked Jenny if we could stop there for an ice pop. It had become a tradition at the end of each day at the beach.

"It's going to rain soon," said Jenny, looking up at the overcast sky.

"It'll only take a second," I insisted. I made my bottom lip tremble dramatically. Jenny sighed and we crossed the road. Long afterward, I wondered if our lives would have turned out differently if I hadn't made a fuss. If we'd kept on walking.

That's the thing about mistakes. Not all of them can be fixed. I can't bring the dead back to life, no matter how much I might wish it.

The gas station was run by a man called

Rick, whose face was set in a permanent scowl and who never had a kind word to say to us. He'd shout at us for treading sand into the gas station's convenience store when we hadn't even been to the beach, or yell at us for opening the freezer door when we hadn't touched it. "You Stills girls don't have two cents to rub together. If you're not going to buy anything, then get out," he told us once when we came in during a thunderstorm. I'd been afraid of him ever since.

I waited near the gas pumps while Jenny went inside to buy my ice pop. My feet were sandy and I didn't want to give Rick a reason to snap at me. I watched through the windows as Jenny looked into the freezer and selected a red ice pop. She crossed the store to the cashier area to pay Rick. Through the reflection of the shopwindow, I saw a pickup truck pull up at a gas tank.

Three teenage boys were in the cab. A fourth sat in the back. I recognized him immediately. He was the boy with gray eyes who'd asked for our phone number that day at the beach. As his friends emerged from the pickup, I recognized them, too. I didn't know their names. All I knew was that those boys always hung out together on the sand dunes, smoking and playing loud music on their boom box. I instinctively knew that it was best to give them a wide <u>berth</u>.

Light rain sprinkled across the cracked raw concrete of the gas station driveway. It was only a matter of time until a downpour erupted.

"You live at the end of the Old Mill Road, don't you? It's going to storm soon. I can give you a ride home if you don't want to get wet," said the driver, holding the nozzle as he pumped gasoline into his truck.

My eyes flicked to the store. Jenny was waiting for Rick to serve her. He appeared to be adding up a long column in his <u>ledger</u>, and even though he must have known she was there, he kept her waiting until he was done.

"Do you want a ride or not?" the driver asked me again.

"I have to ask my sister."

Jenny came out of the store and handed me the ice pop. "We'd better hurry home before the rain hits," she said, picking up the beach bag that had been lying by my feet and walking quickly past the pickup.

"He offered us a ride home," I called out, my eagerness to get home outweighing my wariness.

"We'll walk. There's still time," Jenny said, motioning me to catch up with her. "Hurry up, Hannah."

"My foot's sore. I'm getting a blister," I complained, lifting up my shoulder stubbornly. "I don't feel like walking in the rain."

"We're going your way. I can drop you off," said the driver as he screwed on his fuel cap. "It's no trouble."

"Please, Jenny," I begged, looking up at the ominous sky. "I don't want to walk in a thunderstorm."

"All right," she relented grudgingly. She threw the beach bag into the back of the truck and I scrambled in with it. Jenny was about to climb over the side to sit with me when the driver opened the passenger door.

"There's space here," he said, waiting until Jenny reluctantly slipped inside.

His three friends came out of the store. The one with the gray eyes lit up a cigarette, ignoring a no-smoking sign by the fuel pumps, and sucked in the smoke like a starving man getting a long-awaited meal. The other two triumphantly removed a selection of candy from under their shirts as they scrambled into the cab next to Jenny. They'd obviously stolen their stash without Rick noticing. Jenny was stuck in the middle. The driver sat next to her and the other two boys sat between her and the front passenger door. I could tell that she wasn't happy about being boxed in.

The one with gray eyes jumped into the back with me, staring into space as he sucked on his cigarette. Through the glass partition, I saw the two boys in front swigging from a half-empty liquor bottle as they turned on the truck engine and drove out of the gas station. One of them offered Jenny a sip directly from the bottle. She shook her head.

When we reached the road, we made a turn so fast that I catapulted against the truck, bruising my shoulder so painfully that I had to bite my tongue to stop myself from crying. The boy with the gray eyes helped me up. He told me to hold tight on to the side of the truck so I wouldn't hurt myself again.

"Please tell him to drive slower," I pleaded.

"I'll tell him first chance I get. What's your name?" he asked, trying to distract me.

"Hannah," I answered. "What's your name?"

"Bobby," he said.

We stopped abruptly by the one-way bridge. We had to wait for two cars and a pickup to cross over before it was our turn. While we waited, Bobby jumped down and spoke to the driver. I don't know what he said. They were arguing about something.

He didn't return to the truck. He walked off back toward the gas station, smoking his cigarette. A couple of times he turned around, like he was unsure about something. But he kept walking anyway. I watched him disappear in a cloud of dust as we drove off, across the bridge and up the hill toward my house.

We drove so fast that my knuckles were white from holding the side of the truck so tight. My hair was blowing across my face. I couldn't see a thing. When we came around a turn, the truck slowed down. I was relieved to see the square smudge of our white house and the faint red of our rusty roof set among the pine trees. I expected we'd be dropped off by our front door, or at least at the start of the dirt driveway that led to our house from the main road. Instead, the truck pulled up on the main road, halfway up the hill. We still had to cross the field to get home.

"You can get out now," the driver shouted through the partially open window. I tossed out the beach bag and jumped down. I walked over to the passenger door of the cab and waited for Jenny to get out.

She was trapped between them in the middle of the cab. She couldn't get out unless either the driver or the other passengers climbed out first. Nobody made any attempt to move. Jenny sat stiffly as they drank from the liquor bottle, passing it to each other over her lap. It was starting to rain heavily and I was getting drenched.

I knocked on the passenger window. The boy sitting right next to it rolled down the window, leaving a narrow gap.

"Your sister says she wants to go fishing with us," he shouted over the blustering engine. I choked from the foul stench of liquor on his breath, which wafted in my face through the narrow gap.

"Jenny hates fishing," I said.

"I reckon by the time we're done teaching her, fishing is going to be her favorite sport." He smirked. "She'll be home soon."

With a screech, the truck sped off in the opposite direction from the sea.

18
RACHEL

The radio station receptionist who'd greeted Rachel hours earlier when she'd arrived had long gone when she emerged from the soundproof room after recording the podcast. The overhead office lights were off. The only people around were recording the evening program inside a studio with a red "On Air" sign illuminated above the closed doors.

Rachel let herself out of the building. It was early evening and she was exhausted. The cumulative effects of four to five hours' sleep each night were taking a toll. She was well aware that she needed to break the unhealthy pattern she'd fallen into since arriving in Neapolis. Too little sleep, too much fast food on the run. No regular exercise. Back home she ran four mornings a week. Since arriving in Neapolis, she hadn't done a single proper run unless sprinting across the park to visit the City Hall archive counted as a workout.

As she crossed the road to her car, Rachel saw a letter fluttering on her windshield. She sighed. She was getting tired of Hannah's games. Rachel tossed the letter onto the front passenger seat and put on her seat belt. She had no intention of hastily tearing the envelope open and reading the letter from behind the steering wheel as she'd done at the highway rest stop. It was time to try a new tack. To show no interest in Hannah's letters. Perhaps that was the way to draw Hannah out so they could meet, and talk in person, rather than play this cat-and-mouse game — the purpose of which Rachel couldn't begin to fathom.

Pete was right. The podcast needed to be Rachel's sole focus. There wasn't time to investigate Jenny Stills's death. Maybe, Rachel thought, once the trial was over she'd stay in Neapolis for a few days longer and see what she could find out. In the meantime, she needed to give all her attention to the podcast. The last thing she needed was a distraction. There was too much at stake.

Rachel drove toward the hotel, where she'd planned to eat dinner at the lobby cafe while reading her files on the Blair family. Pete had managed to swing her an interview with Greg, Scott Blair's father. She wanted to read all his press interviews again before she met him and his wife the next day. Rachel glanced at Hannah's letter on the seat next to her. She was tempted to read it, but she couldn't allow herself to be drawn in again. She didn't have time to be Hannah's savior, or Jenny's avenger. She briefly considered tearing it up and tossing the pieces out of the window.

Rachel made it two blocks before pulling her car to an abrupt stop on the side of the road. She put on her hazard lights and ripped open the letter. When she was done reading Hannah's wavy, sometimes barely legible handwriting, she tossed the pages back onto the front passenger seat and restarted the car engine.

Instinctively, Rachel made a furious U-turn and headed south in the direction of the Old Mill Road gas station. Rachel wondered if Rick still worked there and, if he did, if he remembered the driver and passengers of the pickup truck Hannah described in her letter. Rachel got the impression that the truck and its rowdy crew had been regulars at his gas station.

As Rachel drove down the coastal road, she spotted the Morrison's Point jetty, a gray outline against a darkening sky. Again without thinking it through, Rachel turned off the road and into the beach parking lot. She pulled her car to a stop facing the ocean. It was twilight. Rachel figured she had enough time to quickly go down to the jetty to see if the sign warning swimmers not to jump into the water had been erected, just as the newspaper article she'd read at the archive said.

The evening coastal winds were so strong that Rachel struggled to get out of her car. As she walked across the beach, sand blew into her face, hitting her skin like pinpricks. Rachel spotted the sign. It was hung on a rusted pole stuck into a thick lump of concrete on the shoreline, just out of reach of the waves. Its faded warning to swimmers looked decades old. She hadn't noticed it the last time she was there, but then, she hadn't been looking for it.

Rachel stepped onto the jetty. It was unsteady under her feet. She had to hold the rail as she walked, pummeled by the wind and stung by salt sprays from unruly waves. The foamy water looked opaque in the waning light.

When Rachel reached the inscription that Hannah had carved in the timber, she squatted down to read it again: *In loving memory of Jenny Stills, who was viciously murdered here when she was just 16. Justice will be done.*

Rachel didn't hear the jetty creak behind her over the loud rush of wind. Nor did she notice the looming outline of a man emerge from the dark behind her.

"Who are you?" His sudden, angry voice shocked Rachel to her feet.

She swung around to confront the intruder but was immediately blinded by a flashlight beam shining directly into her eyes. From what Rachel could make out, he was a heavyset man dressed in jeans and a plaid shirt soaked with sweat so strong she could smell it. His arms and neck were covered in tattoos, and the left side of his face was crisscrossed by the angry ridges of knife scars.

"I asked you a question," he growled, stepping toward her. Rachel instinctively moved back until her spine was pressed into the timber rail. He pointed his flashlight down to where Rachel had been squatting and moved the beam across the inscription as he read it. He paused the light over the words *viciously murdered.*

"What do you know about this?" he asked.

"Not much," said Rachel. "I heard she drowned here. Hit her head on some rocks when she jumped off the jetty."

"People are stupid. They'll believe anything," he spat. "There ain't no rocks to hit. The ocean floor is pure sand around here. And the water is deep. Real deep. If I remember correctly, she was a real good swimmer."

"If it wasn't an accident, then how did she die?" Rachel pressed. It was the first time someone had come close to confirming what she was starting to suspect — that Jenny's drowning had been no accident at all.

"You need to scram," he growled, taking another step closer. Rachel saw a flash of metal near his leg. It looked as if he was holding a switchblade. "Get out. And make sure I don't see you around again."

Rachel's heart beat rapidly as she stepped away and left the jetty. She headed to her car, walking fast across the beach. She deliberately held back from a full-blown sprint, even though the roar of wind was too loud for her to know if he was behind her. Catching up. She resisted the temptation to look back over her shoulder. She had no intention of letting him think that he frightened her.

When Rachel reached her car, it took all her physical strength to open the driver's door in the strong gusts. She slid inside and pulled it shut. The deafening howl of wind stopped immediately. Rachel took a moment to revel in the silence before turning on her car engine and driving away. As she did, she looked out toward the jetty. The man was leaning over the rail, watching her.

Rachel drove toward Old Mill Road, where she found the gas station at the corner, just as Hannah had described. Rachel filled up with fuel before going inside to pay. The convenience store was brightly lit, with a white-tiled floor and neatly packed shelves. Along the back of the store were self-service coffee and soft-drink machines. There was a cabinet with a heating rack that contained jelly doughnuts and burritos in silver-foil bags.

"Does Rick still work here?" she asked the cashier.

"Don't know any Rick," the attendant said, without looking up from his phone. He shoved across a credit card machine so that she could pay for the gas.

"He owned this gas station, or worked here a few years ago," Rachel said as she swiped her credit card. More like a few decades, she thought.

"Never heard of him," said the attendant, still looking at his phone.

"Would someone else here know him?"

The attendant looked up. "Know who?"

"Rick. The man who used to work here," said Rachel, swallowing her irritation.

The attendant rolled his eyes. "Try Sally Crawford. Her house is about a mile that way." He jabbed his finger in the direction of town. "First house after the empty block. She's been around for — ev — er," he said, stretching out the syllables as if it was a curse word. "If Rick worked here, she'd know."

Sally Crawford's house was a single-story home with a ramshackle appearance from several additions built over the years. The lawn was overgrown with long grass and weeds, which also poked out through the packed dirt of the driveway. On the front lawn was a rusty old camper van and a boat hidden under a mildewed canvas cover. Rachel heard dogs barking in the back garden as she walked down the driveway toward the front door.

Rachel pressed the doorbell. There was no answer. She could see light through the frosted hall window and hear enough noise to tell her that people were home. She pressed the bell again, holding her thumb against it for a couple of seconds longer than necessary.

The door swung open to reveal a man in

his early twenties, holding an open beer bottle. He wore shorts. No shirt. He had long hair and a scraggly beard.

"You're not here to sell face cream or some other shit, are you?" he asked Rachel.

"I'm not selling anything. I'm here for a quick word with Sally. It's kind of private," said Rachel, trying to give the impression that she knew Sally so that he would let her inside.

He grunted and turned around, walking back up the hall, leaving Rachel to make her own way inside. When Rachel reached the kitchen, she saw a woman she assumed was Sally. She was a large woman with bright red hair and she was standing behind the kitchen counter cutting watermelon with a stainless-steel butcher's knife. Her son was using his elbow to open the sliding doors to the back garden, where a group of people were standing around by a barbecue.

"Luke said you want to discuss something," said Sally, without looking up as she cut the melon.

"I was told you might be able to help me with information on the town's history," said Rachel.

Sally looked up at Rachel, taking in Rachel's wild hair and windblown appearance. "You look like you've been out sailing in

160

gale-force winds," she said.

"I was at Morrison's Point before I came here."

"It's not smart to go there at night. The town's garbage hangs out there when it's dark. Vagrants. Addicts. I see syringes there all the time when I take the dogs for a run on the beach on Sunday mornings," said Sally. She cut the watermelon into slices as she spoke, using her whole ample body weight to get the blade through the thick dark green rind of the melon.

"There was a man on the jetty with scars on his face. He scared the heck out of me. Do you know who he is?" Rachel asked.

"Sounds like it's that homeless man I've told the cops about," muttered Sally. "Heard he drops his crab pots off the jetty at night. He's not supposed to," she said, glancing at Rachel. "He's dangerous. Unstable. Cops should have gotten rid of him the second he moved here a couple of years back. They've gone soft," she said to herself as she tossed cut watermelon slices on an oversized plate. She added abruptly: "You said you wanted information on the town's history What exactly did you want to ask? I don't have much time. We're going to eat soon."

"I'm looking for the guy who used to run the gas station at the Old Mill Road," said

Rachel. "His name is Rick. I don't know his family name."

"I know who you mean," said Sally. "He sold to one of those franchise chains a good few years ago. Heard he lives in an old people's homes now. What do you want with him?"

"His name came up in a letter about a girl who grew up here. I was told that Rick might have known her."

"I worked at the elementary school for over twenty years. I bet I know better than Rick. What's her name?"

"Hannah Stills," said Rachel.

"Sure, I remember her." Sally put down the knife on the cutting board. "She was a quiet little thing with long brown hair and sad eyes. Lost all her family within a month. Wouldn't talk afterward. They brought in a psychologist, but she refused to say a word. Not a sound. After that she left town," she said. "Foster care," she added ominously.

"Where did you hear that?" Rachel asked.

"Rumors," Sally said cagily "There was no family to take care of her once her sister Jenny drowned and the cancer took her mother."

"I heard the mother believed that Jenny was murdered. That it wasn't a drowning."

"That's garbage," Sally snapped. "Jenny

162

Stills was never murdered. Her mother was in denial. Jenny would go night swimming. Boys got to hear about it and they'd join in. It involved a lot more than swimming, if you get my drift," she said. "One night, she got drunk and jumped off the jetty. Hit her head and drowned herself. It was nobody's fault but her own. I don't like to speak badly of the dead, but that Jenny was a wild girl. In every way."

"What exactly do you mean by 'wild'?" Rachel asked coldly.

"Isn't it obvious? Jenny Stills was 'the town bike,' " said Sally Crawford scornfully. "She had a bad reputation. And I mean bad with a capital *B*. That girl was just like her mother. Promiscuous. I felt bad for the little sister, but that Jenny was out of control. Getting raised by a new family was the best thing to happen to Hannah Stills. The Stills family were —. Well, they had a name around here. Even the grandfather, Ed. He was crazy as a bat. No wonder his daughter went bad, and then his granddaughter after that. And then her kid, Jenny. They say the apple never falls far from the tree."

"Food's ready," someone called from the backyard.

"Okay, okay," said Sally, picking up the watermelon platter. "I'm coming."

She turned to face Rachel at the sliding door to the backyard. "Word of advice," she said. "Don't dig up the past when it comes to Jenny Stills. It's one thing for a girl to go bad. It's another for her to take down good people with her. She caused terrible tragedy, that girl. Ruined lives. Doesn't deserve a shred of sympathy. You hear me? Not a shred."

19
HANNAH

I get the impression that you're enjoying your time in Neapolis, Rachel. Me, I'm not so sure. It's hard for me to process the strangeness of returning here after all this time. I truly thought I'd never come back. When I heard you were heading to Neapolis, I thought to myself that if you could do it then so could I. And so, much to my surprise, I did.

Rachel, let me say that I'm truly sorry we haven't met in person. I'd hoped we'd already know each other by now. I have admittedly chickened out several times. It's nothing to do with you. It's all me. I don't want you to meet me the way that I am right now. A basket case, to be perfectly frank. Vulnerable. Sad. Terribly angry when I see people I recognize and remember how badly they treated us.

Neapolis is a pretty place, if I put aside all my emotional baggage and look at it objectively. The historic district is as good as any you'll find anywhere south of the Mason-Dixon Line. The cuisine is simple but really, really good. The best crab cakes I ever tasted, I guess they call them burgers now, were in Neapolis. The one you ate at that marina cafe was pretty tasty, but it wasn't even close to the crab burgers my mom made when I was a kid. My ex-boyfriend, who <u>fancied</u> himself a chef, called that type of food seafood chic. He said those dishes always sound better than they taste. But then he never tasted the crab cakes in Neapolis.

The town has changed. At least compared to my recollection. It's less sleepy. Not as <u>provincial</u>. Bigger. Busier. Still, some things have stayed the same. I visited my old elementary school yesterday. It looked exactly as I remembered it. Same hallway color scheme. Same yard. Even the aging playground equipment looked the same. I walked past cute fifth-grade kids lining up to go into class. Hard to believe that I stood there once with the same unsuspecting bright-eyed innocence. I didn't have the faintest idea of what life had in store for me.

I suppose you're wondering what happened to Jenny that day she went off with those boys. To tell you the truth, I don't really know. She never said a word about it. All I can say is that by the time she arrived home in the middle of the night, she was a different person.

Mom was asleep when I got back to the house that afternoon after Jenny was taken in the truck by those boys. I eventually fell asleep myself, curled up at the bottom of Mom's bed like a puppy. I woke when I heard a hesitant knock on the front door. It was the middle of the night. I rushed across the house to get the door. The drapes had been left open and the house was filled with fleeting shadows from pine trees outside.

"Who's there?" My voice trembled.

"It's Jenny. Let me in." A shiver ran through me. I knew that she was broken. I could hear it in her voice. I released the latch and swung the door wide open.

Jenny pushed past me while I stuck my head out into the night. No truck headlights were visible in the dark and there was no sound of an engine. No sound of anything at all except for trees rustling in the wind. I closed the door and shut the bolt.

"Why were you gone for so long?" I asked.

There was no response. I turned around and saw that she'd disappeared down the hall. A sliver of light was visible underneath the bathroom door. The taps whined and water pounded relentlessly against the cheap enamel of the bathtub. I knocked on the door, but Jenny either didn't hear me, or didn't want to answer. I went back to Mom's room and lay pressed between her body and the wall, listening to the water run until I fell asleep.

When I woke, Mom's fingers were tangled in my hair. I had to slowly unwrap them so as not to disturb her when I crept out of bed to my room to check on Jenny. She was fast asleep in my bottom bunk, my teddy bear pressed to her stomach. The quilt had fallen off, leaving her exposed. I could see bruises forming on her wrists and legs.

I didn't know what to think and so I didn't. I went about the usual morning routine instead. I ate breakfast and packed our beach bag with towels and sandwiches. When Mom woke, I brought her toast with jelly and a weak coffee. She sat up with the tray on her lap, picking at her food. Noticing the time, she asked why Jenny and I weren't already at the beach. I muttered something about how we were leaving soon. Satisfied, she turned over and went back to sleep.

The heat hung heavily that morning and I was becoming impatient as the day dragged on and Jenny showed no signs of waking. Eventually, I couldn't wait any longer.

"Jenny? It's time to get up." I shook her gently. "It'll be too hot to walk to the beach if we don't go soon."

"Leave me alone. I'm tired," she slurred.

Jenny lay like that for days. Listless. She didn't wash. She barely ate. She'd go entire days without uttering a single sentence.

I had no idea what was wrong. I was a kid. I couldn't even speculate. Either way, I was so consumed with taking care of Mom, who could barely get out of bed most days, that I didn't know how to break through the wall of silence that my sister had erected.

It must have been three or four days later when we ran out of food. Not a slice of bread or a drop of milk was left in the kitchen fridge. We had nothing except for the lemons on our tree and a few carrots and tomatoes that Mom had planted in the spring.

I told Mom we were out of food and she gave me money from her savings to go shopping. She assumed I was going with Jenny. I didn't tell her the truth.

Rick's convenience store was the closest shop to our house and the only one I could reach on foot. I walked down there and filled a shopping basket with a few staples. I paid Rick at the counter. He packed all the groceries into four plastic bags. I carried them, two in each hand, as I walked home on the shoulder of the road. My arms quickly became sore from the weight of the groceries. I had to put the bags down by my feet to take a short break every few minutes.

It was during one of those rest breaks that I heard gravel crunch behind me. I turned to see an open-back truck pull to a stop next to me. It was the same truck and driver who'd given us a ride home that day after the beach. This time, there were no passengers. The driver was alone. His elbow rested casually on the open window as he leaned out to talk to me.

"How's your sister?" he asked.

"She's fine," I lied.

"She around?"

"At home. Why?"

"No reason," he said, shoving an open pack of gum in my direction. Despite my immediate inclination to say no, I took a stick of gum and popped it in my mouth.

"Do you want a ride home?" he asked. "Those bags look heavy. That one has a split in it."

I looked down and saw that the plastic bag with the milk carton was splitting. I was tempted. A ride in the truck would get me home in minutes instead of half an hour struggling uphill with torn grocery bags. As I hesitated, the driver leaned across the cabin and swung the passenger door open.

"Get in," he ordered as if I didn't have any choice. I climbed in and sat as far away from him as I could manage. My grocery bags rested by my feet.

Instead of dropping me on the main road like last time, he took a sharp turn down the rough access road to our house. He stopped outside our front porch, his truck engine running. He looked toward the house. His eyes were searching for something. I guessed he'd hoped to see Jenny. I snatched my shopping bags and clambered out, relieved to be home.

"Thanks for the ride," I called out in a shrill, nervous voice as I stepped onto the porch.

He put the stick shift in gear and the pickup rattled forward. "Tell your sister that I said 'hey,' " he called out. "Tell her I hope to see her real soon."

20

RACHEL

Scott Blair's family home was an ultra-modern architectural masterpiece in the most prestigious neighborhood of Neapolis. It had beach access, a putting green, and a resort-style pool. Rachel had seen the house in a design magazine. Even that didn't prepare her for the real thing when Cynthia Blair opened a double-size front door to reveal a black-and-white-tiled hall with an overhanging chandelier.

"Greg is one of your biggest fans," gushed Cynthia as she escorted Rachel into the living room, where a white leather sofa faced floor-to-ceiling windows with breathtaking ocean views. Cynthia was tall and slim, with long blond hair. She wore figure-hugging white pants and a sleeveless matching top with a deep neckline. Nestled between her breasts was a thick gold necklace with a diamond pendant.

"My wife's right. I am a huge fan, Ra-

172

chel," said Greg Blair as he finished a phone call on the balcony and came inside to meet her. He was dressed in immaculately pressed chinos and an off-white open-collar cotton shirt. He had the same handsome square-jawed good looks as his son and the same blue eyes and light brown hair.

"When your producer contacted me, I told him we're happy to cooperate in any way we can. We have nothing to hide. We're an open book. Anything you need, you let me know."

Rachel knew exactly what she needed: an interview with Scott Blair. Even though the family had already said twice it wouldn't happen, she decided to put Greg Blair's generous offer to the test. "Is Scott home? I'd love for him to join us for our chat today," she said.

"I wish Scott could talk. To you. To the networks. To everyone," Greg replied. "I really do. Scotty's good name and reputation have been dragged through the mud. He hasn't been able to defend himself. In fact, his new attorney has given strict instructions that he can't talk until after the trial," Greg said. "I told your producer — Pete, was it?"

Rachel nodded.

"I told Pete that we'd cooperate as much

as possible but that an interview with Scott is out of the question. After the trial, it's a different story," he said. "What we are really hoping for — and Rachel, your reputation precedes you in this regard — is fairness. We are hoping that your podcast will be fair and balanced even if you can't talk to Scott until the trial is over."

Rachel nodded noncommittally as she changed the subject by feigning interest in the long lap pool she could see through a side window. "Is that where Scott swims these days?" she asked.

"Yes," said Greg, walking her to the window so she could get a better view of the four-lane Olympic-length lap pool with an ocean view. "Scott couldn't swim at the local pool. The media were staking it out. He had to go through a gauntlet of cameras each morning. Fortunately, we'd put in the lap pool for me. I still swim two, three miles a day. Force of habit. I hate using our family pool. It's good for parties but bad for serious swimming. So we built the lap pool for me and so that Scott could continue his training."

"Scott still trains?"

"When he can," said Greg, his voice tight and bitter. He escorted Rachel back to the living room where he lowered himself onto the white leather sofa and motioned for her to do the same. "Scott hasn't been allowed to swim competitively for months. For a swimmer of Scott's caliber, that alone could set back his career permanently. He never did what he's been accused of doing. His trial hasn't begun, as you know, but his punishment started right after the accusations were first made. The law says he's supposed to be presumed innocent. In reality, it's quite the opposite."

"Kelly Moore says that Scott raped her," Rachel said. "If that's true, then swimming training is the least of his problems."

"It's not true. They went skinny dipping and then had consensual sex," Greg responded. "I don't know what motivated the girl to make false accusations. Maybe she was looking for fame. Or perhaps revenge, because Scott stupidly rated her, uh, sexual performance poorly in a message to his friend and she saw it. I don't know her motivation. But I know my son and he didn't do it. He had everything to lose and nothing to gain other than some pus—" He stopped abruptly.

The last syllable reverberated through the room. He and Rachel both knew what he had been about to say. He cleared his throat awkwardly.

"You were going to say 'pussy'?" Rachel filled in the blank.

"That was uncalled for," he said without missing a beat. "You have to understand that I haven't slept in days and we're all very stressed. But that's no excuse. I apologize," he said, rising from the sofa and clapping his hands together as if to suggest that episode was over. "Let me show you something."

Greg led Rachel into an adjacent room with custom-made mahogany shelves of different lengths arranged in a minimalist asymmetrical design on stark white walls. On each shelf were trophies and medals from swimming competitions.

One shelf displayed awards from when Greg was a champion swimmer. The second had Scott's awards all lined up: elementary school prizes all the way to state swimming medals and national awards.

Greg held up one of his gold medals. "This medal was from the national championships. I won gold. Broke two national records." He picked up a silver medal. "I won this in the World Championships. Lost by a tenth of a second. I made the Olympic team and was in the final weeks of preparation when I got pulled with a shoulder injury."

"It must have been heartbreaking," Rachel sympathized.

"It was. I had to have major surgery. I was only twenty. Never got my form back. I tried, but I couldn't return to elite swimming. It meant a lot to me that my son decided to follow in my footsteps. I never pushed him into it. Scott chose swimming all by himself. If anything, I discouraged it. I knew the discipline and focus it required. The agony of disappointment. But it was his passion. It was his dream to make the Olympics. He gave it his all. So many years of hard work." He sighed.

Greg went into a detailed rundown of Scott's career, starting from his first win when he was eleven at a state competition. "He barely trained. It was raw talent that won it for him," said Greg. After that, Scott exploded onto the swimming scene with win after win, at sixteen breaking his own father's state freestyle record. Later that year, he won the junior national championships in freestyle and backstroke.

"Ask any swimming coach. Any swimming commentator. They will tell you that Scott could be one of the greatest swimmers this country has seen. And then this happens."

As if to emphasize his point, Greg opened a file on his desk and lifted up a thick pile of newspaper clippings. He held up the top clipping. It was a front page newspaper article with a photo of police officers hauling Scott out of a swimming pool. A second photo showed Scott being handcuffed while dripping wet in his Speedo. "Champion Swimmer Arrested for Raping Teen," the headline read.

"Why would a teenage girl make these accusations if they were false?" Rachel asked Greg once they were seated by a glass table on the balcony, overlooking the sea.

"I have no idea. And I don't need to know. What I do know is that he didn't do it. Scott has so many girls coming after him. He doesn't need to rape an unwilling teenager when there are plenty of attractive young women who are more than willing. Models. Actresses. It makes no sense," he said. "It's as if everyone is out for his blood. They hate his success."

"Do you really think it's all a conspiracy to cut him down to size?" Rachel asked skeptically.

"My son didn't do it!" Greg said firmly. "Scott could spend the next decade or more in jail. Lose the best years of his life. For what? Because a girl changed her mind after the fact? He was a kid himself. Just eighteen. Drunk. Dumb. He should have known bet-

178

ter than to get mixed up with a girl like that. With her family connections and all. Her grandfather was the police chief. The police take care of their own."

He sat back and looked out at the panoramic ocean view while he collected his thoughts.

"Scott didn't rape that girl. He didn't. But he's already being treated like a rapist."

"In what way?" Rachel asked.

"Well, for one thing, based on this girl's word alone, he is suspended from competitive swimming. He lost his college scholarship and his sponsorships. My fear is that he will always be known as the swimmer who was accused of rape. That it will be a permanent smear. Doesn't matter that he didn't do it," said Greg. "I just hope the jury sees the truth and acquits Scott so he can still fulfill his potential and win those gold medals that he's been working so hard for all his life. Scotty's still young. He has years of swimming ahead of him. If we can only get people to see that he has been wrongly accused."

He paused as the sliding door opened and a man wearing jeans and a navy shirt joined them on the balcony. His fawn hair was blowing in the wind.

Rachel knew Dale Quinn on sight. He was

a rock-star lawyer who'd cut his teeth by successfully defending a husband accused of throwing his wife off their eleventh-floor balcony. Quinn managed to get the husband acquitted by convincing the jury that the woman might have jumped off the balcony after an argument.

"Do you know why I chose Dale to defend Scott?" Greg asked. "And it has nothing to do with the fact that we're old high school buddies from when Dale lived here in his junior year, while his old man was posted at the marine base out of town."

"I have no idea." Rachel asked the question even though she could guess the answer. Juries loved Dale Quinn. He was good-looking, with a boyish charm and a virtuoso talent at playing heartstrings. She'd seen him in action in a courtroom when she was a newspaper reporter. It had been like watching a master class in winning friends and influencing people. Except in Quinn's case, his specialty was winning over jurors.

"Six years ago, Dale defended a boy around Scott's age. Similar scenario. Tell her, Dale," Greg urged.

"My client and a girl had sex on the college quad during a party. Consensual. He takes her back to her room out of a sense of chivalry, where she bursts into tears and runs into the bathroom. He waits around to make sure she's okay. Leaves his phone number before he goes," Quinn said. "Next morning, he gets arrested for rape. During the trial, my private investigator finds out that the victim has done this before. Twice. False allegations each time. She was a minor. It was all sealed. The judge ruled it was exculpatory, so we can't bring it up at trial. The only way out of this mess is for me to get her to admit some of this stuff in the redirect.

"I was nice as pie to her. Asked her questions every which way. Next thing you know, she's telling the court that she had sex with him to spite an ex-boyfriend who was at the party. She admits on the stand that she never said no and consented at the time. Afterward, she regretted it. Claimed she wasn't all that enthusiastic. Says he should have realized. Law doesn't allow for retroactive withdrawal of consent."

"It went to the jury," Greg interrupted. "They deliberated for an hour and found him not guilty."

"You got him off. That means the system works," said Rachel, looking at her own reflection in Dale Quinn's dark sunglasses.

"He jumped off a bridge onto a highway three days later," said Quinn. He paused dramatically to let that sink in. "The stress, the depression, killed him. He knew he'd never get his old life back. That his good name was stained forever. He lost a prestigious internship. Had no hope of getting into a tier one firm when he graduated. His career was dead before it began."

Rachel remembered hearing about the case. The boy's parents had given a tearful interview on a current affairs program after he died. Before he was charged with rape their son had been offered a highly sought-after internship with a congressman. He lost the internship and he was suspended from college in the middle of the semester. His GPA free-fell. He was struggling with depression.

"What's your point?" Rachel asked.

"What happens during a moment of intimacy is complicated and confusing. When we put it under a spotlight in a court of law we discover that, a lot of the time, there is no black and white. Just shades of gray," said Quinn. "Juries don't like gray. The law doesn't like gray," he said, standing up. "If I was Mitch Alkins, I'd be worried. It's tough to get a conviction when all you can offer is gray."

Quinn took off his sunglasses and tucked them into his pocket as he turned to leave.

"I'd better get going. I have a trial that starts in under forty-eight hours and I haven't written a word of my opening statement."

A maid arrived with a bottle of Riesling. Greg poured them each a glass. Rachel didn't drink hers. The Blairs' conviviality seemed like a thinly disguised bid to get Rachel on their side. It annoyed her.

What interested her most was the war room upstairs, where Scott was obviously meeting with his defense team. The doorbell rang three times. Each time, Cynthia excused herself to let more lawyers into the house. Rachel heard hushed murmurs and the sound of footsteps as people walked up the staircase to the second floor. Then the sound of a door shutting and the murmurs would immediately stop.

All the while, Greg Blair was thumbing through old albums, showing her photos of Scott as an infant, a toddler, a five-year-old with no front teeth. Scott beaming on the winner's podium when he received his first gold medal. The Blairs wanted to humanize Scott. To an extent, they'd succeeded. By the time Cynthia walked her to her car, Rachel was surprised to feel more sympathy than she'd expected.

"All we're asking is that you have an open mind," said Cynthia. "There has been a terrible rush to judgment. We want Scott to have a fair hearing in court and in the court of public opinion. Surely that's not too much to ask?"

21
GUILTY OR NOT GUILTY

SEASON 3, EPISODE 5: THE DRIVE
I have no doubt that K would have instantly recognized Scott Blair when she saw him standing in the playground that night.

How can I be sure? Because in this day and age of social media–driven <u>ersatz</u> fame, Scott Blair was a local celebrity the likes of which Neapolis had never really seen before.

There were articles about Scott in the local newspaper and interviews with him on television. At K's high school, a huge framed photo of Scott was in pride of place in the Hall of Fame trophy cabinet. The local swim center had a life-sized photo of Scott swimming freestyle hanging next to the doors leading to the indoor swimming pool. Incidentally, both photos have since been removed following requests from K's family after Scott Blair was charged with her rape and sexual assault.

Scott's celebrity status was powered especially by social media. Like many kids at Ne-

185

apolis High, K was one of Scott's one hundred and seventy-two thousand Instagram followers. After all, he was the most famous graduate from their school. Scott posted photos regularly before he was charged. Scott doing his swimming training. Scott weight training. Scott running. I'm sure you get the picture.

If you look at old posts on his Instagram account, you can see photos of food piled up on the table before Scott tucked into his breakfast. Three bowls of cereal. A pile of toast covered in the equivalent of a small jar of peanut butter. Three glasses of orange juice. I don't even want to think about what he ate for lunch and dinner!

There are photos of Scott in the gym lifting weights. Underwater shots of him swimming. Above-water shots of his muscles rippling as his arms cut into the water during swim meets. Action shots of his powerful kick as he sliced through the water. He documented every aspect of his training to all his adoring fans.

Ever since the cops charged Scott with rape, there are a startling number of Instagram posts with photos of him volunteering at his church, ladling out stew at a soup kitchen, and teaching swimming to disadvantaged kids.

Of course, maybe that's just me being cynical. Maybe Scott really did devote himself to philanthropy long before he was charged with several class A sexual assault felonies.

In the months before he was named as a suspect in the K case, Scott Blair was on a grueling pre-Olympics training schedule. He woke at dawn to train. He swam two hours in the pool in the morning. Two hours in the evening. An hour around midday in the gym working with free weights. He did this brutal training program six days a week. Nothing unusual for a champion swimmer with Olympic prospects.

During this training, Scott sustained a calf injury. It was a niggling injury that was affecting his swimming times. His swim coach told him to go home for the weekend. Take a few days off from training and get his focus back. That's why Scott was back in Neapolis that Saturday night.

In one of the interviews that Scott gave before his new lawyer, Dale Quinn, stopped him from talking to the media, he said that when he was back home on weekend visits he sometimes went to the same playground where K disappeared to meet up with old friends and to relax from the stresses of competitive swimming. He'd grown up in the neighborhood. That's how he and Harris knew each other even though they were almost two years apart in age.

Scott said he was stressed that night. He had crucial tryouts coming up in a month and he was worried about that niggling calf injury. So he went to the park to soak up the atmosphere of his old "hood." To chill. Stare at the stars. Very poetic.

The prosecution's claims are less poetic. They say he was there because he'd arranged for Harris Wilson to follow K back from Lexi's party and keep her at the playground until he could get there and whisk her away in his car. Which is exactly what he did.

Whether you believe the prosecution or Scott Blair himself, the fact is that Scott was there that night. He saw K on the swing. He gave her a ride in his car.

She went with him voluntarily. We know that because there is CCTV footage of the two of them leaving the playground. It was taken from the house opposite the playground, which had cameras pointing into the street due to an ongoing graffiti problem. The owners of the house hoped to catch the vandals in the act of spray-painting their fence.

Instead, the camera caught Scott Blair opening his car door for K and then driving off with her in his silver sports car. The footage was broadcast on a local news channel after he was charged.

Scott didn't take K home, as he promised

her before she voluntarily stepped into his car. If he had, everything would have turned out differently. He claims that once they were in the car, K asked to go for a spin in his new convertible. It had leather seats and that new-car smell. He claims that he put the top down at K's request, even though it was October. Neapolis gets biting winds from the Atlantic in October. It would have been freezing driving around in a convertible that night.

They drove along the coast. After a while, they stopped at an all-night pizza place. More footage documents that visit, this time released to the media by the owner of the pizza place. I guess the pizza store owner believes in the old adage that any publicity is good publicity, especially when it's free.

Anyway, the footage shows Scott and K standing next to each other at the counter as they order. They sit and talk while they wait for their pizzas to be made. After about ten minutes, Scott gets up and collects two boxes of pizza and two sodas in those oversized cups.

Scott walks out of the pizza place carrying the pizza boxes. He has a baseball cap worn backward on his head, jeans, and a dark T-shirt. K is behind him carrying the sodas. You can see her clearly in the CCTV footage.

The defense will argue that she could have

hung back. She could have asked the staff at the pizza place to call the cops or used their phone to call her dad/ She could have run for it. She didn't. She followed Scott to his car and the two of them drove off. That indicates that she was with him willingly, which the defense will argue is indicative of her state of mind that night./

Scott drove to a beach. He chose the last beaches before the national park, south of Neapolis. There are a few boat sheds on the beach to store Jet Skis and motorboats for water-skiing./ Scott's parents keep a boat there. Scott would have known that nobody goes there. That it's out of the way and usually deserted.

In comments to reporters after he was first charged, he said that he and K sat on the beach and ate pizza./ They listened to music and talked. It was fun. Romantic. And then one thing led to another and they had sex./

Here's what his lawyer says: "My client, Scott Blair, and K went swimming together on the night in question after which they engaged in consensual sex./ There was no violence, rape, or coercion of any kind. Everything that happened that night, including sexual activity, was entirely consensual at the time that it took place./ If there were regrets afterward, then that is unfortunate, but it has nothing to do with the way my client acted that night. Scott is innocent of the charges against him."

The prosecutors give a very different story in their indictment. They say that Scott lured K into his car with the promise of a ride home. Instead, he took her for a drive and stopped to buy pizza, which they took to an isolated beach where he raped K repeatedly, after which he abandoned her and made the three-hour drive back to his college apartment so he would have an alibi.

They say that Scott Blair raped K because he was in a competition with a friend to see who could have sex with the most girls in a thirty-day period. K was going to be a notch on his bedpost. Whether she wanted it or not.

I'm trying really hard here to be objective. I need to give Scott the benefit of the doubt. You know, innocent until proven guilty. Plus, it's my job to keep an open mind.

The question that keeps bugging me is: Why did Scott leave K alone at the beach and drive back to his college apartment? Why do that if it was an innocent sexual tryst?

Scott's parents claim that K asked Scott to drop her at the bus stop. That she told Scott she'd rather take the bus home in the morning so that nobody would see him dropping her off. She didn't want her parents to find out that she'd spent the night with him.

Was Scott abandoning K to make her own way home the act of an innocent young man who had truly done nothing wrong? Or the act of a man with a very guilty conscience trying to cover up for a crime he knew that he'd committed? We'll figure it out together when the trial begins tomorrow.

I'm Rachel Krall and this is *Guilty or Not Guilty,* the podcast that puts you in the jury box.

22
RACHEL

The southern lawn of the Neapolis courthouse was cordoned off as TV reporters did
live broadcasts with the redbrick neo-
Georgian building as a backdrop. The
courthouse dated to the late nineteenth
century, when Neapolis had aspirations of
becoming a major seaport. It had an expansive plaza with a stone staircase that led to a
white-trimmed pillared portico at the entrance.

Rachel joined a group of locals watching
from behind a barrier as a TV reporter
finished the tail end of a Q&A with a studio
host during a live broadcast.

"The trial has divided this small coastal
town. Some say that Scott Blair, the swimming star on trial for raping a high school
student, is innocent and has been scape-
goated by political correctness gone over-
board. Others are worried the verdict in this
case will affect the willingness of rape

victims to come forward," said the reporter, pausing to listen to the next question coming through her earpiece.

Rachel didn't stay to hear the reporter's answer to the follow-up question. A long line was forming on the upstairs portico to pass through the metal detectors just inside the glass-door entrance of the courthouse. Rachel rushed to join the line, zigzagging through the crowded plaza and taking the stairs two at a time after flashing her journalist's credentials at an impassive police officer manning the barricade.

She looked down at the plaza from the top of the stairs as she waited to go through the metal detectors. The area was bustling with a festive atmosphere that seemed to Rachel to be in poor taste, given it was the start of a rape trial. Food trucks were doing a roaring trade in coffee, doughnuts, and breakfast burritos. Protesters with black T-shirts that said "Stop Rapists" were waving "Lock Him Up" placards. Locals stood around taking selfies.

When the Blair family's car pulled in, there was a sudden high-pitched scream so loud that heads turned to see what was going on. "Castrate him," a protester screeched. It was followed by incoherent chanting that became louder as Scott Blair and his parents moved through the crowded plaza, flanked by a two-man security detail. Rachel realized the protesters were chanting, "Cut it off, cut it off," as they followed the Blair family to the courthouse steps. They were shouted down by a rival group of mostly women wearing white T-shirts with Scott Blair's photo printed above the word "Innocent."

The courtroom was half-empty when Rachel pushed through its imposing polished doors and settled in her reserved seat in the media gallery. The court had original timber benches, paneled walls, and a gray stone floor. Filtered light came through clear lead windows set high up on the walls. They softened the harsh summer light and gave the court the atmosphere of a church.

The relative quiet was disrupted by the chaotic thump of files being unloaded onto tables by paralegals. Court clerks turned on computers and arranged paperwork as they prepared for the judge's arrival. A hum of chatter rose into a din as the courtroom quickly filled to capacity.

Scott Blair arrived, surrounded by a phalanx of lawyers. He wore dark pants and a light blue V-neck sweater that made him look wholesome and younger than his nineteen years.

Cynthia Blair walked behind him in an austere navy dress. Her hair was styled straight; her makeup, natural. Her jewelry was almost nonexistent other than her wedding ring. Rachel found it hard to believe that she was the same glamorous, bejeweled woman she'd met two days ago. Greg Blair wore a middle-of-the-range suit that Rachel cynically suspected was carefully chosen to make the jury forget that the Blairs were the wealthiest family in town.

Dale Quinn had chosen an equally forgettable suit-and-tie ensemble in his bid to play the role of local boy done good rather than the brash out-of-towner. Quinn had used every media opportunity leading up to the trial, including a profile puff piece in the local newspaper, to wax nostalgic about growing up in Neapolis. Even though, from what Rachel knew, he'd lived there only briefly.

With those carefully placed interviews, he'd courted the future jurors before they even received their letters in the mail summoning them to jury duty. Quinn well knew the power of pretrial publicity. "It's never too early to start influencing a jury," he was fond of saying, as Rachel had learned from watching YouTube videos of his lectures and interviews as part of her own pretrial research.

The bailiff's booming voice brought every-one to their feet as a wood-paneled door opened and the judge entered the court-room. Judge Nathaniel Shaw was a shortish man with a wiry frame evident despite the billowing folds of his black robe. His tanned face was testament to his reputation as an avid sailor and cyclist. Rachel had heard the judge was sometimes known to cycle to court on his racing bike. The gray tinges to his light brown hair gave him a gravitas beyond his forty-something years. His sharp blue eyes scanned the court with a haughty authority that told everyone, without him having to utter a single word, that he did not suffer fools gladly.

Judge Shaw was known to have an aver-sion to long-winded arguments and court-room theatrics. He had a low threshold for legal maneuverings of any kind if they slowed the wheels of justice unnecessarily. His judgments were terse and rather color-less in their legal prose, though sometimes interesting in points of law. He had zero tolerance for grandstanding, and most notably, he loathed journalists with a pas-sionate intensity. He glared at the reporters in the media gallery as if to remind them of that fact.

Rachel felt that his most withering scowl

was reserved for her. She'd been told confidentially when she picked up her media accreditation badge that Judge Shaw was not happy that she'd be covering the trial for the podcast. He'd found out from his staff that her investigative work in Season 1 of *Guilty or Not Guilty* had resulted in Frank Murphy being let out of prison after Rachel found fresh evidence that quashed the popular high school coach's murder conviction.

For the past seven of the eleven years in which Judge Shaw had been a judge, he hadn't been reversed. Not once. He'd told his staff that no podcaster was going to ruin his near-exemplary record. Or at least that's what Rachel was told by her source, a court administrator who was a fan of her podcast and had become a wealth of information on the inner workings of the courthouse.

Judge Shaw had already banned video and audio recordings of the trial. The last thing Rachel needed was for the judge to micromanage her coverage or restrict her access. It was with relief that Rachel heard from the same court administrator that Judge Shaw was a self-confessed Luddite who had never listened to a podcast in his life and didn't even own a smartphone. "Let's hope it stays that way," she'd told Pete.

After the jury filed in, the Moore family entered the courtroom. Kelly's parents held their daughter's arms, propping her up and shielding her from seeing Scott Blair at the defendant's table as they made their way to a row of seats behind the prosecutors. Kelly had been allowed in court to listen to the prosecution's opening arguments. After that, she and her mother would have to leave, as they were both being called as witnesses and the rules of court prohibited them from being present until they testified. Dan Moore had told Rachel that he would sit through the entire trial to represent the family.

The first hour was spent on tiresome administrative matters that made everyone restless as they waited for the trial to begin in earnest. An almost perceptible sigh of relief ran through the court when Judge Shaw called on the prosecution to present its opening arguments.

Mitch Alkins stood to his full imposing height. He had dark hair and the broad shoulders of a lumberjack. His thunderous baritone could scare the bejesus out of witnesses when used to full effect. Seasoned police detectives were known to leave the stand in a quivering, sweaty mess after going a few rounds with Alkins when he'd

199

been a defense lawyer. Rachel had no doubt that he was equally intimidating as a prosecutor. Just the sound of his thunderous voice was enough to make people quake, which is why she guessed he used it judiciously. There was a fine balance between having the jury in awe of him and terrifying the jurors to death.

Alkins's decision to switch from criminal defense to prosecution was one of the great mysteries of the criminal law world. Some said it was penance for getting a child rapist acquitted. Others said it was a stepping-stone to politics. Speculation was rife, but nobody knew the truth. The only person who did was Mitch Alkins, and he wasn't talking.

Alkins stood before the jury and surveyed their faces over the tops of the pages of his opening statement. He always wore the same tie on the first day of a trial, yellow with navy diagonal stripes. He was not superstitious about anything except that tie, which he kept in an old tobacco box in his office desk drawer.

Without saying a word, he tossed the prepared speech into a trash bin by his table. It was as if he was telling the jury that he trusted them enough to give them the raw, unvarnished truth. No subterfuge. No pretense. The jury was craning to listen to him before he'd said a single word.

Rachel's pen hovered over her notebook as she waited for Alkins to start talking. She intended to take down every word, if she could keep up. She'd post a transcript of his opening statement on the podcast website after court recessed that afternoon.

Alkins opened his address softly, introducing himself and telling the jury a little about the case. By the end of the trial, he said, there would be enough evidence for them to find the defendant guilty beyond a reasonable doubt of the multiple counts of rape, sexual assault, and sexual battery of which he was accused.

He gestured in the direction of the defense table, where Scott Blair stared straight ahead, trying not to squirm under the jury's piercing appraisal. He had a contrite, vacant expression that made him look as if he couldn't harm a fly. Rachel thought it looked rehearsed, just like everything else about the Blair family's presence at court that morning, from the understated clothes to the somber demeanor.

"The victim, Kelly Moore, had her whole life ahead of her on the afternoon of October 11 when she went to her friend Lexi Rourke's house." Alkins's smooth voice filled the courtroom.

"Kelly was sixteen. She was a happy, well-adjusted girl. An excellent student. A gifted athlete. She was looking forward to all the usual rites of passage of her teenage years, getting her driver's license, her junior prom. Maybe even her first boyfriend. Kelly worked hard in school. She wanted to become a physiotherapist, or work in education with disadvantaged children. Those were her dreams. Simple dreams." Alkins locked eyes with each juror as he spoke.

"All of that changed when the defendant lured Kelly to an isolated beach in the middle of the night where he raped her. Repeatedly. And sexually assaulted her. And brutalized her.

"Kelly will appear before you as a witness. She will tell you in her own words what happened to her and the terrible things that were done to her body and to her spirit. No person, let alone a young girl, should ever have to endure such treatment. Kelly was left with deep emotional wounds that may take years to heal. If ever. Let us not diminish the impact of a sexual assault on a victim's life."

Dale Quinn and his team shifted restlessly in their squeaky chairs as Alkins moved on to detail the evidence that he would present. Judge Shaw gave them several sharp looks but he didn't admonish them. There was no need to intervene. The noise was lost on the jury. Their attention didn't waver from Alkins as he effortlessly commanded the courtroom.

"Kelly's mother and her therapist will take the stand. They will tell you how the rape has affected Kelly and her family in ways that have, frankly, left me heartsore. You will hear testimony from doctors, nurses, and police investigators about physical evidence that supports Kelly's description of what happened to her.

"You'll hear how the defendant, Scott Blair, and his college roommate were having a competition to see who could have sex with the most girls in a thirty-day period. They were to take a photo and rate each girl. The friend was winning. The defendant, Mr. Blair, did not like to lose. Not in his competitive swimming meets and certainly not in this sordid sex competition with his roommate," said Alkins. "When he saw Kelly walk off from the party and was wrongly told that she was interested in him, he decided he'd have sex with her that night. What she wanted was of no interest to him." He paused. "He had a motive to rape Kelly. And he raped her. He even took a photo and rated her so she'd be added to his tally."

At the mention of his name, Scott Blair looked up at Alkins defiantly. Rachel saw Dale Quinn surreptitiously kick his client's shoe and Scott quickly lowered his eyes and hunched his shoulders like a victimized schoolboy.

"You will hear from Harris Wilson, who will testify about the predatory, premeditated steps Scott Blair took to have sex with Kelly that night, while trying his best to establish an alibi. Mr. Blair told Harris that he was not interested in whether Kelly consented to sexual intercourse because he would have sex with her regardless. And she did not consent, as Kelly herself will tell you when she takes the stand. In addition, we will enter into evidence the heartless boastful message that Mr. Blair sent his friend after he raped Kelly. He wasn't ashamed of what he'd done. He was proud."

Alkins did not point out that Kelly was sitting in court with her parents' arms around her, a pale face cocooned by her family's love. It might have added to the dramatic effect. Rachel saw him hesitate for a fraction of a second as if he was considering it, but he moved on.

"The party hosted by Kelly's friend Lexi

was supposed to have been a small get-together, but word got around on social media, as seems to happen frequently these days. More than sixty people turned up, including college kids and high school seniors. Among the kids who crashed the party were Scott Blair and his friend Harris Wilson.

"Kelly had a couple of beers, as did most of the partygoers. She hadn't eaten anything that night, which made the effects of the alcohol worse. When she started feeling drunk, she drank a couple of cups of soda to sober up. She didn't know that someone had spiked the soda bottle with vodka, and thus she inadvertently became very drunk. Not long after, Kelly had an argument with her friend Lexi, apparently over a boy they both liked, and she was locked out of the house and forced to walk home in the dark.

"Kelly is not on trial," said Alkins. "We're not here to judge the wisdom of her actions that night. Is it illegal for a girl her age to drink alcohol? Yes. But Kelly has not been charged with underage drinking. Nor have any of the kids at that party. And you are not here to pass judgment on that matter. Was it a poor decision for Kelly to walk home in the dark? Any one of you who has raised teenagers knows they routinely make poor decisions. Does that justify them being hurt, or assaulted, or raped? No, it does not. A person should be able to walk home, even in the dark, even through an isolated field, and arrive home safely."

Alkins moved into a detailed description of how Scott Blair told Harris to follow Kelly back from the party and keep her distracted at a local playground until he could get there. "Kelly had no idea that she was being set up. That she was walking into a trap."

Rachel flexed her cramped hand as Alkins paused to let it all sink in. He moved into a vivid description of how Kelly came to be in Scott's car and their visit to the pizza place.

"Scott Blair offered her a ride home. But instead of driving her home, the defendant took Kelly to an isolated beach where he raped and sexually assaulted her. When he was done, he left her to make her own way home by bus and he fled to his college apartment, where, he later falsely claimed, he'd spent the night."

The jurors sat transfixed as Alkins wove a narrative so convincing that one of the jurors glared at Scott Blair when Alkins described how he'd left Kelly Moore to make her own way home by bus, slipping her money for a ticket but not bothering to check the schedule to see if there were any buses running. Kelly had to wait for hours at a lone bus stop by the car park next to the deserted beach before a bus arrived. It was out-of-season and the beach was only serviced by two buses a day.

"Scott did everything he could to cover up before and after the crime. He convinced Harris to lure Kelly to the playground so that he wouldn't be seen with her in advance of the rape. He then abandoned her and drove back to his apartment after he raped her. He even ensured that she washed after the rape in a failed attempt to eradicate forensic evidence of his assault," said Alkins.

"Scott Blair committed a grave and terrible crime," he said. "He did it knowingly. He did it violently. And he did it with the arrogance of someone who believed that he could get away with it. He believed that his fame and family connections put him above the law," said Alkins, taking a step closer to the jury as he wrapped up.

"Scott Blair ignored Kelly's desperate requests for him to stop having sex with her because he didn't care what she wanted. It was of zero interest to him. His only concern was what *he* wanted, which was to satisfy his own carnal desires and to win a sordid and demeaning sex competition," said Alkins. "He did what he did with a clear head. With planning. With forethought. With full knowledge it was wrong. And most of all, with contempt. Contempt for the law. And contempt for the rights and choices of young Kelly. The evidence will prove this beyond a reasonable doubt. When it does, it will be your duty to convict Scott Blair on all charges."

23
RACHEL

The effect of Alkins's address was hypnotic. His final words hung in the air as he walked back to his seat slowly and deliberately. For a long moment, the only sound in the courtroom was the tap of his shoes against the stone floor. The electric silence reminded Rachel of the hush in a theater before the audience rises to its feet for a thunderous standing ovation.

Sitting at the defense table, Dale Quinn flicked through the pages of his legal pad with pretend nonchalance while he waited for Judge Shaw's instructions. Rachel knew that Quinn would come out fighting harder than ever to win the jury back from Alkins.

During the brief pause that followed Alkins's address, Rachel checked her phone discreetly to see if Pete had made any headway finding Hannah. In the last few days, Hannah had abruptly stopped sending letters. Rachel had asked Pete to check hotels and even car rental places in the greater Neapolis area to locate her. If that didn't work, then Rachel had decided to do a callout at the end of her podcast. Hannah claimed to be a fan. She'd hear the callout and, Rachel hoped, contact her again.

Rachel turned to a fresh page on her notepad as Judge Shaw invited Quinn to deliver his opening statement. She hoped to have a pretty comprehensive, perhaps even word-perfect transcript of both opening statements on the website by the end of the day. She wanted her audience to feel that they were in court themselves, getting all the relevant information so they could come up with an informed verdict. She wanted them to feel as if they were in the jury box.

Quinn stood abruptly, with what seemed to be nervous clumsiness. He took a sip of water and promptly spilled some on his shirt in full view of the jury.

Rachel, who'd studied Quinn's playbook in her pretrial research, knew it was a trick he'd learned from a legendary trial lawyer he'd interned with during law school. His mentor's go-to move was to stumble over something in court, be it a briefcase or a table leg. It didn't matter what he tripped over so long as he tripped. It immediately broke an invisible barrier with the jurors.

They connected to him as a person, and by extension to his client.

Quinn made a show of pulling out a handkerchief and dabbing at his water-stained shirt as the jury looked on sympathetically. Judge Shaw, who knew all the tricks of the trade, was less tolerant.

"Mr. Quinn." The judge's chair squeaked as he leaned into his microphone. "I believe we're waiting."

"Of course, Your Honor," said Quinn. He gave one final dab to his wet shirt and smiled bashfully at the jury. He seemed young and inept compared to Alkins, even though Rachel was pretty sure they were around the same age.

Rachel admired the way Quinn had turned himself into an underdog. After all, who doesn't like an underdog? The spell that Alkins had cast over the courtroom was broken by the time Quinn opened his mouth to speak.

"About three months ago, I received a telephone call at my offices in Memphis asking me to defend a young swimmer who I'd never heard of before. I don't much follow swimming. My wife and I have twin babies at home. When I'm not in court, I'm helping her feed and bathe them. So I didn't know who Scott Blair was when I received the call./I certainly didn't know he was a potential Olympian when I heard the uncertain voice of a young man asking if I would take his case," he said. Rachel raced to keep up with him, her pen tearing across the pages of her notebook./

"Well, I immediately said that I would not take any case outside of Tennessee, even though I am licensed to practice law in North Carolina. By the way, that's nothing against this fine state/ I grew up here and have many fond memories of Neapolis. It's because I promised Beth when she had the twins that I wouldn't do any traveling until the girls were older./I like to think that I am a man of my word./

"Scott begged me to hear him out. He told me what happened that night last October, the facts of which are as different as day is from night from the version Mr. Alkins gave you," he said, his grim tone giving extra weight to his words.| "That was when I understood that a real miscarriage of justice was taking place here in Neapolis./ It bothered me greatly to hear of this boy's problems./ But I could not take his case. I told him so. I had given a solemn promise to my wife.

"I told Beth about his call that night over dinner. Beth insisted that I telephone that boy first thing the next morning to tell him I'd represent him. She told me she'd manage with the babies while I was away. That I couldn't let this boy's life be ruined by an unjust conviction.

"So it's thanks to Beth that I am standing before you to tell you all that Scott, well, he has been unfairly maligned and wrongly charged for a crime that he did not commit. Scott is innocent. Under our judicial system, he is presumed innocent. Unfortunately, long before the trial began, Scott's good name was dragged through the mud. His reputation has been stained so deeply that I am not sure it can ever be washed clean.

"He has been suspended from the state swim team and barred from attending the national swimming championships. His Olympic dreams are in shambles. His college scholarship has been revoked. His sponsors have abandoned him. This boy's life is in ruins due to allegations of a crime that he did not commit," Quinn said.

"Let me tell you a little about Scott. He is nineteen years old and has already set half a dozen state swim records in freestyle. If that's not enough, he's come within a razor's edge of setting national records. Some of our nation's top swimmers and coaches have said that Scott has the potential to be 'the greatest swimmer of his generation.'

"It takes a lot to reach this elite level. While all of us were fast asleep in our beds over the years, Scott has dived into the cold water of an Olympic swimming pool before dawn to swim for two hours. He's been doing it since he was nine years old. Six days a week, forty miles a week. So it's amazing to me that Scott has still had time for family, his church, and of course his studies." Quinn put his hands in his pockets as he softened his voice.

"But that's not all that he's had time for. In a society in which young people are sadly all too often self-absorbed, Scott devotes his spare time to helping those less fortunate than himself, in his church and in the wider community. You will hear about Scott's good works that attest to his true character. You will hear powerful forensic testimony from a world-renowned medical expert from Harvard who will tell you that there was no indication of force on the complainant's body. You will see CCTV footage that shows Scott and the complainant enjoying each other's company that night.

"The prosecution will not be able to offer you a scrap of actual hard evidence that Scott committed the crimes for which he is on trial. Here. In this courtroom. Why? Because there is no evidence. Not a shred. The prosecution may offer you innuendo and supposition, but it won't offer you evidence. It can't. Because my client didn't do it.

"Scott has lost his college scholarship, his income, his place in the national championships. And now his very freedom is threatened. All due to unsubstantiated accusations. Rumor and innuendo." Quinn's voice filled with outrage.

"It is frightening to think that a promising young man's life can be ruined by a baseless accusation. With no evidence," he sighed. "I guess that's the world we live in today. A world where accusations sway opinion. A world where evidence doesn't matter. A world where a person is deemed guilty without any proof.

"Scott's dad, Greg Blair, had his own Olympic swimming career cut short due to a shoulder injury when he was just twenty. He told me yesterday that the devastation he felt when he had to pull out of the Olympics was nothing compared to the day he saw his son hauled by police out of an Olympic swimming pool while training for the national titles. It was done in full view of media cameras to humiliate Scott. To give the false impression he was guilty.

"Scott's hands were cuffed behind his back. He was frogmarched by police out of the pool in a dripping-wet Speedo and shoved into a police car while news cameras photographed him. The mob decided Scott was guilty without a shred of evidence. Not a shred.

"You the jury have the chance to <u>r</u>ectif<u>y</u> that terrible wrong that has been done to Scott, because Scott did not rape or sexually assault Kelly Moore. The prosecutor, Mr. Alkins, won't be able to give you evidence, let alone evidence beyond a reasonable doubt, for the simple reason that none exists. Scott here, well, he did not commit these crimes. He is innocent." Quinn paused to let the words sink in.

"There was no rape. No sexual assault. That's just not true," Quinn continued. "What did happen was that Scott and the complainant had <u>consensual</u> sex and the complainant regretted it afterward. Sure, Scott acted like a <u>ca</u>d after their tryst by boasting about it to <u>his</u> friends. He was only eighteen at the time. Boys can be imm<u>a</u>ture. To cover up for her embarrassment, the complainant claimed that what happened was against her will. It wasn't," Quinn said. "She was a willing participant. That's why there is no evidence to prove her story. Scott is innocent of all charges."

Rachel could tell that Quinn had gotten through to some of the jurors. It helped, too, that Scott Blair had sat contritely throughout his lawyer's address with the slumped shoulders and shocked expression of the wrongly accused. His puzzled blue eyes matched the baby blue of his V-neck sweater. A couple of the jurors nodded to themselves as Quinn returned to the defense table, pausing to squeeze Scott's shoulder reassuringly as his final words reverberated through the courtroom.

Quinn had sowed a kernel of doubt in the hearts of the jurors. Rachel expected that he'd cultivate that kernel through the trial until, by the time the jury went into deliberations, that kernel would have grown big enough for at least some of the jurors to fight for Scott in the jury room. All it took was one juror to get a hung jury, thought Rachel. Just one.

When the jury filed out for the lunch recess, some of the jurors seemed weighed down by the enormity of the task, discerning a needle of truth in a haystack of subterfuge and legal doublespeak. Rachel didn't envy them one bit.

24
GUILTY OR NOT GUILTY

SEASON 3, EPISODE 6: JURY DUTY
About six years ago, I was called for jury duty. It was not long after my marriage broke up. The divorce papers had been filed, but we were still unpicking the Gordian knot of our lives together.

It wasn't so much about who got what. We were both flat broke. But who would keep Millie, our King Charles spaniel? How we would divide up the wedding presents? And who'd take over the loan on the car? And the apartment lease? Not to mention arranging a payment schedule for paying off our credit card debt.

My family was furious with me. They loved my ex. Still do. Mom invites him for Thanksgiving every year. Me she can take or leave. But Ted, he gets to sit at the head of the table and the menu is carefully planned with all his food preferences in mind.

Anyway, I had this awful job working the

graveyard shift in a newsroom in the months after the breakup, I was permanently jet-lagged. Sleeping during the day. Working at night. If you've ever done that kind of job, you'll know that after a while it grinds you into dust.

Then the letter arrived. Summoning me for jury duty. Some people will do anything to get out of jury duty. You wouldn't believe the stories they'll tell. I heard the wildest things the day I turned up at the courthouse for jury selection. One guy said he had a back condition that precluded sitting for long periods of time. Another said she had claustrophobia and would get panic attacks if she was locked in a small room. The really smart ones simply said they were not capable of being objective.

Me, I was excited. I wanted my *Twelve Angry Men* moment. I wanted to play armchair detective. To sway fellow jurors with my righteous indignation. Yup, as you can gather, I had no idea what I was getting myself in for.

I sat with the other potential jurors in a crowded room drinking cheap coffee in Styrofoam cups, hunched over our phones while waiting to go through the voir dire, which is the fancy Latin name for selecting a jury.

There was a unanimous groan when we were told that it was a financial crimes trial and not a murder case. "Fraud," someone said with distaste. "I got fraud last time," another potential juror complained. "What does it take to get murder?"

Whether murder or fraud, the fact was that for most of the jury pool, getting called for jury duty was a major pain in the ass. Most of them were hardworking people, juggling kids and minimum-wage jobs. Few of them were college educated. Most were struggling to get by. They needed jury duty like they needed a hole in their heads.

Eventually it was my turn to be grilled by the lawyers. I didn't last long. The second the defense attorney heard I had two college degrees, he used a preemptory challenge to have me dismissed. He did the same for other college-educated potential jurors until he'd whittled down the jurors to those with little more than a high school education.

I left court that day with the feeling that the jury system was being gamed. That it's all psychological manipulations and obfuscations. That it's about winning. And losing. A game of wits and ego. That it has nothing to do with law, let alone order. Guilt, or innocence. Justice. Or truth.

That feeling was reinforced when, out of curiosity, I watched the trial for a couple of days when it was in full swing. I sat in the public gallery and listened to a befuddling array of evidence and witness testimony that I could barely follow. The jurors looked as if they were suffering from a form of death by a thousand cuts as they listened to the dry-as-dust testimony of a forensic accountant breaking down the details of one forged receipt after the next.

I left court with the impression that particular financial fraud case was so complex that even my brother, a financial accountant, would have had trouble keeping up with the complexities of the case. Let alone a jury of ordinary people without much exposure to the intricacies of the financial world.

It didn't surprise me when I heard the jury had found the defendant guilty in record time. Anything to get out of there and go back to their lives.

The theatrics from Mitch Alkins and Dale Quinn underscored that impression today in court on the first day of the trial. They tried every trick in the book to get the jury's sympathy. And quite a few tricks that aren't in any books. Yet.

They were good. Among the best. They modulated their voices to the right pitch. Their pauses were perfectly timed. Their hand gestures were choreographed to perfection. The wily way they selected facts to suit their arguments while undermining any suggestion they might be wrong. They played each juror. They played their emotions, and they played their perception of the case. They vied for the sympathy of each and every juror.

To be fair, maybe, I'm underestimating the jury. Maybe the jurors in the Blair trial will ignore the theatrics and focus on piecing together the granules of truth that will come out during the trial until they have a big enough picture to reach a fair verdict. I hope that happens. That's what they're there for after all.

There are thirteen jurors. That includes one alternate juror who has to listen to the evidence and testimony but will almost certainly not be allowed to deliberate. Not unless one of the other jurors drops out or is kicked out for breaking one of Judge Shaw's rules. Such as listening to my podcast or following other media coverage of the case.

There are seven men on the jury. Six women. All but three of the jurors are over the age of forty. Word is that such a composition favors the defense. Older women are said to be more judgmental of rape victims. The oldest jurors are in their late sixties. The youngest juror is in his mid-twenties. He is expected to be partial to the defense as well because he's a guy and the same approximate age as the defendant. That makes them kindred spirits, so the theory goes. In reality, who knows?

Three of the jurors visibly resent being in the jury. Their eyes wander longingly to the courtroom doors. You'd have to be blind not to notice that they wish they were anywhere else.

That's a point in favor of the prosecution, because research shows that reluctant jurors tend to take out their wrath on the defendant. They're more likely to convict. One of the three is an accountant. The other is in sales. The third is a plumber who runs his own small business. He begged Judge Shaw to recuse him from jury duty. He's gone so far as to bring his accounting ledger to court to show the judge how desperately he needs to be working full-time. Judge Shaw was unsympathetic. It wasn't easy finding jurors who could be impartial, who didn't know the parties in this case. Not in a town like Neapolis, where the old families go back generations.

The jury foreman is a hardware store manager. He's the only juror who volunteered to be foreman. I guess he figured that since he runs a store, he can run a jury, too. There's another juror who I think will be influential. He's a construction supervisor. Burly, with dark brown hair and laughing eyes. He is charismatic. The other jurors seem to defer to him. Dale Quinn made a special effort to connect with him when he gave his opening statement.

The jurors are still getting to know each other. Still breaking the ice. We're watching them closely. Watching their gestures and their personal tics as they listen to testimony.

I've covered my share of trials. I've seen a few juries in my time. One thing is always the same. The jurors avoid looking at the defendant when the trial begins. By the time closing arguments are delivered, they will stare him down as if trying to see into his soul. Their job is simple. It's to convict the defendant if he is guilty. Or acquit if he is innocent. The problem is: What happens if they get it wrong?

This is Rachel Krall for *Guilty or Not Guilty,* the podcast that puts you in the jury box.

Before you go, in my short time in Neapolis I've learned about another girl who lived in this town. Her name was Jenny and she died a quarter of a century ago. I first learned about Jenny in a letter delivered to me in a, shall we say, unorthodox way. I want the writer to know: You have my attention. You know where to find me. Let's talk. I mean, really talk. I'm game if you are.

25
RACHEL

Harris Wilson was a bundle of nerves as he walked across the courtroom and took the stand. He pulled at his tie as if it were choking him and exhaled loudly after taking his oath.

Rachel watched the courtroom artist next to her draw Harris as a gangly young man with bad acne, sitting awkwardly in the witness stand. His tie was almost comical around his scrawny neck. Standing alongside him in the courtroom sketch was Mitch Alkins. His dark hair brushed across his forehead, his hands in his pockets. Even in that relaxed pose, he looked like a cobra. Ready to strike.

"Are you nervous, Harris?" Alkins asked.

"A little."

"Must be nerve-wracking to testify at such a young age. I gather you've only recently turned eighteen?"

"Yeah. Three weeks ago."

"Your Honor," Dale Quinn interrupted. "The defense acknowledges that Harris Wilson is young and nervous. Perhaps that will allow Mr. Alkins to get to the point."

"Let's move it along here, Counselor," Judge Shaw directed.

Rachel bent down to check her phone as Alkins guided Harris through the events of the night of Lexi's party.

Rachel had been waiting all morning for Hannah to respond to the callout on the podcast by sending another letter or email to the podcast email address. So far there was nothing from Hannah, and no messages from Pete other than to say that he'd come up empty-handed after calling every hotel in Neapolis. *And I mean every single hotel, motel, and bed-and-breakfast place within twenty miles of town,* he'd written. *There's nobody named Hannah staying at any of them.*

Rachel returned her attention to Harris, who was sitting on the edge of his seat and talking too fast as he answered Alkins's questions about the night of Lexi's party.

"Scott told me to go after Kelly and meet him at the playground near my house," said Harris. "He said that when he got there, I should leave because he was going to take her somewhere and have sex with her. He told me he was in this competition with his roommate and he was trailing behind by a few girls. He said he needed an easy lay and that he needed my help to reel her in."

"What did you say in response?" Alkins asked.

"I asked Scott, 'What if she doesn't want to have sex with you?' " Harris recalled. "Scott said, 'Trust me; she knows who I am. She'll be flattered that I'm interested in her. Anyway, I wasn't planning on asking her. She'll do what I want. They always do.' "

A gasp rippled through the courtroom. Alkins paused as heads turned toward Scott Blair. He sat impassively, but Rachel could tell that he was exerting every ounce of self-control to avoid reacting. His parents, behind him, were equally still, like gazelles freezing to avoid catching the attention of a predator. Gradually, despite Scott's best efforts, a pink tinge ran up his neck.

Alkins nodded slightly as if to tell the jury that he wasn't surprised at the red flush of guilt. He moved on, asking Harris to describe what happened once he'd brought Kelly to the playground and waited for Scott's next move.

"Scott texted me to say he was in his car next to the playground and that I should leave so he could be alone with Kelly. He used an emoji that means sex. I hesitated.

Kelly seemed nice. I was worried about Scott. He'd drunk a lot that night. Usually he didn't drink because of his swimming. That night he was plastered. Scott can get pretty unpredictable when he's drunk."

"But you left her anyway?"

"I stayed for a little, thinking that maybe Scott would change his mind if he saw that I wasn't leaving. Then he sent me another text telling me to 'beat it' with an emoji of a finger across a throat. It scared me . . . and — I left," said Harris.

Alkins asked Harris to read the text messages that Scott had sent that night. After Harris read the messages out loud in a trembling voice, Alkins moved into a series of questions to show the jury that Scott had planned to rape Kelly Moore that night. That it wasn't done in the heat of passion, or out of drunkenness. It was premeditated.

"Did you see Scott on your way home?" Alkins asked.

"I passed Scott's car. When he saw me, he put his hand out the window to fist bump me. I fist bumped him back. Once I crossed the road to my house, I turned and saw him get out of his car. I should have gone back and stopped him," said Harris. "I'm sorry I didn't do anything. Although I'm not sure it would have helped. Scott always gets what he wants. That night he wanted Kelly."

When Alkins was done with his witness, Harris scrambled to his feet, his relief visible. He seemed about to bolt from the witness stand when the judge leaned forward to his microphone.

"It's just a wild guess here, Mr. Wilson, but I'm thinking there's a chance Mr. Quinn might have a few questions for you."

"What did you and Kelly do for so long? Were you stargazing?" Quinn asked, his tone friendly, his right hand casually tucked inside his front pant pocket. Rachel could tell this was a precursor to a brutal cross-examination. She'd spoken with Harris on the phone. Talked to his dad, too. He was a good enough kid but not the sharpest knife in the drawer. Rachel almost felt bad for him. He wouldn't know what had hit him once Quinn really got into his stride.

"We talked. And drank," said Harris. "I had a flask and we shared it."

"What was in the flask?"

"It was bourbon."

"Where did you get that bourbon from? You're too young to buy it legally."

"It was my dad's bourbon."

"When I was your age, if I asked my daddy for bourbon he would have said, 'No chance.' What did your dad say when you asked him for liquor?"

"Nothing," Harris muttered.

"Is it possible that you didn't ask your dad?" Quinn asked. "Did you perhaps take the bourbon without your father's permission? Did you steal the bourbon, Mr. Wilson?"

"I guess I did," he admitted.

"Mr. Wilson, I notice that you're flushed. Are you hot? Should we ask for the air conditioner to be turned up? Or tissues to wipe the perspiration off your forehead?" Quinn asked, with barely concealed sarcasm.

"Your Honor, Mr. Quinn is badgering the witness." Alkins's voice thundered across the court.

"I am merely being solicitous," said Quinn.

"Move it along," snapped Judge Shaw.

Quinn did just that, asking Harris about why he'd changed his testimony since he'd first spoken with police on the day Kelly disappeared.

"Isn't it true that you told the detective who came to your house in the hours after Kelly disappeared that you thought Kelly had walked home from the playground that night?"

"Yes."

"Did you lie to the detective that morning? Or are you lying here in court today?" Quinn asked.

Harris stuttered, lost for words. Quinn went through each and every one of Harris's lies when he was first questioned by Detective Cooper about Kelly's disappearance. Harris's credibility was in shreds by the time that Quinn was done.

"One last question, Mr. Wilson." Quinn swiveled around dramatically, as if a thought had suddenly occurred to him. "Have you received anything for your testimony today?"

"Uh, what do you mean?" Harris mumbled.

"Isn't it true that you agreed to testify today in return for pleading guilty to a lesser charge, a charge that comes with a more lenient sentence?"

Harris stuttered, "Y-y-yes," into his microphone.

"And how much time will you be spending in jail on that lesser charge?"

"Uhm," said Harris. "I don't think I'll be going to jail."

"To clarify, in return for your testimony today, you've been given a get-out-of-jail-free card. Is that correct?"

Alkins stormed to his feet.

"Objection."

"Sustained," said Judge Shaw, allowing Harris to finally step down.

As Harris stumbled off the stand, red-faced and trembling with a combination of fear and sheer relief, Rachel could tell the jurors were divided over his testimony. Several jurors sat with their arms crossed. They wouldn't look his way. It was obvious to Rachel that they simply didn't believe Harris. A few others, mostly the older women in the jury, watched him with some sympathy as he left the stand. It was clear that his life was in shambles from the consequences of that night.

Rachel had spoken briefly to Harris's dad, Bill, before court that morning. He'd said that they'd lost their house because he couldn't cover the mortgage payments and pay the lawyers representing his son when he was fired from his job. His boss, a cousin of Dan Moore, had retrenched Bill after Harris was charged, claiming it was part of a restructuring. The family was now living with Bill's parents an hour's drive from Neapolis while Bill looked for a new job.

When court adjourned for lunch, Rachel watched through the hall window as Harris's dad walked across the southern courthouse lawn to his car, his hand on his son's left shoulder to comfort him. The lawn bore no sign it had been the scene of live news broadcasts across the country other than a few muddy indents in the grass in the shape of broadcast-van wheels.

After Harris and his dad were out of sight, Rachel stood for a moment watching people scatter across the plaza for the lunch recess. There was a line forming outside a food truck across the road. Others headed to cafes down side streets or sat on benches to eat packed lunches.

Rachel spent the lunch recess working on a bench in the hall outside the courtroom. She'd packed a sandwich but didn't have a chance to eat it as she typed up the notes from that morning's testimony. When she was done, she posted the notes on the website and closed her laptop as people started filing back into court for the afternoon session.

Rachel used the remaining time to slip into the ladies' restroom. When she came out of the stall and approached the sink to wash her hands, she saw a small envelope propped against a hand soap dispenser. It had her name on it. The restroom door swung backward and forward as if someone had just left.

26
HANNAH

I heard your message for me at the end of the podcast, Rachel. You want to meet me. I get it. I want to meet you, too. I've been a fan for a long time. But trust me, right now is not the best time. One day, you'll understand. It really is in your own best interests. What's that expression? "Plausible deniability"?

That doesn't mean we haven't met, incidentally. If you can call two strangers passing by each other in a crowded courthouse plaza a meeting. Among other places where we've virtually rubbed shoulders.

In fact, you looked right at me this morning when I was in court today. I came in just before the guard closed the doors for the morning session. The only seat available was in the last row. I was stuck staring at the balding head of the man in the row in front of me, listening to Harris Wilson recount his role in Kelly Moore's rape.

Harris tried to sound unwitting. I didn't buy it. He knew what he was doing when he followed Kelly from the party that night.

Still, I thought Harris's testimony was damaging. I bet Scott Blair never imagined his loyal wingman would turn on him once the prosecutors offered him a plea deal.

I didn't stay for long. I found the testimony too upsetting. Nothing has changed. Everyone is still up to their same tricks. I was so disgusted that I came out and scribbled this note for you instead.

Yesterday I went back to see our house. Of course, it no longer exists. Stupid me to have imagined that it was still there just as I remembered it. I'm sure the locals were happy to see it gone. The last trace of the Stills family erased.

We moved to Neapolis when Jenny was eight. I was a toddler. Too young to remember our momentous arrival in a brown station wagon where we had to sleep for weeks until the house was habitable. Mom's grandfather hadn't cleaned the house in the fourteen years since his wife died. Her name was Hannah, too. Mom never talked about her grandfather, but she kept a photo of her grandmother on her dresser.

Jenny told me once that Mom ran away as a teenager and only returned once her grandfather died because she'd inherited his house, along with the surrounding land. Jenny said it was her first permanent home. It was all she ever said about their life before we moved to Neapolis.

I was told plenty of stories about how Mom and Jenny spent weeks cleaning that house as I toddled around the overgrown garden in my diapers. Once they'd thrown out the junk that Mom's grandfather had hoarded, she and Jenny scraped the dirt off the floors with trowels and grease remover.

When the house was clean, they painted the walls and window frames in a fresh shade of white. They sanded down and wood-washed the timber kitchen cupboards and reworked the grime-filled tiling in the bathroom and kitchen using oddments of bright yellow and blue tiles that Mom bought at a hardware store closing-down sale.

Our furniture was secondhand. Mom would buy furniture at garage sales or flea markets. She used to say that all it took was a few coats of paint and a whole lot of imagination.

She hid our threadbare sofas under painters' throw sheets that she'd dyed crimson in a metal washing basin. She decorated the windowsills with painted glass jam jars that she filled with wild yellow daisies we'd pick from the fields around the house.

When she got sick, I always made sure to put a vase of yellow daisies in her room so that there was something for her to look at on the days when she couldn't get out of bed. She was in bed an awful lot that summer.

As for Jenny, she became skinnier than ever after she was taken by those boys. She was always thin, so that was saying something. Her face became pale and her glossy hair turned brittle and lifeless. Her nails were a disaster. She bit them down almost to the flesh.

Mom was so ill that she had no idea that Jenny was hurting. Maybe I should have told her. God help me, I couldn't bring myself to do it.

I kept the house going as best I could. Mopping the floor and hanging out laundry while standing on my tiptoes to reach the clothesline. It was fortunate that nobody had an appetite. There was no need to cook. I lived off jelly-and-peanut-butter sandwiches and glasses of milk. I spent the days drawing pictures on the porch and riding my bicycle.

One afternoon, I heard tapping on the

screen door while I was slumped on the sofa, watching television. Visitors rarely stopped by. Through the window, I saw a woman. She was snooping around while she waited for me to answer the door.

"Is your mom home?" The lady wore a patterned dress with lipstick too orange for her complexion, her blow-dried hair sagging from the humidity.

"She's not seeing visitors," I said.

"She's expecting me," the woman insisted. "We arranged this meeting weeks ago. Tell her that Mrs. Mason has come to see her."

I went back into the house, leaving the woman waiting outside in the clammy heat. Mom was lying in bed in a loose caftan that she'd made herself on her grandmother's vintage sewing machine.

"There's a lady here," I told her. "She's got ugly lipstick and she's wearing a church dress. She said she's supposed to meet with you. Said her name is Mason, or something."

Mom nodded, like she already knew. She climbed out of bed and shuffled to the living room. Only when she was properly settled in the armchair did I let that woman inside the house.

The woman made an awful din coming up the stairs in her heels. She looked disappointed to see the air conditioner was not turned on and kept waving her hand in front of her face like it was a fan.

Mom didn't stand up or reach out to shake the woman's hand. It wasn't because she was being rude. It took every last drop of her energy for her to sit up straight in the armchair and pretend that everything was fine.

"Hannah, it's time to play outside," Mom ordered when I brought them a pitcher of water.

I deliberately left the door open while I played with a tea set on the back patio. I tried my hardest to listen to what they were saying. It was difficult. Their voices were hushed.

I stayed there until the woman rose from the sofa. I thought she was leaving. Instead, she walked through the house with a clipboard and pen, pausing occasionally to write something down. Mom sat in the armchair, watching the woman helplessly as she opened our refrigerator door and examined the contents.

"Not much food in your fridge," the woman said.

"That's because we're going shopping later," I snapped, shocked at her rudeness. It was a lie. We'd run out of money for groceries and couldn't get more until Mom's welfare check arrived later that week.

That awful Mrs. Mason walked through the rest of the house with her lips pursed. When she opened Mom's bedroom door, I was relieved it was aired out, with clean sheets on the bed. She walked down the hall. Without asking, she pushed open our bedroom door. It was dark with the drapes drawn. She turned on the lights. Jenny, who'd been sleeping, sat up in bed confused at the intrusion.

"My sister has a cold," I told her. "She's very infectious."

The woman quickly turned off the lights and closed the door. When she was done poking around our house like a busybody, she and Mom had a quiet chat. I was once again banished to the backyard. Mom asked me to pick lemons from our tree. I think she wanted to give them to that Mason woman. By the time I came back, that woman had already gone. I stood by the window and watched her little car rattle down the dirt driveway. "Good riddance," I murmured under my breath.

Mom's eyes were closed with relief as we heard the last splutter of Mrs. Mason's car engine.

"Who is she?" I asked.

"She works for the city. She was checking to make sure we're managing," Mom said.

And then as if she suddenly remembered, she asked, "Where's Jenny?"

"She's sick."

"In summer?"

"She has a cold," I answered evasively. "She didn't want you to catch it."

"She hasn't been having enough fruit," said Mom. She went to the kitchen and sliced in half the lemons that I'd picked. Beads of sweat formed on her forehead as she squeezed those lemons by hand and poured the juice into a glass jug. She added ice cubes, water, and sugar. When it was ready she stirred it with a long metal spoon and poured three glasses of lemonade.

"Give this to Jenny. Tell her to drink every drop. It's full of vitamins."

Jenny sat up in bed and drank the whole glass in a single go.

"It tastes like Mom's lemonade."

"It *is* Mom's lemonade. She's feeling better today."

"Can I have more?" Jenny said when her glass was empty.

I brought her my own glass of lemonade from the kitchen. She drank that as well.

The next morning, for the first time in

days, Jenny rose from bed. She spent the day lying on a picnic blanket in the backyard as laundry flapped on the washing line against a pristine sky. I lay near her, content, as I tried to replicate the exact shade of the cloudless cerulean sky with my dollar-store paint set.

27
RACHEL

Scott Blair's former roommate, Dwaine Richards, was a squat nineteen-year-old with a thick neck, wide shoulders, and a buzz cut. He was a college wrestler and he looked the part. He wore a square-cut light gray suit two sizes too big that Rachel suspected belonged to his father, who was watching sourly from the front row of the public gallery.

"We came back to our apartment with some girls after a party," Dwaine Richards was saying, sitting on the edge of his seat as if looking for an escape route as Alkins fired questions at him. "When they left in the morning, me and Scott joked about how many times we'd each scored that night. One thing led to another and Scott bet a thousand dollars that he could sleep with more girls than me in a month. I thought it was a joke, but then Scott put up a chart on our fridge to keep track. He was mad as hell when he came back from a weekend swim-team training camp and saw that I was ahead of him."

Alkins moved on to the night of Lexi's party: "The defendant called you from a party. Can you tell the jury what he said?"

"Scott said that he was crashing a high school party in his hometown and he expected 'to bag at least one girl,' " said Dwaine. "He warned me that he'd catch up to me, and that he planned to win."

"Did you hear from the defendant again that night?" Alkins asked.

"Yup, I did," he said. "Scott woke me up in the middle of the night. Said he'd banged a high school girl just like he'd said. He told me to 'add her to the list.' "

"What did Scott mean by 'add her to the list'?"

"He meant that I should add her name to the list of girls we'd slept with that month on the whiteboard on our refrigerator. We had two columns. One for me and one for him. I was ahead by three girls. Once I added her to Scott's list, I was winning by two."

Alkins asked Dwaine if he recalled seeing a photograph of Scott Blair with a half-naked girl, which Scott had briefly posted to his social media account that night before

244

quickly deleting it. Dwaine said he'd seen the photo. "Scott made a smartass comment in the caption. Can't remember exactly what he said. And then he rated the girl as — I think it was a C or C plus."

"Can you tell the court about the system you and the defendant used to rate girls you'd slept with?" Alkins asked, delving into their sleazy rating system. He questioned Dwaine Richards along these lines until all the jurors had the same disgusted expression on their faces.

When they did, he told the judge that he had no more questions and abruptly sat down. Scott Blair had sat through his former roommate's testimony stone-faced, occasionally whispering to his lawyer as if to imply that Dwaine Richards had said something untrue. Rachel noticed that the tips of Scott Blair's ears were bright red by the time that Alkins was done.

Rachel took Hannah's latest letter from her purse as Judge Shaw conferred with his clerical staff about an administrative matter. To the sound of squeaking chairs and hushed voices talking, Rachel smoothed out the pages of Hannah's letter and reread it. She finished reading as Dale Quinn began his cross-examination.

Quinn started slowly with a few softball

questions. Within minutes, Dwaine was visibly sweating when Quinn asked him whether he'd wanted to get revenge after Scott had unceremoniously kicked him out of the apartment due to his "unpaid rent and disgusting lifestyle" a few weeks after the incident with Kelly Moore.

"Isn't it true that after you were evicted, you threatened my client, Scott? You said you were going to take him down."

"I was angry when he kicked me out even though I was only a few days late on the rent. I didn't mean anything by it," said Dwaine, looking down at his shoes as he spoke.

"I have here copies of your text messages to Scott. You used very, shall we say, colorful language, and some quite specific threats," said Quinn. "How about you read out your texts and we let the jury decide whether you meant them or not," he added, handing Dwaine a wad of stapled sheets.

Rachel left court to the sound of Dwaine Richards reading out his angry texts. She had something more important to do. Rachel had found a possible lead in Hannah's letter, and she was anxious to follow it up. She didn't mind missing the rest of Dwaine Richards's testimony to do so. If truth be told, she couldn't stomach hearing another word from him.

Rachel ran all the way uphill to the City Hall building at the top of the boulevard, her arm aching from the weight of her laptop bag digging into her shoulder.

The social services office was on the third floor. It had a sitting area of chairs next to a table piled with old magazines. The reception desk was unsupervised. From behind a stretch of plaster wall that separated the reception area from the offices came the hum of people talking on phones and typing on keyboards.

Rachel pressed a button on the desk to summon the receptionist. A young woman dressed in a long patterned skirt and button-down shirt came out of the back offices, holding a mug of coffee and finishing off a last bite of food. Rachel had clearly interrupted her lunch.

"I'd like to speak with Mrs. Mason. She was a social worker who handled welfare cases in the early nineties," Rachel explained.

"I haven't heard that name before," said the woman. "I'll ask my colleagues. Maybe someone knows. I'm still quite new here."

She left Rachel to pace around the waiting area as she disappeared back into the offices. Rachel checked her phone. Pete had sent her a text message to let her know that his friend, a white-hat hacker, hadn't been able to restore the original emails that Hannah had sent months earlier, which had been deleted by the intern. Rachel was disappointed. She'd really hoped they'd be able to retrieve the original emails despite the passage of time. It was another dead end.

"I understand you're looking for Barb Mason?"

Rachel whirled around to see a woman with a narrow chin and fine features. Her short dark hair was flecked with gray.

"Yes, I am."

"Barb retired years ago. Last I heard, she lives in Canada with her daughter's family. Is there something I can help with? I worked with Barb for a long time."

"I sure hope so," sighed Rachel. "I'm looking for a girl who was put into care here in the early nineties. Her name is Hannah Stills. I believe she was fostered out when she was around nine or ten. After her mother and sister died."

"The records would be sealed," said the woman, careful not to divulge any information. A flicker of recognition in her eyes suggested that she remembered the case.

"I understand," said Rachel, disappointed but not entirely surprised the woman was strictly sticking to the rules. She wrote down her first name and her cell phone number on a blank piece of paper along with all the details she knew about Hannah. "Please ask Hannah's foster mom, Kitty, to contact me. It's urgent," she said, as she held out the note.

"I'll pass it on. I can't promise you'll hear back. It's entirely up to her if she calls," said the woman, taking the paper and disappearing back into her office.

Rachel arrived back in court during the testimony of a nurse from Neapolis General who'd done Kelly Moore's rape kit. Rachel scooted into an empty seat near the back row. The nurse's name was Tracey Rice. She was taller than average, slim, with shoulder-length light brown hair. She spoke confidently, clearly experienced at testifying in court. Rachel's phone vibrated shortly after she sat down. The call was from a phone number that she didn't recognize. She ducked out of court to answer it.

"Neapolis Social Services gave me your number," said the voice of an obviously older woman. "My name is Kitty McLean. The woman from Social Services said that you want to speak to me urgently about Hannah. What do you want with Hannah? She's not in trouble again, is she?"

"Not that I know of," said Rachel, keeping her voice low. The hall echoed loudly. She didn't want her conversation broadcast to everyone within earshot. "I'm trying to get hold of Hannah. I'm a reporter. I do a podcast and Hannah —"

"A pod-what, dear?" Kitty interrupted. "Speak up; I can't hear very well."

"It's like a radio program on crime." Rachel raised her voice. "Hannah wrote to ask for my help in looking into her sister's murder. I'm trying to get in touch with her, as I have some questions."

"Hannah's sister wasn't murdered, dear. She died in an accident."

"What sort of accident?" Rachel asked carefully.

"Her sister went swimming at night. She drowned. Terrible tragedy, of course, but definitely not murder. I don't know why Hannah says such things."

Rachel asked Kitty for Hannah's contact information. Kitty left her waiting on the phone line while she looked for her address book. It took a couple of minutes until Kitty's frail voice was back on the line as she slowly recited Hannah's phone number.

"I doubt she'll answer you," said Kitty. "She hasn't answered any of my messages. In fact, I haven't been able to get hold of Hannah for weeks."

"You must be worried?"

"Not at all. Hannah's a grown woman. It's her way to disappear every now and again. Sometimes for weeks. Sometimes for months. The last time she disappeared, she went to India. Spent three months at a yoga retreat. Wasn't allowed to talk to anyone the entire time. A vow of total silence. She came back a vegetarian. That didn't last. Maybe she went back again. Always said she would if she had the chance."

"I don't think she went back there," said Rachel. "I think she's in Neapolis."

"Neapolis?" said Kitty, her shock obvious even over the phone line. "Why on earth would Hannah go there? I've never heard her say a good word about the place."

"I think it's to do with her sister's death."

"Well, now that you mentioned it, the anniversary is coming up. Twenty-five years. Hannah does get into a mood at this time of the year," said Kitty, weighing the possibility. "But she always swore she'd never set foot in that town again. I'm sure she's in India at one of those places she likes. An ash-something. What are they called?"

251

"An ashram?" suggested Rachel.

"That's right. One of those. I have your contact details, dear. I'll ask Hannah to call you when she's in touch. Bear in mind that it could take months. It's how Hannah is."

Rachel finished the call, but the guard outside the courtroom wouldn't let her back inside. He told her that she'd have to wait for a recess. Rachel was disappointed. She'd been hoping to use the nurse's testimony on rape kits for her next episode. She texted Pete and asked him to contact the hospital to arrange an interview with Nurse Rice.

Rachel sat on a bench in the hall outside the courtroom and rang the phone number that Kitty had given her. It went straight through to an automated voice mail. Rachel tried several times with the same result. Eventually she left a voicemail: "Hannah, this is Rachel Krall. I'd really like to talk to you. Please call me." Rachel recited her phone number before disconnecting the call.

A loud bang from the courtroom made her look up. The doors had swung open and people were streaming out noisily for a restroom break. Rachel grabbed her bag and headed to the courtroom. As she waited by the doors for the crowds to clear, someone tapped her on the shoulder. Rachel swung around to see the guard holding out a large brown envelope.

"Ma'am, you dropped this," he said, handing her the envelope.

28
HANNAH

I was waiting outside the courtroom the other day. It was the day when kids from Lexi's party testified that Lexi told Scott Blair that Kelly was "easy" after she kicked Kelly out of her party. On the wall above my head was an air conditioner. It rattled something awful. A drop splashed on the old courtroom bench right next to me, and then another. It made me remember something else.

It was the hottest summer for years. The heat was so bad that we had to use our old air conditioner even though it had sprung a leak. It rattled noisily when it worked, dripping water into a steel soup pot we'd left on the floor, until one afternoon the motor spluttered to a grinding halt.

After that, sleep was impossible in our tiny bedroom. Jenny and I took our mattresses to the porch and slept outside. There was a cool breeze that came in at night. Mom managed with a rickety fan in her room, which we turned into a crude air conditioner by hanging a damp towel over the wire cage.

One afternoon, a few days into the heat wave, Jenny and I were lying in the living room watching a TV show and sucking ice cubes when we heard Mom scream our names from the garden.

We rushed in a panic to the backyard, thinking that something terrible had happened. When we reached the rear porch, Mom was standing on the grass in a cotton sundress, translucent from sunbeams behind her. Her arms were outstretched. Her face lifted to the sky. Rain trickled down her sunken cheeks and neck all the way down to her bare feet.

"It's a sun-shower." Mom laughed.

We joined her in the rain, not caring that our tank tops and shorts were soaked through. The rain stopped as suddenly as it had started. Rather than go inside to change clothes, the three of us sat in the garden on upturned plastic crates and watched the garden puddles dry up along with the clothes on our bodies.

"Why aren't you both at the beach?" Mom asked, as if suddenly realizing that we'd been home with her for days.

"We'd rather stay with you," said Jenny,

examining her mud-covered toes.

"There's nothing to do at home. Besides, I'm feeling much better," Mom said. "Tomorrow, go back to the beach. It's the best place to be in this weather."

Mom washed the mud off our feet with the garden hose before ushering us back into the house. That night, Jenny said that she still had a cold and needed to stay in bed the next day. I knew that it was an excuse to get out of going to the beach.

"What you need, Jenny, honey, is sun. The sun heals everything," Mom said. It was on the tip of my tongue to ask why it hadn't healed her.

"I'd rather spend the day at home," Jenny mumbled. Mom looked at her in surprise. Jenny loved the sea. She was at the beach the moment the weather was warm enough to get into the water, and she'd keep going long after summer ended. Jenny's reluctance to go to the beach on a perfect swimming day troubled Mom into a heavy silence that night over dinner. Eventually, Jenny relented. She didn't want to worry our mom.

The next morning, I raced ahead with my towel slung over my shoulders. Jenny straggled behind me. She wore an oversized T-shirt and loose pants instead of her favorite sundress with the crisscrossed back.

Jenny didn't stop at our usual spot when we reached the beach. She headed toward another beach beyond the jetty. That beach had strong currents that made swimming dangerous. Nobody went there, not even the surfers.

"Hey, Jenny."

It was a boy from Jenny's high school. He was athletic, with dark hair and a tanned chest. Around his neck he wore a leather necklace. He and Jenny had hung out together at the beach the previous summer, but I hadn't seen him that summer at all. Jenny had mentioned something about how he had a job at a record store downtown. She never told me outright, but somehow I knew that she liked him.

"Where are you going?" he asked.

"To that beach," she answered, flushing slightly as she pointed farther along the coast at the deserted beach beyond the jetty. "My sister wants to collect shells."

I opened my mouth to say that I wanted to do no such thing, but Jenny swung around and glared at me to shut up.

"Don't waste your time. It's covered in seaweed and there're sand flies," he told us. "Throw your stuff down and come for a swim."

Jenny joined him for a swim while I laid

out our towels near where he and his friends had left their bags. Later that afternoon, while I was lying on my stomach reading a book and Jenny was relaxing on her towel next to the dark-haired boy, I saw those boys again. The ones who'd given me a ride home in their pickup truck and taken Jenny away until late in the night. They were sitting on the dunes talking and smoking. I saw Bobby there, too, with his uncut hair and gray eyes. A cigarette hung out of his mouth. He sat a little away from the main group and seemed embarrassed to see me. I'd last seen him when he jumped out of the truck at the bridge after arguing with the driver the day they gave us a ride.

One of the boys caught me staring. I remembered that he'd sat in the front passenger seat right next to the door. He waved at me in a weird way that made me uncomfortable. I looked away. Jenny glanced up to see what I'd been looking at. When she saw those boys she went white and immediately averted her gaze. She trembled. I could almost see the wave of cold dread wash through her.

Out of the corner of my eye, I saw the boy who'd driven the truck that day wander over to a group of teenage boys from Jenny's year at school who were drying off on their beach towels near the dunes. He told them something with an amused expression. I didn't know what he said, but I saw them laugh out loud when he was done talking and then swivel around to stare at us. Jenny pretended not to be bothered. I could smell her fear. Her body shrank into itself.

"Let's go home, Hannah," Jenny said hoarsely. She shoved my buckets and hats and the rest of our lunch into the bag without trying to shake off the sand.

"It's too hot to walk home now. There's not a strip of shade."

Her eyes darted around, trying to find a way to flee. They filled with resignation when she saw there was no escape. One of the boys from Jenny's year at school stood up and went over to sit with another group of teenagers sitting near them on the beach. He whispered something to a couple of the boys. The same thing happened: Laughter followed. Heads turned. Eyes pierced into our backs. Jenny froze.

The pattern repeated itself until the whispers raced across the beach. It was the same each time. The laughter was the worst. It cut like a knife.

Jenny turned pale as people's heads whirled around toward her. Her hands trembled. She gripped her towel until her knuckles were white. The gossip was coming closer and closer, like an approaching tidal wave. Jenny looked desperate. She said something to the boy with the dark hair. He nodded. They both went down to the jetty and dived together into the water as the hum of gossip reached my spot on the beach.

"She did what?"

"I didn't know that she was the type."

"Of course she is. She's a Stills, isn't she!"

I was nine. I had no idea what they were talking about. I knew it was about my sister and I knew it wasn't very nice. Beyond that, I knew nothing. Jenny stayed in the sea, treading water as the dark-haired boy returned to the beach, where he picked up his towel and left with his friends.

I watched him walk up the sand dunes with his friends. I could see them tell him something. When they reached the top of the dunes, he stopped and turned around to look in Jenny's direction. There was something different about the way he appraised her.

When Jenny emerged from the water long after he'd gone, she was pink from sunburn and her hands were wrinkled from being in the water for too long. We walked home in silence. Just after the gas station, Jenny took a shortcut through the brush, even though she'd told me never to go that way on account of the copperheads.

29

RACHEL

The waiting room outside the ER was half-full with people slumped on plastic bucket seats, looking clammy and ill. Rachel, who'd been sitting in the back row typing up notes from her day in court, moved away from the waiting area to answer a call from Pete.

"Have I caught you at a bad time, Rach?"

"Nope. I'm still at Neapolis General, waiting to interview Tracey Rice about Kelly's rape kit," Rachel said, pressing the phone closer to her ear as a toddler started screaming.

After going through a few podcast issues, she asked Pete if he'd managed to get a copy of Jenny Stills's autopsy report. Rachel wanted to see if the cause of death was listed as drowning, as Kitty insisted was the case.

"The state medical examiner's office said there's no record of an autopsy on their database. That doesn't mean that it wasn't done. Just that it was a long time ago and they'll need to do a manual search in their files to find records. If there are any records," said Pete.

"How long will that take?" Rachel groaned.

"That's the problem. They have a staffing crunch right now. Won't be able to look for the report for a few days. But even if they find it, they won't give you a copy without permission from Jenny's next of kin."

"That would be Hannah," said Rachel. "That's just terrific. Another reason to find her."

"Does it really matter, Rach?" Pete asked. "You don't have time to follow up right now, with the Blair trial in full swing. By the time the verdict comes in, the ME's office will have found the autopsy report and you'll have hopefully met Hannah and have her permission to get a copy."

It all sounded very reasonable, but Rachel was consumed by curiosity. She didn't want to wait that long. When Rachel returned to her seat, the waiting room was quiet. The screaming toddler had gone through the doors into the ER to have his suspected broken finger x-rayed. Most of the other people who'd been waiting either had gone home or were being treated. Nurse Rice stopped by to reassure Rachel that she was almost ready for the interview.

"Is it always this busy?" Rachel asked.

"Sometimes. We're down a doctor and two nurses right now. Summer flu," she sighed. "That's why I'm doing the night shift. I won't be much longer. It's always quiet around dinnertime."

Within half an hour, as she predicted, the waiting room was virtually empty. Rachel was taken by an orderly to a treatment room where Nurse Rice was finishing off her dinner of homemade lasagna in a Tupperware container. Rachel explained that she wanted to find out what Kelly Moore would have gone through when she came in to be examined after the rape.

"I can't talk about her specific case," said Nurse Rice, "but I can tell you about the rape kit process. I'm one of three nurses who've been trained to do them at this hospital."

She took out a sample rape kit and removed its contents: evidence bags, swab collection kits, and piles of forms. All with the same bar code. Everything collected had to be carefully logged and tracked, in case it was presented as evidence in court just as Kelly Moore's rape kit was being presented by Mitch Alkins as part of the prosecution's case.

"The body of a sexual-assault victim is a crime scene," said Nurse Rice. "It's my job to comfort the victim and treat her injuries, while at the same time methodically collecting evidence in a way that preserves the chain of custody and reduces cross-contamination. I think of it as half CSI investigator and half nurse. As you can imagine, it's schizophrenic; the two jobs are polar opposites."

She told Rachel that she was often the first person to question the victim about the rape and it was her job to document accurately every aspect of the sexual assault. If she made a mistake collecting evidence or taking down testimony, it could damage a potential prosecution. A defense attorney would look for any hole in the prosecution's case, including perceived inconsistencies in a rape victim's statements to the nurse and to police, to make the victim look like a liar.

"It's not enough that the victim says where and how the perpetrator penetrated her. We need to know a whole range of quite graphic details, which we document as precisely as possible in these forms. After that, we move on to a physical examination."

Nurse Rice explained how the victim's clothes were put into evidence bags, much like the clear plastic evidence bags containing Kelly Moore's clothes that Alkins had presented in court earlier that day. After that, a sterile paper sheet was put under the victim to capture trace evidence such as hairs, fibers, and body fluid.

"When that's all logged and bagged, we examine every inch of the victim, from the tip of her head to her toes. We document each bruise, scratch, and abrasion. We remove any foreign pubic hairs, semen, fibers. Anything we find. And we take swabs and samples of the victim's own pubic hairs for comparison purposes."

"Do you photograph the victim as well?" Rachel asked.

"If the victim agrees, we photograph all scratches, scrapes, bruises. We use a camera called a colposcope to photograph internal injuries. Lacerations on the genitals. Anything that might be evidence of a sexual assault."

She explained that once the evidence was collected, medical issues were treated. The victim was offered the morning-after pill if there was a risk of pregnancy, or medications for HIV, syphilis, and other STDs if needed. After answering a few more questions, Nurse Rice checked her watch.

"I have to get going. I hope you have what

you need," she said to Rachel, packing up the sample rape kit and putting it back on the top shelf of the examination room cupboard.

She walked Rachel out through the swinging doors of a back entrance to the ER, which led to the ambulance bay and then the car park. There were two ambulances parked in the ambulance bay. A paramedic was wiping down a stretcher alongside the ambulances. He greeted Nurse Rice and they chatted for a moment.

The sight of the ambulances reminded Rachel of the newspaper article on Jenny Stills's death. It said that Jenny was brought to the hospital and pronounced dead on arrival. She wondered if the original ambulance crew was still around. Maybe they'd be able to shed light on what happened that night.

"Do you know the paramedics well?" Rachel asked Nurse Rice. "I'd like to speak to someone who was on the job in the early nineties? It's about another case that I'm investigating."

"I don't think any of the paramedics go back that far," answered Nurse Rice. "They're all young. In their twenties, or thirties. The burnout rate in that job is high so they generally quit after a few years and do something else. What do you want to ask them about?"

"A teenage girl who drowned when she was sixteen. Back in '92. She was brought by ambulance to this hospital. Already dead from what I can gather," said Rachel. "I was hoping someone might remember bringing her in."

"DOAs go to the hospital morgue. You could go down and speak to Stuart. Pretty sure he's on night shift this week. Stuart's worked here for decades. He might remember. What was the girl's name?"

"Jenny Stills," said Rachel. She could tell from the shocked expression that immediately appeared on Nurse Rice's face that she recognized the name. "You've heard of her?" Rachel asked.

"Sure, I've heard of her. Everyone who went to Neapolis High knows that name," the nurse said with a catch in her voice.

"How come?" Rachel asked in surprise.

Nurse Rice sighed audibly as she tried to find the words to formulate a response. "The name 'Jenny Stills' was like a cautionary tale about what happens when a girl sleeps around," she said. "There used to be songs and jokes about her. Graffiti in the bathrooms. At school her name became slang for being a slut. Always felt awful for

268

that girl, having her name dragged through the mud like that."

Nurse Rice's pager beeped and she paused to check it. "The waiting room's filling up again. I have to get back," she said. She quickly gave Rachel directions to the hospital morgue and rushed through the swinging doors of the ER.

Rachel followed the sign to the morgue, taking the elevator to the lower basement. The morgue was down a long white corridor lit by a row of bright fluorescent lights. Rachel reached the closed door and turned the handle. It was locked. Next to it was an intercom. She pressed the button. Nobody answered.

Rachel was about to turn to leave when she heard footsteps coming down the stairs. She waited until a barrel-chested man with thick arms, a ruddy complexion, and a reddish gray beard emerged from the stairwell. A hospital badge pinned to his blue scrubs identified him as "Stuart."

"Tracey Rice from the ER said you might be able to help me with a question about a DOA," Rachel said.

"Come inside," Stuart replied.

He scanned his hospital key card and pushed open the door to the hospital morgue. Rachel followed him as he led her into an office with a couple of upholstered chairs and a tired framed print of flowers on the wall. At the back were rows of filing cabinets and a desk with an oversized computer screen.

"If you're here about the DOA from this afternoon then he's already been transferred," Stuart said. "The ME decided there will be no autopsy. Apparently, he had a long-standing heart condition."

"Actually," said Rachel, "I want to know if you remember a case from the summer of '92. A teenage girl drowned. I was told that she was brought here and pronounced dead on arrival. Her name was Jenny Stills."

Stuart stared at her, unblinking. When he saw that she was serious, he pulled a crumpled pack of cigarettes out of his hospital scrubs.

"Can we go outside? I'm not allowed to smoke here," he said.

He took her through the morgue itself. It was a white-tiled room that smelled of antiseptic, with a wall of stainless-steel refrigerators for bodies. There was an empty metal stretcher pressed against the wall, blocking access to an external door. He rolled it out of the way and opened the door. They came out into a basement loading area. He lit a cigarette as he leaned back against a raw concrete wall.

"That was a long time ago. Why're you asking about Jenny Stills now?" he asked.

"Her sister asked me to look into her death. I'm an investigator," said Rachel, choosing not to mention the podcast. "Her sister was very young at the time, but she believes that her older sister was murdered. Not drowned, which was apparently the official cause of death."

He nodded and exhaled. "She did drown. Lungs were full of water," Stuart said.

"But?" Rachel prompted, half-shocked and half-excited that he remembered the case.

"There were bruises. All over her body," he said. "Not from hitting rocks, like they said afterward. She'd been hit and kicked. Physically beaten. One bruise was in the pattern of the sole of a shoe. I still remember that. Looked to me as if she'd been badly hurt before she drowned."

"Did you tell anyone?" Rachel asked.

"Did I tell anyone?" he repeated. "Of course I did. I told the medical examiner. Usually he'll discuss a case like that with me. When I asked afterward what had come out of the autopsy and whether the police were investigating, he was evasive. I asked a friend on the force who confirmed there was no police investigation under way. So, I did the only thing that I could do."

"Which was?"

"Went to see the girl's mother. She was in bed. Could barely sit up. Told her that I thought there was more to it than a drowning. That there had been bruises and cuts on her daughter's body that looked suspicious. Told her that if she wrote a letter requesting an inquest then the authorities would have to look into it properly. I told her to ask for them to investigate it as a potential homicide. I waited while she wrote the letter and then I mailed it for her."

"Why did you think it was a homicide?" Rachel asked.

"I don't know if it was a homicide, but it sure was suspicious. Those fresh injuries on her body should have been enough for a homicide investigation. I said as much to the medical examiner at the time. He wouldn't hear a word of it."

"The newspaper said there was no investigation. Why?"

"Town was burying those two boys. They died the same night. Drove into a tree. By the time everyone was done grieving, the girl's mother was dead and there was nobody pushing for an investigation. I'd done everything I could do," he said. "Couldn't do any more without risking my job. I had a young family. Needed the income."

"Is the medical examiner still in town?" Rachel asked.

"In a manner of speaking," said Stuart, dropping his cigarette to the ground and stubbing it out with the toe of his shoe. "He's in town, all right, but six foot under. Dropped dead of a heart attack a good fifteen years ago. Maybe more. We've been through three MEs since then."

He walked back inside, Rachel following behind. "Come with me," he said with the whispered urgency of someone about to share a secret.

He went through the morgue to his office, where he unlocked the bottom corner filing cabinet. From the back, he retrieved a repurposed rectangular cookie tin. He took off the lid and handed it to Rachel. Inside were faded photographs of a young girl lying on a stretcher. Her hair was wet and her eyes were closed. Her skin was a bluish hue of death.

Rachel went through the photos of Jenny Stills's body. There were close-ups of ugly bruises on her legs, shoulders, and stomach. Rachel couldn't imagine how such bruises could have been caused from hitting rocks. More surprising, the photos of Jenny's head didn't seem to show any cuts or abrasions. Surely, if Jenny had died from hitting rocks, there would have been injuries to her head. It made no sense.

"Who took the photos?" Rachel asked.

"The medical examiner took these on the morgue camera immediately after she was brought in here and before she was transferred to the county morgue. A week later, he stopped by and asked me for the camera film. He was in a panic. I smelled a rat," Stuart said.

"In what way?" Rachel asked.

"Can't say exactly. He was very political. Always brownnosing. The way he asked made me suspicious."

"So what did you do?"

"Told him I'd thrown out the camera film undeveloped, said there was no point wasting money developing film of an accidental drowning victim. We had big budget cuts around that time, so it wasn't unusual to do that sort of thing. He never asked me again."

"Why did you keep the photos all these years?" Rachel asked.

"I suppose it was in case someone like you came calling one day. Never expected it would take this long," he said, sorting through the photos and giving Rachel a handful.

274

"Why do you think nobody followed up?" Rachel asked.

"Because it was more convenient for people if that girl's death was put down as an accident."

30
GUILTY OR NOT GUILTY

SEASON 3, EPISODE 7: VICTIM
I've never been raped. Until recently, if you'd asked me, I would have told you that I've never been a victim of a sexual assault. In my mind, that involved being dragged into an alley and forcibly raped by a stranger.

Things are changing. We're starting to admit that rape and sexual assault can happen in a multitude of ways. We're starting to acknowledge that it permeates our lives as women. I guess you could say that society was in denial for, well, really, forever.

If you asked me today, and you said, "Rachel, have you ever been a victim of a sexual assault?" I would have to say yes.

Yes, I have been a victim of a sexual assault. Well, probably several really. Funny how we were conditioned to accept these situations as unpleasant instead of outrageous.

Most of the "several" were the types of things many women encounter. We considered them to be nuisances, part and parcel of being women in a misogynist world. I'm talking about things like groping. Guys squeezing a girl's butt at a college football game. Or a nightclub. One time, when I was in high school, I was sitting on a crowded train and a man with a mustache rubbed his crotch against my arm. Kind of accidentally on purpose. I didn't know whether it was an accident or not until I saw him move forward and do the same thing to another girl farther down the car.

Another time, at a party in college, a guy pushed past me. Rubbed against my breasts. It was all so innocent until his friends burst out laughing. Hilarious.

I'm sure that every one of my female listeners knows exactly what I'm talking about. There were no scars from those incidents, except that ever since I'm really careful about my personal space. I hate being in crowds.

So, yes. I've been groped. But that's not the worst thing that's happened to me. When I was seventeen, my parents divorced and I moved to a new city with my mom. It was kind of traumatic. You know, new town, new high school, new friends.

I was chosen for the track team. I was a pretty good distance runner in those days. A few days after I made the track team, the team's champion sprinter asked me on a date. He had it all in spades. The guy looked like a movie star. All the girls swooned over him. I was flattered and thrilled.

Of course, I accepted. I counted the days in my diary until the date. I did that stupid schoolgirl thing of scribbling out our inter-twined initials in my notebook.

We went to a movie for this date that I'd been so excited about. It was a forgettable rom-com, the type of film that's supposed to leave you floating on air. In fact, if I'm going to be really cynical about it, it's the type of movie that a guy chooses to soften up a girl before trying to move from, I don't know, first base to third base. In the space of an hour.

After the movie we went out for ice creams and then he drove me home. I had a curfew. Instead of turning into my street, he "forgot" to take the turn.

He drove into this parking lot that faced a park with a pretty view of the skyline. Your classic make-out location. What can I say, this guy truly lacked imagination. He kissed me. It was a beautiful kiss. Everything a girl could have wanted.

But instead of stopping at that one kiss, he kissed me again. This time deeper. More ag-gressive. He forced his tongue into my mouth. Put his hands on my breasts. I'd never done any of that before. I was trying to push his hands off me so he'd know he was going too fast when the whole weight of his body was suddenly right on top of me. He was crushing me and pawing me.

I had to fight him off. While I wriggled away, I accidentally turned on the windshield wipers. The wipers distracted him enough that I was able to get out of the car. He apologized profusely through the open window. I was in tears. He looked terrified. He promised he'd take me home. I refused to get back in the car. This went on for a while. Me crying. Him promising he wouldn't lay a finger on me. Begging me to get back in the car. By then he was scared and worried about my mom finding out what he'd tried to pull.

Eventually, I agreed to sit in the back. That's how I arrived home from the big date with the hottest guy in school — sitting in the back seat of his car. Him in front, driving me like a chauffeur.

Until recently, I never thought of it as a sexual assault. I chalked it up to a clumsy teenage date gone wrong. Now I know that, if things with that boy had gone further out of control, I might have been a rape victim. I might have been a K. And the more that I learn about what a rape victim goes through when her accuser is prosecuted, the more I admire the courage of these survivors. Because, believe me, they are put through the wringer.

I haven't personally met K. She was in court to hear Mitch Alkins, the prosecutor, open his case. Her parents and a social worker supported her. She seemed fragile. Broken.

As you already know, I can't tell you her name as I won't reveal the name of a sexual assault victim on this podcast. What I can tell you is that she is — or rather was — a happy, well-adjusted sixteen-year-old girl before last October. She had friends, worked hard at school, and sure, she partied as well. Why does a girl have to apologize for having fun?

The more that I learn what being a victim in a rape case entails, the more I understand how much courage K has shown in choosing to take this torturous journey.

For one thing, she had to endure a rape kit. I went to the local hospital to find out what happens when a rape kit is done. It's a process that can take hours. The victim is treated like a human crime scene. Except the evidence that needs to be collected is on, or in, the victim. It's embarrassing, invasive, and humiliating. Some experts say it perpetuates the sense of trauma, the helplessness that rape victims feel. Some victims say that a rape kit examination can be as traumatic as the rape itself.

A nurse or doctor goes over every square inch of skin, photographs every abrasion and bruise. It involves having pubic hair combed through and taken for comparison purposes. It involves being photographed internally and externally. And those photos become evidence for a whole lot of other strangers to pore over.

The thing is, while rape kits are used to collect the evidence of an alleged sexual assault, such as the perpetrator's semen and pubic hairs, they rarely provide incontrovertible proof of consent. In the case of stranger rape, it's not really an issue during the trial. It's kind of a given that a victim didn't consent to sex with a violent stranger.

In a case like the one in Neapolis, where the alleged victim knew the alleged perpetrator — I guess for want of a better word you could call it a date-rape case — it usually doesn't meet the "beyond a reasonable doubt" evidentiary threshold just to show there was sexual intercourse. The prosecution needs to prove that the victim did not consent. That's tough when it's "his" word against "her" word.

Over the past few days in court, two charismatic criminal lawyers have lined up in a sort of courtroom duel. For the prosecution, Mitchell Alkins. Intimidating, filled with wrath. For the defense, Dale Quinn. Boyishly handsome.

281

Charming. Born with a silver tongue.

Scott Blair, the defendant, has been there, too, listening to the prosecution's case against him. He is tense. Nervous. What happens in that courtroom over the coming days will determine the course of his life, and his liberty.

The jury solemnly files into court each day. Those twelve ordinary folk will decide whether Scott Blair goes free or goes to jail. That's how the criminal justice system works. Guilty or not guilty. His word, against her word. You'll decide at home. But it's the jury's decision that will count.

I'm Rachel Krall and this is *Guilty or Not Guilty,* the podcast that puts you in the jury box.

31
RACHEL

Mitch Alkins looked downright annoyed when the jury stumbled into court yawning after the lunch recess. Their eyelids heavy, they slouched in their seats as if settling in for an afternoon nap. Alkins was bringing his forensic expert to the stand. He needed a jury that was alert, not dozing after a heavy meal.

"I hope you all had a good lunch?" Judge Shaw bantered with the jury.

"They gave us fried chicken and corn bread with slaw and all that good stuff," said the jury foreman, smacking his lips. Laughter erupted.

"Good to hear my staff is pulling out all the stops," said Judge Shaw, his blue eyes for once twinkling in amusement. Mitch Alkins was the only person in court who did not smile.

Dr. Wendy North was a petite woman in her early fifties. Rachel recognized her from the hotel. Just that morning she'd seen Dr. North eating breakfast at a window table at the hotel cafe.

Dr. North had a natural poise and melodic voice that Rachel thought would endear her to the jury. That is, if they managed to stay awake for her testimony.

Unfortunately for Alkins, Rachel noted, the fried chicken did its work as he moved through his preliminary questions about Dr. North's experience and credentials. One of the jurors yawned. Another followed. Soon the yawning was like a virus spreading through the jury box. Their chairs creaked. They sighed restlessly. They yawned some more.

"Your Honor," said Dale Quinn, during a pause while Dr. North took a sip of water, "to save time and reduce the burden on the jury, the defense is willing to acknowledge that Dr. North is a highly qualified forensic expert witness. We are further willing to acknowledge that the defendant had sexual intercourse with the complainant. We've already said as much."

"That's very thoughtful, Mr. Quinn." Judge Shaw's sarcasm stung. "That point could have been made half an hour ago. I suspect Mr. Alkins may have additional questions for his witness, since she went to the trouble of traveling across the country to get here."

"As it happens, I do, Your Honor," Alkins said, turning to the witness. "Dr. North, were you able to confirm that Miss Moore had sexual relations with the defendant, Mr. Blair?"

"Yes," she said. "Semen traces collected during Kelly Moore's rape kit matched Scott Blair's DNA, taken from a swab of his cheek. It was a one in a hundred million match. We also found pubic hairs belonging to the defendant and traces of his saliva on her body. They all matched the defendant's DNA."

"So we know that the defendant had sexual intercourse with Kelly Moore," Alkins stated. "In your expert opinion, does the evidence show whether Kelly Moore consented to the sexual intercourse?"

Dr. North leaned into the microphone to answer. "It's my opinion after a close study of the forensic evidence that she did not consent," she responded. "That she was sexually assaulted. Raped."

She rose from her seat and approached an easel brought out by Alkins's staff. The jury perked up when they saw the visual exhibit. Anything to break the monotony. On the easel was a chart with a black outline of a female body. Dr. North had placed red circles in various areas within the outline of the body.

"We found bruising, here, here, and here," said Dr. North, pointing at each circle on the diagram to indicate the various locations. "We also found vaginal bruising in the external genitalia and intra-vaginal lacerations. They all indicate nonconsensual intercourse."

"Just to clarify again, you're saying that all these bruises and abrasions documented during Kelly Moore's rape kit show that Scott Blair raped Kelly Moore?" Alkins asked.

"Miss Moore's injuries are the types of injuries commonly sustained by rape victims. Let me show you another example." Dr. North removed the diagram to reveal another board underneath that showed a blown-up photograph of an ugly bruise on Kelly Moore's thigh.

"This bruise was most likely the result of the defendant pushing the victim's legs apart with a level of force that would have hurt her. It suggests she was resisting him. In my opinion, this alone indicates she did not consent and was not a willing participant."

Dr. North handed photos to the jurors

and the judge that showed bruising to Kelly Moore's genitals and internal injuries. The photos were taken using a blue stain that highlighted bruises on a cellular level, invisible to the naked eye. The jurors flinched as they saw the photos for the first time.

"The bruises on the posterior fourchette and labia minor are common injuries from rape," Dr. West said. "Those injuries, along with the bruising on the shoulders and thighs, further indicate that Miss Moore tried to resist the sexual intercourse. By virtue of the fact that she was resisting, she could not therefore have consented," she added.

Dale Quinn rose for his cross-examination when Alkins was done. His expert witness, Professor Carl Braun, was sitting behind him, taking notes as Dr. North testified. In the meantime, Quinn managed to elicit Dr. North's admission that she could not be absolutely certain that Kelly Moore did not consent.

"It's an opinion," she conceded eventually. "Based on years of work in this field."

Rachel tried to catch up to Dr. North after court recessed for the day, but she got stuck in the back of the crowd leaving the courtroom. By the time she came down the stairs onto the plaza, Dr. North had gone.

That evening, Rachel set up her laptop in the lobby cafe at a table near the birdcage. She found her hotel room claustrophobic and, if truth be told, she was hoping to catch Dr. North before she left town. While she waited, Rachel typed a transcript of that day's court testimony for the website and ate a hamburger and fries from the hotel cafe.

"I thought you said this bird sings?" Rachel's concentration was broken by the loud voice of a man. She looked up to see a man with white hair and a green polo shirt who was on the way to dinner with his wife who'd dressed up for the occasion. He had stopped at the birdcage and was tapping it with his palm. "Haven't heard a peep out of this bird since we've been here. Not a peep," he said. "I think it's stuffed. What the heck kind of a songbird doesn't sing?"

"I don't think the poor bird wants to sing, hon," said his wife.

"Rubbish. Nightingales are supposed to sing," the man said, clicking his fingers to get the bird's attention.

"Maybe some nightingales don't want to sing on demand, Keith," the wife muttered, almost to herself.

Rachel spotted Dr. North sitting at a table near the window, sipping a glass of white wine. Rachel walked over to Dr. North's table, where she introduced herself.

"I was wondering if I could ask you something," she said.

"As long as it's got nothing to do with the trial," said Dr. North. "There's still a chance I could be recalled to the stand."

"I promise," said Rachel. She opened her leather satchel and removed the photographs that Stuart had given her.

"These were taken of a young girl who drowned several decades ago. I was wondering whether you can take a look. I'm interested in hearing your views about whether her injuries appear to be consistent with drowning."

Dr. North picked up the photographs and went through them one by one. Squinting at some. Pausing at others. Setting some aside. When she was done, she laid out the photographs on the table in front of Rachel.

"This girl may well have drowned," she said. "But something terrible happened to her in the hours before her death."

"How do you know?" asked Rachel.

"The bruises visible in the photographs would have happened within a few hours before her death. Not right before her death, and certainly not at the time of death. The bruises on her upper legs are similar to the ones I mentioned today in court which we saw on Kelly Moore's thighs. This bruise is the size of a large hand. Most likely male. It's going around the deceased's shoulder, which indicates that she might have been physically restrained. Perhaps pinned to the ground," she said, pointing to a close-up photo of Jenny's naked shoulder.

"Could you hazard a guess as to what might have happened to this girl before she drowned?"

"I think that she was physically assaulted in the hours before her death," said Dr. North. "Why are you asking me? Surely that all came out in the autopsy and subsequent police investigation into her death."

"There was no police investigation, from what I can tell, and I'm not sure that an autopsy was performed," said Rachel.

Dr. North looked shocked. "This girl met with extreme violence before her death. Why on earth would the police not investigate a death this suspicious? I've never heard of such a thing in all the years I've worked in forensic medicine."

32
RACHEL

Kelly Moore's mother conducted herself with enormous grace on the stand as she answered Mitch Alkins's questions about what happened when her daughter finally turned up after taking the bus home from the beach that day.

She told the court that when Kelly arrived home, there was a police car in the driveway and detectives in the living room, setting up a task force to search for Kelly. Nobody noticed when Kelly came through the back sliding door and took the stairs to her bedroom. It was only when her mother went upstairs to use the restroom and saw Kelly's bedroom door was shut that she knew Kelly was home.

Christine tried to open the door, but it was locked. Kelly wouldn't let her in. She sat on her bedroom carpet with her back to the door, barricading herself inside for hours. In a quivering voice, Kelly's mother described to the court how when it started getting dark, Kelly quietly unlocked her bedroom door and allowed her mother to come in. They sat on Kelly's bed and she told her mother what had happened with Scott Blair down at the beach. Christine Moore convinced Kelly to go with her to the hospital. She blinked back tears as she drove, determined to be strong for her daughter. They returned home early the following morning. Kelly had to leave the hospital wearing a borrowed sweatsuit taken from a hospital charity bin, as her clothes were kept as evidence. Her rape kit examination had taken five hours.

The jury was deeply affected by Christine Moore's testimony. Dale Quinn took jabs in cross-examination, but they were delicate jabs, like a reluctant boxer afraid of drawing blood.

Quinn kept pressing the same point with his questions. He established that Kelly's mom wasn't at the beach that night and that she, like everyone else, relied on her daughter's word about what had happened. He also managed to get her to admit that Kelly had not always been truthful in the past, and that Kelly had lied in the note that she'd left in the kitchen saying that Lexi's parents would be home the night of the party.

Rachel bolted out of court quickly after the morning session to move her car. Court had gone later than expected and she'd exceeded the parking limit by twenty minutes. She had a moment of panic when she saw a white parking ticket flapping on her windshield as she turned the corner into the street where her car was parked.

As Rachel came closer, though, she realized it wasn't a ticket. It was another note from Hannah. Rachel read it leaning against her car door. When she was done, instead of feeding the meter and returning to court, she climbed into the driver's seat and drove away.

As she drove, she called Pete for their daily catch-up. He sounded strained when he answered the phone. He'd returned home from the hospital a day earlier and was still adjusting to the lower doses of pain meds.

"What's wrong, Pete?" Rachel asked. "You sound upset. Are you not feeling well?"

"I'm going over social media comments. It's not exactly pretty," he said.

"What do you mean?"

"I've never seen such a divisive reaction. Some listeners have gone ballistic at you.

They think you're blaming the victim and that you're taking it too easy on Scott Blair. Others are accusing you of being biased in favor of Kelly. They're accusing you of hanging Scott out to dry."

"That's ridiculous," said Rachel. "I have to show both sides of the story. Isn't that the point? To be objective?"

"Objectivity is so last century. Didn't you get the memo?" said Pete. "These days everybody has an opinion. Whether they know what they're talking about, or not. Usually it's the latter. Right now their invective is directed at you, Rach."

"That sounds a bit extreme."

"You didn't spend two hours trawling through messages today," Pete said. "It was horrible stuff. None of the social niceties apply online. People will say things they would never in a million years say to someone's face."

"Read me some of the comments. I'm a big girl. I can take it," said Rachel as she turned onto the coastal road.

"Not a chance," said Pete. "Some of the messages have so many expletives that I'd have to wash out my mouth if I read them. You're better off not knowing, Rach. Trust me, you really are."

"So what do I do about it?" Rachel asked.

"Nothing," said Pete. "You're doing great. You're stirring the pot. Like you wanted. You're making people think and talk about rape. Keep doing what you're doing. This kind of response is exactly what we were looking for," he said. "Plus, controversy is great for publicity."

Rachel winced. She hated the idea that anyone might think that she was deliberately courting controversy by choosing a rape trial for her new season. She finished the call with Pete just as she pulled up at the single-lane Old Mill Road bridge, where she had to wait for a truck to cross before she could drive over. After a hairbend turn, she drove uphill until, through the gaps in the trees on the roadside, she saw stone-colored town houses blending into the landscape of a ridge. Rachel was sure the Stills house had been on that ridge. It closely fitted Hannah's descriptions in her letters.

Rachel waved at the guard who was sitting in a security booth with a "Sea Breeze Retirement Villas" sign on the side. The familiarity of her gesture gave the impression that she was a regular and the guard automatically opened the boom gate. Rachel pulled her car into a visitors' parking lot and walked toward a pool area where she could hear splashing and music. As Rachel came in through the pool gate, she saw a handful of women doing low-impact water aerobics while an instructor stood on the edge demonstrating each exercise. Other swimmers swam breaststroke up and down the side lanes.

Farther along, two men slouched over a chess set. "Can't believe I didn't see that coming," said one of the men, slapping his thigh when the other took his bishop.

"Excuse me." Rachel approached them. "I'm wondering if you can tell me what was here before this complex."

"You should ask Estelle." The man gestured toward a woman in her seventies with dyed-blond hair who was lying on a sun lounger. "She knows everything there is to know about the history of this town."

"You're only saying that because she's your wife, Hal," said his friend.

Estelle put down the novel she was reading at the sound of her name. "Take a seat, hon," she told Rachel, patting a chair next to her with red fingernails that matched her one-piece swimsuit. "What is it you want to know?"

"I'm trying to find out about the Stills family. I think they lived around here once."

"Actually, they lived right here," Estelle said. "These condominiums are built where

Edward Stills's house used to be. His land ran all the way up to the river. Would have been worth a fortune today. In those days, nobody wanted to live here. When his granddaughter Hope died, the land was sold cheap to a developer to pay for her funeral and debts."

"Who was the developer?" Rachel asked.

"Hal," she called out. "Who was the developer of Sea Breeze Villas?"

"It was my old tennis buddy Trent's cousin," he called back. "Simon Blair."

"That's right," she said. "His son was a famous swimmer. Grandson too. Kind of a notorious family right now, if you haven't already heard. The Scott Blair trial?" She looked at Rachel to see if she'd heard of it. Rachel nodded.

"Well, in the early nineties, Simon and his son Greg built their first retirement units. Made a lot of money. Enough to build more. And then more. I was at school with Simon. His family was dirt poor. Used to come to school in hand-me-down shoes with holes in them. His dad was a two-bit renovator. These days the family own properties up and down the coast."

"What can you tell me about the Stills family?" Rachel asked.

"I only know bits and pieces," said Estelle.

"Hope came back after Ed Stills died. She had two children, both out of wedlock. In those days, people talked. Hope moved into her grandfather's house and lived there with her daughters. Everyone thought that house was a health hazard. Ed lived like a hermit. But I heard that Hope fixed the place up real nice.

"Hal," she said, handing her husband some coins. "I'm parched. Won't you get us drinks from the vending machine? What's your name, honey?"

"It's Rachel."

"What a lovely name. Very biblical," she said. "Where was I?"

"You were telling me about Hope Stills."

"Such a shame when she came down with cancer. One of those leukemias. She used to work at my local supermarket. Such a bright, vivacious girl. She was a little, you know, out there. She put pink dye in her hair once. Had butterfly tattoos on her ankle. I asked after her when I hadn't seen her for a while. The cashier told me that she was sick. They gave her an office job, but she couldn't manage the hours. A few months later, they said she'd died. I heard her daughter died, too. Jenny. She was the oldest one."

"Do you know anything about her daughters?"

"Jenny had a reputation. Just like her mother. Hope was barely seventeen when she was born. I heard that she didn't even know which boy was the father."

"What do you know about Jenny's death?"

Estelle shrugged. "We were down in Florida for my brother's wedding that summer. I remember it well, though. It was the same summer that we lost two boys in that awful car crash. I played bridge with one of the dead boys' mothers. She was heartbroken. Her only child," she said. "I vaguely remember hearing something about how the older Stills girl went swimming one night and drowned. There was talk that she'd been skinny-dipping with a boy," she said with a meaningful glance. "Apparently she did that a lot." She paused as her husband returned with the soda cans. She passed one to Rachel and then opened her own and took a sip.

"Any chance you might know the name of the boy who went swimming with Jenny that night?" Rachel asked.

"I don't think I ever knew his name," said Estelle. "It was a long time ago. I was a different person then. Younger. Prettier. And with a better memory. Wasn't I, Hal?"

"Nah, you look just as pretty now as you did then," he responded.

"He's a born liar. Used to sell life insurance," she told Rachel conspiratorially. "Honey, you're asking me about things that happened a lifetime ago. Anyway, you're talking to the wrong people. You should be speaking to Jenny's school friends."

"Can you give me some names?"

"Let me see," said Estelle, closing her eyes as she thought back.

"The kids those days were thick as thieves. They spent the summers down at Morrison's Point. My daughter may have some names. I can ask her tonight when she gets back from work. How long are you around for?"

"Two, three weeks," said Rachel. "I'm here for the Scott Blair trial. So till whenever that ends."

"Well, there you go, honey," said Estelle, clapping her hands together with excitement. "You know who you should be talking to?"

"Who?"

"That lawyer. What's his name? Hal" — she turned to her husband — "who's that handsome young lawyer who was in today's newspaper?"

"Mitchell Alkins," he said.

"That's right. Mitchell Alkins knew Jenny Stills. They were at school together. In fact, everyone said he was sweet on her. You should ask him."

33
HANNAH

Earlier today, I visited our old house. It's gone, of course. The land has been turned into a retirement home. How Mom would have laughed to know that people are swimming where our living room used to be. She wouldn't be so happy to know that they pulled out the lemon tree and asphalted over her vegetable garden. The only things that haven't changed are the daisies. The field that was below our old house is blooming with them.

Going there reminded me of something that I'd long forgotten. I was sitting on the front porch, reading a book, when I heard a car approach. It was a pale car. Green, I think, with a dent in the back. The driver was the boy with dark hair and athletic build whom Jenny had swum with at the beach. He was wearing jeans and a button-down shirt. I could see the leather necklace around his neck.

He nervously slicked back his hair as he headed up to the front door, swinging his car keys in one hand. The other hand held a bunch of white and yellow daisies that he must have picked in the field. He tossed the flowers on the ground as he climbed the porch stairs. I guessed that he felt self-conscious.

"Hey," I said, tossing my book aside as he reached the front door.

"Is Jenny around?" His eyes flicked away from me to look for Jenny through the ripped netting of the screen door.

"She's in the back garden. Come this way," I said, leading him into the house and then out again through the back porch.

Jenny was getting in the laundry from the backyard when we came out. She wore shorts and a candy-striped T-shirt. Her cheeks flushed and her eyes sparkled when she saw him.

"Hey, Jenny," he said, putting his right hand in the back pocket of his jeans. He stepped off the porch onto the grass and stood awkwardly next to her as she took clothes off the line and tossed them into a wicker basket.

"I tried to call. Got a message saying the phone was disconnected. So I stopped by," he said.

"We're having problems with the phone line," Jenny lied. She didn't tell him our telephone line was cut because we'd forgotten to pay a bill and it was too expensive to get the line reconnected.

"What did you want to call me about?" Jenny tossed a bedsheet into the laundry basket.

"I thought maybe you'd want to get pizza."

"When?"

"Now?"

"Sure." Jenny took down the last of the laundry and carried the basket inside under her arm. "I'll be ready in ten minutes."

He went outside and leaned back against the hood of his car, tapping his fingers against the metal until Jenny emerged in a cloud of honeysuckle. It was the perfume we'd given her for her sixteenth birthday. She was dressed in jeans and a sleeveless button-down apricot shirt.

She looked prettier than I'd seen her in weeks. Glowing with happiness. Her long hair hung loose down her back. She wore pink lipstick and tiny blue crystal earrings. He opened the car door for her before going around to the driver's seat. I thought to myself that Mom, who was asleep in her room, would have liked that boy if she'd seen the way he treated Jenny.

I fell asleep watching television and woke with a dry mouth and a wooly head when I heard a car approach. I lay back on the sofa, pretending to be asleep, when the screen door creaked open and Jenny came inside. A moment later, I heard a car drive away.

I watched Jenny through half-closed eyes as I lay still as a log. Her hair was messy and stuck with pine needles. The flushed excitement that I'd seen when she'd left had disappeared. She seemed numb and sad. She tossed her house keys onto the hall table and collapsed on an armchair where she buried her head in her hands. I thought she was tired until I saw her shoulders shudder as she swallowed her sobs.

Jenny never said a word to me about what happened on the date to make her cry. As for the boy, he never stopped by again.

Jenny went into town the next day and came back home to tell us that she'd been hired to pack shelves in the supermarket where Mom used to work.

After that, she was barely home. She left the house early for work and came back at dusk most days. With Jenny away, I was stuck at home. Frustrated and bored.

Mom found an old blow-up swimming pool, which she inflated and filled with

305

water. I spent days lying in that pool, watching wisps of clouds drift across the otherwise clear blue afternoon sky like flotsam. Mom lay on a sun lounger and threaded beads onto nylon strings. She had an idea to make beaded necklaces and sell them down at the Sunday market. She said that would give us an income. She'd be able to string beads even when she felt ill and was confined to bed. She said that Jenny and I could do the selling.

Sometimes I'd sit on the front porch stairs and look out longingly toward the sea. One afternoon, Mom saw me and said she was feeling well enough to drive me there.

We arrived late in the afternoon when the light was low and there was nobody around except for surfers out by the headland. I paddled around in the foam near the edge of the water while Mom floated on her back with a straw hat on her head. When I got bored, I flopped down on my towel and drew pictures in the sand with the edge of a broken shell.

"How's that sister of yours?"

I looked up to see the driver from the pickup and his friend Bobby, whose eyes seemed grayer than usual. The driver tossed his cigarette onto the sand, not bothering to extinguish it. Bobby kicked sand over it as if it was his job to clean up the mess.

"I asked how's your sister," the driver repeated.

"She's fine," I answered.

"Haven't seen her for a while," he continued.

"She doesn't come to the beach."

"Why not?"

"She has a job," I answered.

"Where's she working?" I sensed there was nothing casual about the question.

"I don't know," I lied, kicking myself for mentioning the job. Mom, who was in the sea, had stopped swimming to watch me.

The driver stared at me and Mom and then walked off. Bobby tossed me a piece of gum before rushing after his friend. I saw them later with a group of boys by the headland. They were sitting on rocks, drinking from liquor bottles hidden in paper bags.

We stopped at the gas station at the Old Mill Road after we left the beach so Mom could buy me ice cream as a treat. Rick was at the counter. This time he was nice as pie. Told me he'd known my mother since she was knee-high. It was only when we were waiting our turn at the old bridge that Mom asked me what those boys wanted.

"Nothing," I said, licking the last of my ice cream off the stick.

"They sure seemed to have something to say to you."

I shrugged.

"I know those boys," Mom said. "I knew some of their dads, too. They're trouble. The one who gave you the gum follows his friends around like he's their shadow. I reckon he'd do anything they tell him to keep in their good books. He's the only one whose daddy isn't a 'somebody' in this town. The only one with something to prove. That makes him the most dangerous of all."

34
RACHEL

Dr. Katrina Lawrence made a terrible witness, thought Rachel, watching the jury grimace as the thin falsetto of Kelly's therapist came through the sound system so high-pitched that the sketch artist sitting next to Rachel winced as she drew. In her sketchbook was the rough drawing of a tall woman with long straight hair and a tightly buttoned burgundy jacket.

Dr. Lawrence made an affirmation used by atheists instead of taking her oath on the Bible. It was a misstep. It wouldn't have mattered if it were a trial in a big city, but Neapolis was a conservative Southern town with a significant Evangelical population. It antagonized the jury from the start. Rachel suspected that Mitch Alkins had done his best to convey that fact to Dr. Lawrence, who seemed remarkably obtuse for someone who made her living studying the human psyche.

Alkins could see his witness was grating on the jury from the moment he asked her about her credentials. But he needed her testimony. She was, after all, Kelly Moore's therapist. By the same token, he couldn't afford to lose the jury in the process. He skipped whole pages of questions, flipping through his notepad to elicit her key testimony so he could get her off the stand as quickly as possible.

For her own selfish reasons, Rachel hoped Dr. Lawrence's testimony would end quickly. She wanted to corner Alkins at the lunch recess and ask him what he remembered about Jenny Stills. When Rachel returned to her hotel the previous afternoon after talking with Estelle, she immediately tried to contact Alkins. She'd left several messages with his personal assistant but hadn't received a call back from him or his staff.

Rachel stifled a yawn. Alkins worked through his questions, growing increasingly frustrated as the psychotherapist gave long, dry responses when short answers would have both sufficed and gone down much better with the jury.

Rachel took notes as the psychotherapist testified that Kelly had been a well-adjusted teenager before that night with Scott Blair.

Afterward, Kelly exhibited all the symptoms of posttraumatic stress disorder, which Dr. Lawrence said was common among victims of sexual assault. The effects ranged from anxiety and depression to panic attacks and nightmares.

"Dr. Lawrence, what is the normal re-action of a victim in the aftermath of a sexual assault?" Alkins asked.

"It depends," she responded, leaning into the microphone.

"On what?"

"On the victim," she answered. "There's no typical reaction. Some victims become hysterical, cry and so on. Others seem calm and normal, as if nothing happened, and only later show the effects. Others are in shock. They're numb. They don't cry, but they can't cope."

"Dr. Lawrence, is it normal, for instance, for a sexual assault victim to get on a bus, buy a bus ticket, and sit alongside other people without showing any indication of having been assaulted hours earlier?"

This was a crucial question. Dale Quinn was expected to call to the stand the bus driver and several passengers from the bus that Kelly took home that day. Already, some of them had publicly said that Kelly acted normally that day, smiling at the driver when she disembarked, and they didn't believe she'd been raped.

"It's common for the emotional and psychological effects after a sexual assault to be delayed by hours, days. Even weeks," Dr. Lawrence responded. "I believe Kelly was trying to hold herself together emotionally until she was in a safe space. Indeed, once she arrived home, she broke down."

"In your dealings with Kelly, have you found her to be truthful and credible?" Alkins asked.

"In every way," she said.

"Is there a chance that she misinterpreted what happened? Or exaggerated, maybe even lied about some details, or all of it?"

"I've spent more than ten months seeing Kelly as a patient. I have found her account of what happened and her emotional responses to be consistent throughout. I have absolutely no reason to doubt her word on what she says happened that night. No reason at all."

Dale Quinn bounded out of his seat to cross-examine Dr. Lawrence. He happily dragged out his questioning for as long as possible, knowing that the longer she was on the stand, the less the jury liked her, and by extension, the less they'd believe anything she said. He effectively gave her enough rope to hang herself as a witness, thought Rachel. When Quinn was ready, in his softest, folksiest voice he reeled her in for the kill.

"Dr. Lawrence, did you work for an organization called the Women's Rape Network after college?"

"Yes, I did."

"I've been told that the Women's Rape Network's philosophy is that women who say they are the victims of a sexual assault should be believed no matter what. Is that accurate?" Quinn asked.

"Yes," she said.

"Isn't it true that your testimony today is based on that same view, that your role is to support Kelly and not question whether she is telling the truth?"

"I have no reason to doubt Kelly."

"You weren't there that night, were you?" Dale Quinn asked.

"No, I wasn't."

"And you didn't see any of it happen. Did you?"

"No."

When Dr. Lawrence left the stand, Judge Shaw announced they'd take a lunch break. It was already running late enough for Rachel's stomach to rumble.

Rachel hung back until most of the court

had cleared out, except for the lawyers. Mitch Alkins and a young female lawyer on his team were talking and packing files into their briefcases.

"Mr. Alkins," Rachel called out. He paused from packing his briefcase and gave Rachel a hard stare that told her to back off. "Mr. Alkins, I'm a reporter. My name is Rachel Krall; I've been trying to get hold of you."

"She's the one from the podcast I was telling you about," the other attorney whispered to Alkins in a voice loud enough for Rachel to hear.

"Ah, the reporter who believes in crowd-sourcing justice. Why not get rid of the jury system altogether and decide on innocence and guilt with an online poll," he muttered.

"Mr. Alkins, I need to ask you something. In private," Rachel said, ignoring his comments. She had more important things to discuss than the ethics of crime podcasts.

"We're not allowed to talk to reporters until after the case. Judge's orders," he said.

"It's not about the trial," said Rachel. "It's about something else. Mr. Alkins, did you once know a girl by the name of Jenny Stills?"

Alkins froze for the briefest moment. It was so quick that Rachel wondered if she'd

314

imagined it. He put another file in his briefcase, pulled the lid down tightly, and snapped the latches shut. When he was done, he walked right past her without a word and left the courtroom.

35
RACHEL

Rachel shielded her eyes with her hand as she moved from the courthouse into the bright sunshine of the afternoon. The roar of passing traffic was deafening after hours spent in the hushed confines of the courtroom.

Dan Moore was heading down the stairs in front of her. He looked as if he'd aged a decade since the trial began. Being in court every day listening to deeply upsetting testimony about his daughter's sexual assault was taking a heavy toll on him.

"How's Kelly doing?" Rachel asked when she caught up to him in the plaza.

"She's understandably nervous about testifying, but she absolutely insists that she wants to do it," he said. "Her therapist says it will give her closure and help her move on with her life."

Once they parted ways, Rachel headed over to a pretty street of cafes and specialty stores a few blocks from the courthouse. In Rachel's computer bag was the faded bouquet ribbon she'd found at Jenny Stills's grave. Rachel had shown the ribbon to two florists at downtown stores. They both said they'd never used that type of ribbon. It was a high-quality two-toned ribbon made from real fabric. One of the florists suggested that Rachel check at a shop called Antique Flowers, a high-end florist store that specialized in expensive, classical arrangements.

The store had been closed every time Rachel drove past, but that morning while driving to court she'd seen the "Closed" sign had been removed from the door. She'd been running late and didn't have time to go into the store. But now, since court was done for the day, Rachel rushed over to the florist shop so she could ask about the ribbon before the store shut for the day.

Antique Flowers was a corner shop in a heritage building with large bay windows. The store exterior was painted a crisp shade of white. Its name was written in delicate matching white calligraphy on the windows. The brass bell tinkled as Rachel opened the door. She was immediately hit by the unusual combination of furniture polish mixed with a delicate scent of fresh flowers.

"Can I be of assistance?" A diminutive

woman walked in from a back room with an armful of pale roses, which she placed on floristry paper laid out on an antique table. "Are you looking for furniture, or flowers? Or both?" the woman asked. She wore a natural linen apron with the store logo and a matching badge with her name, "Renata."

"I'm just doing the tourist thing and window-shopping," answered Rachel. "I've never seen a store that sells flowers and antiques together, and such beautiful ones at that!"

"The antique store is my dad's business. My mom is a florist. A few years ago they combined the businesses. That way Mom could run the store while Dad went on antique-buying trips," said the woman, as she clipped the stems of the roses.

Rachel was about to introduce herself when the store phone rang. Renata smiled apologetically as she took the call. Rachel used the time to wander around the store. The antiques for sale ranged from the elaborate to the simple. Rachel admired an old farmhouse table with knife marks indented into the timber and a distressed oak pantry cupboard with old-fashioned blue ceramic jars on its shelves.

"Are you enjoying your time here?" Renata asked conversationally when she'd finished the call, and began selecting a combination of cream and light pink roses from the florist's table.

"I am. It's a lovely town," Rachel responded. "You're very lucky to live here."

"Oh, I don't live here anymore. I only come back to see my parents or help run the store when they're on vacation. To tell you the truth, I stay for as short a time as possible and I'm extremely relieved when I go home. But that's just me. Most people love it here."

"Why don't you like it here?" Rachel asked.

"When I grew up, it was an insular town. People got stuck with labels. It was hard for them to, I guess, reinvent themselves," Renata said as she arranged the roses and wrapped it all in floristry paper. She took out a spool and cut a long piece of ribbon, which she expertly tied around the bouquet. Rachel was disappointed to see that the ribbon didn't at all match the ribbon that she'd found at Jenny's grave. She sighed to herself. It was another dead end.

Rachel was about to leave when she decided that she'd show Renata the ribbon anyway in case she knew other stores where Rachel could ask. She was removing the ribbon from her purse when the brass doorbell chimed. A man stepped inside to collect the bouquet that Renata had just finished. Rachel waited as Renata packaged the order in a paper bag with the store's logo and swiped the man's credit card.

"His wife is one lucky lady. That is a stunning bouquet," Rachel said, as the door shut after the man left carrying his wife's anniversary present.

"I was worried that I might be out of practice. The lady who was supposed to have run the store while my parents are on their cruise broke her leg. I couldn't get here until last night, so the store has been closed for the past week," Renata said. "I'm still catching up on orders."

"I'll leave you to your work then. Just one quick question before I go," said Rachel, holding up a plastic bag with the ribbon from the cemetery. "Do you know which florist uses this particular ribbon?"

Renata took one look and immediately opened a drawer under the flower-wrapping table from which she removed an oversized spool containing an expensive two-toned ribbon that was almost an exact match to the ribbon Rachel was holding.

"Dad brings it back from Europe when he visits on antique-buying trips. The ribbon is very expensive, so Mom saves it only for her premium bouquets," Renata explained, leaning forward to examine the one Rachel held. "It's badly faded. Where did you find it?"

"At a grave at the cemetery," said Rachel. "I'm trying to find out who might have left it. Given that it's your ribbon, the flower arrangement must have been from here. Do you keep records for all your orders?"

"Only for delivery orders," said Renata. She clicked open the order database on a laptop next to the cash register. "I can check our old orders. Do you remember where in the cemetery you found it?"

"I found it by a grave. The name on the tombstone was Jenny Stills," said Rachel. "She was a teenage girl who died here in the early nineties."

"Jenny Stills," said Renata, her hand frozen above the keyboard. Her voice was filled with a mixture of recognition and sadness. "I haven't heard her name spoken for years."

"You knew Jenny?" Rachel felt a thrill of excitement. "Were you friends?"

"I knew her from school. We weren't really friends."

"Do you know how Jenny died?" Rachel asked.

"I was in Europe with my parents that summer. It was a sort of sixteenth-birthday present. Dad bought antiques and we vacationed. We were gone for almost three months. Missed the first few weeks of school. By the time I came back, Jenny was long dead. I heard it was in an accident. A couple of boys died in a car crash that summer, so I assumed that's how Jenny died, too."

"You didn't ask?"

"There was nobody to ask. Her mother was dead. Her sister gone. The town had a collective trauma. Nobody wanted to talk about what happened that summer. A few months later, there was a ceremony to install a memorial for the car crash victims. I was surprised that I didn't see Jenny's name on the memorial. I asked my teacher. He said that Jenny wasn't killed in the car accident. That she drowned. I was shocked."

"Why were you shocked?"

"Everyone knew that Jenny was a strong swimmer. I couldn't believe that she of all people would have drowned. It was around that time that the graffiti began to appear, too."

"What graffiti?"

"Rude sexualized drawings with dumb jokes about Jenny. I didn't understand why

322

people would be so mean about a dead girl." Renata flushed suddenly, as if embarrassed by the memory.

"Her tombstone had been graffitied with the word 'WHORE.' Do you know why someone would do that?" Rachel asked.

"Can't believe it still goes on after all these years," sighed Renata. "After Jenny died, her name became synonymous with being a 'slut.' Interchangeable, really. Boys would rate girls on what they called the 'Jenny Stills index.' A girl who put out would get a nine or ten on the 'J.S. index.' That's what they called it. There was other stuff, too, that they used to say which I can't even describe because it was so crude. I'm sure you get the picture. I feel bad. I turned a blind eye like everyone else. I learned that it was better to shut up."

"Why was it better to shut up?"

"There was a girl at school who'd been Jenny's friend. The boys teased her terribly, and made comments suggesting she was easy. I never stood up for that girl. I feel bad about it now. In those days, I was afraid they'd all turn on me. That I'd become the next Jenny Stills. That girl left town for college and never returned." She paused. "Now that I think about it, I guess I did the same."

"Was Jenny bullied when she was alive?

Teased or harassed by boys?"

"Jenny was very pretty and nice, but she wasn't popular. I don't think she could shake off the Stills name. Jenny and her sister didn't look at all alike. Everyone knew that her mother had two kids from separate fathers. In those days, that sort of thing was still scandalous."

"You're the first person I've spoken with who seems to have really known Jenny," Rachel said. "It's amazing to me that you remember her so vividly."

"I've never forgotten her," said Renata. "Mom gave Jenny and her kid sister a ride home once. They'd been waiting out a thunderstorm at the gas station by the Old Mill Road junction. The man in charge wouldn't let them inside the store to take shelter from the rain. Said something about how he'd known the Stills family for years and they were perfectly capable of walking home in any weather," Renata recalled, scooping up another bunch of roses and clipping their stems. "My mom was furious. She flatly refused to put gas in her car at that service station after that incident. Even if she was running on empty. Said she wouldn't give her business to that horrible man."

"Was his name Rick by any chance?" Rachel asked.

"Yes, it was. Actually, Mom donated some flowers to a retirement home a few months ago and she saw him there. He was one of the residents. She told me about it on the phone. Anyway, after that incident with the thunderstorm, Mom tried to help the Stills family. She'd sometimes leave a bag of clothes or a hamper of food on their porch at night. She told me not to say anything if I saw Jenny wearing my hand-me-downs. Said it was kinder to give people charity without them knowing where it came from."

She glanced at her laptop. "I've found something. Mom's received several orders in the past to deliver a premium bouquet to Jenny Stills's grave. They were online order paid for by PayPal. There's no information on the sender. But there's a card. Let's see what it says." Rachel waited while Renata scanned the computer.

"Isn't that strange!" said Renata. "All the orders request the exact same message on the card."

"What's the message?" Rachel asked.

" 'Forgive me,' " Renata read out. "That's the message. It just says: 'Forgive me.' "

36
RACHEL

The Golden Vista retirement village was on the edge of town, opposite a field of overgrown grass littered with rusting car chassis and abandoned tires. The complex consisted of single-level brick buildings in a garden setting. Raggedy pines obscured views of the town dump. The garbage couldn't be seen, but Rachel sure smelled it as she walked to the reception building.

A woman at the reception desk gave Rachel a visitor's badge and directed her to a recreation room down the hall where the residents were relaxing after their early dinner. Most of the residents sat on plastic bucket seats and wheelchairs arranged around a chipped upright piano where a woman with bright lipstick sashayed her shoulders while singing an old Beatles tune.

Rachel beelined to a man sitting in the corner, wearing dark pants and a pale wrinkled shirt. His skin clung to his bones so tightly that Rachel could see the outline of his skull. He grimaced as she approached, flashing nicotine-stained teeth almost as a warning. Like a cat hissing, thought Rachel as she pulled over a chair.

"You're Rick? You used to own the gas station on the Old Mill Road?" Rachel asked.

"What do you want?" Rick snapped.

"Do you remember Jenny and Hannah Stills?"

He shrugged. "There were hundreds of kids who came into my store, stealing when I wasn't looking and tracking in mud. And sand. I never knew their names. Never wanted to know." He closed his eyes and pretended to go to sleep. Rachel could tell from the tautness of his body that he was awake.

"I gave you their names. I never said they were kids," Rachel said carefully. His eyes opened at being caught out.

"I know you know them," said Rachel. "What will it take for you to tell me what you remember?"

"Fish burger and fries," he said, sitting up. "From Admiral's Burgers. Downtown. I tried to get them to deliver once. They said we're outside their delivery zone. The staff here won't get it for me. They say it's high in sodium and cholesterol. Too unhealthy."

He laughed hollowly. "Look at me. I'm a dead man walking and they're worried about my sodium levels."

"I'll arrange your burger and fries if you tell me what you remember about the Stills family," Rachel promised.

"I knew the mom from when she was very small. Her granddad would send her to buy liquor. Never any food. Only liquor. A bottle a day. He'd rather his kid starve than miss out on his drink. Sometimes, little Hope would come in and her face would be swollen. Black eye. Cut lip. When Ed Stills was sober, he adored that girl. When he was drunk, he was as mean a drunk as you'll find anywhere."

"What happened to Hope's daughters. Jenny and Hannah?"

"I told the police everything I knew about those girls," he said.

"Which was?"

"That I didn't see a thing. Nothing. I don't know nothing. Not a thing. And between you and me, even if I did, I wouldn't say."

"There were some teenage boys who used to drive around in a pickup. They'd get gasoline from your store. Sometimes shoplift, too," said Rachel. "Do you remember them?"

"Lots of kids drove pickups in those days. Today they're driving Jeeps. In those days they had trucks," he said dismissively.

"This pickup was a regular. Try to remember," Rachel pressed. "It's important. I think they might have been involved in Jenny Stills's death."

"All I can tell you is that I called the ambulance that night because that little kid was messing up my floor with all that blood. I took her down to the beach in my old truck. I was shutting down for the night anyway, so I drove her. Got there before the cops and the ambulance."

"What did you see?"

"It was dark. There were no lights around there at night. It was hard to see anything at all. The little sister jumped out. I was going to go after her when I heard sirens coming. Figured she didn't need me anymore. Turned the car around to drive home. Almost ran over that boy."

"What boy?" Rachel asked.

"I don't remember," Rick added quickly, realizing he'd said too much. "I'm eighty-one. Memory isn't what it was."

"You remember everything, Rick," corrected Rachel. "Who was that boy you almost ran over? What was his name?"

"I saw him here. Two, three summers

ago," he said, warming to the subject and Rachel's attention. "Saw him one afternoon in the garden. They take us out to get sun like we're fucking tomatoes that need to be ripened. I went up to him and told him I remember what he did all those summers ago. He looked rattled. Left soon after. Never saw him again." He laughed wryly. "Not surprised. Always running. Like a rat."

"What was his name, Rick?"

"Rat," said Rick hoarsely, as his laughter became a cough. "That's what they should have called him. Looked like a rat. Ran like a rat."

"Rick," said Rachel. "What was his name?"

"Better to forget some things. There are folks in this world that a man can't afford to cross," he rasped in between coughs. "I'm senile but not that senile. All these years I kept my mouth shut. Why would I open it now?"

The old man's spasm of coughing worsened so that Rachel could barely make out his last words. She rushed to a water cooler in the corner of the room and quickly filled a cup with water. By the time she returned, he was bent over, spluttering into his hands. When he lifted up his head, his lips were covered with blood.

"What's wrong with him?" Rachel asked a uniformed nurse who'd rushed over, decked out with a mask and gloves.

"Lung cancer," the nurse whispered grimly.

The nurse approached Rick and talked to him in a loud voice, as if he were deaf. "We'll have to move you to the clinic. I need you to stand up so we can get you in the wheelchair." She grabbed Rick's arm and helped him stand while an orderly maneuvered a wheelchair in place.

Rachel watched Rick being wheeled away for treatment as he continued to cough uncontrollably into a wad of Kleenexes the nurse had given him. Rachel wished there was a way to get him to cooperate. To appeal to his better nature. The problem was that Rachel doubted that Rick had a better nature.

On the way out, Rachel took a brochure off a stand in the reception area. It had the same glossy Photoshopped pictures of blossoming gardens and breathtaking views of paddocks that she'd seen on the website. At the back of the brochure was corporate information. The retirement home was owned by Blair Developments. That shouldn't have surprised her. The Blair family's interests were, after all, extensive.

Rachel was driving back to the hotel when she realized her phone was vibrating. She answered it on speaker while signaling to make a left turn.

"Is that Rachel?"

"Yes," Rachel answered over the click of her turn signal.

"This is Renata. From the florist shop. I was so focused on looking for old orders that I didn't look at the current orders. There's an order for a premium bouquet to be delivered to Jenny Stills's grave tomorrow morning, eight A.M. sharp. My courier isn't too happy to be working so early."

37
GUILTY OR NOT GUILTY

SEASON 3, EPISODE 8: CONSENT
If you've been following this podcast, then you'll know that this trial is all about consent.

Prove that K consented to sex that night, and then Scott Blair walks free. Prove that she didn't, and he goes to jail. It really is that simple. And complicated. Because therein lies the rub.

Since K and Scott Blair were the only ones on the beach that night, there are only two people who know what happened. Scott Blair, the defendant. And K, the complainant. This case will depend almost entirely on who the jury believes more.

Will it be Scott Blair? A champion swimmer born and raised in Neapolis. A local boy expected to put his hometown on the map by winning big at the next Olympics. Many people in this town are rooting for Scott, and they're vocal about their belief that he's been falsely accused. Others see him as a sexual predator.

Or will the jury believe K, the teenage girl who says that Scott Blair raped her? The girl with the bright smile and big dreams of becoming a physiotherapist before the events of last October brought her world crashing down. K has had to move schools. Twice. She's now being homeschooled. She's been attacked on every front. Her morals have been questioned. Her motives for accusing Scott Blair have been questioned. She's lost friends. There are people in this town who won't talk to her family. She can't even leave her house because in a town like this, everyone knows, everyone stares.

K can't defend herself publicly. She's a material witness in the trial and she can't say a word until after she testifies, due to the risk it could damage the prosecution's case. She and her family have had to take all the abuse being directed at her without being able to say a single word in her defense.

Tomorrow, K will finally have her chance to speak. She'll take the stand and provide the most crucial testimony of the trial. And the most harrowing.

To remind you, K is only sixteen. Yet she will have to relive every single thing that happened to her that night. She'll have to do it in public. To a room full of strangers. In excruciating detail. She'll be asked the most intimate questions imaginable. How many times he penetrated her. Where. How. And so on. Think about that for a second. She's a teenage girl. . . .

If that's not horrible enough, then K will have to do it all over again during cross-examination. Defense attorney Dale Quinn will try to trip her up. Twist her words. Do everything that he can to damage her credibility, to portray her as a liar. Or a fantasist. Or both. He'll put on his best manners. His softest voice. He'll be considerate. He will feign concern.

Let there be no doubt that it will be ugly. Dale Quinn's job is to defend his client. The sad reality is that the only way he can do that effectively is by decimating K's testimony.

That's how trials work. It's medieval. It's not about getting to the truth. It's about who can put on a better show. And Mitch Alkins and Dale Quinn are among the best showmen around.

Scott Blair, incidentally, gets to choose whether he testifies. He could get through this entire trial without ever opening his mouth. It's up to his lawyers to decide whether he takes the stand, or never utters a single word in his own defense. The decision of whether he testifies will likely depend on how damaging

K's testimony is.

Most defense lawyers prefer their clients not to testify. Their reasoning is that it's the prosecutor's job to make the case. The defense doesn't have to make any case at all. So why put their client on the stand and risk something damaging coming out during a brutal cross-examination? That's the logic anyway.

So we have this unfair disparity in rape cases where the victim gets — let's call it what it is — violated. Twice. The first time in the attack. The second time in court.

Meanwhile, the defendant — the man accused of perpetrating the brutal crimes against K — well, he does not have to make a peep. All he has to do is turn up in court each day with a solemn face and the shell-shocked demeanor of the falsely accused.

K will not have an easy time of it on the stand. She will likely spend hours testifying for the prosecution. She may spend even longer being grilled by the defense. Her testimony will be put under a microscope. It will be poked and prodded by Scott Blair's formidable legal team as they look for lies, or inconsistencies. Anything to damage K's credibility. Anything to get their client acquitted.

The process is so awful that it makes me wonder why a teenage girl would go through this nightmare experience if her accusations are false. If she is making it up.

I'm Rachel Krall and this is *Guilty or Not Guilty*, the podcast that puts you in the jury box.

38
RACHEL

The dark outlines of fishing trawlers moved slowly against a pink-tinged sky as Rachel did hamstring stretches by a bench overlooking the sea. Dawn was breaking over Neapolis on the most important day of the trial.

Rachel should have been fast asleep in her hotel room bed, given that she'd gone to sleep at midnight after working late in the recording studio. Instead, she woke before dawn and dressed in running shorts and a sleeveless Lycra top for a brief morning jog along the boardwalk to clear her head before spending the day in court. Kelly Moore was due to take the stand in what was expected to be an intense and emotional day of testimony.

Rachel finished her stretches and then shuffled into a jog, gradually speeding up until she was running down the boardwalk in long, smooth strides. As she ran, she veered away from her intended route and crossed the road, heading toward downtown Neapolis, a few blocks away. She passed a row of shuttered shops, pursued by the clatter of a garbage truck emptying Dumpsters behind her.

She ran past the cafe next to the library, where a waiter was opening yellow umbrellas at outdoor tables while a barista wearing a black cloth apron picked up a crate of milk cartons that had been left outside the cafe door. She ran across the road to the city park, where the hiss of sprinklers forced her off the grass and onto a bicycle path that led to the heritage section of Neapolis. Rachel passed the dark and silent courthouse and continued running through a maze of side streets until she reached the gloomy entrance of the cemetery.

It was only when she checked her watch as she approached the cast-iron cemetery gate that she admitted to herself that, deep down, she'd always intended to be at the cemetery that morning. Renata's flower arrangement would be delivered to Jenny Stills's grave by a special courier at 8:00 A.M. sharp. The delivery time was very specific. It made Rachel think that someone was turning up at the cemetery to place the bouquet on the grave. Rachel hoped that person would be the elusive Hannah, who hadn't been in touch for days.

Rachel should have been getting dressed, reviewing notes, eating a filling breakfast to sustain her through the long day ahead. The last thing she should have been doing on the morning of the most important day of the trial was running to a cemetery to watch flowers being delivered to the grave of a girl who had died decades earlier, in the faint hope that Jenny's grieving sister might appear.

The cemetery gate creaked sharply as Rachel pushed it open and walked past a row of ivy-covered gravestones. The air was cool and still as she moved through the labyrinth of crumbling tombstones down the sycamore tree–lined path that connected the old and the new sections of the cemetery.

When Rachel caught sight of Jenny's grave, she stepped off the path and hid among the trees, watching and waiting as the rapid beat of her heart returned to normal.

A young man arrived at 8:00 A.M. sharp. Right on time. He held a black motorcycle helmet under his arm and carried an elaborate bouquet of flowers. He strode to Jenny's grave, where he casually tossed the bouquet, and walked away, putting on his motorcycle helmet as he disappeared through a rear service gate.

Rachel heard the roar of a motorcycle as he drove off. She waited ten minutes. And then fifteen. It was twenty-five after eight in the morning and nobody had arrived. She couldn't wait any longer. She had to return to the hotel to get ready for court or she'd never make it in time.

Suddenly, Rachel heard footsteps coming from the direction of the old cemetery. Someone was walking toward her. She slipped farther into the trees as the crunch of gravel became louder. She was so far inside the foliage that her view was blocked by thick-leafed branches. Rachel couldn't move to a better vantage point without crackling leaves underfoot and forcing branches to sway. Not wanting to draw attention to herself, she waited in frozen silence, holding her breath as the footsteps briefly paused.

She detected a hint of hesitation before the steady pace passed her hiding spot. She didn't move at all until the footsteps became more distant and she could tell the visitor was heading toward the new section of the cemetery. Toward Jenny's grave. Rachel moved closer to the path so that she could see the visitor. She was surprised to see that it wasn't Hannah at all. It was a dark-haired man in a navy suit.

Rachel didn't need to see Mitch Alkins's face to know it was him. His powerful build and towering height were dead giveaways. He reached the grave and bent down to pick up the flower arrangement the courier had tossed there. He placed the bouquet gently on the grave and stood for a moment with his head bowed in mourning before stepping back and whirling around.

Rachel quickly moved deeper into the shadows between the trees as he returned in her direction. He walked faster. For a frightening second, she wondered if he'd seen her and was coming to confront her. The cemetery was so silent that she was afraid he'd hear her heart pounding as he passed by.

As he came close, she saw his eyes were bloodshot. Rachel guessed he'd been up late preparing for court. She was relieved when he quickly disappeared the way he had come. The metal clang of the old cemetery gate banging shut confirmed he had left. She ran ahead and watched through the fence as Mitch Alkins drove away.

The line going through the metal detectors at the courthouse entrance was halfway down the stairs when Rachel arrived. She was frazzled from the mad rush to get ready for court.

She hadn't had time to blow-dry her hair or put on any makeup. She'd dressed hastily, and her tight gray skirt and white shirt felt twisted and uncomfortable on her clammy skin. Deciding to take a taxi and avoid wasting time looking for a parking space, Rachel had used the brief journey to fix her hair and apply lip gloss in the back seat as the taxi took a shortcut to the courthouse, driving at breakneck speed before pulling to a stop by the plaza. Court was almost full when Rachel entered and took her seat in the front row of the media gallery.

Mitch Alkins was flicking through a notepad filled with tight, black writing at the prosecution's table. He was wearing the same suit he'd worn at the cemetery. His face was inscrutable. His eyes were set in concentration. He appeared oblivious to the impatient murmurs across the courtroom and the squeaking of chairs as the clerks settled into their seats. He'd shifted mental gears from mourner to prosecutor in the space of an hour.

Why go to the cemetery on such an important day? The question troubled Rachel until she remembered what Kitty, Hannah's adoptive mother, had told her. Today must be the anniversary of Jenny's death, Rachel realized. That's why Mitch Alkins had ordered the flowers and visited the grave before court. The card he'd ordered with the flowers had said simply: *Forgive me.* Rachel wondered what he had done to Jenny Stills that warranted a lifetime of forgiveness.

Her thoughts were interrupted by the arrival of Sophia, the court sketch artist whose corner seat in the media box next to Rachel offered the best view of the courtroom and plenty of elbow room for sketching. Sophia placed a selection of pastel shades on the timber ledge in front of her as she prepared for a long session.

She was a veteran courtroom artist who'd sketched at over sixty trials. Since cameras were banned at the Blair trial, Sophia's drawings were the only visual depictions of the trial that the outside world would see. Her sketches had run on TV news broadcasts every night since the trial began. Rachel had also connected her to Pete, who'd commissioned a series of black ink drawings of the trial for the podcast website. Each day, a drawing related to that day's testimony was posted.

"You've seen more than a few trials in your time. What do you think, Sophia?" asked Rachel once Sophia had organized her drawing equipment. "Do you think the evidence the prosecution has presented so far is enough for a conviction?"

"Not likely," Sophia answered. "Dale Quinn did a brilliant job at twisting the prosecution's witnesses into knots and highlighting every conceivable inconsistency to make them look like liars. Plus he showed that several of the witnesses had an axe to grind against Scott Blair. I just can't see the jury convicting based on what's been presented so far."

"What about the forensic evidence?" Rachel asked. "I thought Dr. North did a convincing job of analyzing the forensics from the rape kit to show that Kelly's injuries strongly indicated that she didn't consent."

"Maybe," sighed Sophia. "The problem is that I've seen Dale Quinn's expert witness on the stand. He's the best that money can buy. He'll demolish Dr. North's testimony." She was going to say more but she was cut off by the bailiff's call for everyone to rise for Judge Shaw. "I'm sorry to say that this case lives or dies on Kelly Moore's testimony," Sophia whispered furtively to Rachel as the judge entered the courtroom.

39
RACHEL

Kelly Moore's mother covered her mouth with her palm in distress as her daughter swayed on her feet after swearing in on the Bible. Instead of fainting, Kelly clutched the polished timber of the witness stand. Her knuckles were white as she lowered herself into the chair.

The fragile young woman in the witness box bore almost no resemblance to the vibrant, outgoing girl in the photographs that Rachel had seen in Dan Moore's office. Her eyes were wide and her face was ashen against the dark fabric of her blouse as she waited for Mitch Alkins to ask his first question.

Alkins's voice was laced with compassion as he slowly eased Kelly into a series of questions about that night. From her walk back from the party with Harris Wilson, to the stab of fear when she saw a man standing in front of her by the swing in the park that night, to the sheer relief that ran through her when she realized the stranger was the famous Scott Blair.

"I knew who he was," she said in a soft voice. "I'd never met him before, but we all knew Scott Blair. He'd gone to our high school. I knew that he was a famous swimmer. He was in advertisements and magazines and stuff. Everyone at Lexi's party was talking about how he'd crashed her party."

"Did you feel less afraid once you recognized that the stranger was Scott Blair?"

"Yes. A lot less afraid. He was really nice. He apologized for scaring me. He told me that Harris texted him to drop me at home because his parents had caught him sneaking into the house and they wouldn't let him out again," she answered.

Kelly described how she walked with Scott to his car. It was a silver sports car with soft leather seats and a new-car smell. He opened the front passenger door for her and made sure she put on her seat belt before he drove off. Kelly told him her address. He said he knew the street, which is why she was surprised when he drove right past it.

"I told him that he'd missed the turn. He said not to worry. That he'd loop around."

"And did he?" Alkins asked.

"He offered to take me for a drive first. I'd never driven around in a convertible with the top down. I said, 'Sure.' We drove along the coast. We were heading home when he suggested we get food," she said. "He asked me what kind of food I liked. I said pizza. He said he liked pizza, too."

Alkins showed Kelly the CCTV footage from the pizza place. He asked her why she didn't alert the staff at the pizza parlor or ask to use their phone to call her parents. "Why did you return with Scott to his car?" Alkins asked.

She told him that she had no concerns about Scott's behavior at that point. He'd been friendly and attentive. She believed he would take her home right after they'd eaten, just as he'd promised. In the car, he suggested they eat the pizza at the beach. She wasn't crazy about the idea, but she didn't want to be difficult, so she agreed. He drove to a beach. Kelly had lost her bearings by then because it was late at night and very dark. She didn't know where she was, but she knew they weren't near town because she couldn't see the bright lights of the marina from the stretch of beach where they sat.

"We ate pizza and listened to waves. Scott brought beer from his car. I drank a bottle," said Kelly. "He drank two bottles. He said he didn't have to be up at dawn to train, so he could have fun."

"What happened when you finished eating the pizza and drinking the beer?"

"Scott told me that I was really beautiful and that he liked me a lot. And then he kissed me."

"And did you kiss him back?"

"Yeah, I did. We made out a bit. Nothing serious. Just kissing."

"And then what happened?"

"He put his hands under my top. I pushed them off me and said that I just wanted to kiss."

"What did he say to that?"

"He said he didn't bring me out there and buy me pizza and all to get a few kisses. And then he pushed me back on the ground and put his hands inside my clothes. I tried to get out from under him, but he put his weight on me. He was strong. He was kissing me and touching me and grinding into me; I couldn't move." Kelly paused to wipe the tears that had collected in her eyes.

"Did you say anything to him?"

"I was shocked by how he went from being nice to being aggressive. I told him I didn't want to do anything like that. I tried my hardest to get out from under him."

"And then what happened?"

"He tried to unzip my jeans zipper." Kelly let out a sob. "I pushed his hand away. He sat on me and restrained my hands. He told me to stop fighting. His voice was mean. Like a snarl. I was afraid of him."

"What did you do when he did that, Kelly?"

Kelly tried to speak, but each time the sobs overwhelmed her and she wasn't able to say anything audible.

"Take your time, Kelly," Alkins said gently as she gulped emotionally, unable to formulate a single sentence.

"I said to him that I wanted to go home and to please let me go home. And I cried. Kind of like I'm crying now. I begged him to take me home," choked Kelly.

"What was the defendant's response?"

"He told me that I'd go home when he was ready for me to go home and then he kissed me again, this time with his tongue, and he unzipped my jeans. He was strong. I couldn't get away. Even if I did, where would I go? It was dark. I had no idea where I was. I didn't have a phone." Her shoulders heaved again. Tears streamed down her face.

"Could you have broken free, Kelly?"

"No, he was holding me down while he pulled off my pants Then he pushed his leg between mine."

"And then what happened, Kelly?"

"He raped me."

Alkins waited for Kelly to stop crying. The courtroom was silent except for the sound of her wracking sobs. Eventually, the bailiff handed her a glass of water. Kelly sipped the water, dabbed at her eyes, and nodded. Alkins took her through more questions, breaking down the rape into short, graphic details.

"Did you at any point tell him to stop? Or let him know that you didn't want it?"

"I cried the whole time. He told me to 'shut up.' He knew I was crying. When he was finished he sat up and shoved a beer bottle at me. Told me to drink it. That it would make me feel better."

Kelly said she drank the rest of the beer while he downed a fresh bottle. When they were done drinking, Scott told her that he wanted to go for a swim. "You can't beat skinny dipping after sex," he'd told her as he pulled her up from the sand. She swam with him in the cold rough water, terrified that he might drown her to cover up for what he'd done to her.

"When we came back to the beach, he raped me all over again."

Rachel watched Sophia draw Scott Blair's

handsome face and pursed mouth as he listened to Kelly's testimony. His face was impassive. His jaw was tight.

"I told him that I was bleeding. I begged him to take me home."

"What did he say to that, Kelly?" Alkins asked.

"He said something like, 'Not yet. I'm not done.'"

"Is it at all possible the defendant did not realize that you were not consenting to the sexual intercourse that occurred that night?"

"I told him that I didn't want to do it. I told him over and over again. I tried to get away. I cried. I begged for him to let me go. He had to know that I didn't want it."

"How long did it last?" Alkins asked.

"I lost track of time. After it ended, he made me pose for a photo with him. A selfie. He put his arm around me and said, 'Smile.' He showed me the picture. I was naked from the waist up. He had his arms around me to cover my breasts. He texted the photo to someone and put it on Instagram."

"What did you do?"

"I was so embarrassed," she said. "I begged him to take it down. He said something like, 'You're right. That was a dumb move.' He took it down, but a couple of his friends had already texted him back emojis like a tongue hanging out of a mouth. One of them asked him whether I was any good. He showed me that text. He wrote back: 'C minus.' He showed me that, too."

"Were you offended that he'd rated you like that?" Alkins asked.

"He'd raped me. I didn't care about his stupid rating. I was scared that he'd do it again."

Kelly described how she fell asleep on the sand. She suspected that Scott had put something in her beer, because she was very sleepy. She said she woke briefly to find a musty old shirt tucked over her like a blanket. She didn't know where the shirt came from, because she said that Scott hadn't worn a shirt like that. She was grateful for the shirt. It was cold on the beach. Its warmth helped Kelly drift off again.

"It felt is if someone was watching me sleep. I must have been dreaming, because Scott wasn't there. I woke up to the sound of his car door opening and then slamming closed. I looked up and I saw Scott walk over holding a sports bag. He opened it up and threw out a bar of soap, shampoo, and a towel. He ordered me to wash in the outdoor shower on the beach. And then told me to get dressed."

"Once you were dressed, what did he do?"

"He threatened me. He told me next time he'd bring friends," she said. "He also said that he'd make sure that everyone knew I was a slut if I said a word to anyone. That the only way to keep my 'good girl' reputation was to shut up."

By the time Judge Shaw called a late lunch recess, four hours had passed. Rachel had no appetite. She doubted that anyone else did, either. She saw a social worker taking Kelly Moore down a corridor into a private room. Kelly would have the lunch recess to compose herself for the cross-examination.

40
GUILTY OR NOT GUILTY

SEASON 3, EPISODE 9: THE TESTIMONY

As soon as court was adjourned for the day, I rushed out of the courtroom to the ladies' restroom where — well, I'll spare you the gory details. Other than to say that I've never felt as sick as I did that afternoon after watching a sixteen-year-old girl get tortured on the stand. All in the name of justice.

Rape cases can be more traumatic to try than murder cases because the brutalized victim is there to describe what happened to her. More than that. She lives with the nightmare every . . . single . . . day . . . of . . . her life.

Today K took the stand. She was asked about every tiny detail of what happened. And I mean every single detail. Did he ejaculate. Sexual positions. Everything. Can you imagine at the age of sixteen — hell, at any age — having to go into that level of detail to a room full of strangers? It was awful.

Her parents clutched each other's hands as they listened to their daughter recall the worst night of her life. Her mother went through a packet of tissues. Her father, well, he's an ex–naval officer. He's been pretty stoic in court so far. But tears streamed down his cheeks as he listened to his daughter recount what happened to her on that lonely beach last October.

There wasn't a sound in court except the rustle of paper as Mitch Akins went through a thick legal pad full of questions written out on page after page after page.

K never strayed from her testimony. Over and over and over again, she consistently said that she told Scott Blair to stop. She pushed his hands away. She told him that she wanted to go home. She told him that she didn't want to have sex with him. He didn't listen. He raped her. And when he was done, he raped her again. And again.

K's testimony left me feeling queasy. I'm sure that it sickened the jury as well. Every day since the trial started, it's been a running joke between the jury and the judge about what meal they would get for their lunch. Today it was obvious that the jury wasn't interested in food when we adjourned. Who could possibly have an appetite after hearing that horrific testimony?

The defendant had a tendency to stare into space during K's testimony. Dale Quinn, and his team of lawyers, scribbled furiously on their notepads and traded notes as K testified. They were already preparing for their redirect even before K left the stand.

Judge Shaw, who throughout the trial has been quick-tempered and sharp-tongued, was unusually pensive. He's probably presided over his fair share of rape trials, but by the end of the session he looked drained.

K's answer each time was consistently "no." K insisted that nobody could possibly have mistaken her responses — weeping, struggling to get away, begging to go home, the way she tried to wriggle out of his grasp, holding her legs together and covering her genitals — as suggesting that she was a willing participant.

So, yeah, I was nauseous after I heard her testimony. But not half as sick as when K took the stand after the lunch recess for cross-examination.

Dale Quinn is charming. He comes across as a regular guy. He loves to mention his wife and twin babies. We know their names. We know that he and his wife put bands on their daughters' wrists to tell them apart. He acts scatterbrained. Drops stuff. Spills stuff. And then pretends to forget his train of thought before going for the jugular with a question that nobody sees coming.

He acts dopey. He seems kind, and considerate and very friendly. It's hard not to like him. If a survey was done, then I'm betting that Dale Quinn's congeniality rating would be through the roof.

But when it came to shredding K's testimony through cross-examination, Quinn was brutal. Not in an aggressive way. He kept his voice soft; he maintained his "aw shucks" routine. But he hammered away at K with question after question. It felt as if he was very slowly and carefully destroying her.

He asked her whether she got into the car voluntarily. She said, "Yes."

He asked whether Scott was nice to her. She said, "Yes."

He asked if she screamed in fear.

"I tried to scream at first, but nothing came out. I was so scared that I was paralyzed," K answered.

"How was Scott to know that you were paralyzed with fear if you didn't say anything?" he asked.

"I cried and begged him to leave me alone. And I kept on saying, 'Please, no, please.'"

"How could you be paralyzed with fear and, at the same time, scream and beg him to leave you alone? Which one was it? Were you

359

paralyzed with fear? Or did you scream and beg him to leave you alone?" He badgered her. "It can't be all three.

"Isn't it true that you wanted to sleep with Scott Blair? He's famous. Good-looking. You wanted to have sex with him. Didn't you?" Quinn asked her.

K broke down about ten minutes into the cross-examination. Quinn asked a detailed question about the rape. I can't remember his exact question, but I think it was something about whether she'd moaned in pleasure. K turned deathly white. Her hands trembled. She took in a series of loud, sharp breaths. She was hyperventilating on the stand. Then she made a primal sound that I've only heard once before at a slaughterhouse. It was a deep, retching howl of pain that sent chills up the spine.

We all thought K was about to collapse. She was having a full-on panic attack. She had her face in her hands. She sounded as if she was choking. Her father held her mother back while a social worker attended to her.

"Your Honor," said Alkins. "The witness has been on the stand for over four hours. It's becoming too much. She's just a child. Can we adjourn for the day?"

Dale Quinn tried to score points with the jury by showing he was equally concerned about her well-being. He rushed to bring her a glass of water and then made a big show of acting magnanimously by agreeing that she could leave the stand until she was feeling well enough to continue testifying. At the same time, he made it clear that he wasn't done with her. Not by a long shot.

Quietly, during a sidebar I overheard, he told the judge that he hadn't come close to finishing his cross-examination. "Eleven minutes, Your Honor," he said. "The complainant testified for hours. All I had was eleven minutes with her. I can't defend my client in eleven minutes."

K is not done yet. She'll have to come back to court to complete her cross-examination. She barely lasted eleven minutes today. Next time, it could last hours. Perhaps even days.

Mitch Alkins looked extremely concerned as he left court today. This from a man renowned for his poker face. He doesn't have much of a case without her testimony. He needs K back on the stand. But at what cost?

One of the questions I keep asking myself is whether it's worth it. When a person goes through a terrible trauma, her mind is conditioned to forget what happened. Memory loss from trauma is a protective mechanism. It helps us stay sane.

In this case, a sixteen-year-old girl is being

asked to recount, in front of a large group of strangers, in public, every single traumatic, horrific moment of that night on the beach so that maybe, just maybe, her alleged rapist will be punished for what he did to her.

Is she doing that for herself, or for the public good? Will it give her closure if he goes to prison? Will it vindicate her? Or will it destroy her? The pain and trauma that she has to endure to get him convicted took a terrible toll on K today. She was trembling uncontrollably. Her eyes were glassy. Her expression was agonized.

The trauma of testifying in open court is one of the main reasons why so many rape victims opt not to testify and why so many rapes are never prosecuted.

We saw K barely able to formulate a sentence at times. We saw her grief, and her despair. We saw the way a social worker had to support her so that her legs wouldn't buckle under her when she took the stand. And how that same social worker almost had to carry her away because she could barely walk when she got off the stand after that brief cross-examination.

We heard her saying "Sorry," as she passed the prosecutors' table, because she couldn't bring herself to answer the horribly detailed and accusatory questions of the defense.

The question now is whether K will return to the stand to finish her cross-examination. If she doesn't, then Scott Blair may well walk free. This is Rachel Krall on *Guilty or Not Guilty,* the podcast that puts you in the jury box.

41
RACHEL

Rachel could see the spring in Dale Quinn's step as he arrived in court, brimming with confidence. He would be presenting the first defense witnesses that day: character witnesses to shore up Scott Blair's bona fides as a card-carrying saint.

The trial had taken an unusual turn. Kelly Moore's sudden departure from the stand and her failure to return to finish her testimony put Judge Shaw in a quandary. He couldn't hold up the trial indefinitely while waiting for Kelly. In the end, he ruled the defense would present its case and Kelly would return to the stand later in the trial. It was unorthodox, but judges had some leeway in sexual assault cases.

Alkins looked grim when he walked into the courtroom. Rachel thought that he had good reason to be concerned, if there was any truth to the rumors that Kelly Moore had suffered a breakdown and might not return to the stand at all. That would be a death blow to the prosecution's case. Without Kelly's testimony, it was hard to imagine a scenario in which Scott Blair did not go free.

While Rachel waited for the court session to start, she checked her messages. There was a text from Dave, an old boyfriend, telling her he'd be in Philadelphia the following week for work. He asked if she was free to meet for dinner. Rachel found it charming that Dave didn't listen to the podcast and had no idea that she was away covering the Scott Blair trial. She responded asking for a rain check. There were several other texts from close friends telling Rachel how much they loved the new season.

Finally, Rachel reached a text message from Pete, saying that he'd gone through the podcast's clogged inbox and found an email from Hannah, sent two days earlier. He'd just forwarded it to her. Rachel was about to open the email when the bailiff called on them to rise for the judge. She had no choice but to turn off her phone and drop it into her handbag as she stood up.

Dale Quinn's first witness was Pastor Mark Fleming of the First Southern Baptist Church, which the Blair family attended. Quinn's questions stuck to the guidelines set by Judge Shaw, who had ruled that character witnesses could testify only about Scott Blair's truthfulness, his general morality, and his past treatment of women. Quinn was not allowed to ask the character witnesses whether they believed Scott Blair had raped Kelly Moore, or whether they thought he was capable of such an act.

Pastor Fleming told the court that he'd known Scott since he was a child. He described Scott in glowing terms and insisted there had never been any suggestion that he behaved inappropriately with girls, including when he was the water polo coach for the girls' team while in high school. "Those girls couldn't say enough good things about that boy," said the pastor.

The second character witness, Tom Tarant, had been a coach at Neapolis High for well over nineteen years. He was a well-known figure in the town. He had the heavyset build of a former athlete who'd beefed up in middle age with a head so bald that it reflected the lights above the witness stand. "I wish all the kids I coached were like Scott. He was a pleasure to teach," he told the court. "Believe me, I'd have a lot more hair on my head if they'd all been like him," he said, prompting titters from the jury.

"Mr. Tarant," Alkins said when it was his

turn to cross-examine the coach. "From your testimony it sounds as if the defendant was an exemplary student. If I may say, he sounds almost too good to be true. Surely the defendant wasn't perfectly behaved all the time? He must have done something wrong at least once in the time you knew him?"

"Can't think of anything," said Coach Tarant.

"What about hazing?"

"I'm not sure what you mean," said the coach hesitantly.

"Was the defendant ever suspended from school for hazing another swimmer?"

"There was a prank that went a little out of control," the coach admitted. "Don't think it can be called hazing."

"Can you tell the jury about this prank?" Alkins asked, sitting on the edge of his table with his arms crossed.

"It was some t-t-time ago," the coach stammered. "I'm not sure if I recall it clearly."

"Let me refresh your memory," said Alkins. "Isn't it true that the defendant brought a pair of scissors into the pool and, while two other swimmers held the arms of a freshman swimmer behind his back, the defendant cut the boy's Speedo off his body? He and his friends then lifted the boy, stark naked, out of the pool, and they called over girls to see the boy's genitals."

"Kids do dumb things," said the coach. "Look, everyone apologized and there were no hurt feelings."

"Do you recall what happened to the swimmer in question?" Alkins persisted.

"He left the school," said the coach stiffly.

"Indeed," said Alkins. "He did leave the school. After he tied a weight around his feet and tried to drown himself in the school pool. I believe you were the one who pulled him to the surface and gave him mouth-to-mouth resuscitation. You saved his life, Coach. I'm surprised you don't remember." Gasps rippled across the courtroom as heads swiveled toward Scott Blair.

During the midday recess, Rachel bought a sandwich and a coffee at a food truck across the street from the courthouse. She ate it while on a bench in the shade of a giant oak on the southern lawn as she read over the email from Hannah Stills that Pete had forwarded her that morning.

When she was done, Rachel walked back across the plaza immersed in thought about how she could get a few minutes alone with Alkins to ask him again about Jenny Stills. It took her a moment to register that her name was being called. She spun around to see Detective Cooper standing in the middle of the plaza with his hands in his pockets and an amused expression on his face as he watched her walk, oblivious to his presence. "You were calling my name, weren't you?" Rachel said, embarrassed.

"You literally walked right past me," he joked.

"I'm so sorry. I was thinking about the trial. It's not looking great for Mitch Alkins right now."

"Is it that bad? I haven't been following it that closely. I'm going to listen to your podcast tonight. I heard that Nath Shaw is riled up about it. Figure it has to be good if it got him all steamed up."

"Nath?" Rachel said. "I didn't know you were on nickname terms with the judge."

"I've known Nath since I was a kid. We lived next door to each other," said Detective Cooper.

"I thought you were from Rhode Island."

"I lived there for a long time, but I grew up here," he said.

"If that's the case then you must have known Mitch Alkins when you were growing up," Rachel said, spotting an opportunity to get information. Ever since the morning she'd seen Alkins lay flowers at

Jenny's grave, she'd wanted to push her way into his orbit and demand that he tell her about his connection to Jenny.

"Mitch is a few years younger than me, but, sure, Mitch and I go way back," Detective Cooper said, his tone cryptic. "Why the interest?"

Rachel hesitated over how far she should push it but figured she had nothing to lose. "I heard that when Mitch Alkins was young, he was close to a girl who was murdered."

Detective Cooper looked at her oddly. "Where did you hear that from?"

"The murdered girl's sister sent me a letter," said Rachel.

"And she named Mitch in the letter?" Cooper asked, a catch in his voice.

"No, she didn't," Rachel admitted. "But I heard from an old-timer here that Alkins knew the girl."

Detective Cooper was about to say something else when his phone rang. He took the call, moving away from her as he spoke while gesturing with his hand that she should wait. He obviously wanted to continue the discussion. His call dragged on and Rachel reluctantly went up the stairs into the courthouse.

Court was already in session by the time that Rachel slipped in and made her way to her assigned seat. She didn't pay any attention to the witness who was being sworn in on the stand until she was settled into her usual place. When she did, she gasped.

It was the man who had frightened her at the Morrison's Point jetty. In the bright light of the courtroom, Rachel was able to see him clearly for the first time. Jagged scars slashed across his cheekbone and forehead, marring what might have been a pleasant face for a man his age, which Rachel put in the mid- to late forties. His muscular arms and the hint of neck tattoos peeking out of his collar seemed out of place against his formal court attire. He wore a pressed suit, a white shirt, and a striped tie that looked a tad short as it hung over his protruding belly, which chafed against the tight fabric of his polyester shirt.

"Mr. Knox, can you tell me how you met Scott?" Quinn asked.

"It was a good three years ago, around the time I moved to Neapolis. I was at the surf beach south of town when a family got in trouble in the water. Tourists," the witness said, as if that explained it. "They were pulled out to sea by crosscurrents. I swam in. Managed to pull one kid to shore. I tried to help the mother. She was fighting. Scratched and kicked me. Wanted me to leave her and get her other kid who was drifting further out and panicking. Worst thing you can do! If I'd left her, she would have drowned for sure. I didn't know what to do. Next thing, a teenage boy swam out to the kid thrashing in the water. He grabbed the kid and brought him to shore while I helped the mother."

"Is the teenager who rescued the drowning child here in the courtroom?" asked Quinn.

"Yes," said the witness.

"Can you point him out for the court, Mr. Knox?" Quinn pushed, trying to hide his frustration with his own character witness, who needed to be prompted for every detail.

"He's sitting over there," the witness, whose full name, Rachel gathered from when he was sworn in, was Vince Knox, nodded toward the defense table, looking directly at Scott Blair.

"Is it your testimony that Scott was a hero? That he bravely risked his life to save the life of a drowning child?" Quinn prompted again.

". . . He won a bravery award, so I suppose that makes him a hero," Knox said after a prolonged hesitation. "Not too many people have the guts to risk their life for a stranger. Got to give credit where credit's due," he added in a flat voice that hardly sounded enthusiastic. His faint praise of Scott's brave act struck Rachel as strange, but she supposed it fitted in with his gruff manner.

Quinn was visibly annoyed by his own witness's terse answers. He'd obviously hoped for a far more enthusiastic account of Scott Blair's courageous feat, diving into treacherous seas and risking his life to save a child from almost certain death. Quinn wrapped up questioning quickly. He'd elicited enough testimony to paint Scott Blair as a hero, a virtual Boy Scout who'd shown great courage by diving into the sea to save a drowning stranger.

Alkins opted not to cross-examine Vince Knox, though he reserved the right to recall him to the stand. Rachel figured that Alkins saw no upside in rehashing the defense witness's testimony about Scott Blair's bravery.

As Vince Knox left court, Rachel left her seat and followed him out of the courthouse, even though it meant missing Quinn's next witness. Knox went down the steps and crossed the southern lawn. Rachel did so, too, holding back so that nobody would notice that she was following him. There was something about Knox's testimony that bothered Rachel, and she wanted to ask him a few questions once he'd left the vicinity of the courthouse.

Knox turned a corner, putting him out of Rachel's line of sight as she straggled behind him. She sped up so as not to lose him. When she turned onto the street where he'd disappeared, she immediately saw him standing by the curb, talking to a man in a black Lincoln. The car window was all the way down, and the engine was running.

The two men's voices were slightly raised, as if arguing. The man in the car passed something to Vince Knox, which the latter stared at for a moment and then almost reluctantly stuffed into his pocket. The electric car window slid shut and the car drove off. Rachel glimpsed the driver through the windshield glass as his car slowed to turn at a traffic sign near where she was standing.

He had thick light gray hair and a neatly trimmed beard. Rachel had seen him before, but she couldn't recall exactly where until she reached the courthouse and remembered that she'd seen him walking with the Blair family from their car, across the plaza, to the courthouse stairs on the first day of the trial. He'd been in a sort of security detail to protect the family from protesters.

Rachel was certain that the man in the Lincoln was on the Blair family's payroll.

When Rachel reached the courtroom, the enormous polished doors were firmly shut. She was loath to annoy Judge Shaw by walking into court during witness testimony for a second time that afternoon. She settled herself on a bench by a window overlooking the plaza and texted Pete to ask him to pull information on Vince Knox. Then she read Hannah's email again.

42
HANNAH

I'm sitting here on the jetty at Morrison's Point. My feet are hanging over the edge. The water is rough. The wind is wild. The light is fading. I can't believe that it's been twenty-five years since Jenny died. I've been throwing daisies picked from the field near where our old house used to be into the waves to mark Jenny's death. She would have liked that.

As I look out at the familiar coastal landscape of my childhood, I find it hard to believe that I am sitting here on the creaking timber of this old jetty, a grown woman, while my big sister will be a teenager for eternity. I've tried to live my life for both of us. Not always wisely. A trail of broken relationships. I've had issues with prescription medication. And alcohol. I never came close to fulfilling the potential they said I had when I won first place in a national award for promising young artists and was given a full scholarship to art school in Paris. There were such high expectations.

I tend to run away from success. It's guilt, I think, if I were to self-diagnose. I live my life plagued by guilt. Jenny never had the chances that I've had in life. She never had the chance to love or to be loved, to find her way in this world. To discover her talents and passions. To travel. She never ventured beyond Neapolis. I find it impossible not to blame myself for what happened.

I've been fortunate. I've had a blessed life, thanks to my adoptive family. Kitty is in a wheelchair now. Her health is failing. She's always been devoted to me even though I haven't been the best or most attentive of daughters. When Kitty first took me in, I was resentful. She did everything she could to try to bring me around.

One time, she took me to see a movie. As the opening credits flashed on the screen, I pushed past her and rushed out of the theater. Kitty found me in tears in the lobby. No amount of candy or popcorn could get me to return.

Kitty assumed I'd panicked when the lights were dimmed. The next day, she bought me a night-light. She told me that lots of children were afraid of the dark. I pretended to be grateful. I didn't tell her that my terror had nothing to do with the dark. I didn't tell her what happened when I'd last been in a movie theater.

Mom had asked Jenny to take me to the movies on her next day off from work. It was supposed to be a special treat to make up for the long, boring days that I'd spent alone while Mom rested and Jenny worked at the supermarket. We took the lunchtime bus into town. We went to the drugstore first to get Mom's prescriptions, and then walked two streets over to the theater to purchase our tickets.

The Neapolis movie theater had old-fashioned upholstered chairs and a burgundy carpet covered with soda stains so deep they'd become part of the pattern. There was a traditional wood-polished box office and a glass-cased snack bar in the lobby. In the theater itself was a velvet brocade curtain with gold thread that opened to reveal the movie screen at the start of the show.

Jenny gave me our ticket stubs and told me to stand in line by the doors while she bought popcorn. I was shifting from one foot to the other, restlessly waiting for her to join me, when I heard a commotion. Everyone turned to look. A girl with long hair from Jenny's school was standing next to the counter, calling Jenny horrible names.

"Take it back," shouted Jenny. The girl shook her head. "I said, take it back!"

"Don't tell me what to do. Slut." The girl shoved Jenny, making her popcorn spill across the floor like confetti. Jenny walked back to me, holding the half-empty box of popcorn under her arm. Her face was scarlet. Her lips trembled. Everyone was staring. Whispering. Jenny kept her head up and her eyes straight ahead until an usher showed us to our seats. When the lights dimmed, she wiped her eyes with the back of her hand.

As the opening credits appeared on the screen, something soft hit me in the face. It was popcorn. Pretty soon we were being pelted by a combination of popcorn and ice shards from soda cups. Others joined in until it felt as if we were being attacked from all directions.

"Stop," I called out. Jenny tried to shush me. "Don't say anything. Otherwise it'll get worse," she said. I was overcome with anger — at the kids taunting us, but mostly I was angry at Jenny for being so passive, for allowing us to be treated this way.

"Let's go," Jenny said eventually, when someone began chanting, "Slut, slut." She tugged at my arm until she was practically dragging me out of the theater and onto the street.

Once we were on the bus home, we realized that we'd left the drugstore bag with Mom's medications on the floor by our seats. Jenny had to buy them all over again the next day.

Jenny went straight into the bathroom when we got home. When she emerged, her beautiful long golden hair had been chopped unevenly to her shoulders. Later, I found clumps of Jenny's hair in the bathroom trash, all stuck together with pink gum. A boy sitting behind her at the movies had put gum in her hair.

After that trip to the movies, Jenny retreated into herself. Mom noticed. She asked if I knew what was worrying Jenny. I said that she was probably bored like me and wanted to get back to school.

I suppose I could have told Mom about how we'd fled the theater as kids pelted us, and about the terrible names they used. I couldn't bear to do it. Jenny and I didn't talk about that afternoon at all. It was almost as if we'd made a silent pact never to discuss it.

Jenny returned to her routine of working and coming home in the evening to make dinner, wash her uniform, and leave it to dry on the porch overnight. She would go to sleep while it was light, with the excuse that she had to wake early for work. I returned to riding my bicycle on the gravel road in front of our house. Backward and forward. The distant haze of the sea beckoned.

The woman with the blow-dried hair and church dress came to our house again. This time, she came with another woman who was plump and carried a nurse's bag.

Mom was expecting them. She told me that visitors would be stopping by after lunch and when they arrived I should play outside. When I heard a knock on the screen door, I let them into the living room, where Mom was waiting in an armchair, wearing a colorful sundress. She'd even done her nails. Despite all her efforts to look well, the brightly patterned dress accentuated her skeletal arms and sunken chest and made her look sicker than ever.

I looked through a window into the living room as the nurse took Mom's blood pressure and listened to her chest with a stethoscope before taking blood samples with a syringe. When she was done, the other woman passed Mom documents. Mom leaned over and signed them with wet eyes.

■ ■ ■ ■

After they'd gone, Mom was so exhausted that she fell asleep on top of her bed. I put a tartan blanket over her and went to wait for Jenny's bus on the main road at the other side of the hill from our house.

I was always excited to see what Jenny had brought home from work. The store manager often gave her leftover deli meat close to expiration and fruit and vegetables that were about to spoil. He knew how sick Mom was and I guess felt an obligation to help us out.

To keep myself amused while I waited for Jenny's bus to pull in, I walked along the white line on the shoulder of the road, pretending I was a gymnast on a balance beam. Down the hill, I saw the bus thundering toward me from a distance. It pulled to a stop near the bus stop sign. The hydraulic doors opened with a hiss. Jenny stepped out in her tan supermarket uniform, carrying two large grocery bags.

We walked in silence to the sound of rustling grass and the occasional whine of a car engine passing by. Me in front, Jenny, a few yards behind. We didn't talk. In the space of a few short weeks, Jenny had become introverted and brooding.

I picked up a long stick and scraped it on the dirt path behind me as I walked. When the path veered away from the road around a clump of trees, I followed it. My feet kicked up dust and my eyes were downcast as I focused on drawing an unbroken line with the stick. The trees blocked the road from view and acted as a buffer from the noise of passing cars.

The path eventually curved back to the road after the trees. Eventually, I realized that I hadn't heard Jenny's footsteps or the rustle of shopping bags for a while. I assumed I was walking too fast and Jenny had fallen behind. I stopped and waited. When Jenny still didn't appear, I called to her.

"Jenny?"

No response.

"Jenny? Where are you?" I called out. She didn't emerge from the path.

"Hurry up, Jenny!" I was annoyed she was taking so long.

"Jenny?"

I huffed in frustration at the silence that followed. I ran back along the path. When I found no trace of my sister, I walked into the road to look for her. There was no sign of her walking along the road on either side. All I saw was a red apple that had rolled onto the asphalt.

I picked up the apple. That's when I saw Jenny's shopping bags lying in the long grass by the side of the road. One bag had tipped over. Loose fruit had spilled onto the ground. The other bag was upright. There was no sign of Jenny. She was gone. I ran uphill, pushing long strands of grass out of my way until I reached the top.

Puffing loudly from running, my lungs burning, I stopped at the pinnacle and scanned the landscape below. I didn't see Jenny. But I did see a familiar pickup truck driving slowly down an unpaved road leading to the mouth of the forest. I ran down the other side of the hill in the direction of the truck. I crossed the road and followed it into the forest.

I moved off the dirt road, walking among the trees into the darkness as the foliage became denser. I darted around tree trunks and bent under unruly branches that scratched my arms. Deep in the forest, I saw the pickup. It had been parked hastily on the side of the road. A canvas cover lay in a heap on the back of the truck alongside a half-empty box of beer. I heard voices and laughter coming from a clearing. Cruel laughter. As I moved closer, I saw a boy lying on top of Jenny while two others stood by and watched. Jeering.

I was filled with rage. I instinctively picked up a rock to charge at the boy who was hurting Jenny. I raced toward him, the rock raised in my right hand. Before I reached the clearing, a hand slapped onto my face like a suction cup. I couldn't scream or say a word as I was lifted off the ground. My feet hung in the air as I was carried through the forest, restrained by powerful arms. My sandals slipped off. I tried to kick and struggle free. It was impossible. His grip was crushing.

43
RACHEL

Rachel ran against a lava-lamp sky of navy cut with orange. Dawn had broken by the time she'd reached the Morrison's Point jetty. Her breathing was labored as she leaned over the rails and looked into the dark, impenetrable water.

Long gone were the wildflowers that Hannah had scattered in the waves a few days earlier to commemorate her sister's death. That had been the last message that Rachel had received from her. Pete was checking the podcast inbox several times a day in case Hannah reached out again. There had been plenty of mail from fans and detractors alike. Nothing from Hannah. Rachel had repeatedly called the phone number for Hannah that Kitty had given her, but it went to an automated voice mail each time. She'd left several voice messages for Hannah, but she hadn't received any response.

It may take time for me to get you the last

letter. I keep starting it and stopping, Hannah had written at the end of the email. *It will take all my strength to put into words what happened to Jenny that night. Maybe I shouldn't tell you. Maybe I should leave the past alone. Let it die with me.*

Hannah's last words left Rachel deeply worried. Hannah had intimated a few times in her correspondence to Rachel that she'd contemplated death. Rachel wished there was a way for her to reach out to Hannah. To reassure her. To get her help if she needed it. But Rachel couldn't help someone who was so determined to stay out of reach. It was almost as if Hannah wanted to keep Rachel at arm's length. It was, Rachel thought as she watched the pink dawn drain from the sky, as if she was a pawn in a game, the rules of which only Hannah knew.

Pete had called Rachel late the previous night to share the results of the background check he'd run on Vince Knox. "Four years ago, a man by the name of Vince Knox died of a heart attack in prison," Pete told her. Rachel had been drifting to sleep when he called, his voice filled with enough urgency to immediately wake her. "The character witness who testified about Scott Blair saving that drowning boy can't possibly be Vince Knox, Rach. For one thing, all records of his existence date back to exactly a week to the day after the Vince Knox I mentioned died in prison. I believe the character witness took the name Vince Knox after the real Vince Knox died, but he wasn't born with that name. He's actually someone else. The question is who?"

"Maybe I should ask him," said Rachel. "Do you have an address for him?"

"No fixed address. He's a vagrant. Apparently, he sometimes sleeps on the beaches south of town in the summer."

"That's a big area," said Rachel, yawning. "There are a lot of beaches south of town."

"If it helps, I just got off the phone with a charity worker who works with the poor in Neapolis and she said that he's been known to sleep in a boat shed near the marine reserve," said Pete.

Rachel knew the beach Pete was referring to. Right next to the national park was a sheltered beach with a row of boat sheds and a ramp. On the map, it was called Anderson's Beach. But Rachel knew it in another context. It was the beach where Scott Blair had taken Kelly Moore for pizza and then allegedly raped her.

After Rachel finished the call with Pete, she set her alarm to wake her before dawn. She wanted to run along the beach south of

Morrison's Point in case she stumbled across Vince Knox sleeping rough in one of his usual haunts.

After catching her breath on the jetty, Rachel continued running south to the national marine park, darting over clumps of glistening seaweed that had littered the beaches overnight. When she came around the last peninsula, she saw a row of boat sheds in the distance, painted in faded pastel hues. From across the beach, Rachel heard a repeated banging noise. It was coming from a boatshed door, which was slamming open and closed in the wind. She ran across the sand to the shed to close the door. Otherwise it would tear off its hinges from the repeated banging.

As she approached, the door blew wide open in a fresh gust, giving Rachel a clear view inside. There was an old fiberglass boat with an outboard motor. Men's work clothes hung off nails banged into the timber. On the concrete floor was a makeshift bed and a pile of blankets. On the walls, newspaper clippings fluttered in the early morning breeze.

Rachel stepped into the boat shed, her eyes drawn to the wall decorated with the newspaper clippings. She was shocked to see they were all about the Scott Blair case.

They'd been carefully torn out and hammered into the timber walls with rusty nails. There were black-and-white photos of Scott Blair coming into court, and photos of Mitch Alkins and Dale Quinn walking down the courthouse stairs, their expressions blank.

An article about Kelly Moore's testimony was pinned prominently on the wall. Sections of text were circled with a ballpoint pen. As Rachel moved closer to read the text in the dim light, the door banged shut behind her. It cast the room in an opaque blackness that made it impossible for Rachel to see.

Rachel instinctively moved blindly in the direction of the door, shoving it hard with her shoulder. The door swung open violently. Rachel tripped and stumbled out into the bright glare of morning and straight into the naked chest of a man.

The right side of his bare torso was horribly disfigured with severe burn scars, puckered and patched by skin grafts. The parts of his chest unmarred by scars were covered with tattoos. Rachel recognized one as a homemade gangland prison tattoo. She raised her head to look at the stranger's face. Vince Knox's eyes were narrow and they burned with rage.

"What are you doing sneaking around here?" he rasped. His lip lifted in a half snarl as Rachel moved back in surprise.

He lurched toward her as if to scare her. It instinctively made her want to step back to put space between them, but she resisted the urge. If she stepped back then he'd be able to corral her into the boat shed and lock her in. Rachel took a step to the side, which at least offered the possibility of outrunning him across the sand dunes.

Except Rachel didn't run. She didn't need to. He'd turned his attention away from her and bent down to caress a quivering seagull, which was bundled up in a plaid shirt near his feet. His gentle touch and the deep concern that creased his face as he tended to the bird was a sharp departure from his anger toward Rachel a moment earlier.

"I didn't know that someone lived here," Rachel said, by way of an apology. She figured that the only way to defuse the situation was to act normal. "I thought the boat shed lock had broken off."

"I left the door unlocked when I went for a swim." He rose, looming over Rachel to intimidate her again. She held her ground. "What are you doing here? You're not a cop, are you?" he hissed. "I hate cops."

"I'm a reporter covering the trial. I saw

391

you testify for Scott Blair. You didn't look like you were enjoying it. After you left court, I saw you talking to some guy who works for Greg Blair. Did Greg Blair buy your testimony, Mr. Knox?"

"No," he said. "Everything I said in court was true. Scott Blair saved that kid's life that day. Swam out and pulled him in. That's the God's honest truth."

"Then what's the connection between you and Greg Blair?" Rachel asked.

"It's none of your goddamn business," he roared. Realizing that he'd startled the bird, he bent down again to soothe the frightened creature in a hushed voice.

"Maybe it's not my business," said Rachel. "It is the business of the prosecutor, Mitch Alkins. He might be very interested, especially if Greg Blair paid for your testimony."

"Every word that I said was true. That trial, it ain't got nothing to do with me," Vince Knox said. "I don't have time for your dumb questions. I need to put a splint on this bird's wing before she goes into shock." He moved into the boat shed and returned a moment later with a box of bandages. He squatted down and expertly repaired the injured bird's wing with a crude splint and bandages as Rachel watched.

"How long have you been living here?" Rachel asked a few minutes later as he cut up scraps of fresh fish with a pocketknife which he fed to the injured gull, now swathed in bandages.

"I stay sometimes in the summer. Get paid to keep an eye on the boats. There's a shower and toilets. A coin barbecue so I can cook. That's all I need."

"Where do you live in the winter?"

"I get by," he said. "If I make enough money in the summer then I rent a room. Mostly I mind my own business. You should try it sometime."

Rachel flushed. He was right. She had no right to barge into this man's life with her questions.

"Tell me about how you know Greg Blair and I'll go," she said.

"I knew Greg once," he said. "He remembered me. Asked me to testify for his son about that time I saw him save that kid from drowning. Said if I didn't then he'd remind people of something that I did a long time ago. All I want is a quiet life, so I agreed. Didn't say anything that wasn't true in court. I made sure of it."

"I had the feeling that you know more than you said in court. That you were holding back on something," Rachel said softly.

393

"What makes you think that?" He stared at her with an expression that she couldn't decipher.

"Instinct," she said.

"Your instincts are wrong," he snapped.

"How did you get your injuries?" Rachel asked as he put on his plaid shirt and buttoned it up to cover the puckered burn scars on his chest.

"Knife fight," he said, pointing to the scars that slashed the side of his face.

"What about the burns? They look pretty bad."

"They're from a childhood accident. Have I satisfied your curiosity now?" he asked. "I might not look like much. And I might not have much. But there are a lot more dangerous people than me in this town. They wear suits and look respectable, but there ain't nothing respectable about the things they're willing do to get what they want. Nothing."

Rachel thought about his remark as she ran across the beach back toward town. Wisps of clouds marred the otherwise perfect sky as she jogged toward her hotel in the far distance. It was Friday, the last court session before the weekend. Rachel's gut feeling told her that it would be a dramatic one.

All week, court had started the same way.

Judge Shaw asked Mitch Alkins if Kelly Moore was returning to the stand. Alkins told the judge that Kelly's psychiatrist said she wasn't quite ready. That she needed a little more time. Alkins had bought time all week with that response. He wouldn't get away with it for much longer. Dale Quinn was running out of witnesses and Judge Shaw was running out of patience.

44
GUILTY OR NOT GUILTY

CROSS-EXAMINATION

Tempers are short in court as we get to the business end of the trial. There's been no more banter about what the jurors ate for lunch. The mood is too tense. Judge Shaw is on edge. His tongue is pure acid. I've heard people say they haven't seen him this acerbic since he was last reversed by an appeals court seven years ago.

The jury is showing signs of exhaustion. Too many long days of hearing testimony that is complex and oftentimes harrowing. It gets to a person after a while, trying to figure out who to believe.

Today the jury heard the forensic expert for the defense give his testimony. Professor Carl Braun earned an estimated thirty thousand dollars to tear apart the prosecution's forensic case with surgical precision. He said there was zero evidence that indicated K was sexually assaulted. Zero. That is reasonable doubt right there. If the jury believes him, that is.

Remember Dr. Wendy North. She was the expert witness for the prosecution. She's considered one of the leading forensic sexual assault experts in the country.

Professor Braun contradicted all her findings with a certainty that I found staggering. The Harvard academic who hasn't been in clinical practice for decades said repeatedly on the stand that there was no indication of sexual assault. Just signs of rough sex. Two clumsy teenagers rolling in the hay. That's the way that he tried to make it sound.

Professor Braun is a tall man. Six foot two, I'd say, at a guess. He has wiry steel-colored hair. He wears rimless reading glasses and tucks a handkerchief in his jacket pocket. He's old-school. He talks in a deep baritone that resonates with a godlike authority. This is a man who has no doubts. At least not about his opinions. Sure, the jurors liked Dr. North. But Professor Braun is in a league of his own when it comes to confidence.

The prosecution's forensic case had been strong, until Braun ripped it apart. I can't say whether his points had any basis to them. To tell you the truth, at times it sounded to me like doublespeak. But it was doublespeak delivered with an arrogant assurance that would be hard for a jury to dismiss. We may not have seen the last of Professor Braun. He may be recalled to the stand after K testifies, presumably to undermine whatever she says during cross-examination from a forensics point of view.

Regardless, there is no doubt that Braun's testimony changed the stakes. The defense has thrown a good dose of reasonable doubt on every aspect of the prosecution's case. Braun's testimony has severely damaged the prosecution's forensic evidence. Now more than ever, K needs to return to the stand.

Today in court, Dale Quinn asked Judge Shaw to set a deadline. He said it can't drag out much longer. Here are his exact words: "Every day that passes without me being able to test the complainant's evidence through cross-examination hurts my client's chances of a fair trial. Her unchallenged testimony gets further embedded in the jury's minds. I believe the defense has been patient, but we need a date. When will she testify?"

Judge Shaw fidgeted with his reading glasses, evidently just as perturbed by the delay. "This is a sexual assault case. I have some latitude to give the complainant time. However," he said, turning toward Alkins, "the court's patience in this matter is not endless."

"She is a young girl going through a very

bad time," said Alkins. "I urge the court to be sympathetic and patient. We are very close."

Quinn's chair scraped the floor as he pushed it back and rose to his feet. "I couldn't be more sympathetic about the complainant's emotional troubles," he said. "But it can't be at the detriment of my client's rights under the law. Our inability to cross-examine her severely damages my client's constitutional right to a fair trial. I can cite dozens of cases."

Judge Shaw leaned forward in his seat and snapped into the microphone, "I am aware of the Constitution, Counselor, and the relevant case law."

Judge Shaw's eyes flashed with anger at his being put in such an awkward position. He turned to Alkins and told him in no uncertain terms that he expected K to be in court on Monday, ready to testify. He said the upcoming weekend should give K's parents and doctors enough time to get her ready for the stand.

Judge Shaw didn't say what would happen if K wasn't on the stand on Monday, but it doesn't take a rocket scientist to figure it out. If, by Monday morning, K isn't in court testifying, then Scott Blair will likely walk free. Whether he can rebuild his reputation and relaunch his champion swimming career is a different matter. But freedom he shall have.

I've been watching Mitch Alkins closely throughout this trial. He keeps his cool. He never shows his emotions. But today in court, he looked as if he knew that his case hung by a tenuous thread.

In his only statements to the media, when Scott Blair was first charged, Mitch Alkins said this case was an important step toward showing women that their right to say no is inviolable.

What message will it send if Scott Blair is acquitted? I tried to ask Mitch Alkins that question in the hall outside the courtroom after today's session. I didn't get an answer. He pushed past me and headed to his office, where I hear his team is in crisis mode. The case seems to be slipping away from him.

I drove past K's house today. The blinds were down. There was a big sign on the lawn telling people it was private property and asking them to stay away. It is heartbreaking to think about what K and her family are going through as she decides whether she has the strength to endure a grueling cross-examination by Dale Quinn. Her parents would be well aware of the terrible implications of her decision. Put simply, if K doesn't take the stand, then the trial is over and Scott Blair wins.

This is Rachel Krall for *Guilty or Not Guilty,* the podcast that puts you in the jury box.

This is Rachel Krall for Guilty or Not Guilty. I'm pleased that quite you in the jury box.

45
RACHEL

Rachel gave her breakfast order to the waitress without looking at the menu. She'd been staying at the hotel long enough to know the options by heart. She drank a mug of coffee while reading the Saturday edition of the *Neapolis Gazette,* which she'd taken from a newspaper rack in the lobby.

The front page featured an enormous photograph of Scott Blair being hauled out of the Olympic-sized swimming pool on the day that he was arrested. His muscular arms were cuffed behind his back. He wore his stars-and-stripes Speedo and a matching swimming cap. Drops of water ran down his skin.

The headline said: "Blair Trial May End on Monday." Rachel didn't have to read the article to know its point. Without Kelly's testimony, Scott would be free.

"Good morning, Rachel."

Detective Cooper's blond stubble looked

darker in the atmospheric lighting of the hotel cafe. He was wearing jeans and a T-shirt with a sports jacket zipped over it. He sat opposite Rachel without asking, just as the waitress arrived with her glass of orange juice and acai bowl.

"I'm surprised to see you here," said Rachel. "Scott Blair is about to get off. Surely, the entire police department is out looking for evidence to save the day."

"It only works that way on television. The sex-crimes unit investigated this case for months and they already handed over whatever evidence they could find. The case rests on Kelly Moore."

"It shouldn't have to rest on whether a teenage girl will allow herself to be traumatized and humiliated again on the stand," Rachel argued.

"Unfortunately," said Detective Cooper softly, "that's how the system works." He called over a waitress and gave his order of eggs, over easy, on whole-wheat toast with a coffee.

"Mitch Alkins would like to meet you," he said when the waitress had gone.

"So he sent you to bring me to him?"

"He knows that on Saturday mornings I'm out early checking my boat, which is docked in the marina right across the road from your hotel. He asked me last night if I'd stop by and see if you're still interested in talking to him."

"How does Mitch Alkins know so much about your weekend sailing routine?" Rachel asked, her eyes focused on his as she took another sip of coffee.

"Before this town became a glorified retirement village, it was small enough that just about everyone knew everyone. As it happens, Mitch is also my cousin," he said. "And he's a late riser. I'll check if he's ready to see you. That is, if you're okay to meet him?"

Rachel nodded. She'd been wanting to talk to Mitch Alkins for days. She was hardly going to pass up the opportunity.

While Detective Cooper ate his breakfast, Rachel checked her phone for messages from Pete. He texted her to say there were over eight hundred emails in the podcast inbox following the latest episode. If there was any message from Hannah, he'd let her know straightaway, but he warned that it would take time for him to trawl through them all.

Cooper's phone beeped as the waitress cleared away the dishes. He read the text, looking up at Rachel cryptically.

"Mitch is up early after all," he said. "He

says we should come now. My car is parked across the road at the marina. I'll drive you there."

They drove through the light Saturday morning traffic. Detective Cooper's left elbow rested casually on his open window. His golden hair was tousled by the wind. Rachel could see the shadow of a gun in a shoulder holster inside his gaping jacket.

"I thought Alkins would be at his office," said Rachel in surprise when she noticed they were driving out of the city limits and into a rural area to the north of Neapolis.

"Didn't I mention that he's working from his home?" said Detective Cooper. His voice was strangely contemplative. "It's not much further."

They drove past a strip of luxury homes on the gated estate where the Blair family home was located in its own compound. There was extra security detail at the entrance. Rachel presumed it was to keep away the protesters who jeered at Scott Blair every day when he came into court.

Detective Cooper veered off the main road five miles later. He turned down a narrow road filled with potholes that ran inland around a peninsula. At one point, the road came close enough to the cliff that Rachel could see waves crashing against boulders in the ocean as they drove by. The area was wild and uninhabited. It was hard to imagine *anyone* living there — let alone Mitch Alkins. Rachel shifted uncomfortably in her seat. She eyed her door. It was locked. The window was shut, too. It was all operated by the central locking system on the driver's control panel.

Rachel became even more unsettled a few miles later as they took the right fork of a gravel road that cut through a dense forested area. The bumpy road was so narrow that bushes brushed against the car. The road finally widened to reveal a Jeep parked in a small clearing.

"Where are we?" Rachel asked hesitantly as she climbed out of the car into the silent solitariness of the remote scrub.

"Follow me," Detective Cooper said, leading her down a crude path hewn between overgrown bushes. Rachel swallowed hard, trying not to show how vulnerable she felt being taken to such an unexpectedly isolated place. As she walked through the brush, she thought to herself that it felt like a place where the Mafia would take someone to execute them and dump the body in a shallow grave. Rachel stopped walking the moment she saw the view between the gap in the trees.

Below them was a breathtaking beach in its own cove. Overlooking it was a house made of timber and mirrored glass that reflected its surroundings of ocean and forest.

"That's Mitch's house," said Detective Cooper. He walked down the sloping pathway toward the house perched on the edge of a cliff. Rachel followed behind.

Mitch Alkins was standing by the steel rails on the balcony, looking out to sea. He wore jeans and a navy button-down shirt that flapped in the wind.

"I'm not supposed to talk with journalists about the trial," Alkins told Rachel when she reached him. "The last thing I need is to be accused of colluding with an influential podcaster. So I'm not talking with you. This conversation isn't happening. Do you understand?"

"Absolutely," she said, turning around to look for Detective Cooper. Through the enormous glass windows of the house, she could see him walking through the minimalist living room down a floating staircase until he disappeared out of sight.

"You've been trying to talk to me for days. What did you want to discuss?" Alkins asked, his eyes fixed out on the blue expanse of sea.

"Jenny Stills. Do you remember her?"

"Of course I remember her," he said. "Jenny was my first crush."

"How old were you then?" she asked.

"I must have been around fourteen, fifteen. Jenny was two years below me at school. I spent what felt like years trying to pluck up the courage to talk with her. Eventually I did. We became friendly. Sometimes we'd hang out together at the beach. I still didn't have the courage to ask her out, though."

"What happened to Jenny the summer she died?" Rachel asked.

She found herself staring at her own reflection in the lenses of Alkins's sunglasses as he turned away from the view to face her. He looked angry at her impertinence, but there was another emotion on his face. Rachel's throat tightened in fear as it dawned on her that it was guilt.

"I know that you leave flowers for her every year. Asking her to forgive you," Rachel said. "What terrible thing did you do all those years ago that you want Jenny to forgive?"

"You're asking if I killed Jenny?"

Rachel swallowed hard and nodded. Mitch Alkins was a formidable man at the best of times. A man who was never lost for words.

His stormy expression told Rachel that she had one hell of a nerve interrogating him. Yet he said nothing as he turned away and stared out to sea.

"Did you hurt Jenny Stills?" Rachel prompted.

"The answer is yes," he admitted finally. "I did hurt Jenny."

Rachel's heart pounded as she realized that she was in perilous territory. She looked down at the precipice, more aware than ever before of the steep drop from the balcony where she stood to the bottom of the cliff.

"We had the beginning of something beautiful and I destroyed it with my stupidity. I heard rumors that she was sleeping around. That she'd sleep with any boy who asked her. So I figured I'd try my luck. It wasn't rape. It didn't get that far. But I think my one-track mind that night devastated her, nevertheless. Does that answer your question?"

Rachel nodded. Her mouth was dry. "You're the boy that she met at the beach that summer. You took her out on a date. Pizza, I think."

"Yes," he said. "How do you know about that?"

"Hannah, her sister, wrote about it in a letter that she sent me. She didn't know

409

your name, but she clearly remembered the night you came to take Jenny on a date. She says you brought a bunch of wildflowers to give Jenny, but you were embarrassed and dropped the flowers on the ground before you went inside."

"I was stupid and selfish and so influenced by rumors and my own hormones that I didn't realize I was destroying something precious. Maybe I broke Jenny's heart that night. But I never hurt her physically."

"So who did it?" Rachel asked. "Who killed Jenny Stills?"

"They said she drowned herself," said Alkins.

"Do you really believe that?"

"There was no reason to doubt it. Anyway, I wasn't here when she died. I was so disgusted with myself and the way that I'd treated Jenny that I went to stay with my granddad up north before starting college," he said. "Why are you so interested in Jenny Stills? That was a lifetime ago."

"I think that Jenny was murdered," said Rachel. "And I may have some evidence. I need your help. I need a copy of Jenny's autopsy report and I'd like to speak to the cops who handled the investigation. I don't have access to that information. You do."

"I'll make some calls and get you whatever

information you need," he said. "If it's true that Jenny Stills was killed then I'll reopen the case. I let her down once. I won't do it again."

On the beach below, Detective Cooper was scrambling over rocks as he walked to a short pier where a motorboat was tethered. He jumped into the boat, released the ropes, and turned on the engine. They watched in silence as he steered the boat into the sea, bouncing so high off incoming waves that it looked as if he might get airborne.

"The coast here is deceptive," Alkins murmured as he watched the motorboat cutting through the water. "One minute, it looks placid. The next, a storm sweeps in. People die in the water around here all the time. The coastline is a graveyard of sunken ships and memorials to the dead. Us locals learn from the time we're young to read the mood of the ocean, but even we get it wrong sometimes."

"I keep forgetting that you grew up here," said Rachel. "Are you enjoying being back?"

"I don't know if 'enjoy' is the right word. It's where I belong. I always intended to come back someday, but I ended up doing it sooner than I'd planned."

"If you don't mind me saying so, it's certainly a strange career change," said Ra-

411

chel. "You were a highly sought-after defense attorney. You were making a fortune. Why make the switch and become a prosecutor and then move back to what is really a backwater town?"

"Because I sleep better at night," answered Alkins as he watched his cousin stop the motorboat and lean over the side to check a net in the water. "Nick's checking some lines. He'll return in a few minutes and take you back to your hotel. I have to get on with my work for the trial next week."

"The trial might end on Monday," Rachel reminded him.

"I'm hoping that Kelly will come through. Otherwise" — he sighed — "you may well be right."

"So you think that Scott might get acquitted, too," said Rachel, reading between the lines of his comment. "If Scott Blair gets off unpunished, it would be devastating for Kelly."

"For Kelly and for many other rape victims," Alkins said. "There's not a lot I can do. We need her testimony. Without it, we don't have much of a case."

His voice sounded exhausted, yet there was also a thread of steely determination that suggested he wouldn't give up so easily. He turned to face her. "I asked Nick to bring you here because I have a favor to ask," he said. "I spent most of last evening at the Moores' home, trying to get Kelly's parents to understand that without their daughter's testimony, the case is lost. Except I couldn't get through to them. They're completely unrealistic about our chances of winning without Kelly's testimony. They told me they're confident the jury will convict regardless of whether Kelly testifies."

"I don't see how the jury will convict if Kelly's evidence is thrown out," said Rachel.

"Precisely," Alkins responded. "That's why I wanted to talk to you. It might carry more weight if they hear it from someone without any stick in all of this. An outsider," he told Rachel. "You're influential. I gather Dan Moore is a fan of your podcast. Maybe they'll listen to you."

Rachel looked up at Alkins. Her eyes searched his face to see whether he was serious. All she could see was her own face in the dark lenses of his aviator sunglasses. As if realizing that she needed confirmation, he took the sunglasses off and leaned against the steel railings so he could look directly at her. "If you think Scott Blair is guilty and deserves to be punished then talk to Kelly's parents, Rachel. Convince them to let their daughter return to the stand."

"I shouldn't get involved. . . ." Rachel hesitated. "I'm supposed to be a neutral bystander."

"All I can do is ask you," he said. "Ultimately, the decision is up to you. If there's one thing that I've learned in my life, it's that a good person's conscience usually leads them to do the right thing."

"I'm not making any promises," said Rachel carefully. "But I will think about it."

"I'm not asking for promises," he said. They could hear the rising roar of the speedboat engine as Cooper steered the boat back to shore over the choppy waves.

"I want to make one thing clear," he said as his cousin pulled the boat up to the rickety jetty and tied the ropes. "Unlike Dan Moore, I'm not a fan of your podcast. I don't understand people's fascination with other people's tragedies. It's modern-day rubbernecking. Ghoulish. Podcasts like yours feed that obsession. If I'd had my way, Judge Shaw would have never allowed you to cover the trial," he said. "I want you to know that, because even if you do get Dan and Christine Moore to listen to you, I will still be on your case. I don't do quid pro quo."

Rachel appreciated Mitch Alkins's honesty. At least she knew where she stood. Down on the beach, Cooper was looking up at them as if asking Alkins's permission to return. Alkins inclined his head slightly and Cooper then crossed the beach and traversed the steep path back to the house.

Detective Cooper drove Rachel to town the way they'd come, along the scenic coastal road. This time, he drove at a leisurely pace, slowing to point out panoramic views and points of interest. As they reached the outskirts of town, Rachel's phone beeped. It was a text message from Pete to let her know that Hannah had sent another email.

46
HANNAH

Dear Rachel,
It's hard to put into words what happened that night. I've never written it down or told a single person. All my adult life, I've tried to forget. The memories inevitably return. Always at the worst possible time, when something good is happening in my life. Sometimes the pain of remembering is so bad that I consider giving up. Letting myself slip away.

I still remember seeing the forest floor sway unsteadily under my bare feet as I was carried away from the clearing, from Jenny, trapped in the steel grip of a stranger. I couldn't scream or call for help. There was nobody there to hear my calls. Nobody who could save Jenny, or me.
I heard drunken laughter. Nasty and cruel. Someone threw a beer bottle against

a tree trunk. It shattered. Laughter followed. More bottles broke as they turned it into a game. And then pitiful cries. It was Jenny. They were hurting her. There wasn't a thing that I could do to stop it as I was carried across the forest like a rag doll, my feet dancing helplessly in the air.

"Please," I tried to say. My words were muffled by the hand over my mouth. "Please, stop hurting her."

We came around a large tree trunk. I could hear Jenny whimper like an injured kitten too weak to let out more than the softest cry. I struggled to wriggle out of the iron grip. I wanted to reach out to her. To touch her. To reassure her that somehow it would all be all right.

But her cries were becoming more distant. We were moving away from her. He held me tighter, locking me in the unbreakable manacles of his arms as he changed course. Moving in a different direction. Deeper into the forest. Away from Jenny. I tried to kick him, but I was no match against his strength and my legs hung limply in the air.

He stopped very suddenly not long after. I felt myself being lifted up and then lowered until I was lying on a hard metallic surface. Metal ridges dug into my skin. I was lying in the back of a truck.

His hand was on my mouth. I couldn't scream. But I was no longer being restrained by those powerful arms. I lay faceup and looked into the eyes of my captor. Gray eyes that I recognized, even in the gloomy light of the forest.

I flinched in terror as Bobby lowered his face to mine.

He lifted his finger and pressed it to my lips.

"Shh," he said.

He pushed me down so that I was lying flat. He pulled the canvas sheet over my head. That's when I understood that he was hiding me. Protecting me. Not long after, I felt the vehicle sink under the weight of people getting into the truck.

Bobby climbed into the back with his legs outstretched alongside me and his back pressed against the cab. There was a light thud as someone was lowered into the back of the truck next to him. I heard a whimper. It was Jenny.

Doors slammed shut. Someone threw an unopened beer can into the back of the truck. It slammed against the metal and bounced onto my leg. It hurt so bad.

We drove off in a loud skid. Jenny was trembling so badly I could hear her teeth chattering. I peered out from under the canvas sheet. Bobby was unbuttoning his shirt. It frightened me to see him get undressed. When he'd removed his shirt, he put it over Jenny and tucked it under her like a blanket. He reached for my hand and squeezed it reassuringly as the truck tore through the forest road, lurching violently when we hit potholes.

"Bobby, make sure she doesn't fall out. We're not done with her yet," someone shouted through an open window. Drunken laughter echoed.

With a squeal of tires, the truck turned sharply onto smooth asphalt. We were on the main road. The drive was faster. Less bumpy. The wind rushed in my ears.

Bobby's hand was on Jenny's back. She was lying next to him. He seemed to be comforting her. I tried to lean over to comfort her, too. He pushed me down abruptly as we drove faster along the road. When the truck eventually stopped, I heard the roar of the ocean and smelled the unmistakable smell of sea and salt.

"Where is she?" It was a male voice. Thick and unsteady. He was leaning over the side of the truck. Drunk. I flinched as he almost touched me.

"She's over there." Another slurred voice.

"Maybe we should let her go now." A

deeper voice. This one inflected with fear.

"Why would we do that?"

"Yeah, man. We all want to have another go. Maybe Bobby will change his mind and take a turn? What do you say, Bobby?"

My heart pounded. I lay without moving, terrified they would discover me under the canvas sheet. Bobby sat next to me stiffly. It felt as if he was shielding me from them.

"No. Not again. Please. I can't." It was Jenny. "Let me go. I want to go home now."

"Stop crying, you slut," someone shouted. "Get up."

Jenny scrambled to her feet. The truck shifted again as she jumped down. They trampled through the sand onto the beach with Jenny.

Bobby, who'd climbed out of the truck, lifted the canvas so he could see my face. "Run," he whispered. "I'll try to get them to leave her alone, but you need to get out of here." I stared at him as he lifted up a crate of beer cans and bottles. "Run," he urged again, before turning to join his friends on the beach.

I didn't listen to him. I hid in the bushes. I couldn't bring myself to leave my sister. As my eyes adjusted to the dark, I saw the familiar outlines of the Morrison's Point jetty. It was strangely reassuring to know our location.

Light flickered from the beach, followed by the noxious smell of gasoline as they built a bonfire on the sand. Their dark silhouettes were set against the fire as they stood by its flames and drank beer, clinking the bottles together.

There was a public phone booth across the parking lot, near the toilet block. I didn't have money, but I figured that I could dial the operator and ask her to call the police. I walked across the lot quietly, hunching down so there was no chance that I could be seen. My shoes had fallen off when I was in the forest. I was in my bare feet. The dirt parking lot was littered with sharp stones that dug into the soles of my feet. Despite the pain, I didn't cry out or make any sound at all.

I had to run out into the open to get to the telephone booth. I did so quickly but was delayed getting inside as I fumbled to open the door in the dark. Finally, I pushed my way inside. I lifted the receiver and dialed the operator, my hands shaking so badly that it took a few attempts to press the correct buttons.

"How can I assist you?" the operator said.

"Please," I mumbled; my throat was so dry that no sound came out. I cleared it

and spoke more loudly: "I need to speak to
—"

The phone booth door was pushed open abruptly, hitting me painfully in the shoulder. A hand reached inside and pressed down the receiver to disconnect the call. I turned around slowly. It was Bobby's friend, one of the boys who stole candy from Rick when they gave us a ride home that first time. He stank of liquor. It was so overpowering that I leaned as far away as I could until my back pressed painfully against the telephone console.

"Well, if it isn't the little sister," he snarled. He curled his hand into my hair and pulled me close to his hot drunken face.

47
RACHEL

They met at the boardwalk at dusk. Dan and Christine Moore approached Rachel arm in arm, baseball caps pulled low to obscure their faces. They were dressed like twins in matching jeans and tees under unbuttoned shirts. Denim for him. White linen for her. Their shirts blew in the wind like parachute canopies.

The three of them stepped off the board-walk onto the beach, passing stragglers shaking sand off their towels before flipping them over their shoulders and heading home. At the far end of the beach, surfers were paddling to shore, pushed out of the ocean against their will by the ebbing light.

Dan had told Rachel when they'd set up the meeting over the phone that he and Christine were happy to talk with her, but not in the house. Mitch Alkins had been there the night before. It upset Kelly to know that she was being discussed downstairs while she stayed in her room, with her grandmother looking in on her intermittently. They never left Kelly alone for long.

Meeting at a restaurant was out of the question. So was Rachel's hotel. There was so much publicity around the case, so much scrutiny, that Kelly's parents hadn't gone out in public since the trial began. Dan told Rachel they were going stir crazy. His strained voice indicated that he was neither joking nor exaggerating.

Kelly's name had been withheld by the media but nothing could suppress the town's rumor mill. It was common knowledge in Neapolis that Kelly Moore was the girl at the center of the rape trial. She'd had to leave her high school, and then a second school, because of the constant buzz of gossip as she walked down the halls. Her mother had taken to ordering groceries online long before the trial started. She didn't dare go into a supermarket, let alone a restaurant. Kelly had anonymity in name only.

Rachel had suggested she meet Kelly's parents at the beach at twilight. It would be dark enough that nobody would recognize them and deserted enough that they'd be able to talk privately without being overheard. They'd agreed their discussion would be off the record.

The farther they walked from the marina, the fewer people they saw, until it was just the three of them strolling on the edge of the shore, their outlines dark against the intermingling ink blots of sea and sky as night began to fall.

"How's Kelly doing?" Rachel asked.

"Not great," said Christine. Her sigh said more than her words. "She goes into full-on panic mode at the thought of returning to court."

Christine explained that Kelly was on high doses of anti-anxiety medication to keep her calm. The medication made it hard for her to think coherently. When her doctor lowered her medication, Kelly became anxious. "It's a vicious cycle," Christine said. The exhausted dark rings under her eyes told their own story.

"Christine doesn't want Kelly to go back on the stand," said Dan, looking down at the pattern the soles of his shoes made in the sand as he walked.

"You don't agree. You want Kelly to finish testifying," Rachel surmised.

"Yes." He looked up. "Mitch Alkins told us that he won't get a conviction without Kelly. I was up all night thinking about what he said. Kelly needs to do it. She needs to do it so that son of a bitch goes to prison. She needs to do it so she can move on," he said firmly. "She'll regret it for the rest of her life if she doesn't finish the job. If Scott Blair gets to go free and enjoy his life unpunished."

Christine shook her head as her husband spoke. It was clearly a major point of contention between the two of them. Time was running out and they still hadn't reached any joint agreement.

"What do Kelly's doctors think she should do?" Rachel asked.

"Her therapist is against it," said Christine. "She worries that it could tip Kelly over the edge. She is emotionally fragile right now. But Dan —" She looked at her husband. "Dan wants blood."

She fumbled in her pocket for a Kleenex and wiped her wet eyes. "He doesn't understand that we might lose Kelly in the process."

Dan put his arms around his wife and hugged her to his chest as she sobbed, their backs to the darkening sea. He looked over Christine's head at Rachel, pleading for her to break the deadlock. She lowered her eyes and turned away, walking ahead along the beach to give them privacy.

"What's your view, Rachel?" asked Dan,

when, composed again, they'd caught up to her. "You've been in court every day. You've seen the evidence and heard the testimony. Do you think the jury will convict if Kelly doesn't return to the stand?"

Rachel looked into the far distance, where she could see the distinctive shape of the Morrison's Point jetty stretching into the water. Kelly's parents huddled, together waiting expectantly for her answer. Rachel considered sugarcoating it. Then she remembered what Mitch Alkins had told her. They needed the truth. Raw and unvarnished.

"If Kelly doesn't take the stand, Dale Quinn will argue that Kelly's testimony should be struck from the record. All of it. Because she's a material witness and he wasn't able to cross-examine her properly. Without Kelly's testimony, I don't believe there's enough evidence for the jury to convict."

They both flinched at the brutal honesty of her words. Christine wrapped her arms around herself, chilled. "Kelly didn't make it up. He raped her. Why does the burden have to be on Kelly to prove it? She's a kid. She's the one hurting."

Rachel didn't have an answer. There was no answer. She'd collected shells as they'd

427

walked, and paused now to toss them into the ocean, one shell at a time. The crash of the surf muffled the soft splashes of the shells hitting the water.

"You think that Judge Shaw will go for that?" Dan asked. "Strike all of Kelly's testimony from the record."

"He won't have much choice," said Rachel. "He can't allow her testimony to stand if Dale Quinn didn't get a decent shot at cross-examining her."

Dan and Christine stood with their arms around each other's waists. Rachel knew that Mitch Alkins had said something similar, although perhaps less diplomatic, the previous night when he'd come to their house. Alkins had told Rachel that he'd been blunt with Kelly's parents before he'd left their home. "If Kelly doesn't testify then there's a real chance that Scott Blair will walk," he'd said.

Rachel hoped that Alkins was right, that hearing the same conclusion from her would carry more weight. After all, she didn't have a vested interest in the outcome. It wasn't her reputation as a prosecutor on the line. Plus, she knew the evidence inside and out; she was in court every day, listening to testimony, taking notes, reporting on the trial for the podcast.

They faced a terrible choice. Putting Kelly on the stand could destroy their daughter. Letting Scott Blair go free could destroy her even more. A gull cried as it flew over the beach, looking for a place to roost for the night.

"We can't do this to Kelly." Christine turned to face her husband.

"We have to. How can we let him get off? His name untarnished. His reputation intact. He needs to suffer. He deserves to be punished," Dan shot back. "Let someone do to him in prison what he did to Kelly."

Christine pummeled his torso softly with her palms, sobs wracking her body. "Every time Kelly talks about it, and I mean every single time, she relives that night. Over. And over. And over again. It's eating into whatever is left of her spirit. We can't make her do it. We are her parents. We have to think beyond getting justice. Or revenge. It's our job to help her heal."

"Testifying is what will help her heal. It will be painful at first, but it will be worth it. He'll be punished and her name will be cleared. She'll be vindicated," said Dan, kicking a clump of seaweed across the sand until it flopped into the water.

"Kelly doesn't need her name cleared. She didn't do anything wrong. She isn't —"

Christine's voice shook with anger.

Rachel didn't hear the rest as she moved ahead to give them space to talk. It was clear to her they'd been having the same discussion for days. Going round and round in circles. They were running out of time. It was Saturday night. If Kelly was to testify on Monday morning, they'd need to spend all of Sunday getting her emotionally prepared. Perhaps even letting Mitch Alkins or his people prepare her for the cross-examination.

Dan strode past Rachel, walking off after the angry exchange with his wife. Rachel hung back, waiting for Christine, who was dabbing her eyes when she caught up to Rachel. Both women walked together in silence, deliberately lagging behind Dan, not even trying to catch up. He walked fast and disappeared around the next headland, out of their line of sight.

It was getting darker and visibility was becoming poor. They walked a little longer until they heard the groan of timber as the Morrison's Point jetty swayed in the wind and tide farther along.

When they caught up with him, he was waiting, staring at the dark outline of the jetty as if afraid to get too close. "I didn't realize that we'd come so far." He gave a

430

shiver. "Always hated this place." He abruptly turned away and marched back toward the marina.

"He looks as if he's being chased by the devil," Rachel said to Christine as they watched him stride ahead down the beach.

"Dan blames himself for what happened to Kelly," Christine said. "He says it would never have happened if he had agreed to move to Portland to live near my folks when he left the navy. Instead, we came here. He insisted on it. Despite his terrible childhood, he felt this was where he belonged."

"In what way was his childhood terrible?" Rachel asked in surprise. His father was the town's police chief. Rachel had assumed that he'd had an easy, protected childhood.

Christine shook her head sadly. She told Rachel that when Dan was twelve his dad had beaten him so brutally that he was taken to the hospital with a skull fracture. Chief Moore told the attending doctor that Dan had gone flying while doing a dangerous jump on his skateboard. "The doctor bought it," she said. "He had no reason to doubt Police Chief Russ Moore.

"Dan's mom killed herself a year earlier. The medical examiner said it was an accidental overdose. Nobody accidentally takes a dozen Valium. Dan said she couldn't take the beatings anymore. Once his mother had gone, his childhood was spent trying to keep out of his father's way. Thank goodness for the navy. It was the making of him."

"In what way?" Rachel asked.

"It softened his rough edges. It grounded him. It gave him values. He's a devoted father, and a wonderful husband," she said. "Dan does a lot of charity work. He cares about the community. He cares about this town. That's why this situation has hit him especially hard. The way the town has become divided. The acrimony. People turning against Kelly, against our family. Casting aspersions on her character. He can't let it go. It's killing him."

She lowered her voice when she saw her husband had stopped and was waiting for them on the boardwalk. The tide was coming in hard, eating up the beach. The two women climbed back onto the boardwalk together. The lights of the marina flickered in the distance. As they came closer, they could hear music from the outdoor restaurants.

"I'll miss Neapolis once we're gone," said Christine wistfully.

"You're leaving town?" Rachel asked.

"I'm taking Kelly to live near my parents. Dan will stay to sell the business and the house. He'll join us as soon as he can," Christine said. But there was a tinge to her voice that suggested he might never join them. Rachel got the impression that if Dan Moore insisted his daughter take the stand the family — and the marriage — would never recover.

When they reached the car, Dan took his wife's hands and looked into her eyes. "On the walk back, I thought about what you said, honey. I've made a lot of mistakes in my life, but I'm not going to make any more. I won't fight you on Kelly. I have to believe that Scott Blair will be punished. Sometime, somewhere, he will be punished for what he did to my little girl." He shook his head. "But you are right; Kelly doesn't have to be the one to make that happen."

Rachel watched Dan and Christine drive away. Their minds were made up. Kelly Moore was not taking the stand on Monday. The trial was over.

48
RACHEL

Rachel sat on her bed listening to the dial tone. Mitch Alkins hadn't sounded surprised when she told him that Kelly would not be in court come Monday. It was almost as if he'd already resigned himself to that outcome. He must have known the fierce protectiveness of Kelly's mother would win out against her father's thirst for revenge.

Alkins had sounded so dejected that Rachel couldn't bring herself to ask if he'd located Jenny Stills's autopsy report or found out anything about the circumstances surrounding her death. He'd promised he would look into it, and she believed him. Once the trial was over, Rachel was certain that he'd follow through.

Hannah's last email had troubled Rachel greatly. Remembering what had happened that night was clearly taking a terrible toll on her. Rachel could feel it in every word, every syllable. She'd briefly considered sharing the letters with Detective Cooper but decided against it. She didn't have Hannah's permission to share her story, and Rachel didn't want to betray her trust.

Rachel brushed her teeth and prepared for bed, feeling restless and sad after her nighttime walk with Kelly's parents. Scott Blair would go free. His good name would likely be restored. He'd claim that he was the victim of a false accusation. Many would believe him.

Maybe he'd make it to the Olympics and win gold, as his father had proudly predicted that day when Rachel visited their house. Or maybe his name would be tarnished enough, or his confidence and fitness so damaged by his suspension from competitive swimming, that he'd never get back to peak athletic condition. Time would tell.

While Scott would never spend a night in prison, Rachel was certain that Kelly's name would be mud forever, much like Jenny's. The Blair supporters would smear her as a vindictive teenager who'd refused to be cross-examined to avoid being exposed as a liar.

As for Kelly's supporters, they wouldn't forgive Kelly for giving up. Deep down, they would resent her failure to stay the course, and they'd secretly blame her for making it harder for other victims to come forward in the future.

Kelly would never be free. Never fully recover. Her childhood had been irreparably damaged by that night on the beach. Her family was fleeing town like persecuted emigres. Their lives and livelihood uprooted so she could start fresh in a new town, a new school. Perhaps even with a new name. Christine was right. It shouldn't rest on the shoulders of a young girl. But it did.

Rachel collapsed on her bed, lying on top of the covers and staring at the ceiling. She'd been so consumed with the podcast and the minutiae of the trial that she hadn't had a chance to take a step back. To get perspective. As she lay on her bed, she was hit by a niggling feeling that she'd missed something. She'd had that feeling before and brushed it off. But this time she was certain.

Rachel scrambled through the pile of notebooks on her desk until she'd found the notebook filled with her own messy shorthand of Kelly Moore's testimony. She flicked through the pages until she was three-quarters of the way through the notebook.

There was an old plaid shirt on me. It was a huge shirt. It was tucked under me like a blanket. I don't know where the shirt came from because Scott hadn't worn a shirt like that.

Rachel pulled out her file with Hannah's letters. She lay flat on the bed and read the letters one by one. The green glow of the clock shifted its shape as time passed. As Rachel finished each letter, she tossed it on her bed and unfolded another one. And another. Until she reached the latest emails from Hannah. Rachel found something that made her jolt up in surprise. She turned on the lamp next to her bed to read the passage again. She wanted to be certain.

Jenny was trembling so badly I could hear her teeth chattering. I peered out from under the canvas sheet. Bobby was unbuttoning his shirt. It frightened me to see him get undressed. When he'd removed his shirt, he put it over Jenny and tucked it under her like a blanket.

Similar descriptions. Two rapes. Twenty-five years apart. In the same town. As she crawled under the covers of her bed, Hannah's letters scattered across the sheets, Rachel told herself it was a fluke coincidence. It was only while she was drifting off that she remembered something that made her realize there was no coincidence at all.

It was still dark when Rachel rolled out of

bed and dressed in running gear. Even though it was a good hour before dawn, it might as well have been the middle of the night when Rachel pushed through the revolving doors of the hotel and emerged onto the deserted street. The streetlights were on and the traffic lights were changing colors, but there was not a single vehicle on the road that ran parallel to the beach.

Rachel ran along the boardwalk, retracing the route she'd walked with Dan and Christine Moore the night before. By the time she reached Morrison's Point, the sky was a lighter shade of dark blue. Dawn would break soon. Rachel didn't stop at the jetty. She kept running, passing one beach after the next until her face was flushed and her breathing labored.

The boat sheds rattled in the breeze as she came onto the last beach. It was so close to the marine reserve that she could see the timber-and-stone visitors' station with its maps and illustrations of local bird and marine life. Rachel moved between the boathouses quietly, sticking to the shifting shadows.

She pressed herself against a shed and waited. As dawn broke, a door slammed open. The hulking figure of Vince Knox — or whatever his real name was — pushed a small fiberglass boat out of the timber shed and down a sandy incline toward the water. The outboard motor was lifted up so it wouldn't drag on the sand.

When the boat was on the edge of the water and would go no farther, he went into the water and grabbed the ropes, pulling the boat off the beach until it was floating.

Rachel ran down to the beach and waved to get his attention. He didn't see her at first. He was arranging crab cages on the bottom of the boat so the weight was evenly distributed. When he raised his head, he looked confused and then angry to see Rachel waiting by the shore.

"You again! What do you want this time?" His voice was rough.

"How's the bird doing?" Rachel asked.

"She's drinking and eating," he said. "I'll release her in a couple of days."

"That's good news," said Rachel, still standing her ground. He went about his work but glanced at her every now and again as if to ask why she was still there.

"I need to ask you about something important."

"I don't answer questions. Not yours. Not anyone else's. Now get the hell off my beach," he called back.

"It's about the Scott Blair trial," she said.

He looked at her in irritation. They'd already discussed that the last time she'd turned up uninvited. He jumped out of his boat and waded back onto the beach. Rachel thought he was coming to talk to her. Instead, he walked straight past her and kept walking up to the boat shed. When he returned, he was carrying a big white bucket for his catch, and a rusted pike. Rachel suspected it was to lift the crab cages out of the water, but he held on to it like it was a spear, and she got the impression that he was hoping it would intimidate her.

"You lied by omission on the stand. I want to know what really happened," Rachel called out as he walked past her.

"I don't have to tell you shit about nothing," he said, tossing the bucket into the boat. He pointed the metal pike at Rachel as if to scare her off. Rachel kept her hands on her hips. Vince Knox didn't scare her one bit.

"There's nobody around except for you and me. If you were a smart lady, you'd turn around and get the hell out of here," he warned her.

"Listen to me for two minutes," Rachel insisted.

Finally, he put down the bucket, listening to her speak as he stared down at his bare feet. His shorts and T-shirt were soaked through from pulling the motorboat into the water. Rachel gave him an abridged version of what she needed. And why. His expression was impassive as she explained.

"I can't help you," he said when she was done. "I told you before. I mind my own business. It's the only way I can survive, living the life that I live."

"Sometimes a man has to speak up or be responsible for the repercussions of his silence," Rachel told him.

He turned back to the boat and tossed in the pike with a clatter before climbing in. The boat rocked unsteadily as he scrambled to a seat next to the outboard motor. Rachel slipped off her sneakers and waded barefoot into the water.

"Wait," Rachel called out, approaching the boat.

He ignored her and pulled the cord to turn on the engine. It spluttered. He reached out to pull the cord a second time when Rachel called out again.

"Bobby, wait," she shouted. He dropped the cord and looked up at her.

"How do you know my real name?"

"A girl who once knew you, she wrote me some letters that mentioned a boy with gray eyes called Bobby," said Rachel. "Bobby helped her injured sister by taking off his shirt and wrapping it around her like a blanket to keep her warm. To stop her from going into shock. Just like the way you did with the seagull. And just like the way you did on this very beach last year when you found —" Her words were swallowed by the wind.

"Who is the girl who wrote the letters?" he interrupted. "What's her name?"

"Her name is Hannah Stills. Her sister was Jenny Stills," said Rachel. "Do you remember them?"

"A little," he said. "My memory is bad from that time, on account of the accident."

"What accident?"

"I drove a truck into a tree when I was younger. Killed my two friends. I survived. If you can call looking like this surviving," he said, lifting his T-shirt to display the third-degree burns she'd seen before on his chest. He laughed, an angry, bitter laugh. "I was in the hospital for nearly a year after that. Had skin graft after skin graft. Fourteen surgeries in all. That whole period is a haze. I remembered only what I was told. That I'd driven into a tree and killed my friends. I reckon that these scars here are a small price to pay for what I did."

"Maybe you don't remember Jenny Stills,"

Rachel said. "But you remember another girl you helped on this beach. You were there that night. Weren't you?"

He didn't hear her. He'd turned on the outboard motor and was heading out into the ocean. Rachel listened to the whine of the motor as he navigated the boat through the crests of incoming waves until he had escaped the pull of the tide and was out at sea.

When he returned, two hours later, Rachel was sitting cross-legged on the beach, waiting for him. Once he'd secured his boat and stepped onshore, he looked at her and nodded.

49

RACHEL

Dale Quinn failed to hide his elation when he saw the dejected slump of Mitch Alkins's shoulders at the prosecutors' table as he walked into court on Monday morning. Victory was within touching distance.

Quinn took his seat at the defense table and leaned back for a lighthearted exchange with Greg Blair. The courtroom was crackling with anticipation by the time Judge Shaw entered in his black robe. His eyes were steely when he asked Mitch Alkins, as he'd done every morning the previous week, whether the complainant was ready to resume her cross-examination.

"Your Honor," said Alkins, "Miss Moore's parents and therapist have advised that her mental state is too fragile for further questioning in open court. However, she can provide written answers, or videotape her answers to a list of questions provided by the defense. I ask for latitude in this regard.

She is very young and very traumatized and I am certain we can elicit her testimony under cross-examination without tormenting her further by bringing her back into this courtroom."

"Your Honor." Dale Quinn bounded to his feet. "I need to cross-examine the witness myself before the jury. Anything less would prejudice my client's right —"

"Yes, yes, I know, Mr. Quinn," interrupted Judge Shaw. "Your client's right to a fair trial. Believe me, Counselor, we are doing contortions here to keep it as fair as possible."

Judge Shaw gestured for Quinn and Alkins to approach the bench. Nobody so much as cleared their throat as the judge conferred with the two attorneys at a sidebar, everyone straining to hear their hushed discussion. Sophia, the courtroom artist next to Rachel, stopped sketching while they spoke. It was impossible to know exactly what had been discussed when Judge Shaw finally ordered Quinn and Alkins to step away from the bar and return to their seats.

Mitch Alkins's shoulders were hunched and he scratched the side of his forehead as if he was deeply unsatisfied with the outcome as he returned to the prosecutors' table. Rachel guessed that Judge Shaw had refused his request to allow Kelly to provide testimony in writing or by video.

Back at the defense table, Dale Quinn stood up, trying not to look jubilant as he buttoned his jacket. "Your Honor," Quinn said. "Since the complainant, Miss Moore, is unavailable today, which was the deadline for her to return to court for cross-examination, I move that her entire testimony be struck from the record."

"I am inclined to agree with Mr. Quinn," said Judge Shaw.

"Your Honor," Alkins interrupted.

"I've given you ample time, Mr. Alkins," Judge Shaw said. He instructed the jury to disregard all of Kelly Moore's testimony. The jury would not be able to draw on anything she said when she took the witness stand earlier in the trial. All of her testimony would be erased, as if she'd never said a word.

The courtroom was hushed as Quinn asked the judge if he could make one further request. He was one chess move away from winning the case. "Your Honor, in light of your decision to strike Miss Moore's testimony from the record, I ask that this case be dismissed, with prejudice, due to insufficient evidence."

"Mr. Alkins, I believe Mr. Quinn has a

strong argument. Do you have anything to say?" Judge Shaw leaned forward into his microphone.

"Your Honor," said Alkins, standing up. "I would like to recall a witness before you consider the defense's request."

"You have already rested your case," snapped Judge Shaw. "You can't go calling witnesses now."

"The witness that I'd like to call was a witness for the defense. Mr. Quinn has not yet rested the defense's case."

"Who would you like to recall, Mr. Alkins?" huffed Judge Shaw.

"I would like to recall Mr. Vince Knox."

A hum rippled across the courtroom. They all remembered Vince Knox as the surly character witness, his face and neck disfigured by tattoos and healed gashes from switchblade attacks. He'd testified to Scott Blair's heroism for saving the life of a drowning boy.

"Mr. Alkins, why are you wasting the court's time by bringing a character witness for the defense back to the stand?" the judge asked impatiently.

"I believe that Mr. Knox may have information that is of material value to this case, beyond his testimony as a character witness for the defendant."

"I'll allow it," said Judge Shaw, looking anything but happy about the direction the trial was taking. "You're on razor-thin ice, Mr. Alkins. I suggest you get to the point with this witness. In record time."

Dale Quinn leaned toward Scott Blair and whispered in his ear. Scott shrugged. It was obvious to Rachel that Quinn had asked his client if he knew what Mitch Alkins might want to extract from Vince Knox, of all people.

Trying to buy time, Quinn asked Judge Shaw for a half-day adjournment to prepare for the witness. Judge Shaw ruled it out. He pointed out curtly that the witness was in fact a defense witness being recalled to the stand and Quinn had already had ample time to prepare. Quinn then tried for a brief recess to confer with his client.

"No," intoned Judge Shaw, as if he were talking to a preschooler nagging for a restroom break. "You may not have a short recess. We have just started for the day. Bailiff, bring in the witness."

The courtroom doors opened to let Vince Knox into the courtroom. He wasn't in the borrowed suit he'd worn the last time he'd testified. This time he wore neatly pressed denim work pants and a worn work shirt with the sleeves rolled up to his elbows.

The courtroom artist drew Vince Knox as the judge reminded him that he was still under oath. The good side of his face was weathered and ruddy from the outdoors. The other side had puckered knife scars, one of which made his eye droop. This time he made no effort to cover up his neck tattoos under his shirt collar.

"Your name is Vince Knox, is that correct?" Alkins asked.

"Yes, sir. It is."

"You were also known by another name in the past. What was it?"

"I used to be called Bobby. Bobby Green," said the witness. A frisson of surprise ran through the courtroom, but the witness seemed oblivious as he waited for Alkins's next question.

"Why did you change your name, Mr. Knox?" Alkins asked.

"A friend of mine once told me that if you change your name, you change your luck. I decided I'd come back here with a new name. Start a new chapter. Neapolis is where I grew up. I've always loved it here: the ocean, the birds. It's where I want to live out the rest of my life."

As the witness spoke, Quinn turned around and gave Greg Blair a withering look before whispering into the ear of an associate, who immediately rushed out of the courtroom. Rachel suspected the junior lawyer had gone to collect dirt on Vince Knox's past, when he was known as Bobby Green, to give Quinn ammunition for his redirect.

Alkins asked Knox where he had been on the night when Kelly Moore was raped. He explained that he'd been living in one of the boat sheds. "It was more comfortable than sleeping in my car. Also there's toilet and shower facilities on the beach, and a barbecue that takes quarters. It's too cold to stay there over the winter," Knox said. "But I was there when that girl was hurt."

"What happened that night?" Alkins asked.

"I was in the boat shed trying to sleep. The wind howls when it blows into that rickety old shed and I'm a deep sleeper, so for a long while I didn't know that anyone else was there. Later in the night, I came out to pee and I found a half-naked girl lying on the sand. At first I thought she was dead, because she didn't move and her eyes were closed, but then she made a whining sound. Like an injured animal. I realized that she was awake, but she wasn't responsive. It looked to me like she was drugged, or delirious. She was in obvious pain, but not so much physical. More emotional. It's hard to explain."

"Did the girl say anything to you?" Alkins asked.

"I don't think she realized that I was there. She kept whimpering and saying things like, 'Let me go. Let me go.' "

Alkins showed Knox a series of photos of teenage girls and asked him to identify the girl he'd seen on the beach that night. He immediately picked out the photograph of Kelly Moore.

"As the only other person who was at the beach that night, did you hear or see anything that indicates whether Scott Blair raped Kelly Moore?" Alkins asked.

"Oh, he raped her all right." said Knox. "After I found that poor girl, I saw and heard enough to know without a shadow of doubt that she didn't want any of it."

50
GUILTY OR NOT GUILTY

The most incriminating testimony against Scott Blair may well be the word of a drifter. His name is Vince Knox. That's not his real name. He changed it when he got out of prison. Aside from a criminal record, he has a history of vagrancy. For the past few years, he's been living in Neapolis. He gets work where he can find it. Odd jobs mostly. He mows lawns, clears gutters. On weekends, he pushes a wheelbarrow down the beach to collect discarded cans and bottles for cash deposits.

He owns a rusty station wagon and a small outboard motor boat. He takes it out most mornings to catch crabs. He sells his haul to local restaurants to supplement his income. He cares for injured birds with damaged wings; he wraps them up in his own shirts to keep them warm. And he keeps his own company. He doesn't have friends. Not unless you count the birds and strays he feeds and cares for when they're injured.

He sleeps wherever he can lay his head. In good times, it's a room, if he can find one cheap. In bad times, he sleeps in the back of his car. Sometimes he sleeps on the beach or in a boat shed. That's where he was on the night in question. The night that K was allegedly raped.

Vince Knox was one of the character witnesses called by Scott Blair's defense lawyer earlier in the trial. He told the court how, three years ago, Scott dived into the sea in dangerous conditions and saved a drowning boy who'd been pulled out by the currents. Vince Knox said Scott was a hero.

Today in court, he testified again. This time, he didn't call Scott a hero. He called him a rapist.

Vince Knox told the court that he was living in a boat shed last year when he came out early in the morning and saw K lying half-naked on the sand. He thought she was dead.

When she whimpered, he realized that she was alive. He recalled seeing bruises on her body. It looked to him as if she'd been assaulted. He suspected she'd been raped. He took off his shirt and covered her nakedness with it. Then he tucked it around her like a blanket. Just the way he does with the injured birds that he saves. He was worried she'd go into shock.

He returned to the boathouse and kept watch from the gap between the timber slats. He said he didn't want to frighten her if she came to and saw him. He's an intimidating man. Frightening to look at. He has scars on his face from a knife attack in prison and tattoos that go all the way up his neck.

He didn't call the police or an ambulance that night. He claims his mobile phone battery was dead. He admitted that he could have taken her to the hospital in the back of his station wagon. He didn't. He was afraid that he'd get jammed up. Perhaps be accused of raping the girl himself. Or get hit with a vagrancy and trespassing charge. This is a man who's spent so much of his life in prison that he doesn't trust the authorities to leave him be.

So he watched K to make sure she was safe while he was hiding in the boat shed. Peering through the cracks in the timber slats, he saw Scott Blair walk onto the beach from his sports car. Scott was carrying a small navy sports bag. The girl had woken by then. The shirt Vince Knox left on her body slid off as she sat up, visibly disoriented. From his hiding place in the shed, Vince Knox assumed that Scott was there to help the girl. Instead, Scott kicked her lightly in her thigh with his sneaker. Like he was rousing a stray dog.

Scott ordered her to get up. He told her to shower in the icy outdoor beach shower. He gave her soap and shampoo, which he'd brought in the sports bag. He told her that if she didn't wash off all the evidence, then he'd do it himself. "Better be careful," he threatened with a smirk as he groped her naked body. "One thing might lead to another. I might get carried away."

When she'd showered and dressed, Scott pushed her against the boat shed where Vince Knox was hiding. Scott warned her not to tell anyone what he'd done to her. Vince Knox recalled that Scott took specific pleasure in mentioning some of the sex acts he'd forced on her. He heard Scott tell the girl that he'd destroy her reputation if she told on him. After that, Scott gave her cash and told her to use it to catch a bus home.

Because K's testimony was struck from the record, whatever she said that day in court does not exist. It never happened. The jury can't refer to it. They can't even remember it. This is why Vince Knox's eyewitness testimony is so crucial. And his testimony was damning.

Despite his gruff, abrupt manner, I think the

jurors found him sincere. A simple man who spoke from the heart in simple words. They appreciated his candor. They realized that he had nothing to gain from coming forward, other than telling the truth. The jury, like all of us, is suffering from trial fatigue. I could tell they liked his authenticity.

When it was his turn, Dale Quinn threw everything he had at Vince Knox. He accused Knox of being a voyeur who spied on two teenagers having a romantic interlude at the beach. He suggested Knox's testimony was motivated by anger against Scott Blair's dad, who'd hired him in the past to do ground maintenance work but never followed through with a full-time job. Once he was done casting aspersions on Vince Knox's character, he focused his attention on finding inconsistencies in his testimony. In trying to trap him in lies.

"Are you asking the court to believe you slept through a rape?" Quinn asked.

"The wind rattles those sheds something awful," Knox responded.

"If the shed rattles so loudly that you can't hear a girl being raped, then how did you miraculously hear the defendant discussing his crimes with the complainant, as you have claimed? Isn't it true that you're lying when you say you overheard this purported conver-

sation between my client and the complainant?"

"I'm not lying. I heard every word because
he pushed her against the side of the boathouse where I was hiding. I was right on the
other side of that thin wall. Less than an inch
away from them. I heard every word. I ain't
deaf. Not yet, anyway."

"Why did you not mention any of this when
you were on the stand last time?" Quinn
asked.

"You didn't ask me if Scott Blair did it. If he
raped that girl. You just asked me about how
he rescued that drowning kid all those years
ago. If you'd asked me whether he did it, then
I would have told you."

It went on like this for a while, until Dale
Quinn was handed a folder of notes from the
associate whom he'd sent out earlier. Quinn
skimmed the notes in the file and then asked
the judge's permission to have a sidebar
conversation with the associate who'd prepared the material. There was obviously
something that he wasn't expecting. We all
watched and wondered what was going on as
he turned to Scott Blair's father and the two
men whispered to each other angrily. It ended
with both men looking furious. The judge
intervened. He said Quinn had enough time
to consult and he should continue with his

questioning.

"Why should the jury believe a man who killed two of his friends by driving drunk into a tree?" Quinn asked. "You were in jail for killing those boys, weren't you, Bobby Green? Then you came back here and changed your name so that nobody would know your criminal past." There was an eerie silence in the court among those who remembered the story of Bobby Green.

"I changed my name just like I said earlier, because I wanted a new beginning. I served time with Vince Knox. He saved my life. More than once. I wanted to honor his memory. That's why I use his name. I knew that nobody here would have given me any peace if they'd known I was Bobby Green," Knox responded.

When he was eighteen, Vince Knox, who was then known as Bobby Green, drove a pickup into a tree one summer night. His blood alcohol content was twice the legal limit. The vehicle turned into a fireball. His friends died. He was badly burned. He almost died. He was hospitalized for months and underwent multiple lifesaving surgeries. He'll carry those scars to his dying day. After he recovered, he pleaded guilty to manslaughter and served time. In the years that followed, he spent more time in prison than out of it until he returned to Neapolis to start his life afresh several years ago.

If Quinn thought that delving into the open wounds of Vince Knox's past would provoke him to explode on the stand, then he couldn't have been more wrong.

Vince Knox stood up, a burly man with thinning brown hair and a protruding belly. His tattooed neck and scars from being stabbed in prison attested to his troubled life.

With tears in his eyes, he turned to the jury. "I've never said I was a good man. I've done plenty wrong in my life. Plenty to be ashamed of. I killed my friends. Drove that truck straight into a tree. But that's got nothing to do with what happened that night. Scott, he did something bad to that girl. He raped her. And then he told her he'd do it again if she ever told anyone. I heard him say it. Every word of it."

Vince Knox's testimony was enough for Judge Shaw to reject Dale Quinn's request to dismiss the case due to lack of evidence. Quinn looked crestfallen. He'd walked into court that morning expecting the case would be over by lunchtime. He walked out like the rest of us, unsure where the verdict was headed.

Mitch Alkins and Dale Quinn gave powerful closing arguments. In Alkins's version, Scott Blair was a predatory rapist. Cruel, calculating. He knowingly and with full premeditation entrapped a teenage girl and raped her to win a competition. His conscience was guilty from the start. He tried to arrange an alibi and did his best to wash away the evidence. In Dale Quinn's account, Scott Blair was, at worst, an immature jock falsely accused after a consensual sexual tryst that the girl regretted in hindsight, spurred on by her angry, vengeful parents and a prosecutor's office trying to use Scott as a high-profile scapegoat to satisfy a public lust to jail men accused of sex crimes.

As the jurors filed out of court to deliberate the verdict, I felt as if I were saying goodbye to old friends. At the start of the trial, the jurors were strangers. To each other. To me. To everyone in court.

Over the course of the trial, I've come to know them as individuals. Their facial gestures. Their nervous tics. I've seen them cry. And laugh. Roll their eyes in disbelief. Mostly I've seen them stifle yawns while they discreetly checked the time. After two weeks of testimony, they're now tasked with determining whether Scott Blair is guilty beyond a reasonable doubt of rape and sexual assault.

There are some who say that the reasonable doubt burden is one of the reasons why so few rape cases end in a conviction. It's a difficult standard to meet when it comes to

460

sexual assault, because rarely are there witnesses other than the parties themselves.

The idea that guilt must be proven beyond a reasonable doubt dates back to the eighteenth-century British jurist Sir William Blackstone, who wrote in his seminal works that underpin our legal system: "Better that ten guilty persons escape, than that one innocent suffer."

Studies show that rapists tend to be repeat offenders more than other criminals. They go on to rape again, at a rate of around five rapes in their lifetime. That means the ten guilty rapists who escape, to paraphrase Sir Blackstone, might go on to rape another forty innocent women. I wonder what Sir William Blackstone would say about that?

The jurors will review the evidence and argue the merits of the case. Then they will vote until they reach a unanimous verdict. Either they will find Scott Blair guilty. Or they will find him not guilty. We will find out in the coming hours or days.

I'm Rachel Krall and this is *Guilty or Not Guilty,* the podcast that puts you in the jury box.

Dear Rachel,

Let me start by apologizing. I promised myself that I would respect your boundaries. I've restrained myself. I haven't left letters on your car or anywhere else intrusive for some time. Yet here I am, downstairs in the lobby of your hotel, writing this note. I promise that I'll leave it just outside your door, followed by a loud knock to ensure that you'll get out of bed to collect it.

I'm ready to meet you, Rachel. Tonight. At the Morrison's Point jetty. I'll go there as soon as I drop off the letter. I know it's late, but please come. I don't think I can do this alone.

I know who killed Jenny. I'd tell the cops, but after watching the Scott Blair rape trial unravel, I'm not confident a jury would ever convict. The lack of forensic evidence and

462

the passage of time would work against a successful prosecution. There's one witness from the night Jenny was killed. A reluctant witness. A dying witness. You led me to him when I followed your car to the Golden Vista retirement home.

Rick saw Jenny's killer. He told me so when I spoke with him this morning, after he was discharged from the hospital wing. At first Rick pleaded ignorance, but he eventually relented. He said that it didn't much matter anymore if the truth came out. Apparently, he has weeks to live. "They can't do anything to me in hell." He laughed dryly. And then he told me what he remembered from that night. He told me the name of the boy he'd seen running away from the beach.

Thanks to Rick's recollections, and my own hazy memories, I believe he's right. The only way to find out for sure is to ask him straight out. To ask Jenny's killer. His confession might be all we get.

Below is the letter that I've been writing to you over the past few days, about what happened the night that Jenny died. I wrote it in fits and starts, in different pens, and in handwriting that changed with my moods. I hope it's legible enough for you to read.

■ ■ ■

After that drunk boy disconnected my call, he smashed the phone with the receiver until it was a mess of wires. When he was done, he kicked the glass phone booth door until it shattered. All the while, he held my upper arm so tightly that it was bruised for days afterward. My feet were bare. By the time he'd dragged me across the concrete toward the beach, the soles of my feet were slashed and embedded with glass.

He threw me on the sand next to Jenny. She was lying on the ground near the fire as the boys stood over her, drinking.

"Your little sister came to tell you that you need to go home." He laughed. Jenny stared at me. The numb expression on her face turned to panic.

"She's the kid sister," said a drunk voice from the dark. "What do we do with her?"

"Let's take a look at her. Maybe she's old enough."

I felt a hand grab my chest. "Flat as a pancake," he said. "Definitely underage."

He flicked up the skirt of my dress. I tried to pull it down. It made him laugh. He flicked it up again. I grabbed the folds of my dress and held them tightly to my body.

"What do we have here?" He pushed my hands away and pulled my skirt up anyway so they could all see my underwear.

"Hello Kitty panties. Such pretty panties." He pulled me toward him and whispered into my ear with his stale drunken breath, "Do you know what a grown-up kitty is called?" I shook my head.

"Please. I'll do whatever you want. Leave her alone. She's just a kid." Jenny's voice was hoarse.

"I don't do little girls," said one. "That's disgusting."

"What do you think, Bobby?" the boy holding me called out. "Which do you prefer, big sister or little sister? You haven't shown any interest in banging the big sister. Maybe you'd like to give the little one a go."

"Leave her alone," shouted Bobby.

"Are you sweet on her, Bobby?" the boy teased. "I always figured you liked them young," he said, flicking up my skirt again and laughing as I tried to hold it down.

Bobby dived at the boy and pushed him to the ground. Those boys were strong, but nothing compared to Bobby Green in a rage. He punched one of them until he'd turned his face into a bloody pulp. One of the others kicked him in the ribs to get him to stop. They dived on him and rolled together in the direction of the bonfire until I heard Bobby scream. I didn't know why until I smelled burning human flesh. After that, everything was a blur. There were panicked shouts about taking him to the hospital and howls of agonized pain from Bobby. They carried him to the truck. Someone ran back and kicked sand over the bonfire to douse the flames. It was the one who'd been driving the truck that very first day.

"You listen to me, you slutty little bitch," he snarled, lifting up Jenny's head by her hair as he spoke to her. "If you ever tell anyone what happened, then we'll do to your little sister what we did to you. But worse. Much worse. Do you understand?"

Jenny nodded.

"You learn fast."

He ran to join the others, leaving us lying in a heap on the beach, clutching each other as we watched the truck reverse, its headlights on as it sped out of the parking lot.

"Jenny," I choked. "Are you all right? Let's go home. Can you walk?"

"No," she mumbled. "I need an ambulance."

"The telephone booth is broken and there's nobody around to help. I can't get an ambulance."

"The gas station," she whispered. "It's still open."

"Come with me," I sobbed. "I don't want to leave you."

"Can't walk." Jenny groaned. "They're gone now. I'll be okay. I'll wait for you here."

Reluctantly, I left Jenny curled up on the beach and trudged through the sand. Sharp stones cut into my damaged feet as I crossed the parking lot and walked along the shoulder of the road to the gas station. I blocked the pain, focusing on getting to the gas station before it closed for the night.

It was shutting down when I arrived. Fortunately, a light by the cash register was still on. I entered through the automatic doors, unaware that I was leaving a trail of blood across the white-tiled floor. "We're closed," said Rick without looking up.

"I need help." My voice trembled. Snot ran down my face, mixing with tears. "I need to call an ambulance."

He looked up and saw the bloody trail that I'd left on the floor and immediately passed me the phone. While I dialed 911 and asked for an ambulance, I heard him complaining about the mess of blood and mud that he'd have to clean up. But by the time I'd hung up the phone, Rick seemed shamefaced at his initial reaction. He drove me back to the beach in his truck so I could wait with Jenny for the ambulance to arrive.

I jumped out when he pulled into the parking lot. I limped onto the beach toward the smoldering remnants of the bonfire. Jenny was all curled up in the same position that she'd been in when I'd gone to get help. It was only when I was very close that I understood that she wasn't there at all. What I thought was Jenny was the shirt that Bobby had put over her to keep her warm.

"Jenny?" I called out. "Jenny?"

I wandered aimlessly across the beach, looking for Jenny, until the dark sky was colored by the bright lights of sirens. Uniformed figures ran down to the beach. I stumbled toward them, stuttering that my sister had gone missing. I shivered as I watched them stand on the beach and comb the water with powerful flashlights.

"I see something," someone called out from near the jetty. He waded waist deep into the water, while another held his flashlight unsteadily pointing into the ocean.

I ran to the edge of the surf. The policeman who'd gone into the water was coming out, pulling something through the white foam of a broken wave. It was Jenny. Her blond hair had spread across the water like a mermaid.

468

"Jenny?" I screamed. Her eyes were open, but they were unblinking. "Jenny!"

I fell onto her the moment they pulled her out of the water. She was cold. Ice cold. Someone pulled me away from her. "She's gone," he said as I heard a siren approach. "She's gone."

I screamed, but not a sound came out.

52
RACHEL

The jetty groaned under the assault of wind and midnight tides as Rachel walked into the black mist that shrouded the coastline.

When she reached the end of the jetty, she looked out to sea but saw nothing. It looked as if the ocean and the sky had merged into a black abyss. She stood with both hands on the rail, her face whipped by the icy Atlantic wind as she enjoyed the sensation of being alone with the elements.

A sliver of moon from a shifting cloud eased the darkness enough for Rachel to see her surroundings. That's when she realized that she wasn't alone. A figure in the corner had been observing her.

Hannah was shorter than Rachel, with cropped dark hair and bright eyes. She wore a black crocheted cardigan that reached down to her knees, and dark jeans with black high-heel boots. She waited shyly for Rachel to approach, uncertain of what reception she'd get.

Rachel moved toward her wordlessly. When they were close, she wrapped her arms around Hannah in a warm embrace.

"I'm sorry for everything you've been through," said Rachel, her voice thick with the sadness that had clung to her since she'd read Hannah's final letter.

"I'm so grateful that you came," said Hannah. "I was worried that I'd have to do this alone."

They rested their backs against the jetty handrail, buffeted by wind, as they looked out to shore, waiting for Jenny's killer to arrive.

"Maybe it's not him," said Rachel with a shiver when minutes passed and he still hadn't arrived. A breaking wave splashed across the weathered timber beams, soaking her sneakers and wetting her jeans. She zipped up her waterproof jacket and put the hood over her head to cover her auburn hair, which had become unruly in the wind.

Hannah shrugged uncertainly. "We'll find out soon enough. If he turns up, it will confirm that he did it. Only a guilty man would come here tonight. Let's wait a little longer."

"What are you hoping to get from him? And me?"

"I want him to confess. And I want you to be a witness to his confession. It might be the only evidence we ever get." Hannah hesitated. "If you feel like it's too danger- ous, you can go. I'll wait. I've waited a lifetime. I can wait a little longer."

"I'll stay," said Rachel. "I'll be your wit- ness. I won't let it be your word against his." She crossed her shivering arms to stay warm as she looked out in the direction of the beach. The sweeping coastal landscape that had become so familiar to her had turned into a vast swath of impenetrable darkness in the night.

Minutes later, they saw two bright orbs moving along the coastal road. The orbs slowed down and turned toward the beach parking lot. They were car headlights. The headlights stopped moving, but they re- mained lit as they pointed toward the jetty on high beam. The driver had parked the car facing the ocean, looking for them. Eventually the lights turned off and every- thing was dark again.

Rachel and Hannah both knew that he was walking toward them, even though they couldn't see him at all in the dark. Nor could they hear his footsteps over the howl- ing wind. Rachel had retreated to the far corner of the jetty so that he wouldn't realize that Hannah wasn't alone.

It was only when he'd reached the end of the jetty and he was close enough for Rachel to see his face that she felt a coldness in the pit of her stomach. It couldn't be him. It had to be a terrible mistake.

"I got your note. I came to say that I'm sorry," he said to Hannah. "And to ask you to leave the past alone."

He hadn't yet noticed Rachel, who had blended into the thick fog of night in her dark clothes and upturned jacket hood and collar. She stayed silent as she listened to them talk, discreetly opening the voice recorder app on her phone in her pocket so that she could record the conversation.

"How have you lived with yourself all these years, after what you did?" Hannah asked.

"I was a different person in those days. A kid. Messed up on drugs and alcohol. I hated the world," he said. "I'm ashamed of what I did. I hate who I was in those days. I'm nothing like that person anymore." His voice cracked with emotion. "I've agonized over what happened every day since."

"You raped and murdered my sister," said Hannah.

"What makes you think I killed her?" he said. Hidden in the shadows, Rachel couldn't help noticing that he hadn't denied the first accusation.

"I know it was you. Why did you do it?"

Finally, he broke down as he spoke in a choking voice. "I didn't plan to kill her. It just happened," he said. "We left her lying on the sand while we carried Bobby to the truck to drive him to the hospital. I panicked and told my friend Lucas to pull over at the next beach. I realized that she was evidence of what we did. That we'd go to prison because of her. Either for her rape, or Bobby's death if he didn't make it. Or both. She was what my father called 'a sloppy loose end.' I carried her onto the jetty. Just over there." He pointed to a side rail in the middle of the jetty, his face pained. "And I dropped her into the water and returned to my friends in the truck."

"You'd already hurt her so much," sobbed Hannah. "Why did you have to kill her? Why did you have to take her from me?"

"I'm sorry," he said. "I'm sorry for all of it."

"If you really are sorry, then you'll tell the cops what you did," said Hannah.

He rubbed his agonized face with his hands. Then slowly, as if fighting his worst instincts, he put his hand in the back of his jeans and removed a handgun from the waistband. He pointed it at Hannah with a hand as steady as his voice.

"I won't be doing any confessing," he said. "Why couldn't you leave the past alone?"

"Because it's time the truth came out. It's time that everyone knew that Jenny didn't drown. That she was gang-raped and murdered here. By you and your friends."

He took the safety catch off the gun with his finger. "There's no evidence that I did it. Nothing at all. He made sure of that."

"Who made sure of that?" Rachel asked, stepping out of the shadows.

Rachel pulled off the hood of her jacket so that he could see her. They'd met enough times before that he recognized her voice even before he saw her distinctive auburn hair.

Dan Moore's face turned pale. He turned toward Hannah in confusion, waving the gun unsteadily in her general direction.

"You told me it would just be the two of us," he told Hannah.

"And you brought a gun," she noted.

"I'll do whatever is needed to protect my family," he said. "It would crush Kelly if she knew what happened all those years ago. I was a kid then. Why can't you both understand that I have changed? I was in a dark place. My father was abusive. All I ever knew was violence. It took what happened to Jenny to make me realize that I was becoming like my father. I've spent all these years making amends."

Rachel moved toward him. "Hannah's lived her whole life wondering what happened that night. Tell her and then maybe she'll agree not to take this to the authorities. She'll move on with her life and allow you to move on with yours. Isn't that what you want?"

Dan ran his hand through his light hair, trying to decide on his next move. He sighed and then unburdened himself in a rush of words.

"After I threw Jenny into the water, I went back to the pickup. Bobby had fainted from the pain. The other two had drunk the rest of our liquor stash while they waited. They were in no condition to drive. I took the car keys and drove on the back roads to the north of town. We argued about what we should do with Bobby. I wanted to take him to the hospital. The others said we should kill him. We were all arguing about it and I lost control and slammed into a tree. I had no idea what to do. My friends were dead. Or close to it. I called my dad from a pay phone further down the road. He came within minutes. He put Bobby in the driver's seat and set fire to the truck. Said it was the only way to explain Bobby's burns," he said. "We went home. He beat me senseless in the garage, fractured my arm, and then told me if anyone asked that I should say we'd spent a father-son evening together watching a baseball game." He let out a bitter laugh. "My father was my alibi. You can't get a better alibi witness than the chief of police."

"It didn't all go according to plan, though. Somehow Bobby got out of the truck," said Rachel.

"Bobby must have become conscious before the fire reached the cab and the truck blew up. He walked a few steps and collapsed in a ditch. Someone reported the explosion to nine-one-one, and the cops came and took him to the hospital. It was touch and go for days. We honestly thought he'd die. He pulled through, but he never remembered anything about that night. When they charged him for reckless driving and manslaughter he pleaded guilty and served the time."

"And the boys who were killed?" Rachel asked.

"They were the real ringleaders. They'd planned the whole thing. Aaron and Lucas.

They'd had a thing for Jenny for a long time. Both Bobby and I were younger than them. We were pulled into their gang for our own reasons. For me, it was a way to escape my dad's fists. For Bobby, well, he was looking to belong," Dan said. "I regret what happened, more than I can ever tell you." His voice broke. "Sometimes, I think that what happened to Kelly was punishment for what I did to Jenny."

"If you regret it, then put the gun down," said Rachel.

"If it was just about me, then I wouldn't care. But I can't allow this to come out," he responded, his eyes narrowed in concentration. He shifted the weapon to the center of Rachel's chest and then back to Hannah, as if trying to decide which one of them to shoot first. "I can't allow Kelly to find out. It would kill her to know that her father was once a monster."

"You're still a monster," said Rachel. "Look at you. You're willing to kill Hannah and me to cover up for your crimes. You should know that I've recorded everything you said and it's automatically uploaded onto my cloud. Even if I die, the audio will be found by my producer. Killing us will only make things worse for you."

Dan ordered Rachel to hand over her

phone. She tossed it to him. He caught it with his free hand and fumbled with it as he tried to see if she was telling the truth. Eventually, unable to figure it out, he threw the phone into the water.

"Stand on the jetty ledge," he ordered.

Rachel climbed over the jetty rails and Hannah followed suit. Both women had their backs to the rails as they faced the chasm of the ocean. The waves hit their feet and splashed against their clothes. Rachel's arms ached from reaching behind her back to clutch the rail so she wouldn't fall into the water, the jetty shifting each time it was hit by a strong wave.

She had lied when she'd said the recording of their conversation was on her cloud. It didn't automatically upload. And even if it had, the noise from the wind and thrashing waves was so loud that she doubted anything recorded would be audible.

Rachel and Hannah stood next to each other against the jetty rails, facing the ocean, their arms cramping and their body trembling from cold as minutes passed. It was only when Rachel turned her head and saw car headlights moving in the darkness toward the road that she realized he'd left them there and made a getaway.

"He's gone," Rachel whispered to Hannah. Hannah didn't respond. Rachel turned and saw that Hannah wasn't there anymore. She'd dropped into the sea and was being enveloped by waves.

Rachel jumped into the water, scrambling around until she was clutching Hannah by her arm, trying to keep both their heads above water. They'd drifted far enough away from the jetty that she couldn't climb back up. They would have to swim to shore.

Rachel felt the weight of her wet clothes and Hannah's weighing them down into the rough water. She used all her strength to get Hannah to lie flat and float, but it was impossible. Hannah's long cardigan was dragging her underwater. Rachel ripped the sweater off Hannah's shoulders, pulling the heavy fabric off her until it floated away. She grabbed Hannah and pulled her along to the shore.

"Stay with me, Hannah," Rachel soothed. "You're going to be okay. I promise."

Rachel's eyes stung from the salt water, and her body ached from trying to stay afloat and guide Hannah to safety in the choppy waves. When she ran out of strength, she relaxed and allowed them to drift in the surf until she felt sand under her feet. Slowly, she crawled out of the water, pulling Hannah with her until they were lying on the beach.

Rachel breathed heavily, her pulse racing. Hannah's eyes were open, but she was trembling violently from the cold.

In the distance, Rachel heard sirens. They rose to a crescendo and then stopped abruptly. Moments later, she saw dark figures running and then beams of flashlights swept across the beach. "We're here," Rachel called out, waving her hand limply.

Rachel sat slumped in an armchair next to the hospital bed where Hannah was fast asleep. She herself had slept little that night, waking intermittently as doctors and nurses came in and out of the room through the night to check on Hannah.

Detective Cooper had met the ambulance at the hospital. Hannah was rushed into the ER and immediately treated for hypothermia and ingesting water. Rachel had insisted that she didn't need medical attention. All she wanted was a hot shower and a fresh change of clothes. Detective Cooper had driven her back to the hotel so she could get just that. She'd told him on the drive over what had happened and how she'd texted Pete surreptitiously when Dan Moore pulled out the gun. He told her grimly that it was lucky that Pete had been awake and called emergency services.

When Rachel was showered and dressed, she insisted on returning to check on Hannah. Detective Cooper had dropped Rachel back at the hospital and she'd spent what remained of the night sleeping under a blanket in the armchair next to Hannah's bed.

Rachel opened her eyes to see Detective Cooper standing over her, holding out a large takeout coffee and a white paper bag. "I brought you some breakfast," he said as Rachel pushed away the blanket and sat up. She rubbed her eyes and stifled a yawn as she took the coffee cup.

"Has Dan Moore been arrested yet?" Rachel asked.

Hannah shifted slightly in her sleep but didn't wake. The sedative the doctors had given her hadn't worn off yet.

"His car was found abandoned. We went to the family house, but there was nobody there. A neighbor told us that Kelly and her mother left town the day that she was supposed to have testified again," Detective Cooper said. "They've relocated to the West Coast. As for Dan, he's on the run."

His bloodshot eyes attested to the fact that he hadn't slept at all since he'd been woken by a call from Rachel at the back of the ambulance, asking him to meet her at the hospital.

He pulled the blinds back slightly so he could see out into the bright sunshine of the morning. He turned around to look at Hannah, still fast asleep. Her skin was almost as white as the hospital sheets and her face looked innocent, and childlike, as she slept.

"You never forget your first death notification," he said. "Jenny Stills was mine. I never imagined that I was being sent out to her mother's house to deliver that terrible news because the police chief wanted me out of the way so he could get my partner to cover up Jenny's rape and murder."

"Didn't you ask questions afterward, given how closely you were involved in the case, helping Hannah and giving the death notification to her mother?" Rachel asked.

He shook his head. "I was sent straight from Jenny's house to work a roadblock near the car-accident scene. After that, I went home and slept. When I returned to work, my partner told me he had good news, that someone had dropped out of a police-training course that I'd applied for in Charlotte. There was a spot for me, but I had to leave right away. When I finished the course, I was immediately offered a junior

483

detective job in Rhode Island," he said.

"Was Russ Moore's hand in that, too?" Rachel asked.

"Probably. The chief in Rhode Island was an old friend of Russ Moore. I'm sure he called in a favor," he said, looking back out the window. "Mitch asked me to get hold of the autopsy report for Jenny Stills. I spoke to a friend. They found the file, but there was nothing in it. Russ did a thorough job of destroying any evidence she was murdered."

Rachel poured a packet of brown sugar into her coffee and stirred it in the silence that followed. Russ Moore had owned the town when he was police chief. He'd had so much power that he was able to do whatever he wanted. He'd terrorized his wife and son, driving his wife to suicide. He'd framed Bobby Green as the perpetrator of the fatal car crash that had shocked Neapolis, even though his own son had been behind the wheel. And, perhaps most horrifyingly, he'd made sure his most loyal police officers covered up the rape and murder of Jenny Stills. Detective Cooper's phone beeped. He took it out of his pocket and read the message.

"It's from Mitch," he said. "The jury has reached a verdict."

53
GUILTY OR NOT GUILTY

SEASON 3, EPISODE 12: THE VERDICT

Today Scott Blair woke up in his bed. Maybe for the last time in a long time. He dressed in navy pants and a blue sweater. He brushed his teeth. He shaved. He probably had breakfast, despite what I'm sure were nervous butterflies in his stomach.

Before he left for court, maybe he stuck his head into his bedroom for a final look. I'm betting he wondered whether he'd sleep in his bed that night or he'd be in a cell in a prison-issue jumpsuit, serving the first night of a long prison sentence.

When Scott Blair arrived in court, surrounded by his lawyers, his parents nervously shuffling in behind him, he looked like a deer caught in headlights. He'd lost control of his life to twelve ordinary people from various walks of life who sat in judgment of him. Twelve strangers who would decide his fate.

485

He knew the power they had over him as he watched the jury file in with fixed expressions and gritted teeth. You could almost see him asking himself the question: "How did I screw up my life so badly that I ended up here?"

It took less than two days for the jury to reach a verdict. They sifted through the evidence methodically and patiently. They asked Judge Shaw for clarification on questions of law. They reviewed thick transcripts of testimony. The jury didn't have K's testimony to consider. That was struck from the record. They didn't have Scott Blair's testimony, either. He never took the stand. Yet they reached a unanimous verdict. By early afternoon, the courtroom was full as we waited to hear their decision.

Judge Shaw asked the defendant to stand. Scott stood and sort of puffed out his cheeks as if he was taking a huge lungful of oxygen as he waited for the verdict to be read out.

The jury foreman passed a slip of paper to the bailiff. Scott Blair's parents tightened their grip on each other's hands as the paper was handed to Judge Shaw. His mother flinched as the judge opened the folded sheet. All eyes were on the judge's expression as he read the jury's verdict. His face was inscrutable.

Then he put the paper down and cleared his throat. Cynthia Blair put her hand over her mouth and closed her eyes. Her son's fate was about to be sealed, one way or the other, and there was nothing she could do about it.

Scott Blair's posture relaxed for an instant when the words "not guilty" rang out. But they were quickly followed by "guilty," "guilty." He flinched each time. It was as if the air had been sucked out of the courtroom.

The jury found Scott Blair "not guilty" of raping K. But it found him guilty on one count of sexual assault and two counts of sexual battery.

Many of you may agree with the verdict after listening to the testimony and reviewing the evidence that we've put on the podcast website. We've also uploaded an analysis from a law professor about why the case might not have met the legal definition of rape in North Carolina, which requires threats, such as the use of a deadly weapon, for a sexual assault to be deemed rape in that state.

Some of you, no doubt, will say that it's a travesty of justice. That Scott Blair should have been convicted on the most serious charge of rape. Others will say that he shouldn't have been convicted at all. That there wasn't enough evidence to convict him beyond a reasonable doubt.

I'm sure I'll get messages from people expressing all sorts of opinions. Believe me,

487

I've heard every possible view during my brief time in Neapolis covering this trial. I've received a flood of messages arguing the merits of chemical castration. And other emails telling me that rapists deserve to die. I've also received plenty of messages in support of Scott Blair, accusing K of all manner of sins, including the sin of lying.

To tell you the truth, I don't get how we can almost unanimously agree that murder is wrong, yet when it comes to rape some people still see shades of gray. At least judging by our inbox and social media, which my producer, Pete, has been monitoring closely over the course of this season.

While the case might be over in court, the appeals will start almost immediately, even before Scott Blair's sentence is handed down. But regardless of how much prison time he gets, Scott will pay for what he did for the rest of his life. His life as he knew it is over. He is now a convicted sex offender. He'll be on the registry. He'll never, ever swim competitively again. Let alone for his country.

As for K, the victim. She's moved away to start a new life somewhere else. Perhaps the verdict will give her a measure of peace. I hope so.

The jurors will return to the mundane worries of their day-to-day lives. Keeping their businesses afloat, or their employers happy. Raising children and grandchildren. Paying mortgages. But I can't help thinking that this case will hang heavily over them in years to come. It's a terrible thing for a person to have to stand in judgment of another.

This is Rachel Krall and this was Season 3 of *Guilty or Not Guilty,* the podcast that puts you in the jury box.

Rachel pulled her suitcase across the hotel lobby. She was looking forward to getting home. The radio reports that morning had warned that a tropical storm out in the Atlantic was strengthening and might be re-categorized as a hurricane as it moved toward the coast. Rachel wanted to be far gone by the time it hit. She paused when she saw a tall man leaning against a faux marble column, his arms crossed.

"You're not staying for the sentencing?" Mitch Alkins asked.

"I have to head back," Rachel said. "What do you think Scott will get?"

"At a guess, around eight to ten years. He's a first-time offender. I don't think Judge Shaw will throw the book at him. But who knows," said Alkins. "One thing is for sure; the defense will appeal. Judge Shaw might lose that nonreversal record he's so proud of."

"I'm sure you'll do everything in your power to make sure that doesn't happen," Rachel said. He smiled determinedly. Rachel had no doubt that Mitch Alkins would see to it that Scott Blair received a hefty prison term and served every day of it.

"Do you have time for a quick drive?" Alkins asked. "I want to show you something." Rachel looked at him questioningly. There was a strange note in his voice. She had a feeling he was hiding something.

Rachel decided to delay her departure even though she'd hoped to get out of town before the highway snarled up with cars leaving before the storm hit. Rachel stored her bags in the hotel luggage area and followed Alkins out to the street where he'd parked his black Jeep. They drove south along the beach road. Alkins didn't say where he was taking her. She didn't need to ask.

When they arrived at the Morrison's Point beach, he parked right next to Detective Cooper's car. She saw the glint of the detective's blond hair at the end of the jetty, where he stood looking out to sea. The sky was overcast and forbidding. There were no boats in the water. It wasn't sailing weather. Fishermen were scattered in their usual spots across the jetty, their lines hanging into the rough water. A couple of teenage boys jumped into the waves, despite the old warning sign.

"Dumb kids," a fisherman complained. "They're scaring all the fish away."

Detective Cooper turned and waved to them as they approached. Standing alongside him was Hannah. She was wearing a striped gypsy skirt and a cropped denim jacket. Rachel could see a hint of a black henna tattoo going down the back of Hannah's neck as she leaned over the edge, throwing flowers into the water.

Rachel had last spoken to Hannah in the hospital. She'd been sitting up in bed picking at her lunch tray when Rachel came into her room with a big bouquet of get-well flowers. They'd talked for a while, until visiting hours had ended.

Hannah had told Rachel that she wasn't sure if she'd slipped into the water that night, or if her arms had given out, or, she conceded, if she had finally answered the beckoning call of the ocean. "Regardless," she'd said, "I'm so grateful to you, Rachel. You risked your life for me."

Hannah turned and smiled at Rachel when she realized that she'd joined them on the jetty. She handed Rachel some flowers and together they tossed the remaining daisies into the water. When they were done, they stood together watching the floating petals get consumed by waves until they disappeared under the surface.

"I can drop you off at Kitty's house on my way back," Rachel offered. "There's a storm coming. You might want to get out of here now while the going's good."

"I don't want to leave so quickly. Storm or no storm, I'm going to stay for a while," Hannah said. "Maybe I'll do some painting. There's a gallery owner who's been pestering me to have an exhibition, and I was thinking I could put together a collection of paintings of Neapolis to go with my other work and hold an exhibition next spring."

She turned to Rachel and touched her arm. "I want to apologize. I manipulated you with my letters so you'd help me find Jenny's murderer, and then I brought you to the jetty and put your life at risk. I had no right to put you in such danger. I was so focused on trying to get him to confess that I didn't consider the possibility that he might kill us both to make sure his crimes stayed a secret."

"Fortunately, that didn't happen. We're both alive and well," said Rachel. "And now, when he's caught, I can testify to his confession."

"Didn't you hear?" said Hannah uncertainly, glancing over Rachel's shoulder at Detective Cooper.

"Hear what?" Rachel asked.

"Dan Moore's body was found early this morning," Detective Cooper said. "He was in the water, tied by a rope to one of his boats. He tried to make it look like a boating accident, but he was an experienced sailor. A man like that with all his naval experience doesn't get caught in rigging and drown. Not unless he intends it."

"I guess he did it for his daughter?" Rachel said. "So she wouldn't have to cope with him being put on trial after everything else she's had to deal with?"

"Probably," said Detective Cooper. "It's unfortunate, though. Dan Moore deserved to be punished for what he did to Jenny, and to Bobby Green. He knew Bobby Green never killed those boys in that car crash, but he let him serve years in prison for it. Ruined his life," he said, shaking his head. "I spoke to Bobby earlier and told him he was never responsible for those boys dying in that accident. I told him what really happened that night and how he got burned. He sobbed like a baby."

"He ruined my life, too," whispered Hannah. "Not anymore. From now on, I'm doing right by my sister and my mother. I'm going to live a full life instead of one consumed by guilt."

"You have nothing to feel guilty about. You never did anything wrong, Hannah," said Rachel softly. "You were a kid."

"I know that now," Hannah said. "I'll never be able to thank you enough for what you did for me, Rachel. You could have ignored me, put me down as a crazy stalker, but you believed me and you were there for me that night on the jetty. We finally know what happened to Jenny."

"I'd like to show you something," said Mitch Alkins, his voice husky. "You too, Rachel."

He led them all down the jetty until they reached the halfway point. Embedded in the timber handrail was a brass plaque commemorating the death of Jenny Stills. It was signed *The People of Neapolis.*

"It was engraved immediately after the mayor signed off on it yesterday," Alkins said. "He wanted to honor Jenny's memory here at the place where she was murdered. He said it was long overdue."

Hannah ran her fingers over the engraving on the plaque as tears wet her face. It was a small step but an important one. It corrected the record of what had happened to her sister on that beach twenty-five years earlier.

Rachel and Alkins slowly walked back to his car. It was too loud for them to talk over the roar of wind until they were in the Jeep and the doors were shut.

"Do you regret coming back to live here?" Rachel asked as he drove her back to the hotel.

"Almost every day," he admitted.

"So why come back?" Rachel asked.

"It's a long story that I can't go into without violating attorney-client privilege. Let's just say that I had a case that left me questioning everything I ever believed in." His voice was low and pensive.

When they reached the hotel, Rachel leaned forward and impulsively kissed Mitch on the cheek before climbing out of the car. He sat behind the wheel with the engine still running, watching her go through the revolving door before he slowly drove off.

Rachel collected her luggage from the bellboy and headed toward the basement parking lot elevator. She stopped abruptly as she noticed a tourist standing at the gilded nightingale cage, snapping his fingers as he tried to get the terrified bird to sing. When that didn't work, the man tapped the cage until it rocked and the bird fluttered about in confusion.

The hotel manager was on the phone when Rachel stormed into his office. She helped herself to a chair by his desk while he hastily finished his call, and then she told him in no uncertain terms what she wanted.

Thirty minutes later, Rachel was in her car, driving down the congested main street, heading out of town. She turned up the radio to hear a news update. The newscaster announced that if the storm maintained its current trajectory, it would hit landfall along the coastline within forty-eight hours. "Residents of Neapolis and nearby towns are being told to prepare for the worst and to implement their hurricane-disaster plans," the announcer said. "If you can get out of town, then go. There's still time."

The traffic was heavy on the way out of Neapolis. Rachel stopped at a red light next to a strip mall and watched a tradesman on a ladder hammer a plywood sheet to protect a shopwindow. Rachel put her foot on the accelerator when the light changed and drove through.

She checked her voice mail messages as she merged onto the state highway. "Rachel!" It was Pete. He sounded excited. "I've found a case for Season 4. I've started researching it. I think we're onto something incredible. This will be the best season ever. Call me and I'll tell you about it." Rachel hit delete. There was a long beep before the next message.

"Rachel, this is Cynthia Blair here," said the crisp voice. "I just want to say that I hope you are very satisfied with yourself. You told us when we met that you were covering the trial to get to the truth. Clearly, you don't care about truth. All you care about is fame, and money," she said. "You got your ratings. Didn't you, Rachel? That's what it's all about. You did it by demonizing my son and depriving him of a fair trial. I don't understand how you can live with yourself. I really don't."

Rachel sped up as the message ended abruptly with a click. She drove for a while in silence as she shifted lanes, navigating through the congestion on the highway. She pressed hard on the accelerator until the other cars were well behind her and the charcoal asphalt of the highway stretched so far in front of her that it looked as if it might reach the sky.

Rachel's eyes flicked to her rearview mirror as she heard a flutter from the back seat. The nightingale was rocking contentedly on the perch in the birdcage.

ACKNOWLEDGMENTS

I sometimes joke that writing a novel is the writing equivalent of running a marathon. It's exhausting and solitary work, requires extreme discipline, and there's no assurance of making it to the finish line. The similarity extends beyond the writing because, just as with marathons, there are many people behind the scenes who play critical and often unsung roles. I wish to extend my deepest appreciation to Charles Spicer, for his invaluable advice as I worked on this novel. I am most grateful to Jennifer Enderlin, Sarah Grill, and the rest of the talented team at St. Martin's Press and Macmillan. It is an enormous privilege to have you all in my corner. Thank you to my agent, David Gernert, and Ellen Coughtrey, as well as to Rebecca Gardner and the rest of the team at The Gernert Company. To Ali Watts and the "random penguins" at Penguin Random House Australia, as well as to all my other international publishers and translators, I am most grateful for your support. After my novel *The Escape Room* was published, I was inundated with messages from booksellers and book lovers. Every message touched me. Thank you so much to everyone who wrote to me.

To my husband and sons, who put up with my lengthy absences and constant distraction while I wrote this novel, thank you for your loving support and endless patience. You make it all worthwhile. Thank you also to my parents, brother and sister, and my aunt, who lives oceans away but is always in our hearts. Any mistakes in this novel are my own, either deliberate or otherwise, because fiction is, after all, fiction. The town of Neapolis is a fictional town. Its name is drawn from the Roman name for the town of Shechem, where the biblical account of the rape of Dinah took place.

ABOUT THE AUTHOR

Megan Goldin worked as a correspondent for Reuters and other media outlets where she covered war, peace, international terrorism and financial meltdowns in the Middle East and Asia. She is now based in Melbourne, Australia where she raises three sons and is a foster mum to Labrador puppies learning to be guide dogs. THE NIGHT SWIM is her second novel.